Praise for

MONKEY LOVE

"Juggling life, love, and loony relatives, Holly Heckerling is a lot like Stephanie Plum—only nobody's shooting at her. Holly's hilarious hijinks had me howling out loud. . . . Delicious as a jelly dough-nut!"
　　　　　　　　　　　　　　　　　　　　　—Janet Evanovich

"This is the perfect book to read on an airplane, especially if you want to be one of those annoying passengers who snort and laugh out loud every few minutes."
　　　　　　　—Dan O'Shannon, Writer/Executive Producer
　　　　　　　for *Frasier* and *Cheers*

"A hilarious romp of a novel. If you've ever felt like a monkey in the middle, you'll love this book!"
　　　　　　　—Sarah Mlynowski, bestselling author of
　　　　　　　Milkrun and *Monkey Business*

"Brenda Scott Royce has one of the funniest, freshest voices around. *Monkey Love* is charming in both its oddity and originality, with characters that jump off the page and wind their way into your heart. Royce's writing is read-out-loud-to-your-friends hilarious; I'm a fan!"
　　　　　　　—Lani Diane Rich, author of *Time Off for Good*
　　　　　　　Behavior and *Maybe Baby*

"Fast and funny, this romp of a book introduces you to a writer whose fresh, quirky voice will be around for a long, long time."
　　　　　　　—Bonnie Hearn Hill, author of *Killer Body* and
　　　　　　　If It Bleeds

MonKey LoVe

BrenDa Scott Royce

 NEW AMERICAN LIBRARY

New American Library
Published by New American Library, a division of
Penguin Group (USA) Inc., 375 Hudson Street, New York, New York 10014, USA
Penguin Group (Canada), 90 Eglinton Avenue East, Suite 700, Toronto,
Ontario M4P 2Y3, Canada (a division of Pearson Penguin Canada Inc.)
Penguin Books Ltd., 80 Strand, London WC2R 0RL, England
Penguin Ireland, 25 St. Stephen's Green, Dublin 2,
Ireland (a division of Penguin Books Ltd.)
Penguin Group (Australia), 250 Camberwell Road, Camberwell, Victoria 3124,
Australia (a division of Pearson Australia Group Pty. Ltd.)
Penguin Books India Pvt. Ltd., 11 Community Centre, Panchsheel Park,
New Delhi - 110 017, India
Penguin Group (NZ), cnr Airborne and Rosedale Roads, Albany,
Auckland 1310, New Zealand (a division of Pearson New Zealand Ltd.)
Penguin Books (South Africa) (Pty.) Ltd., 24 Sturdee Avenue,
Rosebank, Johannesburg 2196, South Africa

Penguin Books Ltd., Registered Offices: 80 Strand, London WC2R 0RL, England

First published by New American Library, a division of Penguin Group (USA) Inc.

First Printing, February 2006
10 9 8 7 6 5 4 3 2 1

NEW AMERICAN LIBRARY and logo are trademarks of Penguin Group (USA) Inc.

LIBRARY OF CONGRESS CATALOGING-IN-PUBLICATION DATA:

Royce, Brenda Scott.
    Monkey love / Brenda Scott Royce.
        p. cm.
    ISBN 0-451-21754-3 (trade pbk.)
    1. Women comedians—Fiction.   2. Pet sitting—Fiction.   3. Monkeys—Fiction.
    4. Aunts—Fiction.   I. Title.
    PS3618.O895M66   2006
    813'.6—dc22   2005017823

Set in Simoncini Garamond
Designed by Leonard Telesca

Printed in the United States of America

for Ramón

Acknowledgments

My mother—one of my staunchest supporters and toughest critics—wrote in my baby book that my name would look great on the cover of a book one day. While she always believed I'd write the great American novel, I hope she'll settle for a few laughs in this one. I am indebted to her for not only encouraging me to write, but also teaching me to find the humor in life even when times are tough.

Two other women who have earned my undying respect and gratitude are my agent, Miriam Kriss of the Irene Goodman Literary Agency, and my editor, Kara Cesare. They believed in me and my book from the beginning, and shepherded it through its journey to publication with knowledge, wit, and compassion.

My friend and fellow writer Kristan Ginther was the first person to read any portion of this book. Her enthusiasm for the first few chapters gave me the boost I needed to keep writing. Other friends and early readers offered insightful comments: Madeline McGrail, Corinna Bechko, Kimbria Hays, James Robert Parish, Mollie Gregory, and Lanette Hohl. Lanette was there when I originally conceived of the characters of Holly and Carter more than fifteen years ago, and she refreshed my memory of Manhattan life when I finally got around to telling their stories.

Thanks to the ever-knowledgeable Joe McNeely for advice on everything from contracts to titles, author Bonnie Hearn Hill for helping me refine my pitch, and to all the baristas at all the Starbucks in the greater Los Angeles area, where I wrote the bulk of this book.

Andrea Campbell became a friend when I edited her book, *Bringing Up Ziggy,* which chronicles her years as a foster mom to a capuchin monkey. Tallulah owes her fictional existence in large part to the real-life adventures of Andrea and Ziggy.

Many other people provided inspiration, information, advice, or assistance, including Norm Abbey, Angela Adams, Anthony Vincent Bova, Dan Cubias, Janet Evanovich, Anthony Garcia, Gabriel Hardman, Tony and Marianne Hudz, Tricia Kokoszka, Lynne Koplitz, Deborah and John Landis, Madeline McGrail, Helena "Gramma" Mete, the entire Posada family, Christine Potvin, Lauren Royce, Lori Sheeran and my other primatology professors at Cal State Fullerton, and classmates Tricia Pacinelli, Katie Zeoli, Chrissy Sepulveda, and the rest of the PSA group, who share my love of monkeys. I'd also like to thank all my friends, both two- and four-legged, at the Wildlife Waystation and the Los Angeles Zoo, especially Connie Morgan for giving me the best job in the world.

Most of all, I am grateful to my family, especially my husband, for letting me bounce ideas off him and for helping me find time to write in the midst of busy family life; my stepsons, Emmanuel and Daniel, for sharing their lives and their laughter with me; and my son, Nicholas, who entered the world as I was nearing the end of the writing process. In the early months of his life, I wrote during his nap times, alternating between working on this book and his baby book. Maybe one day *he'll* write the great American novel. At least when he's old enough to read this one, I hope he'll laugh.

1

Theater of Carnage

"Holly's Hobbies," I answered the phone breathless, my keys dangling in the front door lock. My cat, Grouch, was investigating the grocery bag I had deposited in the middle of the floor in my mad dash to get to the phone. It was my business line and I hated missing business calls, especially in the middle of a workday.

"This is the last time, Holly, I promise!" It was Monica, my cousin Gerry's girlfriend.

"The last time for what? Hold on a sec. I left my door open." I retrieved my keys, shut the door, and scooped up the grocery bag just as Grouch was about to sink his teeth into the Pacific salmon I'd splurged on for tonight's dinner. When I picked up the phone again, Monica was already talking.

"So I need a haircut, a perm, I don't know, *something* done to my hair. I look like shit, and I have to be a convincing bitch-in-heels corporate type by tomorrow morning. Dead ends do *not* say 'bitch in heels.' The audition's at nine. You have to help me."

Oh yeah. Now I knew what she meant. The last "last time" Monica Broccoli had called me for a last-minute favor was less than a month ago. She had gotten a part in a touring production of *Starlight Express*. The night before she was to leave town for four months, she called to ask if I could take care of her pet boa constrictor. I said no. I hate snakes. But the next day she was on my doorstep, clutching an aquarium and pleading, "Please, Holly, I can't find anyone else! You just *have* to take care of Rocky for me."

I don't know what it was—certainly not the slithery sight of Rocky the Boa—that made me give in. But I did, silently wishing terrible things to befall Monica on her tour. Before I had a chance to ask what to feed the snake, Monica was gone. But not for long. She broke her leg during a performance in Pittsburgh, the tour's first stop. I didn't even know she was back until I ran into my cousin Gerry at my aunt Kuki's house in Brooklyn. He told me Monica was in town but she couldn't pick up Rocky because of her condition. What about *my* condition, I asked, namely my mortal fear of snakes?

"Monica," I said into the receiver, "you have a bigger problem than your hair. How can you be a bitch in heels if you're on crutches?"

"That's the other thing. I need you to take my cast off. You have a power saw, right? Gerry said you did."

"Yeah, but—"

"Great. I have to run a few errands and then I'll be over."

"Monica, wait—"

"You're the best!"

"No, I can't—"

Click.

"I have a date!" I screamed into the receiver.

I tried calling her back but got her answering machine. So I called my cousin. His roommate said he was out on a catering gig. Great. I had less than two hours to prepare for my date with my semi-sort-of boyfriend Marcus—for whom I had promised to make dinner—and now I also had to do a perm and remove a cast for my cousin's overbearing girlfriend. On top of that, I had actual paying work to do—a rush typing job for a client who was coming by to pick it up in the morning—and I'd promised Danny, my comedy partner, that I'd work up some new material for our act.

I went into my kitchen pantry and slid open the latch on the little door to my milk drop box. My building was built in the 1930s, when milkmen still delivered bottles of milk, butter, and cream door to door. Though in some respects the building has been modernized, they have never gotten rid of the cubbyholes that allowed the milkman to leave his goods if tenants weren't home. Mine still has a dial that the woman of the house could set, indicating the number of milk bottles she desired.

Most of my neighbors have boarded over their milk cubbies, but I've put mine to use. If I'm not home, clients can leave work for me, and I can leave finished work if I'm not going to be around for the pickup. It's bigger than a mail slot and, thankfully, too small for a burglar to crawl through. Still, since New York City probably has more than its quota of midget robbers, I installed a lock on the inside door.

Since I live in a so-called "security" building, there's still the problem of my clients getting inside the building if I'm not home to buzz them in. Fortunately, the building has a resident busybody, Mrs. Mete, an elderly retiree who lives on the seventh floor and spends the day watching game shows and sitting by her front door, observing the comings and goings of the residents. Mrs. Mete will buzz anybody in without question, just because she's curious to see what they look like. If you ever catch up with her in the laundry room, she'll give you a detailed rundown of who visited whom in the last week—complete with physical description and identifying characteristics. Though it didn't help me sleep any easier knowing that Mrs. Mete would indiscriminately allow anyone off the streets to enter the building, it did make it easier to receive packages—I simply instructed all my clients to buzz 7C to get in, day or night.

There was a manila envelope inside the cubbyhole, with my name in block letters on the front. Inside, a stack of lined yellow pages, with a note clipped to the front.

> Thanks for the rush job. Going out of town.
> Will pick up early a.m.

I counted the pages. Twenty-two. O.K., get a grip. I breathed deeply and then, with the resolve of someone for whose lifestyle the word "multitasking" was a severe understatement, I got down to some serious business.

Preheat oven to 375. Turn on computer. Feed the cat. Wash down two Vivarin with a can of Coke. Pop in a Tina Turner CD and get funky. Grab up the dirty clothes on the floor and toss them into the hamper. Drag my thrift store barber's chair out of the closet and roll it into the kitchen, up against the sink. Run a duster over the furniture. Spritz some perfume on my wrists and air freshener in the bathroom. Dab butter on the salmon, add a few dashes of parsley, pepper, and paprika, and stick it in the oven. Set timer. Chop asparagus, add water, put in the microwave. Pop a handful of gummy bears into my mouth in a feeble attempt to curb my appetite until dinnertime. Squirt some gel onto my hair and run a comb through it, striving for a look that says stunning temptress but settling for subdued tumbleweed. Belt out "Private Dancer" while setting the dining room table with the best china Odd Jobs has to offer. Sit at computer and type from the coffee-stained lined notebook pages.

The writing was nice and neat, straight lines, a welcome change from some of my other clients—aspiring screenwriters, novelists, a few doctors, and one psychiatrist. The shrink's notes from his patient sessions are the most interesting to read, but his handwriting is hardest to decipher. And because of the wide range of mental disorders and bizarre patient histories, it's not always easy to figure out the words from the context. One night I spent twenty minutes staring at the black squiggly lines deciding whether Dr. Handelman was calling a patient a suicidal waiter or a stalwart walrus.

Not with this client. No time would be wasted struggling to interpret his precisely lettered prose. He was a new client, and I was determined not only to meet his deadline but to also impress him with my thoroughness and accuracy so that he would continue leaving work in my pantry.

I opened Word and began typing. My fingers moved fast and furiously, pausing only to turn the page. Thanks to my aunt, who insisted I take those damned typing classes in high school, I could type ninety words per minute without breaking a sweat. It was mindless work to me; I usually did it by rote, not pausing to think about what I was reading.

But on the third or fourth page, something struck me, and I stopped typing. I went back a few lines to read what I'd typed:

In the darkness, that's when I still feel her presence. When I'm lying in bed, half asleep, and I hear a sound like a creak of the floorboards, I can almost fool myself into thinking that she's still here. She's in the bathroom, or in the hall, maybe in the kitchen getting a quick snack or on the balcony sneaking a cigarette. If I don't push it, if I just let myself slip half in, half out of sleep, I can almost believe that in just a minute she'll tiptoe back into the bedroom and slide between the sheets. I'll roll over sleepily and put my arm around her and she'll curl up in my embrace. "Go back to sleep," she'll whisper in my ear, and I'll moan, groggily, before sleep reclaims me.

It's so real and yet my mind never fully allows me to be tricked. I always fight the urge to fall into deeper slumber because even as I do, feeling the cottony warmth of her pajama-clad back spooned against me, I know that I'll wake up alone, the bright morning sun betraying my dreams and announcing the truth: My wife is dead.

Ding. The oven timer startled me and I jumped. I saved my work with a few quick keystrokes and raced into the kitchen. The salmon looked delicious. I lowered the temperature to warm, took the asparagus out of the microwave, and looked at the clock. Shit. Marcus was due any minute and I hadn't even put on any makeup.

B-r-r-r-r-r-r-ing. I pressed the intercom button and said hello, trying to convey a composure that I didn't feel.

"It's me, the plaster-casted wonder of Avenue A."

I pressed the buzzer, feeling a mixture of relief and anxiety: relief that it wasn't Marcus, and the anxiety that always comes with an encounter with Monica Broccoli. My stomach heaved, and I wondered if it was possible that the strange feeling was more likely due to the mix of Vivarin, Coke, and gummy bears I'd consumed.

I unlocked the front door and stuck my head out. I couldn't see Monica yet but I lived in a sixth-floor walk-up and she had a broken ankle. I had a few minutes. I went back inside and started Monica-proofing my place.

Monica Broccoli is a force of nature. She moves as fast as she talks, and when she leaves a room, you get the sense that a hurricane has blown through.

I was contemplating which if any of my possessions required safeguarding when the phone rang. Two quick rings rather than one long one. Personal line.

"Hello."

"Hey. It's me. Is Carter there?"

"No, she's not. Listen, Danny, I have to go. I have company, dinner in the oven, and a deadline."

Danny was my partner and one of my best friends. His girlfriend, Carter, was truly my "best" friend; we'd known each other since the sixth grade. Carter was a walking contradiction. A part-time Starbucks barista and part-time yoga instructor/meditation guide, she spent most of each day bouncing around on a caffeine buzz, but when the gong sounded for her next class, she'd shift gears instantaneously, gliding into Zen master mode without apparent effort.

"She's not at Starbucks. She's not at the studio. She's not home—"

"She's not here, either. I gotta go—"

"If you hear from her, have her call me on my cell. Did you finish the mailing?"

Damn. I'd forgotten about the mailing. Danny and I had a showcase at the Cracker Factory in less than two weeks and I was supposed to mail flyers to all the agents and casting people in town.

"Yeah, I mailed them out yesterday. Took 'em to the post office myself," I lied, looking at the stack of envelopes and the fat, flyer-filled Kinko's box on my coffee table.

"Yesterday? They should have been in the mail last week. That was your part of the bargain, remember?"

"Yes, I remember. I had a deadline. Don't worry. They'll get there in time, the showcase will be packed, and you and I will be signed to a development deal with CBS."

"I'd prefer NBC—"

"Bye, Danny."

I hung up the phone and stuck my head out the door again. I could hear Monica struggling up the stairs in her cast. Thump, step, thump, step.

I called down to her, "I have a date coming any minute, so we hafta be quick about this. What did you have in mind? A trim? A wash-and-set?"

Her words came between pants. Living in a sixth-floor walk-up is great for your butt but it doesn't endear you to people, especially the physically challenged. "What's the matter with you, Holly?

Why don'tcha move into a building with a freakin' elevator?" Thump, step, pant. "I'll tell ya what I want. I brought a picture."

"Can you give me a hint? So I can get my supplies ready?"

Thump, step, pant. "Ya got the power saw?"

"Power saw? I thought you were kidding!"

With a final thump, Monica pulled herself onto the sixth-floor landing. Her face was flushed and her expression was one I hadn't seen in a long time—not since my grandmother's funeral, when my cousin Gerry revealed to the assembled solemn masses that Monica Broccoli was still a virgin.

"Does it look like I'm kidding?"

It did not.

Monica Broccoli was dead-set on going to her audition the next morning sans cast, even though her doctor wasn't planning to remove it for another three weeks. She pleaded with me, telling me how badly she needed the gig, and how the only obstacles in her path were the cast and her listless hair. I doubted she stood any chance of landing the role, described by the casting director as Demi Moore in *Disclosure* meets Angelina Jolie in *Tomb Raider*, but what the hell? Monica Broccoli was practically family, and, at times, a paying customer. How could I refuse? Besides, now that she was here, she would have to take her snake back.

I rummaged through the hall closet, pushing aside a small mountain of coats, shoes, and assorted cleaning supplies, until I got down to the hardware section, back left corner. My mother, having been a dyed-in-the-wool tomboy, taught me how to build a bookcase, rewire an electrical outlet, and change the spark plugs in a car before I was twelve. Because I lived in Manhattan, the spark plug thing hadn't been the most practical of the legacies she imparted, but the building thing had come in handy. Not only did I have the coolest floor-to-ceiling bookcases lining the walls of my apartment, but the building super had referred me for a handful of similar construction jobs for other residents. My joy at taking on these jobs was twofold: cash under the table and the surprised look in people's faces when they opened the door and discovered that the builder they'd hired was a *chick*.

Oh yes, I had power tools, and what's more, I knew how to use them.

I hauled out a circular saw and began polishing the blade. It was a purely theatrical move; I was still hoping Monica would come to her senses before I put her leg on the chopping block. While I felt secure in my ability to turn a stack of two-by-fours into a charming end table, I was less confident that I could keep a steady hand with human flesh under my blade.

Unfazed, Monica opened her purse, pulled out a page torn from a magazine, and handed it to me. "Here. I was searching all day for the perfect look for this part and this is it."

I flattened the wrinkled page. A bathing suit layout showed a supermodel frolicking on the beach, masses of chestnut hair trailing in her wake. I winced. All those cascading curls! This was gonna be work.

"You sure? How about a buzz cut instead. You know, like Demi Moore in *G.I. Jane.*"

"It's bitch in heels, not bitch in combat boots."

I looked at my watch. It was five minutes to eight. Even if the perpetually punctual Marcus was late, there was no way I'd be through with Monica in time for our date.

"Hope you like salmon," I said, as I pushed Monica's head back into the kitchen sink with perhaps a tad more force than was necessary.

I had washed and rinsed Monica's hair and was setting it in perm rods when the intercom buzzed. "Come on up," I yelled into the speaker before pressing the button that would open the lobby door.

Unlike Monica's tortured trudge up the staircase, Marcus must have sprinted two steps at a time. I barely had time to fasten the next roller when there was a rapid knock at the door.

"Just a sec—" I started toward the door but it burst open, revealing not my pseudo date, Marcus, but my best friend, Carter. She was bouncing up and down and clutching a small brown bag. Her short spiky hair seemed even more on end than usual.

"Hol, you have to help me. Oh, my God, I gotta pee!"

Sensing that her urgent need to urinate was not what she needed my help with, I reached for the bag. "What is it?"

Still bouncing, she nodded, pointing at the bag. "A pregnancy test. I bought it two hours ago but I was afraid to use it. Plus, I didn't have to pee then. I've been downstairs drinking coffee and contemplating suicide."

I opened the bag and removed the pregnancy kit. The box had been hastily ripped open, the directions marked with finger-smeared chocolate stains. I could picture Carter hunched over in the break room at Starbucks, furtively reading the directions while chomping down a chocolate croissant.

I pointed to the bathroom door. "Well, who's stopping you? You have the kit. What do you need me for?"

"I just needed a place to do it. I can't go home—Danny'll freak out—and I didn't want to do it at work—some sneaky gossipmonger would find it in the trash and it'll make headlines in the next corporate newsletter. 'Store #271 had record sales this month and the assistant manager got herself knocked up.'"

"About Danny . . . he called. He's looking for you."

She grabbed the kit from my hands and raced into the bathroom, screaming behind her, "I know we've been friends forever, but if you breathe a word of this to him, I'll kill you."

The notion that Carter—nobody's picture of the ideal mother—might be pregnant distracted me from the other drama unfolding in my apartment. Monica Broccoli was staring at me with a mixture of surprise and annoyance. "Listen, I don't have all night, and that fishy smell is making me hungry. You got something to munch on?"

She snatched the bag of gummy bears I proffered and began popping them in her mouth. I hurriedly mixed the perm solution, and began applying it to her rolled hair. There was an explosion of noise behind me, and I turned to see Carter, jeans around her ankles, with the expression of wild woman. She lunged toward the kitchen cabinets, bouncing and nearly tripping over her pants. "A mug, a cup, give me something, quick!"

"What?" I asked, rescuing my favorite coffee mug from her clutches.

"I opened the kit on the subway and I must've dropped the little plastic cup you're supposed to pee into. I need something *now!*" There was desperation in her voice.

Monica Broccoli sighed. "Jesus Christ, I thought I was a wreck."

I fumbled through the boxes on the kitchen counter, reached into a home permanent kit, and fished out a plastic vial. "Here," I said, handing the vial to Carter, "it's L'Oréal. You're worth it."

She disappeared into the bathroom and slammed the door. Monica Broccoli said, "Why didn't she get the kind where ya just pee on a stick?"

I finished applying the perm solution to Monica's curlers and wrapped her head in a big towel. I set the oven timer for fifteen minutes, then, remembering the salmon, peered into the oven. The extra time warming in the oven had caused it to shrivel slightly, and while it didn't looked burned, exactly, it was browner than the picture of its inspiration in the *Elegant-but-Easy Dinners* cookbook my aunt Betty had given me for Christmas last year, her subtle way of saying what everyone else in the family put more bluntly: "When are you gonna land a husband?"

The salmon had to be saved from its slow-cooking misery, so, crossing my fingers that Marcus would arrive soon, I transferred the fillets from the broiling pan to a serving dish, placed it on the center of the dining room table, then turned the dial on the microwave to reheat the now cold and wilted asparagus.

Directing my attention to the other task at hand—removing the cast—I approached Monica warily. "You sure you want me to do this?" I asked, picking up my trusty Black and Decker saw.

"Would ya just do it already?"

I lifted Monica's ankle and placed it on a wooden chair, atop a few cushions. If they didn't help to steady her leg, at least they might soak up the blood, I reasoned, envisioning a gory accident. I donned safety goggles, flipped the power switch, and slowly lowered the blade, pausing to consider the best—or least damaging— point of entry. Over the shrill whir of the blade I heard an even shriller noise. A high-pitched scream. Had I hurt her already? I jumped back, inadvertently pulling the power cord out of the wall socket. I lifted my goggles and looked at Monica. She didn't look injured, but was staring over my shoulder with that same mixture of surprise and annoyance.

I turned around. Carter, now fully clothed, was standing there, her mouth agape, her hair looking positively strained from the stress of the day. "Holly, are you crazy? What the hell are you doing to this lady?"

Monica waved a hand impatiently. "A spiral perm, if we can get on with it."

Though Monica had been dating my cousin for nearly two years, Carter hadn't yet had the dubious pleasure of making her acquaintance. I introduced them and Carter squealed, "Oh! The virgin from the funeral!" Monica arched one eyebrow, declining comment.

"So?" I looked at Carter expectantly. She was holding the plastic cup as though it was a ticking time bomb. Perhaps it was. "Is it positive or negative?"

"It takes five minutes. It has to—I don't know, whatever it does—percolate."

I looked at the oven timer. "That's about how much time is left until I have to rinse Monica's hair. We'll just wait for the timer to go off."

She set the plastic cup on the counter, then backed away from it. "I can't look. It's like torture, waiting."

I glanced at the little plastic cup. Considering its contents, I was surprised at the odd coloration. Carter was a chain-smoking caffeine addict who considered beef jerky and Funyuns a square meal. Such a lifestyle could have strange effects on one's bodily fluids, I supposed. "What's it supposed to do?"

"Turn pink if it's positive, blue if it's negative. You drop a pill in the pee and wait."

That would explain the odd tint. I didn't want to discourage Carter, but the liquid was taking on a decidedly rosy hue.

"Why didn't ya get the kind where you pee on a stick?" Monica asked again.

Carter shrugged. "This one was in the clearance bin at Duane Reade, fifty percent off."

"That should tell ya something. It's probably expired." Monica dug her hand into the bag of gummy bears, Halloween rejects that, I'd neglected to tell her, had most definitely expired.

Carter was pacing frantically, glancing around my apartment, fingering knickknacks, sifting through the mail on my counter, petting my cat. "Mmm, gummy bears," she said, reaching her hand toward the bag on Monica's lap.

Monica slapped Carter's hand away. "Lay off. They're mine."

Great. I didn't know if I could survive twenty minutes with either of them, and now they were going at each other. Marcus was late, the salmon was getting cold, and I still had all that typing to do. I thought back briefly to the nice handwriting and the beautiful words "*In the darkness, that's when I still feel her presence. . . .*" Of all the things demanding my attention at that moment, that was the only one that really piqued my interest. In just a few pages, it had sparked something inside me, some emotion I couldn't quite identify. But now there was the salmon, Carter's possible pregnancy, Monica Broccoli's possible amputation, the perm, and . . . and the nagging feeling that I was forgetting something. I looked around the apartment. Rocky the boa constrictor was motionless in his aquarium, oblivious to the fact that he would soon be filling out a change of address card. Grouch had been fed, the apartment was in the ballpark of clean . . . Ah! Memory returned with a jolt when I spotted the Kinko's box. The showcase!

I grabbed Carter by the arm and led her to the coffee table. I opened the Kinko's box and removed a stack of purple flyers. "I've got the perfect thing for you to keep your mind off things. These hafta be in the mail by tomorrow morning. You can fold, seal, and stamp 'em for me." I took one out of the box and demonstrated. "Here's the address labels and postage stamps."

She held up a flyer. "The comedy showcase? I thought you already mailed the flyers. Danny said—"

"What Danny doesn't know won't hurt him." I smiled knowingly, tipping my head in the direction of the pregnancy test percolating in my kitchen.

"Ah, blackmail." Carter nodded. "Excellent strategy." She settled in on the couch and set to work.

Monica Broccoli shouted, "Let me see one of those. Maybe I'll come to the show. Gerry's always saying how funny you are, but I just don't see it."

I sighed. If you make your living as a comedian, people expect you to be constantly "on," to be knee-slappingly funny every moment of your daily life. A trip to the post office, a dash to the dentist, all mundane tasks should be accompanied by a spontaneous monologue of wry observations and witty asides.

To be accurate, I don't make my living as a comedian. I have to supplement my occasional paying gigs with money from my business. Holly's Hobbies is the catch-all name I came up with to cover the assorted enterprises I undertake to support myself while waiting for my comedy career to take off. In addition to word processing and hairstyling, I also pet sit, babysit, sell handmade jewelry, and for one crazy month each year, do income taxes. I'd been thinking of expanding lately, perhaps selling Avon products to my hairstyling clients, a captive audience. Monica was tapping her toes impatiently. She could certainly use some concealer.

I handed her a purple flyer. "I work with a partner. I'm not funny on my own."

"Oh, that must be it."

There was a ding and Carter nearly jumped out of her jeans. "Oh, my God!" She came running into the kitchen, nearly crashing into the perm kits and solution bottles that lined the counter.

"Relax! It's just the microwave." I took the asparagus out and set it on the table. I was beginning to wonder if I'd been stood up. Marcus was never late. I'd give him five more minutes and then it'd be a free-for-all. There wasn't enough salmon for three, but we could supplement with gummy bears.

Monica tapped her cast on my wooden chair. "Hey, can we get a move on here?"

"Okay, let's do it. Carter, help steady her leg." I plugged in the saw, held my breath, and turned it on. The whir of the blade caused my stomach to churn, but I steadied my hands and lowered the saw. As the blade made contact with the cast, tiny bits of plaster shot up into my face—I had forgotten to put the goggles back on. Too late now. I blinked, took a breath, and lowered the blade a tiny fraction of an inch.

B-r-r-r-r-r-r-ing. I shot back again, startled by the noise of the intercom buzzer. Struggling to control the heavy saw, I lost my balance and knocked into Carter, who reeled backward. Arms flailing, Carter jerked herself around in a valiant effort to prevent Monica's outstretched leg from becoming her point of impact. Instead, she body-slammed into the kitchen counter, sending my spice rack and kitchen caddy sliding into the hair accessories and power tools. As spice bottles and cooking supplies rolled down the countertop and collided with the beauty and hardware supplies, Carter lunged toward her plastic vial, screaming, "My test!"

"My leg!" Monica yelled, pulling herself off the barber's chair and hobbling away from the still-whirring blade of the saw, which I held straight out in front of me. My elbows seemed to be locked and I was frozen, unable to turn off the power switch.

B-r-r-r-r-r-r-ing. The buzzer snapped me back to reality. I yanked the saw and the plug came flying out of the outlet. I set it down and pressed the button to let Marcus into the building. Then I surveyed the scene before me. The barber's chair was tipped over on its side and Monica was crouched in a corner, breathing heavily, her calm reserve finally shattered. Carter was crying and stuffing something into a paper bag.

"I'm leaving," she said, pushing past me toward the door. "I'm taking the test with me. I can't bear to look at it yet, and besides, I need to be in a calm place, a peaceful place, when I get the news that could change my life. *This* is not that place." She glanced at Monica. "Besides, if this becomes a crime scene, I don't want to be implicated." She pressed her tearstained cheek to mine in a quick embrace, then placed her hands into yoga prayer position and bowed slightly. "*Namaste.*"

She opened the door and bounded down the staircase. I waited a moment, listening. From her and Marcus's muffled hellos, I guessed he was still about three floors down. Briefly, madly, I considered hurrying to hide some of the evidence of the evening's calamity—then remembered that I had never even finished putting my makeup on, and that alone was more than a three-floor job. There was no point.

I left the door open a crack and shuffled into the kitchen. I began making sense of the mess, separating spice jars from hair supplies, and looking for the jar I'd used to mix the neutralizing solution for Monica's perm. I was aware of Monica calling my name, but I wasn't yet ready for Act 3 of our twisted little theater of carnage.

There was a rap on the door and it fell open. Marcus's tall frame filled the doorway. "Hello . . ." he called, brushing sandy blond hair out of his eyes. A few feet inside, he stopped in his tracks and looked around with a pained expression on his face. In that moment, I realized that I didn't care what he thought. If Marcus Pressman was the man of my dreams, he would understand. He wouldn't look at me with that disdainful expression that asked, "Now what have you gotten yourself into?" Most important, if Marcus Pressman was the man of my dreams, I would have known it by now. We'd been dating for three months, and although I'd convinced myself that I cared for him, the best thing he had going for him was that, unlike my previous boyfriends, he lacked any obvious psychological disturbances.

I'd planned this romantic dinner for two to mark our three-month anniversary, a milestone unequaled in my dating history, and one that should have filled me with flutters of excitement. But now

I had to admit to myself that the only butterflies I'd felt in my stomach all evening involved the use of power tools.

Before I could answer his unspoken question, the oven timer dinged. Monica Broccoli hobbled back into the kitchen. "Time to get this shit out of my hair," she grumbled. As she approached me, I dared a quick glance at her cast and was relieved not to see any evidence of bleeding or disfigurement. Pieces of plaster hung from the three-inch notch I'd managed to make in the cast, but no dangling flesh.

I shouted to Marcus, who was still standing in the doorway, dumbstruck, "Close the door so the cat won't get out! I'll be with you in a sec. Dinner is ready."

"Dinner is *history*," he pronounced, shutting the door. I twitched at his remark. Even if, like me, he'd just concluded that our relationship was going nowhere, he had a lot of nerve to decide that our date was finished before it began. Especially after I'd prepared his favorite meal.

"Excuse me?"

Monica uprighted the barber's chair and pushed its back against the kitchen sink. She said flatly, "Your cat ate your dinner."

That was when I saw what had prompted Marcus's remark. Grouch was atop the dining room table, clearly in heaven amid a smorgasbord of fishy goodness. The salmon had been decimated, its remains scattered across the tablecloth in little flaky chunks. Grouch had gone in for the kill; now he was just picking the table clean.

Marcus was standing, hands on hips, a disapproving smirk on his face. "Salmon. My favorite," he deadpanned. "Now what are we gonna have for dinner?"

"Well, there's asparagus," I suggested weakly, "and gummy bears."

Monica held up the gummy bear bag. It was empty. "All gone," she said, and I pushed her head back under the faucet with decidedly more force than was necessary.

I rinsed Monica's hair and then searched for the vial of neutralizing solution I had prepared earlier. Marcus was in the kitchen now, peering over the items on the counter, at Monica's leg, at the power saw sitting in the middle of the floor.

"I'll explain later," I said as, one by one, I picked through the mess of bottles and vials on the kitchen counter.

"What are you looking for?" he asked.

"Neutralizing solution. It's in a little plastic vial, and it has to be applied now or Monica's hair will be seriously fried." Hearing this, Monica shot bolt upright and assisted the search and recovery effort. "Paprika, cumin, strawberry blond hair dye . . ."

"Is this it?" Marcus was holding a plastic L'Oréal solution container.

"Oh, no."

Monica Broccoli looked panic-stricken, clasping her hands protectively over her wet hair. "What is it?"

I took the vial from Marcus and held it up to the light. The fluorescent overhead lamp illuminated the pinkish hue of the liquid. I looked at Monica Broccoli. "I think your perm is pregnant."

Martin Scorsese's Socks

B-z-z-z-z-z-z-z-z. The alarm buzzer broke into my dreams and yanked me awake with a start. Reaching over, I slammed my fist into the hateful device, hoping that one of the little buttons I'd crushed was marked SNOOZE. Ah, sweet relief. The sonic boom–level noise ceased and I snuggled deeper under the covers, hoping to snatch another few minutes of sleep before the dreaded Sleepblaster Plus sounded its next death toll.

As much as I despised the little bugger, I had to admire how it unerringly performed its function of getting my ass out of bed every morning. Not an easy task, even on a good day, when I hadn't stayed up until the wee hours of the morning picking plaster and salmon out of my carpet. No, no tinkly-winkly alarms for me. No CDs with the soothing sounds of the rain forest to gently ease my body into wakefulness. I need noise. I need power. I need to be shocked from sleep.

I need a life.

Lying in bed, contemplating the day ahead, I was struck by this depressing thought: I am not the controlling force in my own life.

Events swirl around me, sucking me into their vortex. Like tumbleweed caught in the eye of the cyclone, I am just along for the ride. Last night was a perfect example. Carter, Marcus, Monica Broccoli, even Grouch—they all imposed their own agendas on what would have otherwise been a perfectly ordinary evening. Even had it not been for hurricane Carter and tropical storm Broccoli, the night would have held unexpected drama. For, after Monica Broccoli limped out of my apartment, Marcus revealed the reason for his late arrival: He'd been pacing in my lobby for over an hour, practicing his breakup speech. He was seriously bent out of shape when he realized that his news would be eclipsed by far more dire events: Carter's possible pregnancy, Monica's probable dismemberment. If he was expecting tears and pleading, he was sorely disappointed.

"This isn't working, Holly . . ." he'd begun, and I'd cut him off, though I could tell he was just warming up. Marcus, a former captain of his college debate team, was incapable of stating an opinion that wasn't accompanied by a full-blown speech: supporting arguments, colorful anecdotes, concluding remarks, and sometimes, visual aids.

"That's okay. I totally understand," I'd said, patting him on the shoulder consolingly. "Can we talk about this later?"

Despite his obvious dejection at being denied the opportunity to deliver his carefully crafted sayonara speech, Marcus was a good sport. He stuck around—whether out of curiosity or compassion, I'm not sure—to help me deal with Monica.

Monica's perm turned out surprisingly well, and with Marcus's help, we managed to get the cast off her ankle. This time, instead of a power saw, we used a small handheld jeweler's file. The blade was thin enough to slide inside the cast without hurting Monica's leg, while the teeth were sufficiently sharp to cut through the plaster. We had it off in thirty minutes. I don't know why I hadn't thought of it sooner. Actually, I didn't think of it at all. It was Marcus, queasy at the thought of bloodshed, who rifled through the cupboard housing my jewelry-making supplies in search of the saw he remembered once seeing in my possession. He still thought that removing the cast was crazy and tried to reason Monica Broccoli out of it, but many a stronger man has withered in the face of her determination. Poor Marcus didn't stand a chance.

With Monica gone, Marcus wanted to deliver his this-is-going-nowhere speech. I had other things in mind. "That's great. I totally understand," I said, leading him by the hand into the living room. Carter had finished folding the flyers but she hadn't affixed the postage stamps and mailing labels. I explained the problem: the showcase less than two weeks away, next morning's typing deadline, the frequent interruptions. "If you could seal and stamp these flyers while I finish the typing job, then we can have a big heart-to-heart and I promise to cry and go full-tilt histrionic, but right now, there's no time!"

Marcus sighed and gave me his best "Oh, the things I put up with" look, then hauled out his cell phone and punched some numbers in.

"Who are you calling?"

"Village Pizza. You're buying."

I kissed him on the cheek. "You're a lifesaver."

The Sleepblaster Plus struck again, jolting me out of my painful trip down memory lane, and I hauled myself out of bed. I trudged to the bathroom, stumbling over the detritus of last night's adventure. Grouch meowed insistently as I passed by, rubbing his head against the cupboard where I store his food. I normally feed him first thing, but this morning he could wait. Eating twenty dollars' worth of salmon made him *persona non gato* in my book.

I dressed quickly, mentally preparing myself for the day ahead. First stop, the post office to drop off the flyers, which Marcus had finished stamping sometime after midnight. I smiled, thinking how ironic it was that Marcus was the one who helped me out, despite the terminal state of our relationship. I could have been nicer. . . . I could have acknowledged the deep sighs that punctuated his work as what they were: invitations to talk. But instead, when I'd notice that he'd stopped working and was staring in my direction, sighing wistfully, I'd bark, "Lick and stick, Marcus, lick and stick. Mama's got a deadline."

He licked and sticked and I typed. By the time both tasks were finished, we were too tired to talk. At the door, Marcus hugged me good-bye, squeezing me tighter and holding me longer than usual. "You promised histrionics," he said, looking forlorn.

"I'm too tired for histrionics," I answered. "But I promise you I'm gonna curl up in bed and cry myself to sleep."

And I tried. But despite Marcus's many good qualities, I couldn't conjure up tears over our breakup. Instead I found myself thinking about my new client, the man with the elegant handwriting and the dead wife. While racing to finish his typing job, I had been too distracted by Marcus's long-suffering sighs to focus fully on the writing, and I wished I had time to savor it. I had never met the client—we'd only spoken briefly on the phone. I was curious about him, who he was, what he looked like. Lying in bed, I strained to remember his voice, but it had been businesslike, unremarkable.

Then Grouch had leapt onto the bed and settled down on the pillow next to me, his salmon-scented breath a reminder of my disastrous dinner and failed romance. Another one bites the dust, I thought, and this one was so close to passing the three-month marker that spelled the end of most of my relationships. A hopeful thought occurred to me and I glanced at the alarm clock. It was two thirty a.m. Less than an hour had passed since Marcus's departure. Marcus didn't officially put the kibosh on our relationship until after midnight. That meant we had been dating for three months and *one day*. Comforted by this dubious achievement, I rolled over and drifted off to sleep.

As I was putting the stamped flyers in my knapsack, I heard a loud click coming from the pantry—the sound of the outside milk door snapping shut. My client had wanted to pick up the typing job early, so I told him I'd leave it in the milk cubby. On a whim, I had enclosed a flyer for the showcase in the envelope. Still curious to see what he looked like, I opened my front door. I saw no one but heard footsteps retreating down the stairs below. I leaned over the banister, but he was already gone, the lobby door clicking shut behind him.

I contemplated giving chase, breathlessly catching up to him in the street and saying . . . what? Our business was concluded, and there was no reason I had to see him. But for some reason I *wanted* to see him, if only to get a face to go along with the beautiful, soulful writing. I rushed to my window and looked out, but I couldn't pick out any likely candidates from the people passing by, an assembly as heterogeneous as New York itself: a buffed, spandex-clad guy whizzing by on Rollerblades; a walking Brooks Brothers ad hailing a taxi at the corner; and several people briskly walking while talking into cell phones. At the corner, a group of people waiting for the light to change included a couple of smartly dressed women wearing gym shoes with their business suits, a man pushing a stroller, and an elderly black woman wearing a sweatshirt that read GROOVY GRANDMA.

Though I find people-watching in New York a fascinating and instructive pastime, I had more pressing concerns. I finished loading the flyers into my knapsack and headed out the door. Waiting for the light to change at the street corner, I was struck by an overwhelming need for coffee. Coffee was definitely on my agenda, but it wasn't scheduled until after the trip to the post office. I looked down the street at the Starbucks on the next block, salivating at the sight of the familiar green-and-white logo. Suddenly deciding that a trip to the post office was extraneous and wouldn't substantially speed up delivery time, I shoved the flyers into the mailbox on the corner and hustled in the direction of Starbucks.

Carter was behind the register, looking even more tightly wound than usual. She nodded when she saw me, and called my usual order to the barista, Bob. "Grande no whip Mocha Frappuccino."

When I got to the register, we made our customary monetary exchange: I handed her a five-dollar bill; she reached into the register and gave me back five singles. To the casual observer, it would look like she had rung up my sale, but in reality, I had mooched yet another Mocha Frappuccino, a minor crime that occasionally weighed on my conscience. But not this morning.

"You left something at my apartment last night," I said, pocketing the singles and stepping aside for the next customer.

"What color is it?" she asked, ringing up a latte.

"Pink."

She nodded, biting her lip. "Grande decaf vanilla latte!" she screamed at barista Bob.

Miracle of miracles, my favorite seat was empty: a big, stuffed purple chair in the corner near the window. I snagged it just in time, heading off a laptop-laden young man who was eyeing the chair covetously. After enjoying a victory sip of my Frapuccino, I pulled a folder out of my knapsack and began leafing through a hodgepodge of clippings, Post-its, notes scrawled on the backs of envelopes and receipts, and once in a while, an honest-to-God piece of lined notebook paper with legible handwriting in something other than crayon or eyebrow pencil.

I was meeting Danny in half an hour to go over new material for the comedy showcase. Sifting through the jumble of notes in front of me, I hoped that Danny had been more successful in his brain-storming efforts than I had been.

Danny Crane had been my comedy partner for close to three years. We met at a midtown restaurant; he was a waiter, I was a cashier-hostess. For Danny, working at the Broadway Bistro was an obvious career move, waiting tables being pretty much a prerequisite for anyone aspiring to fame and fortune. For me, it was just a part-time job on my road to nowhere in particular. Fresh out of college, I wasn't sure what to do with myself, and my aunt's neighbor mentioned the job opening. "Maybe you'll meet a nice *man* there," my aunt whispered, pressing the phone number into my palm with a wink.

It was easy money but I soon grew bored with seating people and making change. To amuse myself, I'd adopt eccentric personalities and put on different accents, especially when taking phone orders, when my characters weren't limited by physical reality. I gained a reputation, particularly among the elderly regulars, for being "a real card." When Danny was hired, we quickly developed a friendship based on our shared sense of humor. We bounced off each other, inventing characters and pulling impromptu pranks to amuse ourselves during the restaurant's slow periods. Sometimes we'd play estranged lovers; in a fit of anger, I'd yank an imaginary ring off my finger, hurl it in his direction crying, "It's over!" and watch as patrons dove under booths, trying to retrieve the lost ring. More than once we took a charade a little too far, upsetting customers and disrupting the fine dining ambience the Broadway Bistro was striving for. On one such occasion, Danny and I were fired. Ironically, though, it was the restaurant manager who launched our comedy career, urging us to find a better outlet for our creative energies and offering to host our first comedy showcase.

Danny had been attending comedy workshops and had done a few well-received open-mike nights at the Improv. I had no experience and no desire to perform in front of people. But Danny and I clicked, and I didn't want to see that end when I turned in my Broadway Bistro apron. What the hell? I thought. I'll give it a try. That was three years—and six showcases—ago, and in that time we'd built a respectable career for ourselves. True, it wasn't yet supporting either of us full-time—I had my business and Danny held two part-time delivery jobs—but our future seemed bright.

"Looks like the mad scrawlings of a raving lunatic," Carter said, peeking at my notes and wiping down the table next to me.

"I don't mind being insane as long as I'm funny."

Carter glanced around the store, then leaned in and whispered, "Are you sure it was pink?"

I nodded solemnly. "I'm sorry." She was wringing the towel in her hands, looking so forlorn that I had to give her some hope. "But ya know, those things aren't a hundred percent accurate. You should go to a doctor."

She brightened. "I think I might have screwed up, too, with the directions. I was too nervous. And maybe all the caffeine in my system affected the results. I musta had, like, twelve cups of coffee yesterday."

"Yeah, the caffeine could have affected the *results*," I said, with more than a hint of sarcasm. "It also could have affected the *baby*, if there is one. Maybe you should lay off until you know for sure. And the cigarettes, too. And get some sleep. . . ."

She was walking away from me, waving the towel dismissively in my direction.

"And eat a decent meal!" I yelled to her retreating back.

I turned my attention back to my notes, but was doubtful that I could glean anything of comedic value from the disjointed ramblings in front of me. My attention was soon distracted by the father and daughter seated next to me. I don't know what it was that captivated my interest, but I suddenly, simply, fell madly in love. Not with him, nor with her, but with *them*. He looked to be in his late thirties or early forties, with thick, wavy brown hair. He was dressed professionally, but was not a starchy corporate type. I guessed he had a more down-to-earth profession. The little girl, no more than five years old, was dressed in a navy blue skirt, blue tights, and a white sweater with a bunny embroidered on the front. Her dark hair curled in springy tendrils, which fell to her shoulders.

It was the way the two interacted that sparked my instantaneous affection. She looked happy, confident, curious; he protective, proud, gentle. Between sips of cocoa, she'd bounce off her seat, climb onto the extra-wide window ledge, and twirl around ballerina-style. Her father looked on, and I could read so much in his watchful gaze: concern should she fall, encouragement that she spread her wings, joy in her very being.

I knew it was ridiculous, but I found myself imagining that they were mine, that when he leaned over and wiped chocolate off her chin, he whispered, "Let's get going, Mommy's waiting," and then he'd bundle her up and they'd be on their way home, where I would greet them at the door. She'd jump into my arms and squeeze me tight; he'd lean over and kiss me on the cheek, saying, "She did the cutest thing this morning. . . ." Then we'd shut the door and walk back into the apartment.

A cell phone rang, causing at least six patrons to reach into their pockets or purses. It was the dad who answered the phone, and reluctant to let go of my fantasy, I listened to his side of the conversation.

"Hello . . . Yes, we're on our way. We just stopped at Starbucks."

It was probably the mom. I tried to imagine her, but couldn't form a mental picture.

"School pictures? I didn't know that was today. . . . No, I did not get a note. . . . Yes, of course." He sighed heavily, glancing at his watch. "I know I agreed to bring her for a haircut, but—" A hint of irritation crept into his voice. "I'll take care of it."

The little girl tugged on his coat sleeve. "Daddy . . ."

He brought a finger to his lips. "Shh. In a minute." He reached over and brushed the hair out of her eyes. "I have to go. Bye."

"Daddy, I don't want my hairs cut."

"I know, pumpkin, but we promised Mommy. She's going to kill me if you have bangs in your eyes in your school pictures. Finish your cocoa so we can get going."

He dialed another number. The little girl lifted the cup to her lips. "Uh-oh," she said, as cocoa dribbled down her chin and onto her white sweater.

The dad leapt to his feet, grabbing napkins and dabbing at the stain. Then, into the cell phone, "This is Tom Hansen calling for Mr. Algado. . . . He isn't? Is this his secretary? . . . Hi, Donna. Listen, I was supposed to drop off some documents this morning on my way to take my daughter to school, but something has come up and I can't make it. H-a-n-s-e-n. Yes, I'll hold."

Carter was making her way through the store again, wiping down tables, and he flagged her down. "Miss? Could you tell me if there's a SuperCuts or something like that near here?"

Carter shook her head. "Nah. There's a hair salon on fifteenth, but it's kinda pricey and I don't think they're open this early. There is a SuperCuts near Union Square."

"Yes, I know. I was hoping for something closer. Thank you."

"No problem." A line was beginning to form at the counter, so Carter went back to the register.

"Yes, I'm here," the dad was saying into his cell phone. "I know it's important. I had to run a few errands this morning and I got held up. It's picture day at my daughter's school and I was supposed to get her hair cut yesterday but she had a tummy ache."

The door opened and Danny bounded in, nodding hello to me

before heading to the counter. I saw him lean over the register and kiss Carter's cheek.

Danny's arrival reminded me of my task that morning, and I felt guilty at my lack of progress. Still, I couldn't take my attention off the daddy-daughter drama playing out in front of me.

The dad was saying, "There's no way I can get uptown to your office and still make it in time to get her hair cut and drop her off at school. . . . No, no, after that, I have to go straight to work. I'm teaching a ten o'clock class."

He was shifting in his seat, clearly getting agitated, and I felt a strange responsibility toward him, an irrational desire to help him out. I don't know why; he was a complete stranger, and as a New Yorker, I typically go through life in my own little insulated bubble, not pausing to stop and talk to strangers, let alone help them solve their life crises. Sure, I might help a little old lady cross the street now and then, but only if she's going in my direction.

Yet I felt oddly compelled to help the distraught dad. An idea struck, and I leaned forward and tapped his shoulder. "Ask if you can messenger the documents."

He looked startled. He shook his head and whispered, "I don't know a messenger service."

"I do." I pointed to the phone and prodded, "Just ask."

He cleared his throat. "Donna, is it all right if I send the documents by messenger? . . . Yes, I've already had them notarized. . . . I didn't realize that. . . . No, I'm sorry. . . . Yes, I realize that he has to prepare the motion this morning. . . . By nine o'clock? I'll send them right now. . . ."

I leaned forward again. "Ask what kind of coffee she likes."

He turned to me, his expression a mixture of curiosity and annoyance. He mouthed, *"What?"*

I gestured for the phone, and most likely numbed into compliance out of shock, he handed it to me.

"Donna?" I said brightly. "This is Mr. Hansen's . . . assistant. What kind of coffee do you drink, hon? . . . And your boss? Cream and sugar? O.K., you have a nice day, O.K.?"

I hung up the phone and handed it to the dad, who was gaping at me. He started to speak, but I interrupted. "Hold that thought." I waved my arm and shouted in Danny's direction, "Yo, Danny!"

As Danny made his way toward me, I asked the dad for the documents. He took a manila envelope out of his briefcase and began writing the address of an uptown attorney's office.

"Ready to rumble?" Danny asked. "I've got a few ideas—"

"Not yet," I interrupted. "First, I need you to take these documents to the address on the envelope." I held out the envelope, but he was waving me off.

"I'm not on the clock yet. I came early just to meet with *you*, remember? Besides, I can't deliver anything other than coffee and pastry products. You wanna get me fired?"

I picked up the napkin on which I had scrawled Donna's coffee preferences. "This is a bona fide coffee delivery. Here's the order. Consider this"—I thrust the envelope at him—"to be the delivery slip. Just leave it with the coffee."

Danny looked hesitant, so I pleaded. "Please, Danny, it's important. I'll owe ya big time." I pushed him in the direction of the coffee counter. "Tell Carter to put it on my tab," I called after him. "And throw in some scones!"

The dad looked uneasy. "Look, I appreciate what you're trying to do, but I can take care of it."

"No, you can't. I heard you. You need to get your little girl's hair cut and drop her at school and get yourself to work. Oh, I can help you with that, too. I run a hair salon out of my apartment upstairs. I can give her a quick trim in minutes flat . . . and we can work on getting that cocoa stain out, too."

He shook his head, eyeing me doubtfully. "I don't think so. . . ."

I suddenly realized how crazy I must appear to this guy, barging in on his morning coffee break and trying to take over his life. "I'm sorry. Of course you can't just go to some strange woman's apartment on the drop of a dime. I could be a scissor-wielding psycho." I reached into my knapsack, searching for one of my flyers advertising my haircutting service, but came up empty. "But I'm legit, really. . . ."

"Daddy"—the little girl was pulling on his sleeve—"I hafta go to the bathroom," she said, smiling sheepishly.

Carter approached with hands on hips. "I need to talk to you, Holly."

I grabbed her by the arm and smiled at the dad. "Carter can vouch for me. She's the manager here. Carter, tell this man I'm okay. I'm licensed by the state of New York to do hairstyling and income tax preparation."

"Yeah, we're proud of our little Holly. She's the best damned accounting cosmetologist in the whole tristate area."

Unmoved by this testimonial, the dad took his daughter by the hand and asked Carter to point the way to the restroom.

"Who is that guy?" Carter asked, watching them walk away. "And what was that coffee delivery about? You know the delivery program is only on a trial basis, and we're supposed to stay within a ten-block radius. On top of the free coffee, I had to give Danny cab fare! You want me to get fired?"

"Of course not. I'll pay you back. He's just a guy who needed help, and I couldn't resist."

"When did you become freakin' Wonder Woman?"

"I don't know. I just felt sorry for him. Haven't you ever had one of those moments when everything is spiraling out of control, and it would make a world of difference if someone showed up to lend a hand . . . or a little plastic cup to pee in?"

Carter glared at me. "Thank goodness, Danny left." She looked around the store nervously. "You better not say anything to him."

"You can buy my silence by helping me with this guy. I'll throw in dinner and a movie. *Please.*"

"I already sent coffee and scones. What else do you want from me?"

I smiled, a plan forming in my mind. "I'm gonna need your break room."

While Carter, sufficiently bribed into complicity, persuaded the dad to wait in the Starbucks break room, I dashed to my building and raced up the six flights of stairs. I threw some basic haircutting supplies into a bag and was back downstairs, panting and sweating, in mere minutes. Carter had persuaded the little girl to remove her sweater and was working on removing the chocolate stain. The girl, Nicole, was shivering in a little pink undershirt. I propped her up on a stool and wrapped a towel around her neck. Spraying her hair with detangling spray and water, I began combing it out.

"But, Daddy, I don't want my hairs cut," she complained, putting both arms over her head protectively.

"I hate getting my hairs cut, too," I confided. "I promise I won't cut too much off. Would it make you feel better if I cut your daddy's hairs, too?"

She giggled, nodding, but Daddy objected, "Oh, no. There's no time for that."

"Okay," I said, "since your dad is too chicken, how about this: If you let me cut your hairs, I'll let you cut some of mine."

The dad raised his eyebrows in surprise but said nothing. Nicole smiled and nodded in agreement. I cut quickly but carefully; haunted by images of my own school pictures—crooked teeth, bad hair, funny clothes—I would do what I could to protect Nicole from such a fate.

Carter appeared, holding out the bunny sweater to the dad. "It's still a little damp, but the stain's gone."

"Thank you, really—"

She cut him off, turning to me. "Your cousin Gerry's here. I told him to wait out front."

Barista Bob bellowed, "We're out of half-and-half!"

"I'm on it!" Carter yelled back, running out of the break room.

The news that my cousin had arrived was more than a bit disconcerting. Gerry wouldn't track me down at Starbucks for a casual chat. Something must be wrong. Maybe something had happened to Monica Broccoli, wobbling around on her weak ankle. A slip and fall, or worse. Oh, God, it would be *my* fault, wouldn't it?

I finished snipping Nicole's hair; then I rooted around in my bag and pulled out some pink barrettes. I swept some hair back on either side of her face and held it in place with the barrettes. She looked precious; any mom would be pleased to see this face staring back from a school photo. The dad, too, looked satisfied.

Gerry appeared in the break room doorway. "Check it out," he said, grinning. I looked at him curiously, and he reached into a gym bag and held up a pair of black dress socks, beaming proudly. "Martin Scorsese's socks!"

Before I could even contemplate what bizarre chain of events led to my cousin brandishing a famous director's footwear in my face, Carter appeared behind Gerry. Her patience had clearly reached its breaking point.

"I need everyone to clear out of here *now*, before Sheila the Squealer arrives for her shift." She thrust a finger at Gerry's chest. "I told *you* to wait out front. This area is for employees only!"

Cowed, Gerry retreated from the break room, and the dad began shifting uncomfortably. "I didn't mean to cause such trouble. . . ."

"It isn't your fault," Carter said brusquely. "It's mine. I let *her*

talk me into this. She's always getting me into situations like this."
Funny how her way of taking responsibility sounded an awful lot
like blame.

"Me? I'm always the one getting you out of jams. I'm just flotsam," I said.

"What the hell is flotsam?" She was cramming the hair supplies
back into my bag. "Never mind. Just get outta here."

I had removed the towel and was brushing stray hairs off
Nicole's clothes when Danny burst into the break room. "There
you are! Come on, I only have ten minutes before I clock in. What
the heck are you doing?"

"Never mind. How'd the delivery go?"

"Great. The lady was so happy with her cappuccino and chocolate chip scone she nearly had an orgasm."

"Danny!" I hushed him, pointing to Nicole.

"Sorry." He shrugged. "I don't do kids." He left the break
room, saying he'd meet me out front. I looked at Carter, who was
obviously stung by his comment about kids. She shoved the bag at
me and rushed out the door, fighting off tears.

I hurriedly swept the hair up off the floor, while the dad helped
Nicole back into her sweater and lifted her off the stool.

"Wait, Daddy. I didn't get to cut her hairs!"

"Honey, I think she was kidding. . . ."

"Absolutely not! I never renege on a promise." I handed Nicole
the least lethal of my styling shears. "Just one cut, okay? I'd let you
do my whole head but I don't want you to be late for school." I
twisted most of my long hair up atop my head, holding it with one
hand. With my other hand I pointed to the strands left dangling at
the base of my neck. "Pick one and go for it!"

I felt the cold blade on the back of my neck, felt the shears open
and snip shut. I turned around, and Nicole was smiling broadly,
grinning at her accomplishment. I wondered how her mother

would react when she came home boasting that she had cut some strange lady's hair in Starbucks. I hoped I hadn't made things worse for the dad in my attempt to make them better.

Gathering up the last of my things, I led the way back to the front of the store. Danny was in the stuffed chair I had formerly occupied, pawing through my muddled mass of notes with a pained expression on his face. Gerry was at an adjacent table, looking like he was about to jump out of his skin. He saw me glance in his direction and held the black socks over his head, dangling them as though he was teasing a puppy with a chew toy. Nearby patrons looked at him distastefully; the aroma of stinky socks did not complement the cinnamon-infused atmosphere of Starbucks.

The dad looked a little overwhelmed by the morning's events. Reaching for his wallet, he asked, "How much do I owe you?"

"No charge. It's today's special: one free haircut with every cup of cocoa sold."

He held out his hand and I shook it, wishing him luck. He glanced at his watch. "Thanks to you, I think we'll just make it to school. I don't know how to repay you." He hesitated, then said, "Maybe dinner?"

The invitation took me off guard and I hesitated. I had assumed that the dad was married, but of course, he could be single or divorced. I looked for a wedding ring, but he was standing with his left hand in his pocket. Of course, there might not have been any romantic intention behind his invitation. Best to play it cool. "Uh . . . yeah. Dinner would be . . . fine. Or lunch. Whatever. Let me give you my number." I grabbed a napkin and scrawled my phone number. In place of my name, I wrote *Scissor-Wielding Psycho from Starbucks*.

Both Gerry and Danny were demanding my attention, but my curiosity about Martin Scorsese's socks won out over my desire to brainstorm with Danny. Actually, though he wasn't always aware of it, my cousin Gerry often provided material for my comedy act. I got a lot of mileage out of his "virgin" speech at my grandmother's funeral. Perhaps I could kill two birds with one stone. I sat at Gerry's table and gestured for Danny to pull his chair closer.

Delighted to have another audience member for his tale, Gerry thrust the socks into Danny's face, announcing triumphantly, "Martin Scorsese's socks!"

"For real?" Danny asked, backing away from the odiferous display. "Whaddya know, Scorsese's feet stink just like the rest of ours."

"That's *my* foot stink," Gerry said.

Danny wrinkled his nose. "Gross, man, put 'em away."

"Why do you have Martin Scorsese's socks?" I asked.

"Ya know that catering gig I worked last night? It was at Martin Scorsese's place. A bunch of big-wig film people, very chichi party. Full wait staff, little pupu platters, everything. I was coming straight from dance class and I had my uniform in my gym bag. The maid let me change in the guest bathroom. Do you know he's got a TV in every room, including the bathrooms? I guess he doesn't want to miss anything if he has to take a whiz—"

"What about the socks?" I prodded, knowing how long and pointless Gerry's digressions could be.

"So, when I got dressed, I realized I forgot my socks. My suit pants are a little short and my bare ankles were showing. I couldn't wear it like that—"

"Of course not," I said, "not to a chichi party with pupu platters."

"Exactly." Gerry rattled on, explaining how he'd tiptoed out of the bathroom, barefoot, hoping to find a fellow waiter with a spare pair of socks. Instead, he stumbled upon the laundry room, where lo and behold, a load of still-warm clothing was in the dryer. He opened the dryer, rifled through Scorsese's unmentionables, and appropriated a pair of black Armani socks. When the party was over, he returned to the laundry room, planning to sneak the stolen booty back into the dryer, but by then he had grown attached.

Now he was holding the socks up and regarding them reverently. "I'm thinking of selling them on eBay."

Danny snorted. "You can't sell Martin Scorsese's stolen socks on the Internet! First of all, why would anyone believe they're his?"

Gerry paused to consider the question. He shrugged. "I could give them a certificate of authenticity. I'll print one up on my computer."

Danny said, "But you wore them. They look stretched out."

Gerry nodded. "Yeah, his feet are kinda small. I would have expected bigger feet from a director of such magnitude."

I eyed him quizzically. "What are you talking about?"

"Oh come on! *Mean Streets, Raging Bull, The Last Temptation of Christ . . .*"

"I'm not questioning his talent. But I had no idea that foot size was correlated to cinematic vision."

"I'm just sayin', the director of *Taxi Driver* should have at least a size ten."

As Gerry continued to wax poetic over Scorsese's genius, I imagined what would have happened if Gerry had replaced the socks, stretched out and sweaty, in with the clean clothes in the dryer. Only in a truly twisted world could a major motion picture director end up wearing socks soiled by my cousin Gerry.

Having more than satisfied my curiosity, I turned to Danny. "All right, let's get to work."

"Can't," he said, rising from the purple chair. "My shift just started."

Freeze-Dried Mice

Soon after Danny clocked in, Gerry departed Starbucks, eager to show off his prized possession to other members of the family. As he was halfway out the door, I realized I had forgotten to ask about Monica Broccoli. "Gerry, wait up."

I gathered up my things and stopped by the register to say good-bye to Carter. "Come by when you get off work!" I shouted at her.

Gerry was waiting for me on the sidewalk. I asked if Monica had made it home safely from my place.

"Yeah, no problem. She left early this morning for her audition. I helped her into a cab and told her to break a leg. You think I mighta jinxed her?"

"Probably not the best choice of words."

"Yeah, well . . . words never were my thing."

We reached my building, and Gerry gave me a quick hug. "Hey, thanks for helping out with Monica. And for taking that snake off my hands."

I cringed at the memory. The night before, as Monica was ten-derly tiptoeing across my kitchen floor, testing her ankle's ability to carry her weight, I went to the living room and retrieved the aquarium housing her pet boa. "Don't forget your snake." I smiled, setting the aquarium by the front door.

Monica moaned, "But, Holly, I don't think I can carry it all the way down your stairs, and then home on the subway."

"I'll carry it down. And I'll hail you a cab. You shouldn't brave the subway on that ankle."

Monica had whined some more, then finally admitted that she never intended to take the snake back. "Gerry doesn't like it," she explained. "It's a threat to his masculinity."

"What?" Marcus had balked. "What kind of self-respecting man doesn't like snakes?"

"It was a gift from my ex-boyfriend Carlos. Whenever Gerry would see me stroking the snake, he thought I was thinking about Carlos."

Ugh. Surprisingly, I found myself on my cousin's side on this one. I wouldn't want my boyfriend to stroke *anything* belonging to his ex.

"But I'm terrified of him," I protested. "I have to stuff a towel under my bathroom door when I shower because I'm afraid he'll slither under the door when I'm in there naked."

Monica raised one eyebrow. "Holly, I think you have deeper problems. Rocky won't hurt you. Will you, baby?" She was over the aquarium now, unfastening the cover and murmuring baby talk. "My sweet snookums, come to mama. . . ."

"It's not just that. I can't feed him. He hasn't eaten since he's been here. I bought a rat, like you told me, but I couldn't give it to him. Now I'm stuck with a pet rat to take care of!" I pointed to a small plastic cage on a bookshelf, where the rodent I'd christened Felix was chewing on a piece of lettuce.

Monica was struggling with the aquarium cover. "What the hell did you do to this thing? It used to pop right open."

"I know! It was dangerous. I reinforced it with some supergrip metal clasps and a triple-locking guard rail." I showed her how to open the cover, then scurried away as she lifted Rocky out of the aquarium. Lacking anything to use as a shield, I climbed up onto my dining room table, hoping boas weren't particularly good climbers.

Monica was cooing to Rocky and stroking him lovingly. Now that I had a visual, I could sympathize with my cousin's reaction to Rocky. Monica looked up at me. "You don't have to feed him live rats, Holly. You can order them freeze-dried over the Internet and have them delivered once a month by FedEx."

I stared at her incredulously. "What, like a Rat-of-the-Month Club?"

Monica shrugged. "I prefer feeding him live prey. You want me to feed your rat to him before I go?"

"No!" Though I found rats only slightly less desirable as pets than snakes, I had grown strangely protective of young Felix and could not condemn him to such a grisly death. And somehow, between Monica's plaintive pleas, sympathy for my cousin's quandary, and the two hundred bucks Monica handed me at the door, I had relented and agreed to keep Rocky until I could find him another home.

Now Gerry was saying, "That snake drove me crazy. Monica was too touchy feely with him, if you know what I mean."

Unfortunately, I did. I fished my keys out of my bag. "Hey, how'd you know I was at Starbucks, anyway?"

"You weren't home, and it's too early for you to have a gig, so I figured you'd be there. You're not exactly unpredictable, Holly."

"Oh." The little buzz of excitement I'd gotten from playing Starbucks' resident superhero dissipated in an instant. I was predictable. Dull. Boring.

Gerry said, "You goin' to my mom's house for dinner Sunday?"

"I don't know. Depends if I get a gig. Why?"

Gerry said cryptically, "You should go. It's gonna be interesting." He winked, then took off down the street.

* * *

I checked my mail in the lobby and trudged up the six flights to my apartment. Once inside, I went into the pantry to check the milk cubby. There was a bulky brown envelope and a small white one. I felt a little thrill when I saw the handwriting on the small envelope: neat, straight letters spelling out my name. The writer.

I ripped it open. There was a check for the job I'd completed the night before. I was impressed—precious few of my clients were such prompt payers. And since I hated playing bill collector—mailing reminder notices and making those dreadful phone calls asking for money—it was a huge relief to find that my new client was not going to be a problem in that regard. That was assuming his check didn't bounce—another problem I'd encountered more than once. A yellow Post-it note was affixed to the check.

Thanks. I'll be back next week to drop off
more of the same.

The check was drawn on a business account. RBH Enterprises, with a post office box address and no phone number. Unlike the precise lettering of my name and the amount payable, the signature was completely undecipherable. It looked like an excerpt of a polygraph or heart monitor printout: several bold up-and-down strokes with no clear correspondence to any letters in the English alphabet. The check offered no clues as to the writer's identity. Again I struggled to recall my telephone conversation when he first called to inquire about my services, but nothing was forthcoming.

Pushing the writer out of my mind, I opened the second envelope. An I♥NY key chain tumbled out, and I remembered my promise to my upstairs neighbor Brian to take care of his cat while he was away for the weekend. I read the note:

Holly, please check on Kramer once a day. He gets bottled water
    only, please. Dry food is in the cupboard, as always.
    And be sure to leave the TV on for him. Thanks.

There was a twenty-dollar bill attached to the note with a paper
clip. I smiled. Today had been a good day. I put the twenty and the
writer's check in my wallet, where they joined Monica's two hundred dollars. Tomorrow morning I'd stop at the bank. I hoped my
bank account wouldn't die from the shock of the deposit.

"Maybe we'll splurge and buy some Fancy Feast this week," I
said to Grouch, as I filled his bowl with Friskies. Reaching into the
fridge, I ripped a chunk off a half-wilted head of lettuce and
brought it into the living room, where Felix the Rat was reposing in
a nest of shredded paper towels and cedar chips. Having fed the
other animate members of the household, I looked over at Rocky's
aquarium and felt a stab of guilt. I had tried feeding the big guy lettuce and myriad other food items, but he wasn't biting.

I booted up the computer, marveling at the technological ad-
vances that would allow a snakephobic Manhattanite such as myself to have preserved prey delivered right to my doorstep with just
a few clicks of the mouse. Within moments of starting my search, I
had located a smattering of Web sites catering to the Net-savvy
snake owner, with such clever names as FrozenRodent.com and the
Mighty Mouse Merchant.

Ordering a meal for Rocky was going to be no simple matter, I
soon discovered. A wide array of rodents was available, in different
sizes and types. One price chart distinguished between pinkies,
fuzzies, and hoppers. I looked over at Rocky. Was he hankering for
a hopper, or was a fuzzy more to his liking? I did some more searching, and was amazed by the number of Web pages created by snake
enthusiasts. As I read through the advice, I discovered that I had
much to learn about boa constrictors. I was relieved to read that

there wasn't much danger of a boa Rocky's size killing me, though if he mistook my hand for food, he might inflict a painful bite. But I was appalled to find out that adult boas can grow to be eleven feet long! Clearly, my guardianship of Rocky was going to have to be temporary.

One herpetologist's Web site insisted that I needed to know his size and weight in order to figure out what to feed him. As I was pondering the nauseating prospect of weighing a boa constrictor, my business line rang.

I reached for the phone. "Hollie's Hobbies."

"Hi, Holly, this is Virginia Talbot with PAPS." The Patients and Pets Support Network, PAPS, was a nonprofit organization I was involved with from time to time. They provided services to people who were hospitalized and couldn't take care of their pets. I loved the program but thought they could use a better acronym, as hearing from Virginia always made me think of my gynecologist.

"Hi, Virginia. Is it Armand again? Is everything okay?" Armand was a man in my neighborhood who had been in and out of the hospital with kidney problems. Since I was nearby, I usually got the call to take care of his pets, a German shepherd named Fritz and a bunny named Jack.

"No, it's not Armand. I have something . . . unusual for you. A woman contacted us on behalf of her brother, a quadraplegic with a helper monkey."

"Did you say a *monkey*?"

"Yes. The monkey is trained to perform simple tasks for his owner. It's a wonderful program, Holly. The quadraplegic person gets a companion as well as a little relief from being totally dependent on caretakers and family."

"Wow. So what do you need?"

"The brother is going into the hospital for surgery and they called to see if we have someone who can take care of the monkey. I told her that we've never handled anything like this before, but then I remembered the application you filled out when you first came to us. I have it here." She read from the form. "Under education and special skills, you wrote 'unicycling, stand-up comedy, carpentry, palm reading, certificate in tax accountancy, and degree in primatology.' Is that true?"

"I gave up palm reading years ago."

"You have a degree in primatology? That's monkeys, isn't it? And apes?"

"Yes. Columbia University, class of 1998."

"What on earth do you do with a degree in primatology? I never knew there was such a thing."

"You become a palm-reading comedienne who prepares tax returns."

"Seriously, Holly. It's a real degree?"

Her line of questioning recalled long and tortured conversations I'd had with my aunts when I was accepted into the Columbia program. "But, Holly," my aunt Betty would plead, "whaddya gonna do with a degree in monkeys? If you gotta go to college, at least study something that'll help you in life. Doris Cumberland's daughter went through dental hygiene training and now she's married to a dentist." My aunt Kuki would concur. "Whaddya gonna learn in that monkey school anyway? Why don't you sign up for that secretarial course I saw advertised on the TV? Have you called the number I gave you?" Only my aunt Kuki, who measured a woman's achievement by her husband's salary, would consider Columbia University "monkey school."

"Yes, it's a real degree, Virginia. It just doesn't have much practical application outside of Africa or South America." I had wanted to move to Africa once, envisioning myself communing with wild chimpanzees like Jane Goodall had, but once I had my degree in hand, the prospect of leaving Manhattan, with its twenty-four-hour pizza delivery and newsstands on every corner, for Africa, with its malaria-bearing mosquitoes and giant deadly snakes—not to mention a considerable amount of civil unrest—well, let's just say my plans got a bit more realistic. I applied for a zookeeper position at the Bronx Zoo, and when I didn't get it, I took a job waiting tables at the Jungle Room, a theme restaurant decorated like a rain forest, replete with fake trees and animatronic jungle critters. There, my degree was more of a hindrance than a help. It used to drive me batty staring at the faux rain forest where South American monkeys, African gorillas, and Asian orangutans shared bananas in the same little patch of plastic jungle. My constant complaining about the geographical impossibility of the tableau led the manager to decide that I'd be better suited working outside—as a parking lot attendant. So I quit, eventually ending up at the Broadway Bistro, working with Danny, leaving my primatological past behind me.

"So you know all about monkeys?"

"Well, I studied their ecology, social behavior, cognition, that kind of thing. That's not the same as taking care of a *pet* monkey."

"You're the closest I've got. Bless you, Holly."

Here we go again. She was thanking me and I couldn't recall agreeing to anything. "Why can't the sister take care of the monkey?"

"She says they have personality differences."

Great. A monkey with personality problems. Still, I had to admit, I was curious. "Okay," I said. "I'll do it."

After getting the details of my monkey-sitting assignment, I returned to my snake search, printing out several pages of information on the care and feeding of boa constrictors. The more I read, the more guilty I felt. Young boas should eat once a week, and it had been three weeks since Rocky had arrived. I promised myself I'd make up for my shameful neglect that night, ordering him the best rodent meal the Internet had to offer. But first there was the problem of what to order. I tried to call Monica, but there was no answer at her place or Gerry's.

My intercom buzzed. "Yeah?" I yelled into the speaker.

"Buzz me in!" Carter shouted.

I pressed the button and unlocked the front door. While waiting for Carter to climb the six flights, I began ridding my apartment of the final remnants of last night's festivities—sorting the hair supplies from the kitchen accessories and returning everything to its proper place.

At last Carter appeared in the doorway, clutching a large paper bag. She looked brighter and calmer than she had earlier in the day. "Up for a pajama party?" she asked.

I peeked into the bag. "Got any ice cream in there?"

"Rocky road." She nodded, taking a large tub out of the bag and putting it in my freezer. Then she dumped the bag's remaining contents onto the table. Out spilled enough home pregnancy test kits to supply a small drugstore. "I was thinking," she said, "Monica was right. That test I did last night was probably bad. It had expired, plus the directions said for best results use your first morning pee. I went back to the drugstore to get another but I couldn't decide which one was best."

"So you bought them *all*?"

Carter nodded. "I figure I can spend the night here and we'll do them all in the morning. Come on, Hol, we can stay up all night talking about boys, and give each other facials and do yoga and stuff. I told Danny I'm spending the night at my grandma's house."

I considered the evening's prospects. Though I was an attractive, vibrant, single young woman living in New York City, arguably the dating capital of the world, my chances of landing a date for the evening had walked out the door last night with Marcus, the not quite man of my dreams. Believe it or not, spending an evening eating ice cream and watching my best friend pee into plastic vials was the best offer on the table. "O.K.," I told her, "but I need your help with something first."

"What?"

"We have to weigh a snake."

Over a dinner of leftover pizza, Carter and I discussed our respective relationship dilemmas. Hers was obvious: Quite possibly pregnant, she was in love with a guy who could be the poster boy for commitment phobia. I loved Danny dearly, but couldn't imagine him as a husband and father. Part of his charm came from his boyish kid-at-heart attitude. He liked to say that he lacked the responsibility gene. He was not someone you'd entrust with the care of your houseplants, let alone a baby.

Carter certainly didn't radiate maternal vibes with her punk haircut and multiple body piercings, but I had a feeling that deep down she had all the makings of a true-blue, carpooling, cookie-baking, costume-making mom. Having known her since we were both ten, I understood that much of her attitude was artifice. She might talk tough, but she was still the same girl who'd played dress up with me in my aunt Kuki's closet, always favoring a certain pink chiffon gown and cultured pearls.

My dilemma was less apparent. Not at all morose over my breakup with Marcus, I was instead fixated on a man I had never met: the man behind those lined yellow pages that I'd typed the night before. I knew it was ridiculous, but all day long I had been remembering the impassioned words and imagining the man who had written them. I pictured a tall man with tousled blond hair, expressive blue eyes, and a wistful smile. But, as I admitted to Carter, I didn't know anything about him—not even his name.

"Didn't he introduce himself to you on the phone?"

"Yeah, I'm sure he did, but I just can't remember! I was in a rush to get out the door and I couldn't find a piece of paper to write on. So I committed the information to memory."

"Obviously," she said dryly. "He could be married."

"His wife died," I reminded her.

"You don't know that. How do you know he's writing about his real life? It could be fiction."

"Right. But I didn't get the feeling that it was fiction. It reads like journal entries or personal essays."

"Why would he want that stuff typed? Think about it."

I nodded. She had a point. Still, my instincts told me that what I'd read was genuine grief, not fabrication.

"And even if his wife is dead, you don't know what he looks like. He could be eighty, balding, and fat. What if he's a delusional maniac? Maybe he killed his wife!"

"Point taken," I said, clearing our dinner plates. "I don't know who he is, what he looks like, or whether he has a wife, living or dead. I just have a feeling—I can't explain it—but I feel like I'm meant to know him."

Then I told her about my last-minute inclusion of a showcase flyer in the envelope with his typing job. "I know it's a long shot, but maybe he'll show up and introduce himself."

"Why would he? You're obsessed with *him*, not the other way around. To him, you're just the girl who does his typing."

I sighed, my hopes deflated. "Maybe he needs a good laugh."

Carter gulped down the rest of her Coke and smiled patronizingly. She was clearly enjoying this reversal of our roles. Usually I was the one trying to explain the irrationality of her latest notions. "Let's get real here, Holly," she said. "You're fantasizing over some mystery man you've never met, when you had a real live one in your reach today at Starbucks. What was that all about, anyway?"

"That was about helping someone in need. Nothing more. I don't go after married men."

"I don't think he's married. He wasn't wearing a wedding ring."

"You checked?"

"Of course. I see someone giving my best friend the once-over, I check out the ring finger."

"He must've thought I was a lunatic."

"He was smitten," she teased. "I think you should go for him. He may be a little past his sell-by date, but I think he's cute."

I rolled my eyes. To Carter, anyone over thirty was past his prime. "He was attractive," I acknowledged, "but it was more of a package deal. I saw him and his daughter and thought they looked sweet together. On his own, I probably wouldn't have noticed him at all."

"Maybe not, but what is it that your aunt Kuki always said?"

I shrugged. My aunt had a number of memorable aphorisms, not all of them suitable for print. " 'May the lint in your belly button never fuzzy your mind?' "

"No, the one about the treasure under your toes."

Ah yes. " 'The foolish man seeks out treasure in far-distant places; the wise man knows that treasure lies beneath his own shoelaces.' " One of many "pearls of ancient wisdom" my aunt concocted to persuade me not to leave home. "Quoting Aunt Kuki will not win you any points."

"O.K. If you weren't just the teeniest bit interested in the guy, why did you give him your phone number?"

I raised my eyebrows. "You saw that?"

She nodded.

"He caught me off guard. I wasn't sure if he was asking me out or if he was just being polite, offering to repay me. So, yeah, I gave him my number. He's a potential client, after all."

"He's got a lot of potential, all right. Just do me a favor—if you become his kid's regular hairstylist, find yourself a new salon. The Starbucks Corporation frowns upon third-party commercial utilization of its floor space. It's in the manual."

"Don't worry. I'll probably never hear from him."

The words were still hanging in the air when the phone rang. Carter whispered, "I bet it's him!"

Carter's suggestion caused my stomach to become all fluttery, despite my insistence that I wasn't interested. I picked up the receiver and affected a nonchalant tone. "Hello?"

"Holly, what's the matter with you? Your blessed mother, rest her soul, asked me on her deathbed to look after you, and it's taken a toll on my heart, believe you me. Every time I turn around, it's something new. My ticker can only take so much stress."

"I know, Aunt Kuki," I said. "Calm down. What's the matter?"

"Gerry says you took a machete to Monica last night, hacking her cast to pieces. It's lucky the poor girl wasn't maimed."

I balked. "It was a power saw, and I didn't hack it to pieces. She asked me to remove it so she could go on an audition today."

"I know all about that. I don't know which one of you is worse. You, with your power tools, hacking the cast off someone's leg right there in your apartment—and I think it's probably illegal, by the way, and you're lucky no one called the cops—or her, cavorting around town in her underwear trying to be an *actress*."

As a model, Monica Broccoli had done some catalog work, mostly casual wear, but ever since she appeared in a JCPenney circular modeling bras, my aunt has been unable to discuss Monica without making mention of her unmentionables.

Kuki continued. "I can say nothing for her. Who knows what she came from? But you! You should know better."

"You're right," I said placatingly. "I should never have done such a crazy thing. I don't know what I was thinking." I knew from experience that arguing with Aunt Kuki was futile. If you got her dander up, you'd never hear the end of it; it was easier to just give in and let her grumble about what a perpetual disappointment you were.

"That's better. Now tell me you'll be at dinner on Sunday night."

"Sunday night? I'm not sure—"

"Your blessed mother, may she rest in peace, how it would break her heart to see how her only child has cast aside her family. . . ."

Emotional blackmail, works every time. "Sunday night. I'll be there."

"And just remember what I always said—"

" 'May the lint in your belly button never fuzzy your mind?' "

" 'Young ladies with no regard for propriety cause their aunts much anxiety.' "

"You made that up!"

"I did not. It was in *Reader's Digest*. But I'm going to embroider it onto a throw pillow."

"Please don't make me touch it, Holly."

Carter and I were standing over Rocky's cage, planning our strategy. I was reading from the pages I'd downloaded from Big Todd's Snake Lovers' Web site on the safe handling of boa constrictors. Carter had my Crate and Barrel oven mitts over her hands. She was all gung ho about reaching into the tank until I read Big Todd's helpful tip #2: Most bites result from hungry boas mistaking a human hand for food.

"But, Carter, a boa's bite isn't deadly. They kill their prey by coiling around it and squeezing it to death. Look at him. He's a baby boa. He's not big enough to wrap around you once, let alone squeeze the life out of you."

"Maybe so, but I'm not taking any chances. After all, I could be pregnant! You wouldn't want to endanger the life of my unborn child, would you?"

"O.K., I'll pick him up," I groaned, hoping that if I stalled long enough she would talk me out of it. "But first, let's figure out how we're going to weigh him." I had hauled out my bathroom scale, but I was convinced it added ten pounds to my true weight, just like the scales at the doctor's office and my gym. Besides, if we set Rocky on the scale, what would prevent him from slithering away? I also had a postal scale that I used to weigh packages for my business, but it was pretty wobbly and I couldn't imagine how to balance a snake on its small stand. "What if we weigh the entire aquarium with Rocky inside, and then weigh it again without Rocky, and subtract the second weight from the first?"

"Mm," Carter said, considering. "Makes sense. Better yet, we could go buy the exact same aquarium, and all the stuff inside, then see how much that weighs. That way, we don't have to touch the snake."

I had to admit, Carter's plan had the makings of brilliance, except that it involved spending money I didn't have on an aquarium I would never use—not to mention the time it would take running around town trying to duplicate Rocky's abode. No, it was much simpler to just do a quick lift and weigh. That is, as long as I wasn't the one doing the lifting. "What if we wrap your hands in Ace bandages, then put the oven mitts over that. Even if he did bite you, he couldn't puncture very far." I looked hopefully at Carter, who was shaking her head vigorously.

"I have done many crazy things in the name of friendship, but that's asking too much," she said. "Give the damn snake away, or let it loose in the subway or something. But if you want to pick it up, you gotta do it yourself."

"O.K.!" I shouted. "Let's do it then, before I lose my nerve."

First, I scooped Grouch up and locked him in my bedroom. If something went awry, I didn't want an innocent cat to pay the price, especially after reading about the slow, suffocating death that boas inflict on their prey. I set my cordless phone on the coffee table. "If it bites me, call 9-1-1."

Carter nodded. "Do you have a first aid kit? It might take a while for the ambulance to come."

I went to the hall closet and retrieved the first aid kit my aunt Kuki gave me when I moved into my apartment. I opened it up and frowned. I had raided its contents so often without replacing anything that the only things left were two tiny bandages and an alcohol swab. I showed them to Carter. "Well, at least you could disinfect the puncture wound and put bandages on it."

She nodded again. "What about the snake? I mean, if it bites you, you'll drop it, and I'm not gonna stand here playing Florence Nightingale with a python on the loose."

"He's a boa. And that's not gonna happen," I said, unconvinced. "But if it does, just grab the phone and we'll run out of the apartment. You may have to carry me if I'm unconscious."

She nodded and said, "Yeah," but her tone was unconvincing.

"O.K., let's do it." We each grabbed one end of the aquarium and slowly lowered it onto the bathroom scale. It took some maneuvering to shift the aquarium so that it was not obscuring the scale's digital display. When it stabilized, the display read forty-one pounds. It was difficult to guess how much of that was Rocky himself and how much his aquarium and accoutrements. We had to proceed to step two. The step that involved me touching a live snake. I paused to reflect on the circumstances that put me in this position, silently cursing Monica Broccoli and wishing all manner of bodily harm upon her.

Carter snapped me out of my vindictive reverie. "Holly, don't be a wimp. Just do it so we can get on with the ice cream and girl talk."

I donned the oven mitts, unlocked the guard rail, and took the lid off the aquarium. Rocky was motionless, and for a moment, I thought he might be dead. The tiny twinge of guilt I felt at being the cause of his demise was obscured by my overwhelming sense of relief at not having to touch him. Then he blinked. My stomach jumped into my throat.

Carter nudged me. "Just do it!"

I leaned over the aquarium and slowly lowered my mitts. I cautiously placed one hand on each side of his coiled body, applied pressure, and started to lift. The oven mitts made it impossible to get a secure grip, and the snake slid from my grasp. I was repositioning the mitts, trying to figure out the most secure angle, when my buzzer rang.

I glanced at Carter over my shoulder. "Could you get that? My hands are kinda full."

"No way. What if it's Danny? He thinks I'm in Poughkeepsie!"

I grunted. "Keep an eye on the snake."

"Don't worry. I'm not going anywhere."

I pressed the button and Danny's voice came booming over the intercom. "Buzz me up, Holly. I gotta talk to you."

Carter looked at me, her eyes panic-stricken. She was shaking her head vigorously.

"It's not a good time, Danny," I said into the box. "I'm in the middle of something."

I heard Danny say, "Hey, thanks," then, "Hol, your neighbor let me in. I'm on my way up."

Carter was at the door. "I'm outta here."

"He'll see you on the stairs!"

"I can't face him, Holly. You have to hide me." She was looking out my window, examining my fire escape.

I grabbed her by the arm before she could climb out the window. "There's nowhere to hide. Just talk to him."

"I *can't*. Not yet." She looked at me intently. "*Please.*"

A thought struck. I grabbed the I♥NY key chain off my counter and thrust it into her hand. "One flight up, apartment 7B. He's out of town, I'm supposed to feed the cat. Just hang out and watch TV, and I'll come and get you when Danny's gone."

I could still hear Carter's clogs clomping on the steps above me when Danny reached my landing. He brushed past me into my apartment, and swung his backpack onto my kitchen table. "I hope you had no plans tonight, because we have to work up some new material. I'm not doing the showcase cold. Carter's in Poughkeepsie, so we have all night."

"I know we have work to do. But not tonight. I have something else going on."

"Oh, my God!" Danny was gaping at the plethora of pregnancy tests Carter had stacked onto my kitchen counter. He picked up a box and turned it over in his hands. "Are you *pregnant*?"

"No!" I snatched the test from his hand. "It's not for me. It's for—" I was about to say *for a friend,* but that would point the finger of suspicion squarely at Carter. I glanced about the room, looking for inspiration. I saw Rocky's aquarium on the coffee table in the living room. "It's for the snake."

"You're giving a pregnancy test to a *snake*?"

"Do you know a better way to find out if it's pregnant?"

"How could it be pregnant? It lives alone!"

"Well . . . *now* he does. I mean, she does. But she didn't always."

"What makes you think the snake is pregnant? And do you really think a pregnancy test for humans would work on a snake?"

"I'm not sure . . . but I thought it was worth a try. The snake's been acting funny and it looks kind of swollen around the middle."

"That's probably just his last meal." He headed into the living room. "Holly, I don't know what's going on, but if you think I'm buying this bullsh—" He hesitated, frozen in the middle of the living room.

"What?"

He looked at me and inquired in a too casual voice, "Where's the snake?"

Oh, my God. I jumped onto a chair. From my vantage point I could see into Rocky's aquarium. The lid was pushed aside and the aquarium was empty. Everything went black.

My head was throbbing. I looked around. I was on my dining room floor, and Danny was standing over me, waving his arms in my face. I guess I fainted. Please, God, tell me that while I was passed out, Danny recaptured Rocky and the beast was safely ensconced in his aquarium, from which I promised to never, ever remove him so long as we both shall live.

"Are you okay?" Danny asked.

"I . . . guess so. . . . Where's Rocky?"

"I dunno. I was looking around when I heard this big crash and saw you come tumbling down. Did you hit your head?"

I jumped up and climbed onto the dining room table. I didn't care if I had a gaping head wound. There was a reptile on the loose. I have my priorities.

Considering the imminent threat to our lives, Danny seemed relatively placid. I took this as a very good sign. Guys are good with snakes—let him get Rocky back in his cage. He casually peered under the couch and end tables, then opened the closet door. "Why did you let him out? I thought you were afraid of snakes."

"I am." I hesitated. "But I had to give him—I mean, her—the pregnancy test."

He had picked up a ClearResults test kit, and was reading the box. "How exactly do you give a pregnancy test to a snake, anyway? Don't you have to pee on a stick?"

I nodded. "That's why I had to pick him up. I was going to hold him over the stick and wait for him to tinkle."

Danny gave me a bewildered stare, then shook his head. "Who's the guy, Holly?"

"What guy?"

"You have half a dozen pregnancy tests on your counter. There's got to be a guy."

"There's a boa constrictor loose in my apartment and you're fixated on the pregnancy tests?"

"Holy crap!" Danny yelped, scrambling onto the dining room table. "You didn't tell me it was a *boa constrictor*!"

"I thought you knew."

"What the hell are you doing with a boa constrictor?"

"It's a long story." I looked at Danny, whose face had gone pale. "I suppose this means you're not going to catch it for me."

He reached for the cordless phone. "I'm calling 9-1-1. They'll get Animal Control over here."

"No!" I shouted. "They'll shoot him! I couldn't have that on my conscience. Besides, I think you're supposed to have a permit, and I don't have one. I could get fined, not to mention evicted. I'm pretty sure my lease doesn't allow boa constrictors." I grabbed the receiver and dialed my cousin's number. No answer. I screamed into his machine: "Gerry, when you get this message, come to my apartment immediately and bring Monica Broccoli. It's an emergency!" I hung up, then dialed Monica's number and issued a similar command. Then we stood there for a while, waiting and watching. My stomach was in knots and my nerves were raw.

The phone rang and I nearly jumped out of my skin. "Hello?"

It was Carter. She whispered, "Is he gone yet?"

"Nope."

"Come on. Just tell him to *leave*. I'm bored sitting up here by myself. There's no cable and all the videos are gay porn."

I tried to think on my feet. How to let Carter know that Rocky had escaped without tipping Danny off that she'd been here. "The *cat* is out of the *bag*," I said, hoping she'd get my hidden meaning.

"What?" she screamed. "Oh, my God, I trusted you! How could you tell him?"

Oh, shit. Wrong hidden meaning. Bad choice of words. "No, I didn't—" I protested, but Carter had hung up.

"Oh, no," I groaned, staring at the receiver.

"Who was that?" Danny asked.

"Nothing. Just my aunt. I have to go." I looked to see if there was a clear path to the front door. I had to get upstairs to see Carter. I turned and was about to jump when Danny grabbed me.

"Holly, you're bleeding!" he screamed. "The back of your head."

I put my hand to the back of my head and felt warm, sticky liquid. Then I brought my hand back and looked at it. It was covered with bright red blood. Once again, everything went black.

I must have been out longer this time. When I woke, Danny was sitting on the edge of the table, his legs bouncing nervously. He looked over at me when I groaned. "I called 9-1-1," he said. "They're on the way."

I struggled to sit up. Danny continued. "You have a pretty nasty gash on the back of your head." He tapped the first aid kit I'd left on the table for Carter's use in case of a snake-related emergency. "There's nothing in here but a coupla bandages that wouldn't cover a hangnail." I groaned again and tenderly touched the back of my head. The blood was congealing. I hoped that was a good sign but couldn't remember, having spent most of my seventh-grade health class staring lovingly at the back of Robby Francomano's head.

The phone rang. I hoped it was Carter, but Monica Broccoli was a close second. Wrong on both counts.

"This is Tom Hansen," the caller said. "We met this morning."

"Yes, hi," I said brightly, trying to sound composed.

"Did I catch you at a bad time?" he asked.

"Oh, no, not at all," I chirped. I'm not sure why I felt compelled to put on a pretense of normalcy. What else could I say? *I was just lying here on my dining room table with my head in an ever-widening pool of blood, afraid to move lest I be attacked by a runaway reptile.* The Starbucks dad seemed like the personification of normal, and I didn't want to scare him away.

"Did you make it to school on time?" I asked.

"Yes, we did. I don't know how to thank you."

"It was nothing. I was just trying to help."

He cleared his throat. "I was wondering . . . would you be interested in going out for dinner sometime?"

I felt a fluttery feeling in my stomach. I wasn't sure whether it was the invitation or the massive blood loss. I started, "Um, I'd . . ." Then out of the corner of my eye, I spotted something coiled up on the heating grate in the corner of the living room. I elbowed Danny and pointed. He let out a gasp.

I put a hand over the receiver and whispered at Danny, "Go get him quick, before Animal Control arrives!"

Danny shook his head vigorously. "No way. I don't do snakes."

"Come on, don't be a wimp! You're a guy. Just grab him and put him in the aquarium."

"Are you still there?" the dad was asking. "I'm sorry if I put you on the spot."

"Yes, I'm here. It's just . . ." *It's just that I'm sitting a few feet from a creature that could squeeze the life's breath out of me and then eat me whole.* "It's just, I saw you with your daughter, so I assumed you were married."

"No, I'm divorced. Well, to be honest, divorc*ing*. Those documents you had delivered for me were the final legal papers."

"Oh." I heard heavy footsteps on the stairs; then there was

pounding on my door. I gestured for Danny to open it. He shook his head. "I'm not going down there. It's the paramedics. They can break the door down."

The dad said, "Did someone say paramedics? Is everything okay?"

"Everything's fine. Dinner would be . . . great."

The pounding was accompanied by a scraping sound. They were picking the lock. I decided to get over my squeamishness and just hop down and open up the door. I mentally measured the distance between Rocky and the door. About six feet. Definitely not within my comfort zone. Let 'em break it down.

"I have to go," I said into the phone. "Someone's at the door."

"Okay. I'll call you next week about dinner."

"Great." I hung up just as the door burst open.

My cousin Gerry was standing with his spare key in the lock. Monica Broccoli rushed in wild-eyed. "What the hell happened? Why are you two standing on the table? What's with all the blood?"

I heard sirens downstairs. No time to explain. I gave Monica the abridged version and warned her that Animal Control was on the way. She was even more appalled than I was at the prospect of turning Rocky over to Animal Control. She rushed to the heating grate, scooped him up, and deposited him in the aquarium in one fluid motion. Then she stood there, paralyzed, as clomping footsteps signaled the approach of the paramedics, probably with Animal Control in tow. "I have to hide him," she said. "Where can I go?"

I wondered if Carter was still upstairs at Brian's place. There was no time to find out. I led Monica to the front door. "Go upstairs to number 7B and knock on the door." I leaned in closer and whispered, "Carter should be in there. Danny doesn't know she's up there, so *shhhh*. If she's not there, just keep out of sight until Animal Control leaves."

Monica left, clutching the aquarium and cooing to Rocky, "It's okay, baby. Mama's here."

Gerry was inspecting the wound on my head. Satisfied that it wasn't life-threatening, he started rooting around in my refrigerator for snacks. "Mmm, rocky road," he said.

Danny had climbed down from the dining room table, but was still tiptoeing around cautiously, as if Rocky, the possibly pregnant snake, might have left behind a few offspring.

Gerry sat down beside me. He was eating rocky road ice cream out of the container—a reminder of how my original plan for the evening had gone horribly awry. "You gonna be okay?" he asked.

I nodded. "Yeah."

"Good, then I gotta tell you what happened to me at the gym today. You'll never guess."

I wasn't in the mood for guessing. I grabbed the rocky road and pressed the cold container against the back of my head, which was pounding fiercely.

Gerry reached into his duffel bag, pulled out a pair of large white gym socks, and crowed, "Patrick Swayze's socks!"

Six Little Sticks

I woke the next morning with a pounding headache. The paramedics had taken me to St. Vincent's Hospital, where I received five stitches in the back of my scalp. Danny had taken me home in a cab. He dropped me off in my lobby, saying, "Look at the bright side. At least we have some new material."

Gerry had stayed behind, promising to clean up the blood and to lock my place up using his spare key. He also dealt with the Animal Control officer, who wasn't buying my story that I just *thought* I saw a snake, but couldn't be sure.

"The caller said it was a boa constrictor," the officer pointed out. "That's pretty specific." He peeked around in cupboards and drawers, looking for signs of illegal snake ownership. Luckily for me—but not so for Rocky—there was no sign of anything remotely resembling snake food in my apartment.

Danny said, "Python, boa, rattler . . . they all look the same to me. I didn't actually *see* a snake. I just saw my friend here jump up on the table and pass out."

The officer was unconvinced and threatened a building-wide

search. When Danny and I left with the paramedics, Gerry was telling him the story of how he snagged Patrick Swayze's gym socks when the actor was showering after a workout. Gerry waved the Dirty Dancer's dirty footwear in the officer's face. "Take a whiff," he was saying. "That's genuine Patrick Swayze foot sweat."

I hoped that after the night's events, Monica Broccoli would think better of entrusting her beloved boa to my care, but when I let myself into my apartment, there he was, in his aquarium, in the middle of my dining room table. A note was taped to the side:

> He weighs about two pounds. Give him one fuzzy
> mouse every week.

She must have seen Carter, and gotten the lowdown on our little dilemma. At least that meant Carter hadn't stormed out of Brian's apartment as I had feared, angry and seeking vengeance.

I looked at Rocky, who was curled up in the far corner of his aquarium. "I guess we're stuck with each other," I told him. "Let's make the best of it." Remembering my pledge to order his food that night, I logged on to the Internet and placed an order for a month's worth of freeze-dried mice.

I took one of the pain pills the ER doctor had given me and crawled into bed. Before dozing off, I tried calling Carter, but there was no answer. No answer at Starbucks either. I left plaintive messages at both numbers, insisting that I hadn't done what she thought I did—and not giving too much information in case Danny picked up either message.

Carter and I are among the few remaining people under forty who still don't have cell phones. For me, the reasons are purely financial. Some months I can barely afford to pay my utilities and have enough left over for cat food. A cell phone is a luxury I cannot afford. Carter claims ideological reasons for refusing to join the twenty-first century. Something about the technology interfering with her chi or tao or dharma. She also claims not to need a cell phone, because when someone truly needs to contact her, she can pick up their vibes telepathically.

I closed my eyes and focused on directing my brain waves out into the universe to send a message to Carter. I visualized Carter's face and chanted inwardly, *Call me. Come to me.* Grouch jumped up on the bed and licked my face. I guess my brain waves are tuned to a feline frequency.

I slept fitfully, my dreams punctuated by images of renegade reptiles. I woke to an insistent pounding. It took me a while to realize that the pounding wasn't coming from within my head. Someone was knocking on my door.

I trudged to the door, clutching the back of my head. I opened the door, and Carter rushed in, bouncing up and down. Déjà vu.

"Where are the tests? Get 'em ready, 'cause my first morning pee is gonna be a doozy."

I hugged her. "You're not mad? I was so worried—"

"No. But I will be if you don't stop squeezing me. I drank two margaritas last night before going to bed."

I mobilized into action. I grabbed a large plastic tumbler from the cupboard and handed it to her. "Here, pee into this. Then we can use it to do all the tests at once."

She nodded approvingly. "Sort of like the mother vial." She disappeared into the bathroom.

I started opening the boxes and lining up their contents. I skimmed the instructions for each. They all used basically the same procedure. Dip the stick in the pee—and *wait*.

I screamed through the door. "Where did you go last night? I tried calling."

"I was afraid of running into Danny if I came back here, so I stayed upstairs at your neighbor's. I hope he won't mind I slept on his satin sheets and used up his margarita mix."

I winced. I would have to do a walk-through later to make sure she hadn't left behind any signs of her sojourn.

Carter shouted, "Monica told me about your head. How are you?"

"It hurts like hell. And they had to shave my hair around the wound. I have a bald patch on the back of my head. That should go over well on my date."

The door opened. Carter was zipping up her jeans. "*Date?* What date? When did this happen?"

I told her about the phone call from the Starbucks dad. "His name is Tom, and he asked me out to dinner. I said yes."

She handed me the plastic tumbler, which was nearly filled to overflowing. "That's great, Holly. He seems nice."

"Yeah, but . . ." I trailed off.

"But what?"

I shrugged. I didn't know what the "but" was, but it was there. Something was holding me back from being genuinely excited about my date with Starbucks dad. I glanced toward my pantry. I knew the milk cubby would be empty. The writer said he was going out of town.

Carter groaned. "Oh, no. This is about that writer guy, isn't it? Don't ruin this, Holly. You have a simple choice: fantasy or reality. Choose reality."

"You're in for a little dose of reality yourself. Are you ready?" I had the test kits lined up and was dipping the first stick into the mother vial.

Carter bit her lip. "What am I gonna do if I'm pregnant, Holly? I have no maternal instincts whatsoever. Plus I drink, I smoke, I eat like crap, and I consume so much coffee I may as well be on an intravenous caffeine drip."

"You'll quit drinking and smoking, you'll eat more fruits and vegetables, and you'll switch to decaf."

"*Decaf?* Are you crazy? It's not like people drink coffee for the *taste,* Holly. You drink it for the *buzz.* How can I get through a day of double shifts and back-to-back classes without caffeine?"

"I think you'll manage." I carefully laid the first stick down on the counter and set my egg timer for three minutes. Then I went down the row, following the directions for each one.

Carter looked over my shoulder. "What's supposed to happen?"

I pointed out the salient features of each kit, feeling like a car salesman in a showroom. "This one will give you a plus sign if you're pregnant, whereas with this one, you'll see a solid line. Over here is the classic pink or blue—pink being positive, of course."

"I don't like that one."

"This one also gives you a solid line if it's positive, and this last one is more of a big dot. For most of them, if you see nothing in the second window, it's negative."

"How long do they take?"

"This one is three minutes. The rest will come up within a minute or two after the first."

The phone rang and I moved toward it but Carter grabbed my arm. "Don't you dare answer that. No interruptions. This place is hexed, Holly. You go to the door, and the next thing ya know, either the police or paramedics are involved."

I let the machine pick up. It was my aunt Kuki. Her voice was snappish. "Holly. I'm not going to say I told you so. But I did. Moving into Manhattan was your idea, and now look what has happened. At least in Brooklyn, you were never attacked by snakes or broke your head open falling off a table. I think you should move home now. Don't forget to take your vitamins. Call me." She sighed, a long-suffering sigh I'd heard repeatedly throughout my life, a sigh that allowed her to express all her disappointment and disdain without actually uttering a word. Then she added, "It's Aunt Kuki," as though there were any number of people who call to tell me to take my vitamins and remind me what a disappointment I've been.

Moments later the phone rang again. This time it was Gerry. "Holly, hope you don't mind. I told my mom about last night. I'm sure she'll read you the riot act when you come for dinner on Sunday. Anyways, I gotta talk to you about my collection. I think you can help me out. It's gonna be big. Call me."

Carter raised an eyebrow. "His collection?"

I shrugged. "I don't know what he means, unless—" I shook the thought out of my head. Even my demented cousin wouldn't call two pairs of purloined socks a "collection." Then again . . .

The egg timer dinged and Carter and I edged closer to the counter, where the test kits were lined up. She grabbed my hand and squeezed, her fingernails digging into my palm. "Wait! I can't do this—"

"Yes, you can. It's just six little sticks. They won't bite."

I heaved Carter to the counter and we stood there staring, without speaking. The first test sported an unmistakable plus sign in its window. The second and fourth had solid vertical lines. Number three was a lovely shade of pink, while number six had a big dot. Six out of six. No room for doubt.

I racked my brain, trying to think of the right words. I wanted to say something that showed I understood the magnitude of Carter's situation, but didn't think it was the end of the world. To be sympathetic yet encouraging. I needed to let her know that I was there for her, that I wasn't freaked out by this—when, in truth, I was.

Carter spun on her heels and headed for the door. "Gotta run." She took the stairs at a record-breaking pace. I rushed to the top of the stairs and called down after her, but she never stopped, never looked back.

5

Hugging the Donkey

The next few days were relievedly calm, blessedly calm. Actually, it was more like oddly calm, eerily calm. Calm before the storm calm. Dead calm. I enjoyed the peace and quiet, but knew it was only a temporary reprieve from the insanity that had been creeping into my life and slowly taking over. Danny still didn't know Carter was pregnant. I'd been avoiding him, afraid I'd inadvertently spill the beans. *Inadvertent,* my ass. I was afraid I'd grab him by the throat and scream at him to grow up and take responsibility for his actions. I couldn't keep it up much longer; the showcase was less than a week away and we hadn't rehearsed.

Carter had been mondo incommunicado, not returning any of my calls. At Starbucks, when I'd pop in for my daily caffeine fix, she'd put on her best Little Mary Sunshine persona and pretend nothing was wrong. Her insistence that she was perfectly peachy aside from having a backload of drink orders to fill was unconvincing, but what could I do? Yank her out from behind the counter and force her to face up to her situation? After all, it wasn't my problem. I should stay out of it and let her and Danny deal with it in their own way—or non-way as the case may be. I had my own problems to contend with.

The frozen mice had arrived on my doorstep that morning, and I had fed the first fuzzy to Rocky as soon as it thawed. It had taken some rearranging to find a way for my plentiful stocks of ice cream to coexist in my freezer with Rocky's future meals without the two factions touching. Even though each mouse was hermetically sealed in its own Ziplocked death shroud, psychologically, I knew I would not be able to eat any rocky road if the container had come into contact with a dead rodent.

The gouge on the back of my head was no longer a constant source of pain, but the silver dollar–sized patch of baldness surrounding it was no laughing matter. I had taken to wearing hats so as to avoid the questioning stares of adults and blunt comments of children. One of my haircutting clients had brought her young daughter with her to my place for her monthly appointment. As I was readying my supplies, I heard the little girl whisper to her mother, "Mommy, don't let her do *that* to you!" and turned to see her pointing at the back of my scalp.

I was still worried about how to disguise my wound for my date with Tom, but even more disconcerting was the fact that he hadn't phoned since that initial call. Perhaps he'd come to his senses and changed his mind. Maybe as time passed, the craziness of our first meeting sunk in and he thought better of dating someone who could turn morning coffee into a three-ring circus. The possibility that he'd reconciled with his wife had also presented itself. Receiving the final divorce papers could have shocked one or both of them into rethinking their split.

As I mulled over these possibilities, I also checked my milk cubby at least three times each day, vainly hoping to find an envelope from the writer. He hadn't mentioned when he'd be back in town, and it was unlikely that his first matter of business upon his return would be to drop off pages for me to type, but I still felt myself drawn to the milk cubby with an urgency I hadn't felt since my early teen years, when Robby Francomano from down the street told me he'd sent me a valentine, and I spent hours each day sitting at the window watching for the mail truck to turn onto our street.

I sighed at the memory. When the valentine finally arrived, a week after Valentine's Day, I raced with it to Carter's house and together we examined it for hours, looking for clues to the deeper meaning hidden in the simple card. The preprinted message read *Happy Valentine's Day to a Cool Kid* and was signed plainly *from Robby*.

" 'From,' " I had whined to Carter. "Not 'love.' From."

"A boy isn't going to use the word 'love,' ever," Carter said knowingly. "Like prob'ly not even when they get married. They like to play it cool."

"And what does 'cool kid' mean?" I asked. "*Kid.* Like he doesn't even know I'm a girl."

We continued trying to crack the valentine code until I was called home to dinner by my aunt. By the end of our session, Carter had concluded that Robby was madly in love with me and was secretly planning to marry me one day. If it was true, he sure knew how to keep a secret. Robby barely spoke to me the rest of the school year, and he moved to a different neighborhood over the summer. I never heard from him again.

It was distinctly possible I'd never hear from the writer again, also. Best to take Carter's advice and stick with reality. That is, if reality ever called back.

My workload had been light all week. A few odd jobs here and there, nothing major. My neighbor Brian had returned, but thankfully not before I'd managed to replace the margarita mix Carter had consumed and launder his lime green satin sheets. Tallulah, the capuchin monkey, was due to be delivered to my doorstep on Tuesday morning. That meant I still had two days to monkey-proof my apartment.

Though I didn't even know where to begin prepping my place for a nonhuman primate, I convinced myself it could all be done in a day. *Tomorrow.* Today I had more pressing matters at hand. I was expected at my aunt's house for dinner at seven.

Though I loved my family dearly, I was more than a tad bit apprehensive about what was in store. My aunt would probably let loose with a barrage of admonitions the moment I set foot inside the door. Nothing would be off limits—my lifestyle, my friends, my love life, my career, not to mention my unfortunate injury. I'd been hoping to stay out of my aunt's line of sight until after my head wound had healed and the hair had grown back. But she'd been insistent, as had Gerry, that I attend this family dinner.

As for Gerry, he'd called almost daily wanting to talk about his "collection" of famous socks. He was convinced that he'd stumbled upon a once-in-a-lifetime opportunity and was trying to figure out how to best exploit it. I tried to bring him down to earth, but he was doggedly determined. In fact, I'd never seen him as passionate about anything before. I felt a pang of guilt at the way I'd been acting toward him lately—chiding, sarcastic, dismissive. That morning, he'd called to ask me my advice about setting up a Web site. "I can't decide between www.celebrity-socks.com and www.famous-feet.com. Which is better?" he asked.

I'd replied, "How about www.getalife.com?" and hung up.

I resolved to be more supportive from now on. But I still wasn't looking forward to being cornered by him at dinner and forced to sniff Patrick Swayze's stinky socks.

I wondered what Monica Broccoli must think about this sock business. Monica was a strange duck, but she seemed to inhabit a level of reality at least one full plane higher than my cousin's. Perhaps she could help him to see the folly of his sock obsession. Maybe I could talk to her at dinner, make her my ally. The fact that I was considering Monica Broccoli to be the evening's saving grace says something about the level of dysfunction in my family. My aunt's house would be filled with all of my closest living relatives, and the person with whom I would most closely identify was a snake-loving, loud-talking bra model named after a vegetable.

The phone rang, and I let the machine pick up. It took me a moment to recognize the voice. Regardless of his actual mood, Danny presents a perpetually perky persona, his sprightly speech sprinkled with wisecracks. But today he sounded wretched. He was speaking too fast for me to understand the words, but I got the gist of it: Carter had dumped him.

"What's going on, Holly?" he moaned. "You're her best friend. You have to know what's going on." He sounded close to tears, but even more alarmingly, he didn't crack a single joke.

After he hung up, I replayed the message, this time getting a clearer picture. Apparently, Carter had dropped by Danny's place the night before while he was out. She'd gathered up her belongings and left a cardboard box filled with things he'd left at her place. She also left a note saying that it was over. At Starbucks, he'd learned that she'd just finished her last shift before starting a two-week vacation. He spent the night camped out at her place but she never came home. He was desperate to know where she was and what was going on.

It was wrenching to hear him in such pain. I couldn't stand it. Despite my allegiance to Carter, I felt I owed it to Danny to be up front with him. I dialed his number. When he picked up, his voice sounded so expectant that I hated letting him know it was only me.

"Do you know where she is?" he asked.

I insisted I hadn't seen her in a few days, which was the truth. I honestly didn't know where she'd gone.

When he was convinced I wasn't harboring Carter at my place, he said, "You wanna hang out tonight, Holly? I don't want to sit home alone. It's pathetic. Let's go out drinking. Let's get smashed."

Though I rarely drank to excess, getting snockered with Danny had definite appeal when held up as an alternative to spending the evening with my relatives. I considered ducking out on Kuki's dinner, but knew that I'd have to live down weeks of guilt trips, her ceaseless messages reminding me of her deathbed promises to my dear departed mother and all the sacrifices she'd made for me.

"I can't. I have to go to dinner at my aunt's house."

"You're just avoiding me because you *know* something. Some friend you turned out to be!"

"I *am* your friend. And Carter's. I don't want to see either of you unhappy."

"Too late."

I sighed. Danny sounded truly terrible. I wanted to be there for him, hold his hand, toss out all the trite clichés that you tell someone suffering from a broken heart. To tell the truth, comforting Danny was more of a need than a duty. I felt I was uniquely qualified to commiserate with him. Carter's disappearance had left us both high and dry.

"Come with me." It was more of a command than a request. "Dinner is at seven. Meet me at my place and we'll go together."

I did what I normally do when I'm feeling helpless. I paced. I walked the floors of my apartment, absently opening drawers and cupboards looking for something to take my mind off things until dinner. I checked the milk cubby again. Still empty. I went to the refrigerator and opened the door. Except for a half jar of olives and some wilted lettuce, it was empty. I hoped Kuki would send me home with some leftovers. I moved on to the freezer, hoping to hit the dessert mother lode. Instead, I was reminded that my ice box had been transformed into a mouse mortuary. A stack of rodent body bags was gathering frost. I spied the tiny pink mouth of the rat heretofore known as Rocky's next meal pressed up against the plastic, and lost my appetite—even though a full container of Ben & Jerry's Chunky Monkey sat on the other side of the freezer.

As I swung the freezer door shut, a faded fudge-stained flyer posted to its front caught my attention. It was a class schedule for BodyWorks, the dance studio where Carter taught yoga three afternoons a week. If the flyer was accurate, she had a two o'clock class for beginners. She could ignore my phone calls, she could steer clear of me at Starbucks, but she couldn't avoid me if I plopped my leotard-clad self down in the front row of her class.

My self was a good twelve pounds lighter the last time I squeezed it into a leotard. I was feeling a bit uncomfortable as I left the changing room and walked into BodyWorks' main studio. About a dozen women were stretched out on mats, warming up, but Carter was nowhere to be seen. I grabbed a mat and found a spot, front and center, by the mirror. I lowered myself gingerly, fearful that sudden movements would cause me to split a seam.

I tried to touch my hands to my outstretched feet and winced in pain. It had been a long time since I'd set foot in a dance studio, and I was no longer the limber cheerleader of my high school days. At least it was a beginner's class—I could probably manage that without too much pain.

I heard Yanni being piped through the speakers and looked up from the mat. Carter was walking toward the front of the room, a serene smile on her face. The smile dropped when she saw me; then she quickly recovered. "Good morning, seekers," she intoned sweetly. "Let's begin with some breathing exercises." As I listened to her dulcet-toned instructions for inhaling and exhaling and being mindful of my chakras, I marveled at how completely different

Carter's yoga persona was from her "street" mode. I'm convinced it's not an act—she seems completely different when she's meditating or teaching yoga from when she's hanging out in clubs or working at Starbucks. If any of her yoga students popped in for a latte after class, I doubted they'd recognize the fast-talking, punk-haired barista as their soft-spoken spiritual guru.

Carter was sitting Lotus-style with her eyes closed, demonstrating proper breathing techniques. After a moment, she opened her eyes and looked around the room, assiduously avoiding my gaze. I darted my head to and fro, trying to put myself in her direct line of sight. She stood and walked around the room. "Good, good," she was saying to the students who apparently had the breathing thing down. I never understood the big deal about breathing, anyway. We do it all day long without thinking about it, so why should we pay fifteen dollars a class to do it in a big group?

We moved on to light stretching and then began our yoga poses. The first few poses—sun salutation and downward dog—I remembered from my last ill-fated attempt to get in touch with my body. Despite being dreadfully out of shape, I managed to keep up with the class for these. My confidence was shattered when I tried to twist myself into the next position, a cruel contortion known as embryo inside the womb. Unlike the women on either side of me, who seemed to be holding the pose effortlessly, their placid expressions betraying not one smidgen of discomfort, I was in excruciating pain.

It only got worse from there. I felt like I tore a ligament doing something called the one-legged pigeon, and I quite possibly gave myself an episiotomy achieving the split-legged donkey hug pose. Through the searing pain in my crotch, I tried to look at the bright side: hugging the donkey may have made it easier for me to give birth later in life.

Through it all, I was trying to get Carter's attention, but she steered clear of me. I knew the moment the class ended she would bolt out the door, so this was my only chance. I watched her move around the room, gently placing her hands on students to help them achieve proper alignment, murmuring words of encouragement, nodding and smiling. But apparently my little mat had been demarcated as a hands-off zone; no encouraging words or helpful posture adjustments were forthcoming. So I raised my hand and kept it in the air until she had to respond or risk appearing insensitive to her students' needs.

She smiled and glided toward my mat. She leaned in close and, through gritted teeth, said, "Go away. I can't deal with you now."

Deal with me? What did that mean? I was only trying to help her and Danny. They were the ones whose personal problems were always intruding on my life. Now I was someone who needed to be dealt with?

"Just talk to Danny. If he doesn't hear it from you, he'll hear it somewhere else."

"Is that a threat?" She came around behind me and put one hand on the small of my back, applying gentle pressure. To the rest of the class, she said, "Press through the lower back, stretching the legs, and straightening out the spine." Suddenly, the gentle pressure gave way to forceful shoving, and she pinned me to the mat, my legs splayed out on either side of me. Under her breath she said, "If you tell him, I'll kill you."

Though Carter is prone to hyperbole, something in her manner made me think she wasn't kidding. Maybe it was the way she grabbed my left ankle and thrust it skyward, until my knee was jutting into my ear.

Unable to speak and unsure whether I'd ever walk again, I just shook my head. Carter took center stage and demonstrated a new gravity-defying pose, something she called the tortoise. Sitting with her knees bent, she leaned forward until her chest was nearly flat against the floor, then stretched her arms out to her sides, reaching under her legs. As if that wasn't enough, she wrapped her arms under her legs and around her back, clasping them behind her.

"Advanced students can try the supta kurmasana." As she said this, I watched in disbelief as she lifted one leg, then the other, and crossed them behind her head. Even with her forehead pressed against the floor and her arms and legs twisted up like a pretzel, Carter maintained her mellow tone of voice. "If it helps, you can visualize a soothing color slowly moving through all your joints, loosening up each one as you ease yourself into position." She slowly disentangled her limbs and stood before us, inviting the rest of us to do the tortoise pose.

No way, no how was I going to even attempt to mimic the tortoise pose. Instead, as I waited for my hip joint to pop back into place, I rethought my plan to get in her face and force her to speak to me. I quickly formulated my own version of the tortoise, curling up in a ball and tucking my head between my shoulders. Like a turtle who's been threatened, I hoped to elude my tormenter by pretending there was no one home inside my shell. I heard Carter walking toward me and prayed that she would pass me by. After all, there were other students here, strange people who actually wanted their knees to touch their ears. *Pick on them!*

But she was sashaying back to me. I detected a sadistic smirk behind her tranquil countenance as she said, "Holly will demonstrate the next pose."

I shook my head no. "I'm still trying to find my chakras," I said to the class. To Carter, I whimpered, "Please don't hurt me. I'm just trying to help!"

She took my left leg and pulled it across my body, then did the reverse with my right leg. Then she grasped my right hand and drew it across the front of my body until my fingers wrapped around my left shoulder. She explained to the attentive contortionists that they should raise their legs higher for maximum stretch. To demonstrate, she placed her hands on my crossed legs and began lifting, while whispering in my ear, "What I *need* is *space*"—pushing my legs higher with each word she emphasized—"to clear my *head*. And think about my *options*. Seeing *you* just reminds me of *everything*. You're the only one who knows." She relaxed her grip and my limbs slowly untwisted. "And I'd like it to stay that way."

She stood and walked away. Though I knew it meant risking another torn ligament, I hissed, "You can't keep it a secret forever."

She turned and shot me an angry look. "Maybe I can."

I spent the rest of the class flat on my back staring at the ceiling, in what I later learned is an actual position called corpse pose, which aptly described how I felt. When the rest of the class lowered themselves to their mats and reclined on their backs, I felt like I was ahead of the game for the first time all day. I achieved corpse pose first, dammit, and to prove my yoga prowess, I'll just go on demonstrating my proficiency while the rest of you lightweights skip off to the changing rooms.

I don't know how long I remained in corpse pose, but by the time I began contemplating the arduous task of standing, the yoga students were gone and the room was beginning to fill up with little girls in pink leotards. A junior ballet class. I slowly lifted myself up off my mat and tested my legs' ability to carry my weight. On either side of me, prepubescent girls of all shapes and sizes were stretching on mats, lifting their feet over their heads and pressing their noses into their knees. Feeling suddenly much older than my twenty-nine years, I staggered toward the door.

"It's the hair lady!"

I turned and saw a little girl in a lavender leotard pointing at me. It took a moment before recognition kicked in. "Nicole?"

She nodded and smiled shyly. My crabby countenance and sour

disposition melted instantly. Something about this little girl made me go all gooey inside when I saw her. "How did your school pictures turn out?" I asked.

She shrugged. "I dunno." She looked around the room. "Who's hairs are you cutting?"

"Oh, I'm not here to cut anybody's hair. I was taking a class. Just like you."

"Oh. O.K." Her curiosity about the Hair Lady satisfied, Nicole turned and skipped away. I watched her plop down onto a mat; then I turned to leave. A lurching feeling in my stomach stopped me short. I clutched the doorframe and took deep breaths while trying to identify the cause of my gastric distress. I supposed it was possible that I was experiencing delayed side effects of the yoga class—the one-legged pigeon coming back to poop on my parade—but truth be told I'd had this exact same feeling before. Carter and I had named the phenomenon Male-Related Anxiety Disorder. The fluttery stomach, clammy palms, and nausea that accompanied unexpected encounters with potential love interests. My body had reacted even before my brain put two and two together and realized that if Nicole was in the dance studio, her dad—Tom—would most likely be waiting in the outer room.

A glance in the mirror confirmed my suspicion that the post-yoga class Holly, the Holly who had dashed out of the house without makeup, the Holly who was breaking out in a nervous rash in anticipation of dinner at Kuki's, was not a pretty Holly. Not a best-face-forward Holly. Not a Holly I'd want to expose a potential love interest to. Not yet, anyway.

I tiptoed out of the studio. To the left were the waiting area, reception desk, and exit. To the right was a door marked "private." I knocked on the door and whispered, "Carter?" After a moment, the door opened a crack and a young man popped his head out. "She left," he said. "Can I help you with something?"

I had a feeling he was lying, but what could I do? I tried peering into the room behind him, but I couldn't see much and he wasn't budging. "If you're in there, Carter, I really need your help! *Please.*" The young man was tapping his foot. "I told you, she's not here."

"Is there a back exit to this place?" I asked.

"No." He shut the door.

Feeling trapped, I decided to make a run for it. I darted into a changing room and pulled on my street clothes. I rummaged through my bag looking for makeup, but all I came up with was some cherry ChapStick. Kind of like putting an Elmo bandage on a gaping head wound, but I did it anyway. I gathered up my stuff and sprinted through the waiting room and out the front door. No one looked up from their magazines. No one called out my name. I was home free.

I stopped on the street in front of the studio. Instead of the relief I expected to feel, I was tormented by a more urgent sense of unease. I was pretty certain that the reason I'd made it out of the studio without being spotted by Tom was that he wasn't there. In my hasty retreat, I'd cast a quick glance around the waiting room and hadn't seen any men—just a blur of women. It was foolish of me to assume that Nicole's presence guaranteed Tom's when it was equally plausible that Nicole's *mom* could be sitting in the waiting room.

Burning with curiosity, I pressed my face up against BodyWorks' storefront. Two women were talking and looking at photographs, one was absorbed in conversation on her cell phone while a toddler tugged at her pant leg, and two others were leafing through magazines. Another was standing in the doorway to the dance studio, craning her neck to see the little ballerinas. No Tom. Just moms.

The BodyWorks' receptionist looked out the window in my direction and I feigned interest in one of the flyers posted near the studio door. It was the current month's schedule. I ran a finger over it, pretending to care what body-twisting torture activities were on tap for the coming week. That's when I saw the name of the class I had just endured: Extreme Yoga! The exclamation point was part of the title. The schedule I had at home was out-of-date, obviously. Only mildly relieved that it was an *extreme* yoga class that had knocked me on my ass rather than a *beginners'* class, I resolved to rip the faded flyer off my fridge and use it to line Felix's cage.

Surreptitiously returning my attention to the moms, I tried to deduce which mom belonged to Nicole. Odds were pretty good that one of the women I was spying was Nicole's mother, aka Tom's soon-to-be ex, aka Tom's *wife*. I suddenly felt like the "other woman," an image no doubt intensified by my current stalker stance. Feeling somewhat illicit, I surveyed the women inside. I felt I could safely rule out the woman with the toddler, as Tom hadn't mentioned having any children other than Nicole, but the other ladies were all contenders. They all looked pretty normal. Women I might be friends with, or at least share pleasantries with while I was cutting their hair or doing their taxes. This brought me up short. Since Tom seemed like such a nice, normal guy, I had assumed that the woman he was divorcing had to be a psychotic raving lunatic. None of these women looked psycho or looney, at least on the surface. What if *he* is the lunatic? I wondered, as I slunk away in the direction of home.

Dinner at Kuki's

On the subway ride to Brooklyn, I briefed Danny on what to expect when dining with my family. He'd met some of my relatives before, but never en masse, and never in their own element. A daunting prospect under the best of circumstances, for someone in Danny's depressed state, dinner with my family could be truly disastrous. He was slumped in his seat looking disconsolately out the window of our express train as it whizzed past commuters waiting on local platforms. He'd barely said anything since he picked me up at my apartment, other than extracting my solemn promise that if I heard from Carter, I'd tell him.

"I haven't seen her," I lied, as a spasm of pain tore through my groin. Pinocchio had his nose; my anatomical barometer of truth was destined to lie farther south.

Danny was equally oblivious to my deception and my pelvic pain. When I finished my exhaustive list of the dos and don'ts of dining at Kuki's, he nodded and smiled absently. "Hol, don't worry. How bad can it be?"

* * *

Those words were still hanging in the air as we stood on the stoop of my aunt's brownstone. I adjusted the scarf I was wearing to cover the bald spot on the back of my head, and rang the bell. Before the door was even opened, I was salivating from the savory smell of my aunt's cooking. No doubt she'd made all my favorites. Suddenly my qualms about the evening seemed silly. We'd have a good meal, my aunt would berate me for my life's choices, I'd shrug it off, and we'd go home. Danny was right—how bad could it be?

The door opened wide and I was engulfed in an embrace by my cousin Gerry. "Holly! I'm so glad you could make it!"

"I wasn't aware my attendance was optional," I said dryly.

Gerry pulled me inside, then punched Danny's biceps. "My man! Everyone's in the parlor." He was grinning widely and bouncing on his heels. "Go on." He nudged. "I'm gonna wait on the stoop till Monica gets here."

I took a deep breath and braced myself for the inevitable inquisition. Then I strode into the parlor, Danny trailing close behind.

"Holly's here!" my aunt Betty crowed as soon as I entered the parlor. Though it's too traitorous to admit, Aunt Betty is my favorite of my mother's two sisters. After my mother died, I'd gone to live with my grandmother, but it was Kuki, my mother's oldest sister, who took on the responsibility of caring for me. As my grandmother, addled by Alzheimer's by the time I was in high school, slowly slipped into dementia, Kuki cared for all of us—Nana, me, my uncle Leo, and her own kids, Gerald and Veronica. Aunt Betty and Uncle Bernie lived down the street, and I snuck off to their house whenever I had the chance. At Kuki's, the furniture was all covered in plastic and you had to take off your shoes at the door, but at Betty's you could keep your street shoes on even in the sitting room. Kuki wouldn't let me have any pets, but Betty and Bernie had dogs—big dogs that I could get on the floor and wrestle with.

Kuki's house was always orderly and neat—every last knickknack was dusted twice weekly and replaced on its own embroidered doily on the perfectly polished mahogany furnishings.

Kuki was concerned about keeping up appearances, constantly reminding me to mind my p's and q's and maintain an air of respectability. Betty told me to listen to the beat of my own drummer and called Kuki's pretenses "a bunch of pippity-poppity poppycock."

Kuki had taken me in, put me through college, and taught me a trade—hairstyling, which I learned working alongside her at the barbershop she and my uncle Leo owned. I owed her more than I could ever hope to repay. I would always be grateful to her for everything she'd done for me. But in my heart of hearts, it was Betty I liked best.

Betty rose and made her way toward me, arms outstretched as if preparing to wrap me up in a big bear hug. I knew better. Aunt Betty was no hugger. She was a grabber, a pincher, and at times, even a biter. I'd often wondered what childhood trauma led to her custom of expressing affection by inflicting painful nips and tweaks. I winced as she hobbled near, hoping she wouldn't pinch my cheeks. Last time she'd squeezed so hard she left a bruise.

"Holly, honey," she squealed, boxing my ears with such force I feared a crash course in lip-reading would be in my near future, "let me take a look at you!" She seized my shoulders and eyeballed me head to toe. "You haven't been around in so long, and we hear these dreadful stories about you living alone in the city." Yeah, I could just imagine the stories she'd heard and from whom she'd heard them.

As if on cue, Kuki called out from the kitchen, "Take off your shoes, Holly! I just had the carpet steamed."

"I'm fine, Aunt Betty," I said as I kicked off my shoes and motioned for Danny to do the same. "No need to worry about me, despite what you may hear from certain quarters."

"Are you sure? You look a little green about the gills."

"I'm sure. Never felt better." Never, that is, since two o'clock that afternoon.

She relaxed her grip on my shoulders. "Good."

I took Danny by the arm and led him to the center of the room. "This is my friend, Danny. I invited him to join us for dinner."

My uncles Bernie and Leo sat limp and languid on the sofa. Leo nodded weakly and Bernie managed a wave. Aunt Betty lunged toward Danny. "Holly brought her boyfriend!"

"I'm not—" Danny protested as Betty embraced him, pulling his cheek close to hers.

"What a handsome fellow," she said. "I could just take a bite out of you!"

And she did.

Danny yelped and jumped back, raising his hand to his cheek. "What the—?" He shot me a wounded look. "She bit me!"

I took Betty by the arm and led her away from Danny's accusing stare. "He's not my boyfriend," I insisted, as we slowly made our way across a half dozen woven throw rugs to the sofa. Though most of Betty's joints were held together by metal pins, she looked like a speed sprinter next to me. The searing pain in my pelvis made walking difficult, though I thought I was hiding it well.

"Why are you walking so funny?" Betty asked. So much for the cover-up.

"I hugged a donkey."

She nodded knowingly.

I lowered Betty onto the sofa, where she assumed her usual position next to my uncle Bernie. She glanced over at Danny, who was examining his cheek in an antique mirror. "What's wrong with him?"

"You bit him."

"It was just a little nip." She slapped my arm with a force belying her advanced age. "And I didn't mean *that*. I mean, why isn't he your beau?"

"He's not my 'beau' because we're not in the nineteenth century. And he's not my 'boyfriend' because he's Carter's."

My uncle Bernie perked up. "Carter? Is she here? Where is the little dickens?" Danny looked over upon hearing Carter's name.

"Carter's not coming tonight," I said.

"Did I ever tell you about the time Carter and Holly hid their bras in the cookie jar?" Bernie said, addressing no one in particular.

Oh, God. Not the cookie jar story. "How are the Knicks doing?" I asked, hoping to divert Bernie before he could launch into the tale. I had to cut him off quickly or the enthusiasm would spread like wildfire and my relatives would spend the entire evening regaling Danny with embarrassing stories of my youth. Ever eager for new material, Danny would surely find much fodder for our act in my teenage foibles. I had no problem exploiting my life's current calamities for all their comedic potential, but I drew the line at poking fun of my former gawky self. It had taken me years to gain the self-confidence not only to live on my own, but to start a career in a very public profession—and I felt fiercely protective of the young, insecure me.

Danny strode over. "What's that about bras in the cookie jar?"

Bernie hesitated. Though he fancied himself a raconteur, becoming atypically animated whenever he found virgin ears for the tales of which his family had long ago tired, he was equally allured by the prospect of discussing his favorite team, the New York Knicks—he'd held courtside season tickets since the Eisenhower administration. I crossed my fingers, hoping the Knicks would win out.

Bernie leaned forward and tugged at his shirtsleeves. "Holly couldn't have been more than yea high," he said, his hand marking a spot about four feet off the ground.

Damn Knickerbockers. If they hadn't been smack in the middle of a losing season, perhaps Bernie would have been more eager to discuss them. "Uncle Bernie, Danny doesn't need to hear this—"

"Her aunt had just taken her to get her first brassiere," Bernie pressed on. "Whadda they call it, a starter bra?"

"A *training* bra," Leo corrected him.

My cheeks flushed at the memory. Aunt Kuki had taken me to our neighborhood Woolworth's, with my cousins Gerry and Veronica in tow, to pick out my first bra. She thought it was too much trouble for me to go into a changing room to try it on, couldn't imagine why I might like some privacy. Instead she started taking bras off hangers and fitting them over my burgeoning breasts right in the middle of the sales floor. I was fighting back tears as she fastened one after another brassiere over my blouse and made comments like "You don't quite fill this one out" and "Maybe this one, look at the pretty pink bow." Gerry, meanwhile, was milking the situation for all it was worth, snickering as he composed a ditty about itty-bitty titties. I had never missed my mother more.

"I'll never forget reaching into the cookie jar for a macaroon—" Bernie wheezed, pausing for breath.

"Not the cookie jar story again," Kuki interrupted, standing in the doorway with oven mitts on both hands. "Dinner is almost ready. Where's Gerry?"

"I'll get him!" I volunteered, limping to the foyer. As I reached for the knob, the door opened and Monica Broccoli plowed straight into me, knocking me onto my rear. " 'Scuse me, Holly. Didn't see you there." She was still limping slightly, and I wondered if I'd done the right thing, removing her cast prematurely. Gerry trailed behind her like a puppy dog, helping her with her coat and shoes. Neither offered to help me up, which was just as well since I was certain I'd separated my pelvis in the fall and would require the help of emergency medical technicians in order to move again.

They disappeared into the parlor, and I could hear shouted greetings mingled with Bernie's asthmatic guffaws.

When I returned to the parlor, Kuki was standing in the doorway, wringing her hands and looking at the clock. Everyone was gathered with the exception of my cousin Veronica. "Where in heaven's name *is* she?" Kuki complained.

No one ventured a guess, but if I knew Ronnie, she was somewhere in a liplock with Brooklyn's latest bad boy. Ever since she'd turned seventeen a few years ago, she was never at home, and the last few times I'd bumped into her in public, she was attached at the lip to one in a series of brooding, dangerous-looking young men. She'd come up for air just long enough to say hi and introduce me to Rick, Nick, or Dean. These days I couldn't even picture her face without a young man affixed to it.

I hugged Kuki and thanked her for allowing me to bring Danny on such short notice. "You know your friends are always welcome here." She hugged me back and I felt suddenly silly for fearing the evening would be a disaster.

Then she eyed the scarf I was wearing. "Take that silly thing off," she said, giving it a yank.

"Ouch!" I raised my hands over my head protectively.

"No use covering it up. We all know how you hit your head, chasing after that snake in your apartment." She spun me around. "Let me have a look." She gasped. "Who did this hack job?"

"What, now you're an expert on stitches?"

"Not the stitches! They mangled your hair. It's not even straight. It looks like the time you got a big wad of bubble gum in your hair and your *father* cut it out, right close to the scalp!" On the rare occasions that Kuki actually mentioned my father, her intonation made the word itself sound like an accusation, as though his very relationship to me had been a personal affront to her. I always figured she blamed him for dumping me on her doorstep, another mouth to feed, another set of school clothes to buy, another prepubescent girl to take bra shopping.

"I'm guessing the ER doctor didn't graduate from Flushing Beauty Academy," I said. "And speaking of my *father*, remember that box of his stuff? You always said I could have it when I was old enough."

"This is appalling," she said, still scrutinizing my hair, ignoring my question. She grabbed me by one arm and dragged me into the kitchen, where she propped me on a stool at the far end of the counter, away from the stove. Draping a large dishcloth around my neck, she added, "And you're not old enough."

Before I could challenge her, she disappeared, leaving me to wonder exactly how old I'd have to be before Kuki would begin treating me like an adult. She returned moments later with a pair of styling shears, and I let the subject drop—knowing better than to invoke my father's memory while Kuki was wielding a sharp instrument. I wasn't even sure why I had brought up my father's box—it had been years since I'd even thought about it. When I was moving out of Kuki's house, I'd offered to take it with me, thinking she'd be glad to be rid of it. Instead, she'd insisted it remain where it was, gathering dust in a far corner of the attic. "Leave well enough alone, Holly," she'd said, causing me to wonder what was "well enough" about having nothing more to show for my father's existence than a musty old box.

Kuki spritzed my head with a water bottle and began combing out my hair. At the other end of the counter, a half dozen dishes were simmering in the over and on the stove. The food was so aromatic and my hunger pangs so acute that I soon graduated from salivating to full-blown drooling. Other than the banana I'd scarfed down on my way to Yoga Extreme!, I hadn't eaten anything all day.

Unmindful of the thunderous grumbles emanating from my gastrointestinal tract, Kuki snipped away at the hair surrounding my wound, pausing intermittently to stir sauces, sprinkle seasonings, and pop her head in and out of the oven. Once, when her back was turned, I reached up to the counter and snatched a baby gherkin off a pickle tray. Turning back just in time to witness my treachery, she gave my hand a whack that sent the pickle flying across the kitchen. "Who do you think raised you? A pack of baboons?"

There was a commotion in the parlor and I heard my cousin Veronica's shrill voice above the din. Then Gerry's, accusing, "What's a matter with you? I told you seven o'clock." Shouting something about a stalled IRT train, Ronnie warned him to get out of her way before she clocked him. Then we heard a thump, and the pictures along the wall rattled.

Wagging a finger in my face, Kuki forbade me to move and hastily exited the kitchen, obviously eager to put a stop to the clocking.

My cousins' brawl presented me with a perfect opportunity to engage in some furtive feasting, and this time I moved quickly, though—as time would tell—less than surreptitiously. I hopped off the chair and bounded gracelessly to the stove, clutching the dishcloth around my neck. My eyes darting nervously from the stove to the doorway, I seized a pot holder and jerked the lid off the nearest pan, revealing at least a dozen gloriously golden marinated meatballs. I speared one with a fork and, not risking the time it would take to blow on it to cool it off, hoisted it directly from the frying pan into my mouth—a decision I regretted the instant the fire-hot ball of beef made contact with my tender tongue. Even as it was searing the roof of my mouth, the meatball's savory juices sent a reassuring message to my stomach—that actual home-cooked food was in its near future.

Heavy footsteps signaled Kuki's approach. Whipping my head around to view the kitchen door, I tried to gauge her distance while

I pondered pilfering another beefy morsel. Feeling a draft, I looked down in horror to find that the cloth around my neck had come loose and the snips of hair it had held were now gone. A quick glance confirmed my worst fear: jerking my head around had propelled the clippings across the stovetop, where most came to rest atop the marinated meatballs.

I glumly surveyed the hairy balls while considering my options. Option one: tell Kuki the truth, giving her fresh evidence of my thoughtlessness and ingratitude just when it seemed she was beginning to lighten up. Option two: cover my ass and hide my tracks. I knew, of course, which option was the right one, the morally correct one, but my self-preservation instinct kicked in, easily quashing any ethical objections I may have had. The hairs were too fine to successfully strain out, so my only choice was to conceal them. I grabbed a wooden spoon and stirred the meatballs. Luckily, my reddish tresses blended beautifully with the tomato sauce, and once I'd swept the remaining clippings off the stove and countertop into my hand, there was no evidence to betray my misdeed.

I slid back into the chair and sprinkled the cloth with the few hairs that had managed to miss the meatballs mere seconds before Kuki swung through the kitchen door. She looked startled to see me, as though she'd forgotten leaving me and my half-shaven head in such dangerous proximity to her hors d'oeuvres. "We can serve dinner now," she announced, eyeing the perfectly proportioned platters with suspicion.

Satisfied that not a single gherkin was out of place, she brushed the back of my head and yanked the cloth from around my neck. Ronnie's arrival obviously negating the urgency of repairing my cosmetological nightmare, I'd been dismissed.

I reached up and felt the back of my head. The hair around the bald patch still felt ragged, and the patch itself felt like it had significantly increased in diameter. Rather than repairing the emergency room "hack job," Kuki had made it worse. "Are you sure you're done?" I asked tentatively.

She hmphed. "There was nothing I could do to save it. You should consider a wig."

I returned to the parlor, my guilt over contaminating Kuki's meatballs lessening with every step. I secretly hoped I'd left a strand long enough for her to choke on.

When I returned to the parlor, Danny was on the divan looking downcast; Bernie's blabbering about my itsy-bitsy boobies was apparently insufficient to raise his spirits. Having lost his audience, Bernie had sunk back down into a torpid slump.

I made my way over to Gerry and Monica. "How'd the audition go?"

She shrugged. "Good. I think I'll get a callback, at least."

Gerry whispered something in Monica's ear. She nodded, then spoke. "Hey, Hol, I was wondering about that actor friend of yours . . . the one in your building."

The only actor I knew in my building was Brian, Kramer's owner, but out of respect for his privacy, I hadn't mentioned his profession to either Monica or Carter. "Brian? He's not really a friend. I just take care of his cat when he goes away. What makes you say he's an actor?"

"He had a big stack of headshots on his coffee table, not to mention photos of him and his lover in frames all around the apartment. I recognized him from my soap opera."

Gerry raised his eyebrows, doing a poor job of acting surprised. "What's this? You know a soap opera star, Holly? How come you never told us?"

I cringed, suddenly realizing where this was all heading. So much for enlisting Monica's help in bringing Gerry back to Earth. She was obviously setting me up. "He's not a *star*," I said, "and I don't know him well."

Gerry put his arm around my shoulder. "He's a regular on a soap opera. Ergo, he's a soap star."

I raised one eyebrow, wondering what misalignment of the planets had resulted in my cousin Gerry using words like "ergo." "There's a soap star living on every other block in this city. It's not really noteworthy."

He drew a deep breath and leaned closer. "You have access to his apartment, right? You could get me a pair of his—"

"No way," I cut him off. "I'm not stealing his socks! I have a business reputation. People entrust me with their animals, their apartments. I don't even *touch* their belongings, let alone *steal* anything. It's a matter of principle."

"Puh-*lease*," Monica Broccoli spat in my direction. "Your friend Carter was practically splooging all over his satin sheets the other night. When I got there she was slurping margarita mix straight from the bottle."

Uh-oh. I felt my stomach jump into my throat. Please tell me Danny didn't hear that, I thought. I glowered at Monica, raising a finger to my lips, but it was too late. Danny was making his way toward us.

Gerry, meanwhile, undeterred by my refusal, was pitching his heart out. "I wouldn't ask you if it wasn't important. You can make all the jokes you want about it, but this sock thing—it's totally unique. No one's ever done it before!"

Danny pushed his way past Gerry and confronted me. "You know where Carter is, don't you?"

"No, I swear—"

"I *heard* you guys." He turned to Monica. "You saw her the other night? Where is she staying?"

"I, uh, I—" Monica stuttered.

"She's not there anymore," I answered him. "It was one night. She was at my neighbor's apartment."

"He's a soap star," Gerry offered unhelpfully. Monica whacked the side of his head.

"I swear I don't know where she is now," I said. "I tried to get her to talk to you, and now she won't talk to me either." I wanted to add that she'd physically abused me and threatened my life, but that would bring up another encounter with Carter I'd neglected to tell him about.

Danny's voiced quavered. "So that's what it is. She's sleeping with a soap star?"

"No—" I protested.

Monica interrupted. "Honey, the guy wasn't even there. Besides, he's gayer than Ronald McDonald."

So much for safeguarding Brian's privacy. Monica Broccoli was hardly the type to be discreet, and I wondered how long it would take before she blabbed Brian's business all over Brooklyn.

"Trust me," Monica continued, "it was just us girls. The only tail in that apartment was on a cat."

Danny fell silent, his pained expression out of character on his usually affable face. I felt guilty and aggrieved at the same time. Once again, I was at the center of other people's drama. True, I had kept things from Danny, including one very *big* thing, but it was Carter's place to tell him, not mine. I was trying to maintain a very delicate balance between being Carter's friend and Danny's— hopefully I'd manage to get through it with my pelvic ligaments intact.

Kuki called out that dinner was ready, and Gerry and Monica bounded toward the dining room, the elderly contingent shuffling behind them. I stayed behind to talk to Danny, who looked like he was about to bolt out of Brooklyn.

"I promise, I'll tell you everything I know," I said, meaning it. "But let's just get through dinner first. If you leave now, my aunt will be offended, and I'll never hear the end of it. Please, Danny."

Danny managed a slight, sad smile. "Okay. I'm too hungry to leave without dinner."

"Good," I said, leading the way to the dining room. Pausing at the door, I added confidentially, "Stay away from the marinated meatballs."

I took a seat between Danny and Gerry, opposite my cousin Veronica, who regarded me with a contemptuous sneer. Ever since I'd moved into my aunt's house and she'd been forced to share her bedroom with me—allotting me exactly one and a half drawers in her capacious bureau and one-eighth of the closet space—she'd treated me as a most unwelcome intruder. Though it had been eight years since I'd moved out on my own, her indignant stance, long in-grained, stuck like a bad habit.

"Nice hair," she remarked. "You do that yourself?"

I rolled my eyes in her direction, hoping to convey how boring I found her insults. Her hair, as usual, was perfectly coifed, her appearance beyond reproach. Unlike my emergency room intern, Veronica *had* attended Flushing Beauty Academy—which, Aunt Kuki never hesitated to point out, was far less expensive than monkey school—where she'd diligently mastered the art of the make-over, practicing this art mainly on herself. She changed her look nearly as frequently as she changed boyfriends.

She glanced over at Danny, who looked like someone had killed his pet kitten. "What's with Mr. Perky Pants?"

"He and Carter broke up," I answered. "He's depressed. I thought having dinner with the family might cheer him up."

"If Carter's your friend, why aren't you cheering *her* up?" she asked.

"Danny's my friend, too," I said truthfully. "And Carter's not speaking to me right now."

"No Carter, huh? No wonder you're so cranky. No one to mooch Frappuccinos from."

"Yeah, that's what hurts the most, Ronnie. A lifelong friendship is on the line and I'm mourning the loss of complimentary coffee." Although, now that she mentioned it, I was suffering from a colossal caffeine craving.

I passed a casserole dish in her direction and smiled sweetly. "Have a meatball. They're delicious."

Aunt Kuki subjected me to mercifully little grilling during dinner. Usually, she'd have me on the defensive from the moment I walked in the door, but tonight she'd been oddly genial, even asking after my health and suggesting I rest while she set the table. She only managed one barb, when Uncle Bernie asked if I had any new clients and I mentioned I'd agreed to babysit a monkey.

"A monkey, huh? How much ya get paid for somethin' like that?" Bernie asked.

"It's a volunteer program, so normally I take care of animals for no charge when their owners are in the hospital. But this is an unusual case, and the monkey's owner is paying thirty bucks a day."

Aunt Kuki nodded with mock approval. "Thirty dollars a day? That should offset the twenty grand we spent for your tuition at monkey school."

If anyone noticed the extra ingredient in the marinated meatballs, they didn't say anything. It may have been my imagination, but I thought I noticed Uncle Leo picking at his teeth more than usual, and Gerry spent long intervals staring at his plate perplexedly, as though something was askew.

I'd tried to pass on the meatballs, but Kuki had ladled two onto my plate with a dismissive grunt, as though I didn't have the sense to make such a decision on my own. Later, noticing they remained untouched, she nudged my arm, saying, *"Mangia."* I obediently lifted a piece to my mouth, then nearly gagged when I felt something tickle the back of my throat.

Betty smiled at me from across the table. "You need to keep up your strength, dear."

I realized then that everyone had been oversolicitous of my health since I'd arrived. "Look, it's nice of everyone to be concerned," I said, "but it was a minor head wound. I'm fine."

Kuki and Betty exchanged looks, and Gerry drummed his fingers along the table. Everyone was quiet. I looked around the table, but no one would meet my gaze except Danny, and he looked as lost as I was.

"What's going on?" I asked.

Finally, Ronnie spoke. "Gerry told us about the other night in your apartment."

"Yeah, I know. The snake, the stitches. Everything's out in the open."

"Everything?" Kuki demanded.

I looked at her blankly. "What?"

Ronnie answered for her. "We know about the pregnancy tests. Gerry saw them in your apartment. You knocked up, or what?"

"No!"

Danny spoke up. "Those were for the snake."

"Oh, that explains it!" Aunt Betty smiled, obviously relieved.

"A pregnant snake?" Bernie said, pausing to pick at something between his teeth. I flinched, noting the half-eaten meatball on his plate. "That's something to see."

"Rocky's a *boy*," Monica objected. "And besides, Holly's not the one who's pregnant."

When I was five, I fell headfirst off a set of monkey bars on the school playground. At most it was a six-foot drop, but it seemed like an eternity while I was falling. The knowledge that I would certainly land face-first in the dirt and there was nothing I could do to prevent it caused time to slow, every second lasting a lifetime. If my life passed before my eyes, I don't remember it, or perhaps I hadn't experienced much of a life up to that point. What I recall is seeing the footprints in the dirt below gradually grow larger and wondering how the soft dirt would react to its impending impact with my face.

I had never again experienced such an extreme slowing of time until the moment Monica uttered the words—"Holly's not the one who's pregnant"—at the dinner table. Had I remembered that Monica had been at my apartment when Carter took her first pregnancy test, I would have realized my folly in inviting Danny to dinner. What can I say? I've never been good at keeping secrets. It's too hard to keep track of who knows what.

I shot Monica a look I'd previously reserved for perverts who stood too close to me on the subway, but it didn't seem to register. She plowed on. "It's that friend of hers who's pregnant."

Had I possessed a multitude of friends I might have jumped in and tried to do some damage control. But given my tight circle of friends, anyone with the deductive powers of a slug could have figured out who Monica meant by "that friend of hers."

Danny turned to face me. "Carter?"

Bingo.

"I was going to tell you—" I began.

"Yeah, right." He stood, tossing his napkin onto his plate and pushing away from the table. "Thanks for dinner," he said to Kuki. "I have to go."

I tried to follow him, but he shot out the front door without even stopping to retrieve his shoes from the hall closet. By the time I reached the stoop, he was at the street corner, his outstretched arm hailing a cab. I returned to the dining room and announced that I had to leave, too. I had to catch up to Danny and straighten things out, perhaps even get him and Carter to talk.

Kuki wouldn't hear of it. She grabbed me by the arm and lowered me forcibly into my seat. "You'll stay for dessert. Then you can go find your friend."

"I'm not hungry," I insisted.

"Yes, I could tell by the way you picked at your meatballs." She looked at me with one brow arched and I knew I'd been busted.

After a few moments of strained silence, Aunt Betty tried to lighten the mood by asking Gerry about his "star socks." He responded that he had a lead on a new addition to his collection, but that I was refusing to cooperate. All eyes turned, once again, in my direction.

"He wants me to steal a guy's socks from his apartment," I explained. "I can't do it."

Uncle Bernie said, "It's not like they're valuable. A man has so many socks, he'd never miss one pair."

"You should be more supportive of your cousin," Kuki reprimanded. "He's showing initiative. He's trying to make something of himself."

Leo nodded. "He's got chutzpah."

Even Betty turned on me, suggesting that since I had the keys to Brian's apartment, it wouldn't really be stealing. "Couldn't you just accidentally take a pair of his socks with you when you feed his pussycat? What's he gonna do, call the cops?"

"First of all," I addressed Gerry, "I'm still not clear on how a few pair of socks constitutes a business enterprise. How on earth do you plan to make money? Are you going to sell the socks?"

"At first I thought so, yeah. But then I realized how hard it would be to replenish my inventory. I'm kickin' myself for only taking one pair of Scorsese's socks, but how was I to know I was touching gold?"

How, indeed?

"Now I'm thinkin' "—he paused to clear his throat—"it will be more like an exhibition. I can charge admission—" He began coughing in earnest, sounding like Grouch trying to hack up a hairball. When he regained control of himself, he resumed. "Maybe find some rich sponsors, sell advertising even."

Aunt Betty clapped her hands. "What an entrepreneur!" She leaned over and gave him a congratulatory flick on the forehead.

"Yow!" Gerry cried, rubbing the red welt on his brow. "That means a lot, Aunt Bet."

I was dumbstruck. The whole family was backing Gerry in his ridiculous sock venture. The only one who hadn't chimed in was Veronica. Considering her overall enmity toward her older brother, I figured I could at least count on her to contribute a few barbs and take some of the heat off me.

"What do you think about this sock business, Veronica?" I asked, looking across the table.

She shrugged. "It's cool."

"Stealing stinky socks from celebrities is cool?"

She smiled. "He said if he gets Justin Timberlake I can have first whiff."

Discussion of Gerry's sock collection was diverted when Gerry broke into a coughing fit, his body shaking as the paroxysms mounted. I was on the verge of confessing my culinary crime when he took a deep breath and exhaled. The crisis had past.

"What's the matter with him?" Leo asked. Gerry was staring down at his plate as if the answers to all life's mysteries were written there—if only he could decipher the code encrypted in the stringy meatballs.

He coughed again, then pushed back his chair and sank to his knees. I jumped to my feet, certain that emergency resuscitation was in order and once again wishing I'd paid attention back in health class, instead of fawning over no-good Robby Francomano. How would I live with myself if Gerry choked to death and I couldn't save him? Worse still, how would I survive the recriminations that would follow when the paramedics arrived and discovered the clump of my hair that was surely lodged in his esophagus?

I lunged toward Gerry, my chair toppling over behind me. Though the precise details of the Heimlich maneuver had been lost on me in the seventh grade (my fumbling attempts to perform the maneuver on Resusci-Annie would have surely resulted in her death, my teacher had solemnly informed me), I had the gist of it, and it was clear no one else was going to try. Positioning myself behind Gerry, I clasped my hands together over the midpoint of his rib cage and thrust upward. He gagged and sputtered. A good sign? I couldn't recall.

As I strained to recall what to do next—continue thrusting, check for a pulse, stick my finger in his mouth to check for obstructions—Gerry looked up at me, his face flushed, his eyes pleading. But, as I wondered how many minutes Gerry could survive without oxygen, I began to sense that his expression was not that of a dying man. He shot me a look, which, if I wasn't mistaken, revealed extreme annoyance. At whom? I wondered, looking around. Seeing similar expressions on everyone at the table, I grew more confused. I couldn't fathom why they were all just sitting there, why no one had dialed 9-1-1, why Kuki hadn't made a dash for her rosary beads or smelling salts.

Gerry flung his arms recklessly, landing a surprisingly strong backhand to my jaw, which sent me reeling backward. As the back of my head struck Kuki's china cabinet, she gasped, displaying more alarm over her Wedgwood teacups than her suffocating son.

Kuki held her breath as the china rattled and, finally, settled. Her heirlooms safe for the moment, she exhaled dramatically.

My desire to save Gerry's life waning precipitously, I gaped at him and noted, for the first time, that in the hand he'd slugged me with he was clutching a small black velvet box. Suddenly, a bell went off in my head (actually it was more like Big Ben signaling high noon), and I understood. Gerry had not dropped to his knees because he was choking, but because he was *proposing*, his red cheeks resulting from nervousness, not lack of oxygen. I recalled the wink that accompanied his cryptic invitation to this family dinner, an event for which he was disproportionately excited.

Flooded with relief and embarrassment, I backed away from Gerry, mouthing apologies and attempting invisibility.

Struggling to catch his breath, Gerry watched my retreat warily. Once confident I was out of attack range, he drew a deep breath and turned to Monica Broccoli. "Monica," he wheezed, "will you do me the honor of becoming—" *Cough, gag, hack.*

As he struggled to regain the ability to speak, Gerry pried open the little velvet box, revealing a gleaming ring, whose diamond was surprisingly large for someone for whom peddling famous people's footwear represented a surefire investment strategy.

After one last cough, he sputtered, ". . . my wife?"

All eyes were on Monica now. Kuki and Betty clutched their bosoms. My attention wasn't on Monica, but on my pounding head, and the telltale trickling, which surely meant that blood was oozing from my newly reopened wound. I tried to ignore it, but, propelled by morbid curiosity and fear of the repercussions if my blood stained Kuki's shag carpet, I reached up and touched the back of my head. I traced the stitches with my fingers; the terrain felt slickly wet. I told myself it could be anything—food had gone flying, after all, when I'd lunged across the table, Heimliched Gerry, and then been flung into the china cabinet. But the slick substance on my fingers had neither the consistency of Kuki's mashed potatoes nor the texture of her Pomodoro sauce. I was not surprised, therefore, to see blood on my fingertips when I brought my hand to my face. I was, however, shocked that the person who fainted at the sight of the blood wasn't me.

7

Meeting the Monkey

Being hated was new to me. All my life I've been pretty universally liked. If not for the fact that my father had abandoned me before I was a teenager, I'd have no reason at all to suspect there was anything remotely unlikable about me. To be honest, even my father's abandonment didn't dent my self-esteem too much, because I'd always been secure in my mother's love and I think if kids have at least one parent—or any caring adult—who wholeheartedly adores them, they can't go too far wrong. I had that with my mom and, to a lesser degree, my aunts, who had each in her own way let me know that my dad's leaving was a reflection of *his* character flaws, not my own.

But in the space of a week, I'd managed to alienate my two best friends, my cousin, and my cousin's fiancée. And while I knew that Aunt Kuki could never harbor such a harsh emotion toward her only niece, I feared I might have at least earned a spot in the ice cube tray she used to "freeze people" out of her life. When Kuki believed someone had done her wrong, she wrote their name on a little square of paper, folded it, and placed it in an empty slot of an ice cube tray that she kept—minus ice—in the freezer. Kuki scorned such old-world curses as giving someone the "evil eye," but she fully believed in the retributive power of the ice cube tray. And it seemed to work, too—once someone's name went into the tray, they virtually vanished from our lives; their names were dropped from our Christmas list, their information blacked out of Kuki's address book with bold black strokes.

I used to sneak a peak in the freezer occasionally to see who Kuki had iced. One wad of paper, tucked in one of the farthermost hollows of the tray, had been there even before I'd discovered the reason Kuki kept people instead of ice in her trays. Condensed moisture had caused the ink to run and the paper to freeze to the side of the metal tray. I couldn't make out any letters through the frozen wad, but somehow I knew that the name on the paper was my father's.

If I had made it into the tray, it wouldn't be easy getting out again.

This morning I had not required the services of the Sleepblaster Plus; I'd tossed and turned all night, my mind replaying the events of the previous evening on an endless loop. One image stood out with vicious clarity, that of Aunt Kuki standing over Monica Broccoli with smelling salts, saying, "Holy hell, Holly, what's the matter with you?" It was a question I'd struggled to answer, and upon failing, I'd turned and fled from the house, not waiting for Monica to regain consciousness and respond to Gerry's proposal—knowing that whatever her answer was, it didn't bode well for me being a bridesmaid.

When I'd arrived home, I tried calling both Carter and Danny but neither answered. I hoped now that Danny knew the truth, he had found Carter and they were in the process of working things out. In case Danny hadn't reached her, I felt I should warn her that he knew about the pregnancy. I left messages at her apartment, Body-Works, her grandmother's house, and Starbucks, and even tried another telepathic communiqué. So far, there'd been no response.

I dragged myself out of bed at the ungodly hour of six a.m., hoping to put an end to the mental images. I emptied a can of Fancy

Feast into Grouch's bowl and gave Felix half a wilted carrot. Thankfully, Rocky's next feeding was still a few days away—I was in no mood to handle frozen rodents.

I was in no mood for much of anything, actually. My head was pounding and I'd run out of the painkillers they'd given me in the emergency room. I rummaged through my purse and came up with one teensy little Advil, which I knew would be about as effective as a Tic-Tac in subduing my pain but I popped it in my mouth anyway. Caffeine might help, but that would require the almost Herculean effort—given my multitude of muscle aches—of a trip to Starbucks. The possibility of running into either Carter or Danny when both wanted to inflict bodily injury on me wasn't nearly as daunting as the six freakin' flights of stairs that lay beyond my front door.

Yet I desperately wanted a Mocha Frappuccino. It would help me clear my mind. Remembering the store's new delivery program, I reached for my phone. The service was supposed to be for business clients only, so I adopted my most businesslike tone when a barista named Sue answered.

"Hi, Sue, this is Holly with Holly's Hobbies. I need to place a delivery order."

"We can't deliver this morning. Our delivery guy called in sick."

"Oh. I'm sorry."

"'S'not your fault." Actually, if Danny was today's delivery guy, it probably was.

"Is Carter in today?"

"Nope. She's on leave."

"Still?"

"Yeah. Wanna place an order for pickup?" Sue asked, oblivious to my role in depleting Starbucks of its staff.

"No, thanks."

I hung up the phone, disconsolate. So coffee was not going to be on the morning's agenda. I tried to scrounge up some food, but my apartment had little to offer on that score, also. On top of all my other screwups last night, I'd gone home without any leftovers. It was too early to order takeout, so I nibbled on the other half of Felix's wilted carrot.

I limped around my apartment, trying to get a mental fix on the day ahead. I had no appointments lined up, which was a good thing, considering my overall malaise, but not so good from the perspective of my pocketbook. I knew I should work on my material—the comedy showcase was in three days—but with Danny and me on the outs, I doubted there would even be a showcase. I could try to drum up business by posting flyers for my various services in Laundromats and coffee shops around town, but that would involve a level of physical activity I didn't think I was ready for. Better to sit and sulk.

I had barely embarked upon what I intended as a full day's sitting and sulking when I heard a noise coming from my pantry. It sounded like the milk door snapping shut. I wasn't expecting anyone to drop work off today, and most of my clients called or buzzed first before leaving something. Thinking it could be the Writer, my first impulse was to hurl myself out the front door, stopping him before he could make another silent getaway. But even if I managed to get across my apartment before he made it down the stairs, what would I say to him?

I ran my fingers through my hair. When I reached the ragged edges around my bald patch, I stopped cold. What would I say, indeed? If I dragged my bedraggled self to the door and found the man I'd imagined—tall, blond, with piercing eyes and a slight, sad smile—kneeling by my milk cubby, could I find the words to convince him that his anonymous typist could be the woman of his dreams? Lacking the Writer's wonderful way with words, I doubted such a thing was possible. Better to wait until I looked irresistible. Or at least till my hair grew back.

I waited until I heard footsteps descending the staircase, then staggered to the pantry and undid the lock to the milk cubby. My stomach lurched when I withdrew a manila envelope bearing my name in tidy block letters. My hunch had been right—I instantly recognized the handwriting as belonging to the Writer. I tore the envelope open to find a note clipped to a handful of lined yellow pages. The brief message—*No rush this time. Thanks*—was devoid of any clues to the writer's identity. Damn.

I booted up my computer, propped the yellow pages on a typing stand, and began reading.

Snuggled close, I smell the sweet soapy scent of my daughter, fresh from her nightly bath. She rests her head on my shoulder, her damp hair leaving an impression on my nightshirt. "Read me a story, Daddy," she implores, and I feign disinterest. "Nah, you don't want a story. You'd rather be tickled!" I tease, assuming a wicked smile as my wiggling fingers close in on her slender waist. She screams, a shrill shriek that blends fear and delight, and I can't help but laugh. My daughter is terrified of being tickled, yet no matter how earnest my pretense, she trusts I won't actually do the evil deed. I am staggered by her faith in me; it is the source of my greatest pride and the cause of my deepest shame. Father, protector, vanquisher of demons—I am the hero of her eight-year-old heart. Yet when the time would come, I'd fail to safeguard the one thing she needed most: her mother.

I stopped reading so I could process this new information. The mysterious Writer has a *child*. This required a major adjustment to the mental picture I had formed. Instead of a bereaved loner, he was a widowed father, struggling to care for his daughter in the wake of his wife's death. I was overcome with a jumble of emotions—not the least of which was a mounting desire to know him, talk to him, see what he looked like. Maybe I should have made that mad dash to the front door after all.

The phone rang, interrupting my thoughts. Although I knew the odds were slim that the person on the other end would be someone whose life I hadn't recently ruined, I answered.

"Holly, I'm only going to say this once," my aunt Kuki said. "Last night was a big night for your cousin. Why did you have to go and spoil it for him?"

Groan. "I didn't mean to spoil anything. I thought he was dying. I was trying to save his life!"

"And another thing," she continued. "You ruined my meatballs!" From her tone I could tell she considered the latter offense more disgraceful than the first.

"I didn't—"

"Don't try to deny it. Leo was up half the night picking red hair out of his dentures. He says to tell you if he'd wanted a lock of your hair, he'd have raided your baby book."

"It was an accident," I said in my most contrite tone. "Please forgive me. I feel miserable."

There was a long pause on the other end; then Kuki said, "Good," and hung up.

I tried to call back but the line was busy. Kuki hadn't frozen me out, but she wasn't going to let me off the hook too easily.

Dying to know whether Monica had accepted Gerry's proposal, I dialed Kuki's number at least ten more times over the next half hour, but the line remained busy. Finally, I tried Gerry's apartment. After three rings, his answering machine picked up. His voice sounded professional, businesslike.

"You have reached Gerald Corelli, proprietor of Celebrity Socks, Incorporated. For more information about hosting an exhibition, or to book Mr. Corelli for a speaking engagement, please leave a message after the tone." Now Gerry wanted to do speaking engagements? After recounting how he'd swiped two pair of socks, what was there to talk about? How you, too, can seek your fortune in the footwear of the famous?

I left a brief message, apologizing for turning his proposal dinner into a food-flying fiasco and begging his forgiveness. Then I hung up and dialed the only person I knew I could count on to lend a sympathetic ear.

Aunt Betty answered on the first ring. "Holly, honey. That was something last night, huh? What a debacle."

"Yeah. Does everyone hate me?"

"*I* certainly don't."

"Thanks. That means a lot."

"How's your young man? Did you catch up with him?"

"Danny is not my young man, remember? And no, I haven't seen him. He probably hates me, too."

"Nonsense. Don't get yourself all flummoxed. It'll sort itself out in the wash."

I sighed. "So what happened after I left? Did Monica say yes?"

"Yes, she did—"

"Great! That means Gerry won't hate me too much. He's engaged. He'll be happy, and pretty soon he'll be laughing about all this."

"Well . . ." She hesitated.

Beep.

"Aunt Betty? I have another call coming in. Hold on." I clicked a button on my phone and said hello.

"Thank goodness you're home, Holly. It's Virginia Talbot with PAPS. We have a situation with Tallulah."

"What is it?"

"Mrs. Lipton just phoned. Her brother had to go into the hospital a day earlier than scheduled, so she wants to drop off Tallulah today. I know you weren't expecting her until tomorrow, but—"

Actually, with everything going on, I'd forgotten all about Tallulah's impending visit. I hadn't even begun to monkey-proof my apartment. I looked around, noting the exposed electrical outlets, the cabinets and drawers that would need safety locks, the multitude of small objects that would surely pose a choking hazard.

"Gosh, Virginia . . . I've been kind of having a bad week. Maybe it's not such a good idea, me taking care of a monkey."

"Nonsense! You're the perfect person for the job. And Mrs. Lipton's in a bind. You really *must,* Holly."

I sighed. "I don't have food for a monkey." Unless she likes freeze-dried mice.

"Mrs. Lipton will bring everything you need."

"Well, I guess—"

"Great! Mrs. Lipton says Tallulah just needs to pack a few things. We'll drop her off in an hour."

I switched back to Betty and caught her midsentence. She obviously still hadn't grasped the concept of call-waiting and had never stopping talking. ". . . how they do it is beyond me, but isn't that something? For just seven thousand dollars, you can have any dead body turned into a diamond. I saw it on the TV."

"What?" I said, certain I had missed something important in Betty's train of thought but not sure I wanted to know what it was.

"After all, it's made out of carbon, just like the human body."

"Uh . . . okay."

"I wouldn't mind doing that to Bernie. You know, when he passes. Make myself a nice diamond necklace or something."

"Why don't I just take you to the diamond district and help you pick out a necklace? It'll be a lot cheaper." Not to mention less *icky.*

*   *   *

After allowing Betty to brainstorm over which type of jewelry Bernie's remains would be most suited for, I informed her that I had company coming and I had to go.

I had less than an hour before Tallulah was due to arrive. Not enough time to make a trip to the hardware store to buy the supplies I had in mind for the monkey-proofing job. On second thought, Virginia had said the monkey was well behaved, so maybe I could get by with just tying my cupboards shut with garbage bag fasteners. I searched my kitchen drawers until I came up with a half dozen twist ties, then used them to fasten the cupboard doors shut. I was having doubts about the wisdom of this strategy before I even finished fastening the last tie. The flimsy little paper-coated pieces of wire wouldn't keep a two-year-old out; what chance did they stand against a wily little monkey? Still, I reasoned, it was the best I could do on short notice.

I turned my attention to my drawers, especially those containing sharp utensils. Lacking anything as sophisticated as safety locks, I taped the drawers shut using a roll of heavy-duty duct tape. I had barely finished this task when my buzzer rang. Damn, that's one fast-packing monkey, I thought.

I pressed the intercom button and said hello. To my surprise, my cousin's voice came booming back. "Holly, let me up!"

I buzzed him in. I couldn't imagine what would bring Gerry to my apartment at seven a.m., but I was relieved that he was at least speaking to me again. Few things are as embarrassing as interrupting a marriage proposal with a lifesaving choke hold, but it seemed Gerry wasn't going to hold it against me. My relief at this was almost enough to make me want to break into Brian's apartment and steal a pair of his gym socks.

I heard Gerry reach the landing, and opened the door to greet him. He was wearing jeans and a rumpled T-shirt and looked like he hadn't slept all night. He stuck his hand out, thrusting a pair of battered tennis shoes in my direction. "Your friend left these at Ma's."

I took the shoes and tossed them into the closet as Gerry ambled into my kitchen and poked his head in the fridge. He removed a pitcher of iced tea and set it on the counter, then reached up to open the cupboard where I keep my drinking glasses. He groped, tugged, and pulled the knob, not noticing the little green twist tie holding it closed.

"Let me help," I started toward him, but he waved me away.

"I got it, I got it." He yanked the knob again, but it didn't give way. Finally noticing the twist tie, he regarded it curiously, then shrugged and gave up, sticking his head under the faucet and drinking straight from the tap.

As I watched him guzzle, I revised my earlier estimation of the twist-tie fasteners. If they'd succeeded in keeping my thirty-year-old cousin from getting to my glassware, a little monkey would be no problem.

When he'd satisfied his thirst, Gerry sat down at my kitchen table. He seemed to be struggling to catch his breath, so I began speaking. "I know I embarrassed you last night, and I'm sorry. If I had known you were going to propose—"

"It was supposed to be a surprise," he said. "I couldn't tell you, 'cause I didn't want Monica to find out."

"Well, all's well that end's well, right?"

He looked at me with an openmouthed expression bordering on disgust. "Ends well? Whadda you talkin' about?"

"It's Shakespeare."

"Monica turned me down."

"What? Betty told me Monica said yes."

He shook his head vigorously. "First she said yes, but then she said no."

"She changed her mind?" I wondered what could have changed Monica's mind so suddenly; hopefully it wasn't the realization that her betrothed had been tackled by his younger, daintier cousin. Then again, maybe it was something she ate. "Did she try the meatballs?"

He shook his head again. "She said yes, and she was lookin' at the engagement ring I got her. Then Ronnie asks if she's going to change her name. Ma says of course she'll change her name. It's the proper thing to do. And Aunt Betty says she must be glad to have a chance to get rid of a name like Broccoli."

"So lemme guess. Monica wants to keep her name, and your mother is offended."

"No. She doesn't want to keep her name. But she got upset that everyone thought Monica Broccoli is her real name, and when she asked me to tell them what it was, I couldn't."

"Monica Broccoli isn't her name? Why does everyone call her that?"

" 'Cause when I first met her, I had a real hard time remembering her name, so I made things up to help me remember. You know, like Jimmy Beans."

Jimmy "Beans" was James Balducci, an old neighbor in Brooklyn. When he was younger, Gerry couldn't pronounce Balducci, so he called him Jimmy B, which over the years became Jimmy Beans. Eventually, everyone on the block called him Jimmy Beans, and when anyone came looking for Mr. Balducci, they'd shrug, not knowing who was being referred to.

"She says if I can't remember her name," Gerry continued, "she won't marry me."

That seemed pretty reasonable to me. "You honestly can't remember?"

He stared at me wide-eyed. "Holly, I've been dating her for *two years*. For two years I've been calling her Monica Broccoli. I can't remember anything before that. What am I gonna do?"

I scratched my head. "Can't you ask any of her other friends? Her family?"

"Her family lives in Florida, and I don't know any of her friends. I mean, not to call them. I've met them, but I don't remember their names or nothing."

Good point. If he couldn't pay attention to his fiancée's name, it stood to reason he hadn't registered the names of her friends either. When I thought about it, I realized Gerry probably knew the names of very few people outside the immediate family. He was always calling people "bro," "buddy," or "my man" or, for women, "baby," "sweetie," or "good-lookin'."

He looked at me pleadingly. "Holly, you have to help me. She was, like, your client or something, right?"

I nodded. Considering how infrequently she paid for my services, "or something" was more like it.

"So you must have business records, right? With her name on it? Did you make copies of her checks?"

"When she paid, it was always cash." I walked to my desk and retrieved a green ledger book. "But yes, every time she gave me money, I recorded it. See?" I held the open book in front of him. "Last name, Broccoli; first name, Monica."

"Aw, Holly. Didn't you ask to see some ID?"

"Why would I? She's your girlfriend for Pete's sake."

He hung his head sadly. "Not anymore."

Gerry had brought up a good point. I was going to have to do a better job of learning my clients' names. Here I was on my second typing job for the mysterious Writer, reading what seemed to be his most personal thoughts, and I hadn't a clue who he was.

I glanced over at my desk and saw the neatly lettered yellow pages. I was dying to finish reading them, but with Tallulah due to arrive any minute and Gerry skulking around my kitchen looking miserable, I guessed it would have to wait. My head was still pounding and I was no closer to being fit for a trip to Starbucks than I was upon waking at six. But now I had company.

"How 'bout this: I'll help you figure out what Monica's name is. But first you have to do me a favor."

"What?"

"Coffee. I need coffee so I can think. You run down to Starbucks and pick me up a Mocha Frappuccino, and when you get back, I'll start making some calls."

He looked dubious. "Who you gonna call?"

"I don't know. Monica's a model. Some casting director or agent is going to know who she is. I'll call around."

Gerry brightened. "I knew you'd help me. I'll be right back." He stopped at the door. "Grande?"

"Better make it a Venti," I answered. "It's gonna be a long day."

With Gerry out of my hair for the moment, I hoped I'd have time to read a few more pages of the Writer's prose. But before I could even limp across my apartment to pick up the pages, the phone rang.

"Hello?"

"I'm not saying I'll ever forgive you, but I need to talk to someone." Carter's voice sounded thin and reedy, like she'd been crying.

"Carter! I've been trying to reach you, to warn you. Danny *knows*. I didn't tell him, but it was my fault he found out. I took him to my aunt's for dinner, and Monica Broccoli was there. Did you know that's not her real name?"

"What?"

"Monica Broccoli. Can you believe it?"

"No shit. You thought it was?"

"Well, yeah. Didn't you?"

"Ever since you told me your cousin brought a virgin named Monica Broccoli to your grandmother's funeral, I knew something wasn't right." She paused. "So how did Danny take it?"

"He looked at me like I'd just revealed Anne Frank's where-abouts to the Gestapo. Then he took off—barefoot—and hopped into a cab. Carter, I am so sorry. I should have kept him away from Monica."

"Never trust anyone who'd impersonate a vegetable," she said flatly.

I laughed. "It sounds like you're channeling Aunt Kuki. That's something she would embroider on a throw pillow."

I thought I heard a faint chuckle; then Carter cleared her throat. "O.K., look. It's not your fault. Danny had a right to know. I know that. I just wanted more time to think about things. Now he's pissed because he found out from someone else."

"You heard from him?"

"Yeah. He left me a bunch of messages. He loves me, he wants the baby, he wants to marry me, blah blah blah."

"Well, that's good, isn't it? You were afraid he couldn't handle the responsibility."

"Just because he wants the baby doesn't mean he can handle it," she pointed out.

I had to admit that much was true. "Why don't you come over so we can talk?" I asked.

"I'm still avoiding any place Danny can find me. At least until I get my head together. Why don't you meet me for lunch?"

"I can't. I'm expecting a monkey any minute."

I explained about Tallulah and Carter said she'd meditate on whether it was safe to pay us a visit. I'd just hung up when my buzzer rang. I pressed the intercom button. "Hello?"

Virginia Talbot's voice responded, "We're here."

"I'm on the sixth floor, apartment 6B!" I shouted, before pressing the button that would release the downstairs lock. I scooped Grouch up and locked him in my bedroom, not wanting him to meet the monkey before I'd thoroughly assessed the situation. I un-latched my front door and paced. I found myself curiously con-cerned about what Tallulah would think of my little apartment, whether it would be up to her standards. Once again I wished I'd had more time to prepare.

I popped my head out the door to check on their progress. I heard thunderous footsteps and the sound of packages being dragged up the stairs and thumped against the stairwell. Obviously Tallulah hadn't packed lightly. From all the commotion, it sounded like Mrs. Lipton had brought enough equipment to lead a hiking expedition up Mount Everest.

"Do you need some help with that stuff?" I called down the stairs, desperately hoping the answer was no.

"No, thanks, dear. We ran into one of your neighbors who of-fered to help." I wouldn't be surprised if they'd hired a few sherpas.

When Virginia, the first to ascend, arrived at my landing, she looked startled to have made it in one piece. I opened the door and helped her carry in what looked like a large, collapsed metal cage. Behind her was Brian, who was laden with two large suitcases and a duffel bag.

"Hey, Holly," he said, dumping the stuff inside my door. "I see you got a visitor."

I thanked him for helping, then looked behind him to see Mrs. Lipton trudging up the last few steps. Perched upon her shoulder, dressed in a polka-dotted dress and tethered to Mrs. Lipton by a sturdy-looking leash, was a small brown monkey with a pink face and a white tuft of hair atop her head. Tallulah, I presumed.

Tallulah leapt off Mrs. Lipton's shoulder and onto mine. She clutched me on either side of my head, her long, soft fingers digging into my hair. She cocked her head to one side and stuck her tongue out in my direction.

"Oh, good," Mrs. Lipton said. "She likes you."

* * *

Gerry came up the stairs just behind Mrs. Lipton, bearing two gloriously large Mocha Frappuccinos. I smiled, thinking that my day had definitely taken a turn for the better. I'd heard from the Writer, both Gerry and Carter had forgiven me, and there was a triple shot of espresso in my immediate future. The only problem was Brian was still standing in my doorway, transfixed by Tallulah, and if I didn't hustle him out of there soon, Gerry would realize who he was and start hounding him for his socks. Tallulah climbed onto my back and peered over my shoulder at Brian, who wiggled his fingers in her direction.

I introduced Gerry to Virginia and Mrs. Lipton, hoping he'd assume Brian was just a monkey handler. But when he'd finished shaking hands with the two women, he turned to Brian, who stuck his hand out and introduced himself. "I'm Brian. Holly's neighbor."

Gerry's face lit up. "Brian? Holly tells me she takes care of your cat."

Brian nodded.

I yanked Gerry's arm. "Why don't you help me with Tallulah's things?"

Mrs. Lipton was already busy assembling the portable cage Virginia had hauled up the stairs. "That's O.K. We're almost done here." She slapped the last of the metal sides into place. The cage measured about three feet wide by four feet tall. Mrs. Lipton opened one of the suitcases and removed a tattered blanket and stuffed teddy bear. She placed both inside the cage.

"Then you can help me get everyone something to drink," I said to Gerry, who was eyeing Brian's feet longingly.

Gerry shot me a dirty look and followed me into the kitchen. I removed a pitcher of iced tea from the fridge, while Gerry tugged at the cupboard where I kept my glasses, the mighty twist tie still holding up against his assault. Tallulah leapt off my shoulder, landing on the counter next to Gerry. She reached up with both hands and twisted the green tie round and round until it came off. Then she handed it to Gerry and jumped back onto my shoulder.

O.K., so my cousin lacked the manipulative powers of a monkey. He had other qualities that endeared him to me.

I served the iced tea. Brian demurred, saying he had to run. Gerry followed him to the door. "Yo, Brian. Nice to meetcha."

Brian smiled. "You, too."

Gerry gestured to Brian's running shoes. "Nice kicks."

"Thanks."

"What are you, a size eight? Nine?"

"Nine and a half," Brian answered, regarding Gerry quizzically.

Realizing his line of questioning had veered from standard first-meeting protocol, Gerry offered, "I'm in footwear. My line of work."

Brian nodded, satisfied with this explanation.

Gerry added, "I could float you some samples sometime. Just give me your socks, so I can make sure to get the proper fit."

"Uh, I'm in a bit of a hurry. I'd have to go upstairs to get a clean pair."

Gerry shook his head. "We take used socks. That way we can tell, um, from your imprint, the pressure points of your feet and um, the actual dimensions to, uh, determine the most beneficial shoe for your foot type."

I suppressed a smile, impressed at how well Gerry thought on his feet. This was the same man, after all, who'd just been outmaneuvered by a monkey.

"For real?" Brian smiled. He seemed to suspect he was being put on, and he was almost good-natured enough to go along with it. He paused to consider, then shook his head. "That's O.K., man. I gotta dash. I'll catch up with you later, Holly."

I shouted good-bye and he was gone. Gerry stood at the door, looking dejected as his latest sock museum prospects disappeared down the staircase.

Mrs. Lipton demonstrated how to clean and lock Tallulah's cage and how to get her in and out of her harness. Finally, she opened the duffel bag, which held two dozen baby diapers with holes pre-cut for Tallulah's tail. She explained that Tallulah was trained to go potty in her cage. "But if you value your belongings, you'll encourage her to wear a diaper when she's not in the cage."

Naturally. I recalled my teenage babysitting experiences, struggling to get screaming, writhing toddlers into their Pampers without either of us experiencing bloodshed. I doubted I'd do any better diapering a monkey, but with Tallulah settling in on my shoulder—picking at the stitches on the back of my head and clucking in Kuki-like disapproval of my hatchet hair—it seemed too late to back out now.

Mrs. Lipton removed some papers from her purse and handed them to me. "Here's her health certificate and the number for her veterinarian. And a few notes my brother jotted down about Tallulah. Her likes and dislikes, that kind of thing. So you'll know what to expect."

I read the first item on the likes list. "Regis Philbin?"

Mrs. Lipton nodded. "Oh, yes, she adores Regis. Be sure to put his show on every morning. It's his voice. It calms her."

I wondered if Regis was aware he had the power to soothe small simians with the sound of his voice. I nodded uncertainly, then scanned the rest of the list. "Bananas, grapes, Chex party mix, monkey chow . . ."

"It's all in the other suitcase. There's enough to feed her for four or five days. By then, David should be out of the hospital and she can go home to Daddy."

Tallulah reached a slender arm toward Mrs. Lipton and swatted her across the face.

"Now, Tallulah," Mrs. Lipton said, "don't misbehave. We want Holly to like us, don't we?"

Tallulah cocked her head and stuck her tongue out, a clear indication that "we" didn't care what Holly thought.

Mrs. Lipton smiled. "Don't worry. We keep her fingernails trimmed down short so her little slaps don't hurt one bit." As though taking this as a challenge, Tallulah reached over to Mrs. Lipton and grabbed her by the nose. Virginia smiled warily as though no longer certain that leaving this slap-happy monkey at my apartment was such a good idea.

Unruffled, Mrs. Lipton pried the monkey's fingers out of her nostril and remarked, "She likes to grab. You shouldn't wear any jewelry." She picked up her purse and started toward the doorway. "Oh, and she's a marvelous pickpocket, too. She likes keys, especially. But don't worry. She usually just hides her booty in her cage, and she'll trade it for a piece of candy."

She unzipped a pouch on the duffel bag and extracted what looked like a pen, but was actually a laser pointer. She fished a set of keys out of her purse and set them on the table. She pointed the laser at the keys and pressed a button. Tallulah hopped onto the table, grabbed the keys, and handed them to Mrs. Lipton, who rewarded her with a LifeSaver.

"Impressive," I said.

"She's very well trained. She performs small tasks for my brother. Putting a tape in the VCR, getting a drink from the refrigerator, that kind of thing. Mostly she's a companion." She looked at Tallulah. "He loves her so."

"I'll take good care of her," I promised, walking her to the door. "Does she stay in the cage all the time?"

"Heavens, no," Mrs. Lipton said. "She wouldn't like that. She sleeps in the cage, but if you're home and you keep her locked up, she'll . . . uh . . . express her displeasure with that arrangement."

A whiny monkey, I thought. I can handle that. "What about when I go out? She'll be okay in the cage?"

Mrs. Lipton smiled nervously. "Well, it's best if you can take her with you."

"Really? Take her out in the streets of Manhattan?"

"Well, yes, as long as she's on her harness she's quite well-behaved in public. She likes people, and she loves going for walks. If you leave her home alone too long, she'll . . ."

"Express her displeasure?"

Mrs. Lipton nodded. "Exactly."

8

Alias Monica Broccoli

I soon discovered that Tallulah's primary method of expressing her displeasure was flinging excrement at the object of her distress. This realization came shortly after Mrs. Lipton's departure, when I decided to put Tallulah into her cage for a while so that Gerry and I could enjoy our Frappuccinos while beginning our Monica Broccoli fact-finding mission. As Mrs. Lipton had instructed, I removed Tallulah's diaper before putting her in the cage. Apparently, the boredom of confinement leads her to rip her diaper off and tear it to shreds.

I booted up my computer and logged on to the Internet. After a few minutes' searching, I found a site with a reverse phone directory and typed in Monica's phone number. There was a brief pause and then a screen came up listing the number as being registered to Gabriel Karakowski. I pointed to the screen. "I don't suppose that's Monica's real name?"

Gerry shook his head. "She's got an illegal sublet. Her apartment's not in her name. Utilities neither."

Great. "I don't suppose her name is listed on the building directory for her apartment?"

"Nope."

This was going to be harder than I thought. I pulled out the
phone book and looked up modeling and talent agents, and charged
Gerry with the task of making a list of Monica's recent modeling as-
signments and auditions. I had dialed the first agency in the book
and asked the receptionist if she knew a model named Monica—a
tall, leggy brunette with a personality like a steamroller. The receptionist replied that she couldn't give out information about their
models over the phone, but if I was a client she'd be happy to put me
through to their booking department to set up a shoot.

"No," I said, "I'm just trying to track down my friend. Can't you
at least tell me if you have someone like that on your roster?"

"Sorry. It's against policy."

I had dialed the next number in the book and was about to
launch into my plea when I felt something warm and wet hit my
shirtsleeve. I looked down in horror to find I'd been pelted with
monkey poop.

"Holy crap!" Gerry yelled, pushing his chair out of the line of fire.

I looked over at Tallulah, who looked pleased with herself as she
brushed her fingers along the bars of her cage in a circular motion,
leaving behind swirling brown streaks, which she regarded with
artistic pride. Then she abruptly abandoned her artwork and began
yanking on the cage door lock with both hands.

"She wants out," Gerry said, stating the obvious.

Mrs. Lipton had warned me that Tallulah hated being confined,
so after much consideration I decided to let her out of her cage for
a trial run. After changing into a clean T-shift and persuading Tallulah to stick her hands through the bars so I could clean her fingers, I unlocked the cage. She climbed out, clutching the beat-up
teddy bear. "If you misbehave, it's back in the cage," I warned her.

Gerry helped me get her into a fresh diaper—which proved to be relatively easy once we figured out how to get her tail through the appropriate hole—then I gave her a pile of peanuts to snack on and set her down in front of the TV. I flipped through the channels. Regis wasn't on, but Tallulah seemed intrigued by an old episode of *Hogan's Heroes*. Go figure.

Once satisfied that Tallulah was going to behave, Gerry and I returned to the kitchen table. I looked at Gerry's list. All he'd come up with so far was "TV commercial audition."

"Do you remember the product?" I asked. "The agency? Where she went for the audition?"

He shrugged. "I dunno. I never paid much attention to that stuff."

"Well at least we know her first name is Monica," I said.

Gerry furrowed his brow.

"Oh, no," I said. "Don't tell me."

"Well, I'm not positive. For some reason, I think it may be Karen."

"Oh, brother." I picked up the notepad and smacked Gerry across the head with it. "You proposed to a woman and you don't even know her first name!"

"I know, I know," he moaned. "You can't make me feel worse than I already do." He reached into his pocket, pulled out Monica's rejected engagement ring, and stared at it glumly. Once again I was struck by the magnitude of the gem. As a cater-waiter, Gerry usually only had gigs on weekends. He pulled in decent tips, but I doubted he made enough to afford a rock that size.

"That diamond is huge," I said. "Is it real?"

He held it up to the light. "Of course it's real. But it's not a diamond. It's a diamonelle."

"A diamonelle?"

"It's like a diamond, only more affordable. The guy at the jewelry store said it's totally real. 'One hundred percent genuine faux diamonelle.' I think it's French."

I groaned inwardly, wondering whether I should elucidate for my cousin the meaning of the word "faux" and deciding against it. A genuine faux ring seemed somehow appropriate for a guy who didn't even know the name of his intended bride.

Gerry pocketed the ring and I returned my attention to the task at hand. I decided to start with the highest-profile gig Monica had done since I met her. The touring company of *Starlight Express*. I called the performing arts library at Lincoln Center, and after several minutes on hold, a reference librarian came back on the line. "I have reviews for *Starlight Express* going back to 1987," she said. "Can you narrow it down for me?"

"This was in the past six months. A touring company that played in Pittsburgh. Do you have anything with a cast list?"

I heard papers rustling; then the librarian said, "Here's a review for a production in Pittsburgh from May."

"That's gotta be it! Can you look through the cast list and find anyone with the first name of Monica. She was a dancer in the company."

"No . . . there's no Monica."

"What about Karen?"

"No Karen either. But the review doesn't list the entire cast. After the first several names it says 'and others.' You might want to try contacting the production company directly."

"Okay. Thanks for your help."

It took several minutes of searching the Internet before I found a phone number for ticket sales for the U.S. touring company. I dialed the box office number. A young man answered after several rings. This time I pretended I was a casting director and I'd seen the show in Pittsburgh. "There was a girl in the company who I think would be right for a project I'm working on," I lied.

"What's her name?"

"That's the thing," I said. "I don't know her name. She's tall, brunette, good-looking."

"That could be anybody," he growled.

"Oh! And she broke her leg in Pittsburgh."

"Why didn't you tell me that to begin with? I can work with that."

I heard a piercing screech behind me and, startled, dropped the receiver. Tallulah, apparently bored with the antics of Stalag 13's inmates, had abandoned her post in front of the TV and was bouncing up and down in front of Rocky's cage, shrieking in fear. Flashing back to Primate Behavior 101, I recalled the very basic fact that monkeys do not like snakes.

Since snakes are one of the capuchin's primary predators in the wild, Tallulah's reaction to Rocky wasn't surprising. And I couldn't blame her, given my own mortal dread of reptiles. Her timing was inconvenient, however, as I had been on the verge of a Broccoli breakthrough. I snatched up the phone and apologized for the disruption. "I have the *National Geographic* channel on in the background," I explained lamely, as Tallulah continued to screech.

"Uh-huh. What did you say your name was?"

"Holly Heckerling. I'm a casting director. My partner and I are casting new talent for a showcase, and—"

"Why don't you give me your number? I'll see if I can find out the girl's name and have someone call you back."

"Great," I said, hoping he wasn't just giving me the brush. I rattled off my business number and hung up.

Gerry was beaming. "Good news?" he asked.

"Maybe. The guy in the box office says he'll call back."

I whisked Rocky's aquarium into the bedroom to join Grouch in the monkey-free zone. Once the reptile was out of sight, Tallulah quieted down. I had no idea how she would react to a rat, but to be on the safe side, I put Felix in the bedroom, too.

I returned to find Gerry on the sofa watching TV as Tallulah climbed over him like a jungle gym. She tugged at the neck of his T-shirt, then stuck her head inside as her tail whipped up and smacked him in the face. Seconds later, a furry arm emerged from one sleeve. Gerry adjusted his position each time one of Tallulah's limbs blocked his view of the screen. Eventually Tallulah managed to maneuver her entire body inside his T-shirt, turn around, and pop her head out of the neck hole so that it looked like Gerry had sprouted a smaller, furrier head.

From this position, Tallulah watched as Gerry flipped rapidly between channels, registering her opinion of his viewing selections with a series of high-pitched squeaks. They reminded me of a married couple squabbling over the remote. When he stopped flipping and settled on a football game, Tallulah slapped his face and screeched.

"I don't think she's a sports fan," I remarked.

Gerry flipped back to a sitcom and got to his feet, gingerly extracting Tallulah from his T-shirt, the neck of which was now absurdly stretched out. "I think I'll go watch the game at my place."

"But we have more calls to make," I protested. Besides, I was still a little leery of being left alone with Tallulah.

"You don't need my help. You're the one with the ideas." He stopped at the door. "Thanks a million, Holly. I knew I could count on you."

"Don't count your chickens. We don't know her name yet."

"I have faith. You'll get it. Call me."

I nodded, grateful that he was back on my side. The day was looking up indeed.

*   *   *

I locked the door behind Gerry, then heard him bounding down the stairs. I didn't share his optimism about my success. Calling blindly to modeling agents certainly wasn't going to lead anywhere. In this age of stalkers and other sickos, no one was going to give out information to a stranger over the phone. Especially if it sounded like they were calling from the monkey cage of the Bronx Zoo. I'd have to think of another way to get the dish on Monica Broccoli.

Despite the seeming futility of my quest, I resolved to make a few more calls before lunch. After being rebuffed by the receptionists at six more modeling agencies, I was ready to throw in the towel.

My phone rang, two quick rings. Personal line. Probably Kuki heard I was helping Gerry and was calling to give me a reprieve from my Siberian exile. But instead of old and ornery, the caller's voice was deep and husky.

"Hi, it's Tom Hansen. We met at the coffee shop." I'd just about given up on hearing from the Starbucks dad—figured he'd either reconciled with his wife or come to his senses about taking me out on a date, but here he was, and once again his voice made my stomach all jangly.

"Hi, Tom," I said, affecting a nonchalant tone. "How's it going?"

"Fine. I've been meaning to call, but things have been a little hectic."

"I understand." Heck, hectic is my middle name.

"Is this a good time to talk?"

I looked around my apartment. No slithering snakes, no widening pools of blood. Just a monkey minding her own business, watching *Gilligan's Island*. "Fine. Couldn't be better."

Buzz.

Oops. Spoke too soon. "Can you hold on one second? Someone rang my buzzer."

"Sure."

I set the receiver down and pressed the intercom button. "Hello?"

"Comin' up!" Carter shouted.

I buzzed her in, then unlatched the front door.

"I'm back," I said into the receiver. "I have company, but it will take her a while to climb the stairs, so we can talk."

"O.K.," he said, then paused. "I . . . uh, was calling to see if you'd like to meet for coffee. My afternoon class was canceled, so I have some time."

"This afternoon?" I asked.

"I know it's short notice, but between my daughter and my teaching schedule, it's hard to find free time."

I noticed a flash of light bouncing around my apartment and glanced over at Tallulah, who was still in front of the TV, munching on peanuts and playing with a small, shiny object. My heart skipped a beat when I realized it was Gerry's ring. She must have taken it from Gerry's pocket during their little love fest on the sofa. Mrs. Lipton had said she was an inveterate pickpocket.

"Oh, shit," I muttered.

"Is that a no?" Tom asked.

"No . . . I, uh . . ." I knew I should drop the phone and make a mad dash for the monkey to rescue Gerry's ersatz engagement ring from her clutches, but then again, this was the closest I'd come to having a real date in a long time. My relationship with Marcus had been pretty tepid; I'd never had this fluttery feeling when talking to *him*. Of course, Tom might understand if I told him I had to hang up so I could wrestle a monkey for a genuine faux diamonelle so my cousin could marry his nameless girlfriend and my aunt would forgive me and take my name out of her ice cube tray. Then again, better not take any chances. "I'd love to go out for coffee."

"Great," he said, sounding relieved. "You like Starbucks, right?"

"Are you kidding? I'm going to name my firstborn Mocha Frappuccino."

"I can meet you in half an hour."

I instinctively reached for the back of my head, feeling the bald spot. Making myself presentable in less than thirty minutes would require a makeover miracle worthy of Flushing Beauty Academy's Hall of Fame.

There was a beep on the line and I asked Tom to hold while I switched over to the incoming call. It was Gerry, sounding more high-strung than usual. "I lost Monica's ring! It must have fallen out of my pocket. Please tell me it's at your place."

I glanced over at Tallulah, who was staring at the ring, mesmerized by the way it reflected the light streaming through my living room window. "Yes, it's here," I said, neglecting to add that Tallulah had lifted it to her mouth and was licking its surface.

"Great. Hold on to it for me, will ya? Make sure it's safe."

"You bet," I said, watching as Tallulah stuck the ring in her mouth. "Listen, I'm on another call—"

"No sweat. Talk to ya later."

Gerry hung up and I switched back to the other line. Fearing he'd made a dating faux pas, Tom was backpedaling on his invitation. "We could wait until next week if you'd feel more comfortable." And give him another week to come to his senses about dating the crazy haircutting monkey lady? I don't think so. "Can we make it in an hour? I have to take care of a few things first."

Carter rapped on the door, then turned the knob. I waved her in and, covering the mouthpiece, whispered, "See if you can get the ring away from the monkey."

Carter grimaced, then approached Tallulah with trepidation. "Ya know, Holly, your place is turning into a zoo."

Tom asked, "Shall I pick you up at your place?"

"Let's meet there." I felt our first date should not begin somewhere plagued by renegade reptiles and poop-flinging primates. "The Starbucks where we met."

"See you soon," he said.

"Great. Bye."

I hung up and squealed. "I have a coffee date!"

"The guy with the kid?"

I nodded. "Yeah. His name's Tom."

"I thought you weren't in to him."

"I guess he's growing on me. I know he's not my usual type, but—"

"Good. Maybe he'll stick around longer than three months."

Carter was standing in front of Tallulah, one hand on her hips, the other outstretched. "Fork it over, monkey," she commanded. Tallulah cocked her head to one side and stuck out her tongue. I wondered if that was her standard greeting, or if it was just Carter and me who provoked such a reaction.

"No luck?" I asked.

"What's it look like?"

"It looks like a very expensive diamond engagement ring. Fortunately, it's fake."

Tallulah was no longer holding the ring, and it didn't appear to be in her mouth, either. I searched the area, kneeling down and looking under the sofa and feeling between the cushions. Carter looked around halfheartedly. "So what's the big deal about a Cracker Jack ring?"

"It's the ring Gerry bought for his girlfriend, alias Monica Broccoli."

"Where's the last place you saw it?"

"In Tallulah's mouth."

Carter stopped searching. "Well then, duh, she must have swallowed it."

I shook my head. "Monkeys aren't dumb. They don't go around eating inedible objects for sport. They only eat what tastes good."

Carter shrugged. "You got a monkey on a leash, the ring's

nowhere in the vicinity of said monkey, the monkey was last seen chomping on said ring. You do the math."

I groaned. "What am I gonna do? We gotta get her to cough it up!"

If my attempt to perform the Heimlich maneuver on my cousin hadn't been such a colossal failure, I might have considered trying it on the monkey. I knew, however, that one misplaced thrust would probably cause more damage to her tiny frame than digesting a dozen diamonelles.

Carter shrugged. "Don't worry. Babies eat junk all the time and it comes out the other end. You just have to comb through her poop for the next few days."

An unpleasant thought, but it beat telling Gerry I'd allowed Tallulah to eat Monica's ring because I was on the phone trying to score a date. As I wondered how long it would take for the ring to work its way through Tallulah's digestive tract, I was struck by another thought: What if Mrs. Lipton came to pick the monkey up before the ring finished its trajectory? Not only would Gerry be furious with me, but my reputation with PAPS would be in the toilet. My career as a pet sitter would surely be over if Tallulah went home spewing costume jewelry out of her cute little monkey ass.

"I don't know if I can wait that long!"

"We could speed up the process," Carter suggested. "Got some Ex-Lax?"

I shot down the suggestion. My life was complicated enough already. The last thing I needed was a monkey with the runs.

Carter patted me on the back. "Hey, it's just a crappy ring."

I nodded. "You can say that again."

A quick call to Tallulah's vet alleviated most of my fears. The ring would most likely work its way through her system within twenty-four hours without causing any internal damage. If it didn't turn up by then, I was to bring her in to his office. He promised not to mention my call to Tallulah's owner—there was no need to alarm him unnecessarily, especially when he had his own health problems to worry about. After thanking the doctor profusely, I hung up the phone and hugged Carter. I realized I had been too absorbed with Tom and Tallulah to greet her properly.

"I've missed you," I said, squeezing her tight. "It's tough not having your best friend around."

"I know." She patted my back. "I'm sorry I was so rough on you at yoga."

"That's O.K. Tearing my groin muscles took my mind off my head wound." I released my hold on her and stepped back. "You look good. How do you feel? Any morning sickness?"

"Nah. I feel fine, except I'm having massive withdrawal symptoms."

"Withdrawal from what?" I asked.

"Everything," she said. "Coffee, cigarettes, booze. It's been hell. Especially working at Starbucks, being around coffee all day and not being able to drink it."

"Maybe you should find another job," I said, crossing my fingers that she wouldn't actually take my advice and leave me without my coffee connection.

"Nah, it's O.K. I'm learning to tolerate decaf."

I hugged her again. "I'm proud of you. You're doing the right thing."

"I figure the kid should at least have the right to develop her own addictions, rather than getting stuck with all of mine."

"Her? You know it's a girl already?"

"Nah. Just a feeling."

"But you've been to a doctor?"

"Yes. Everything's fine. Except they've got me on these vitamins the size of horse pills. They make me gag when I swallow them."

It sounded like Carter was really getting her act together, just like I knew she would. Now we just had to work on Danny.

"I talked to my boss at the studio about starting a prenatal yoga class," Carter added. "She said she'd think about it."

"That's great! Just promise me you won't make the pregnant ladies do that turtle torture thing you did to me."

"The tortoise pose? No, it'll just be light stretching and toning for the pregnant chicks."

"You'll develop the class yourself?"

She nodded. "It'll keep my mind off quitting smoking and drinking. I need to have something to keep me busy. I don't know what to do with myself anymore, except eat. I've already gained five pounds."

"I want to hear all about it." I glanced at the clock. Twenty minutes had elapsed since I hung up with Tom and I hadn't even combed my hair. Time to panic. "But I can't. I told Tom I'd meet him for coffee. It shouldn't take long. Could you hang out here until I get back, keep an eye on Tallulah for me?"

Carter raised her eyebrows. "Me? Babysit a monkey?"

"Think of it as practice for the terrible twos."

She regarded Tallulah warily. "You know, with that punk hairdo and goofy smile she kind of looks like she could be me and Danny's offspring."

I smiled. "So you'll stay?"

"You got anything to eat?" she asked, opening my fridge and frowning at its paltry offerings. Then she moved on to the freezer. I could tell by her horrified gasp that she wasn't in the mood for frozen rat. I explained that every morsel of food in my apartment was earmarked for one of its nonhuman inhabitants. We toyed with the idea of raiding Tallulah's food stores—I'm a big fan of Chex party mix—but I didn't think it would be right.

"Why not?" Carter said. "She eats *your* things."

I fished around in my purse and pulled out a twenty. "Order Chinese," I said. "And save some for me."

She took the twenty. "All right, I'll stay. But if the monkey swallows anything else, I'm not responsible."

I changed quickly and teased my hair back into a big, conveniently placed banana clip, which, with the aid of several bobby pins and a pint of hairspray, did a decent job of hiding my hideous head wound.

Carter nodded approvingly. "You look great. He'll fall head over heels."

We returned to the living room to find Tallulah sitting peacefully on the sofa, watching an episode of *Baywatch*. "I can put her back in her cage before I go," I offered, warning Carter about Tallulah's propensity for poop throwing when confined.

"I'll take my chances with her loose."

Tallulah looked downright angelic on the sofa, clutching her teddy bear and ogling the *Baywatch* babes. "O.K.," I said. "I'll only be gone an hour. And if anything goes wrong, I'll be at Starbucks. You know the number."

"If Danny's there, you won't tell him I'm here?"

I shook my head. "I'm no more anxious to see him than you are. But don't worry. I think he called in sick today."

I checked in on Grouch, refilling his food and water, then spritzed myself with perfume and did a quick double-check in the mirror. I might not have been Flushing Beauty Academy material, but I looked pretty good for someone with multiple bodily injuries.

Carter gave me a quick hug at the door and wished me luck. "I guess this means you're over the dude with the dead wife."

"Well . . ." I hedged, casting a glance at the yellow pages sitting on my desk, still unread. I hadn't forgotten, but was saving it for later, when I could savor his words in private. "I'm still intrigued by him. But I've been thinking about what you said. Why fantasize over some guy I know nothing about, when there's a real live man waiting for me at Starbucks?"

"Now you're talking," she said, practically shoving me out the door toward my destiny.

Tom was waiting at Starbucks when I arrived. As he walked toward me, I looked him over, taking in his warm smile and easy manner, his relaxed but confident posture. I could picture him in front of a classroom, his brown eyes sparkling with curiosity as he tried to ignite that same spark in his students. He would win them over with his authoritative yet patient style. Above all he seemed like someone completely at ease with himself—a rare commodity in my world, where neurotic and insecure were the flavors of the day.

This would be the test, I thought as the gap between us closed. When I first met him, I was attracted to the way he interacted with his daughter. Now it was just us—two adults, no cute little girl in a bunny sweater to melt my heart.

He reached out his hand and I shook it. He had a firm grip and strong hand. He smiled, a slightly crooked smile that put me at ease. His brown eyes, which were flecked with gold, reflected the highlights darting through his dark hair. Tom was definitely handsome, but you wouldn't expect him to step out of an International Male catalog. Which was O.K. with me. Living in New York, I'd dated enough models and actors to last a lifetime. I was tired of men whose flawless facial features masked a stunning lack of character development.

Tom gestured to a table by the window, which he had claimed with his briefcase. "What can I get you?" he asked.

As a general rule, I never have more than one espresso drink a day, as too much caffeine makes me giddy and nervous. But even though I'd already met my daily quota—thanks to Gerry's early-morning coffee run—I had zero willpower when it came to Frappuccinos. Standing there in Starbucks, taunted by the roar of the blenders and the aroma of roasted coffee beans mingled with cinnamon and vanilla, I buckled like a crash test dummy in a Ford Escort. "A grande Mocha Frappuccino, please."

While waiting for Tom to return with our drinks, I looked around the store, noting how few of the patrons were actually drinking coffee. Most were either talking on their cell phones or staring at their computer screens, settled in for the long haul, long-empty cups by their sides.

I'd been noting with amazement over the last few years how my neighborhood Starbucks had been transformed from a cozy gathering place for coffee and conversation into a haven for every laptop-toting, cell phone–carrying screenwriter or novelist in the city. Aside from my envy over not being able to afford either a laptop or a cell phone, I didn't mind this trend, except that the scribbling squatters left few seats for the rest of us. Moreover, I was convinced that they were responsible for the drastic drop in ambient temperature at Starbucks citywide. Starbucks' seating capacity hadn't increased commensurate with its popularity, and the stores I frequented seemed to be dealing with the overcrowding by raising the air-conditioning to subarctic levels in an attempt to freeze out all but the most die-hard devotees. As a result, it was not uncommon to see young people in parkas hunched over their keyboards in mid-July, wrapping frostbitten fingers around their coffee mugs for warmth.

Carter steadfastly denied that Starbucks was conspiring to turn its patrons into Popsicles. The store's employees had probably all been sworn to secrecy, their stock options threatened if they revealed the sinister plot. Despite the Big Chill, I couldn't bring myself to switch my allegiance to one of the newer, trendier coffee shops that had sprung up in my neighborhood recently. I'd been frequenting this Starbucks since I moved into my apartment, and I felt I had seniority over the laptop luggers.

Once again, the store was unnecessarily nippy, and I'd forgotten to bring a sweater. I looked out the window, longing to feel the warmth of the afternoon sun. A group of people was standing, coffee in hand, engaged in conversation outside the store. Two men stood apart from the crowd, apparently engaged in a heated debate. One, a bearded man with glasses, was gesturing wildly at the other, a gaunt, younger-looking man. Both wore business suits. Even through the store's thick plate-glass windows, I could make out a string of expletives. Another day in New York.

Tom returned with our drinks and took the seat across from me, moving his briefcase to the floor. We sipped in silence for a moment, each searching for something to say. I was rarely at a loss for words, but I was still feeling a bit thunderstruck by our meeting. Had I minded my own business a week earlier, Tom and his daughter would have gone about their lives, and except for Nicole's school pictures being marred by a cocoa stain and bangs in her eyes, they'd have been none the worse for not having met me. And Danny and I might even have worked up some material for our act.

"I was just thinking of how we met," I said, "and wondering what possessed me to interfere like that."

"You saved my life."

"Don't exaggerate."

"I'm not. My divorce has been quite . . . difficult. I want joint custody of Nicole, and her mom wants full custody, with me having visitation every other weekend. She'll use any little thing she possibly can to show I'm a bad father. Things like me forgetting to take her for her haircut. If Nicole had scruffy hair and a stained sweater in her school pictures, they'd be exhibit A in the custody case, believe me."

So maybe I had made a difference after all. "I'm sorry it's been so difficult. Nicole's lucky."

"Lucky her parents are fighting like cats and dogs?"

"Well, yeah. My dad couldn't handle raising me alone after my mother died, so he left. I haven't seen him since I was twelve."

"I'm sorry."

I shrugged. "I came to terms with it a long time ago. I just brought it up to explain what I meant when I said Nicole is lucky."

"I guess so. I just wish her mother and I could settle things without having to go to court. But we can't seem to agree on anything right now."

I wondered again what Tom's ex was like, then remembered my chance encounter with Nicole. "I saw your daughter," I told Tom, "at BodyWorks, the dance studio. She was taking ballet and I was just finishing a yoga class."

"Nicole loves ballet. I didn't know they also teach yoga there. Maybe we can take a class together sometime."

"Um . . . sure." I smiled weakly as a daggerlike pain tore through my pelvis. "When I'm not so busy."

I took a sip of my Frappuccino and glanced out the window. The two well-dressed men were still arguing. The bearded man was pointing at something on the ground, while the other shook his head.

I turned back to Tom. "So you're a teacher?"

He nodded. "English. I'm teaching freshman composition at NYU, but it's a temporary position. I'm applying for a full-time slot in the fall."

The door opened and the two men who were quarreling outside the window entered the store. The older of the two looked vaguely familiar but I couldn't place him. "You don't know what you're talking about!" he shouted, causing several patrons to look up from their laptops.

The skinny man approached the counter and spoke to the barista. I couldn't hear what he was saying, but it was obvious he wasn't ordering coffee. The bearded man was shaking his head. "Not a coat hanger. You'll make it worse!" The barista disappeared into a back room while the two men continued their argument in hushed tones.

I turned back to Tom. "Does that guy look familiar?" I gestured toward the counter. "The one with the beard?"

Tom followed my gaze. "I heard someone whisper, 'It's John Landis,' when he walked in."

"The director?" I took another look. "Yeah, I think that is him." He was pacing the front of the store, shaking his head. "I wonder what's going on." More important, I wondered if there was any chance I could get him to donate his socks to my cousin's collection. Gerry had forgiven me for upstaging his marriage proposal, but something told me he wouldn't be so understanding when he learned the present whereabouts of Monica's ring. I had to do something to regain his favor. And so far, my mission to find out Monica Broccoli's real name had been a bust.

The barista returned from the stockroom, shaking his head. The skinny man began to speak, but Landis interrupted him. "You go out there and stand guard. Don't let anyone walk over the grate."

I was vaguely aware of Tom's voice, but realized I'd stopped paying attention. "I'm sorry. I was distracted. You were saying?"

He laughed. "It's O.K. A famous director is much more interesting than the fall curriculum." He leaned back and sipped his coffee. I felt terrible for ignoring him. This was definitely not good first-date etiquette. He probably thought I was a starstruck idiot, preparing to pounce on Landis to ask for an autograph. If only it were that simple.

In a rare flash of clarity, I realized that it was not only futile but unnecessary to keep up a pretense of normalcy for Tom's benefit. Unlike my previous boyfriends, I had a feeling he was going to stick around. I might as well let him know what he was in for, sooner rather than later.

I took a deep breath and began. "This may sound bizarre, but my cousin collects celebrities' socks. And I kind of owe him, since I recently ruined his marriage proposal and let a monkey swallow his engagement ring. If I could get John Landis's socks, I could redeem myself with my family."

Tom looked at me askance. He seemed at a loss for words.

"Don't worry. I won't embarrass you," I assured him. "I don't have the nerve to ask for his socks."

Tom straightened in his seat, then looked over at Landis. "Do you want me to do it?"

I was stunned by his offer and knew I should reject it outright—why involve an outsider in my family's lunacy, after all?—but decided it was worthy of consideration. As I mulled it over, I glanced out the window and saw the younger man standing over a subway grate, looking down with a perplexed expression.

Tom said, "I think one of them dropped their keys down there."

Landis was talking into his cell phone and pacing. He was clearly agitated, his voice raised loud enough that everyone in the store could hear his end of the conversation. "They're sitting there about a foot below the grate, dangling over a ledge. Kevin wants to try to fish them out with a coat hanger, but if they move a fraction of an inch, they'll fall down into an abyss. . . . He's a putz—that's why. . . . He jolted me. We were walking toward the car, I had the keys in my hand, and he jolted me." He glanced at his watch. "The rental car company can send a spare key but it'll take them an hour to get here. I'm supposed to be at the Waldorf in twenty minutes. Yes, I could take a cab, but my speech is in the car. . . . I don't want to wing it—that's why I wrote the damn speech." His face was turning red. "No, it's too small. Have you ever *seen* a subway grate? You can't stick your hand through there."

Maybe it was the double dosage of caffeine. Or maybe it was the giddy, euphoric feeling that accompanies the start of a new romance. Whatever it was, I was feeling downright invincible, ready to leap tall buildings in a single bound. I bolted out of my seat and stuck my hand out to Tom. "Give me your cell phone."

He handed it over without question. I headed for the front door, punching in my personal phone number as I walked. The machine picked up. I bypassed the message and shouted, "Carter, pick up. It's an emergency!"

Out on the sidewalk, a small crowd had gathered and people were tossing out suggestions to the skinny guy. "You need to get a magnet," one said. "Tie it to a rope and lower it down there." I peered between them and looked at the subway grate. The spaces between the grating were indeed too small for a hand to fit through. A human hand, anyway.

I heard a click and Carter was on the line. "Wha-a-at?" she said, dragging the word out over three syllables to indicate her annoyance.

"I need a huge favor, quick. There's a black duffel bag by the door. In the front pocket, there's a laser pen. Get that, and also grab a couple pieces of candy, and bring Tallulah to Starbucks. I'll meet you out front."

"What?" Carter screeched. "I can't bring a monkey into Starbucks. The New York City health code—"

"Not *inside*. I'll be out front."

She exhaled dramatically. "This isn't about Danny, is it?"

"Danny's not here! Just make sure Tallulah's leash is fastened tight and get her down here fast. Don't worry. Mrs. Lipton says she's well-behaved outside."

Tom had followed me onto the sidewalk and was staring at me quizzically. I was about to explain my plan to him when John Landis exited the store, followed by a green-aproned barista. The barista looked baffled as he held out a small timer with a magnet affixed to its back. "It's the biggest one I could find," he said apologetically.

Landis looked doubtful. "The keys are too heavy. We need a stronger magnet."

Kevin grabbed the magnet. "It'll work. Give me your tie."

"My wife gave me this tie," Landis protested. "I'm not gonna let you drop it into the sewer. You're the one who jolted me. Use your own tie."

"Fine." Kevin began unknotting his tie. "I didn't jolt you. You tripped."

"Schmuck," Landis muttered under his breath.

"Stop!" I shouted, pushing my way through the mini mob. "I can get the keys." I turned to Landis. "Don't let him lower that magnet down there. It'll knock the keys off the ledge."

"You got a better idea?" Kevin challenged.

"I've got more than an idea. I've got a monkey."

Kevin was determined to try his tie-and-magnet method, but John Landis was blocking his way. As it turned out, Landis was somewhat of a primatology buff himself, and though he favored go-rillas, he was well aware of the manipulative abilities of capuchins. My suggestion that my hairy houseguest could extract the keys brought snickers from the rest of the crowd, but Landis looked in-trigued. "You have a helper monkey?"

I nodded. "I'm watching her for her owner, who's a quadriple-gic. She's trained to retrieve items. The keys will be a cinch for her."

He looked thoughtful. "Where is she now?"

"On her way."

I heard someone call my name and turned to see Carter sprint-ing toward us, a grinning Tallulah riding on her back. Someone shouted, "Make way for the monkey," and a path was cleared.

As Carter turned over Tallulah's leash, I noticed her eyes were red and puffy. I'd obviously interrupted her during a pregnancy-induced crying jag. "Are you O.K.?" I whispered. "Thinking about Danny?"

She shook her head. "I was reading that writer guy's stuff. You left it on your computer table. Ohmigod, Holly, it's so heartwrenching. That poor little girl . . . Just thinking about it's gonna make me start bawling again." She handed me the laser pen and a package of gummy bears. "Here."

Since my own reading of the writer's latest installment had been interrupted, I was burning with curiosity—especially seeing how it had affected the ever-cynical Carter. But with a burgeoning crowd pressing in around us, there was no time to probe her for details.

I let the slack out of Tallulah's leash and the monkey hopped to the ground. Then I pointed the laser at the keys and depressed the button. Tallulah bobbed her head up and down, as though indicating comprehension of the task. She cocked her head to one side and turned around in a circle, her eyes fixed on the keys. Then she leaned onto one side and slid her slender arm through the grate. There was a collective gasp and we all held our breath as Tallulah's tiny hand reached for the keys.

Someone complained, "I can't see!" and was met with a chorus of *shh*'s and *shut up*'s.

I heard the scrape of keys against metal, then watched as Tallulah withdrew her arm. When her hand was almost free, she reached through with the other hand and pulled the key ring out. She held the keys up in the air and the crowd applauded. She handed them to me, then stuck her hand out for a treat. I ripped open the package of gummy bears and popped several in her outstretched hand.

Landis was laughing as I turned over his keys. He thanked me, then added, "I can't wait to tell my wife about this."

Someone in the crowd had a camera and asked Landis to pose for a picture with the monkey. He happily obliged, asking me if it was O.K. for him to hold Tallulah. Tallulah answered for me, leaping into his arms the instant he bent down toward her.

After posing for the picture, Landis headed toward his rental car, explaining that he was on his way to a luncheon for which he was the guest of honor. He clicked a keypad and the car alarm chirped. Kevin opened the passenger door as Landis walked around to the driver's side. My moment of opportunity was slipping away. I had to speak now or forever live with the guilt of having let Gerry down. *Again.*

"Mr. Landis?"

He looked up at me, still smiling. "What's the monkey's name?"

I replied, "Tallulah."

"Tallulah? I'll remember that." He removed his coat jacket and tossed it on the backseat.

"Before you go . . . can I ask you for a favor?"

"Sure. What is it?"

I bit my lip, knowing no matter how I phrased my request, he was going to think I was nuts. I took a deep breath, then blurted, "I'm gonna need your socks."

9

Genuine Faux Diamonelle

I never intended to become Starbucks' resident superhero. But I had to admit, after my recent string of debacles, it felt pretty good to be regarded in a saviory light. Before darting off to teach his afternoon class, Tom had stared at me in wonderment and asked if I was in the habit of hanging around coffee shops, waiting for problem-laden people to happen by.

"Nope," I responded. "You were the first."

"Then I'm a very lucky man." He smiled at me and my insides turned to mush. Then he leaned forward and kissed my cheek, and my lower limbs took on a gelatinous consistency. I wondered if I'd have the strength to walk home.

Tom promised to call, then took off down the street. His step was remarkably bouncy for someone weighed down by a briefcase full of textbooks and term papers.

Having made it as far as the sidewalk, Carter decided to actually go inside Starbucks and pencil herself back into the schedule. I took it as a positive sign that she was ready to face her situation head on.

"But what about our talk?" I asked. "This is the second time we've had our plans interrupted."

"Yeah. First a snake, then a monkey. Trying to work your way through the Chinese zodiac?" She reached into her pocket and extracted my twenty. "Here. I was just getting around to ordering the food when you called."

We hugged good-bye and she turned to leave. She stopped at the door. "Oh, yeah, about the writer guy. Your destinies are intertwined. I have a feeling about this." She launched into a paean of the writer's work, using words like "brilliant" and "poignant."

"Wait a minute," I interrupted. "You're the one who told me to 'choose reality' and go out with Tom instead of fantasizing about the writer."

She nodded in acknowledgment. "I know. Frankly, I thought you were screwy to go gaga over someone you've never met. But now that I've read his stuff, I think there's something there. You should go for it."

"Go for it? How? I don't even know his name or where to find him."

"So," she shrugged. "He knows where to find you."

She said good-bye to Tallulah, who stuck her tongue out in reply, then disappeared inside the store.

Spurred by my success in retrieving John Landis's sewer-bound keys, I headed back to my apartment with renewed determination to solve the Monica Broccoli mystery. Tallulah clung to my back as I walked the two blocks home, Landis's socks literally burning a hole in my pocket. The director had been a good sport, sitting in his car and removing his socks on the spot when I explained they were for my crazy—but harmless—cousin. "It's strange, I know, but he collects famous people's socks," I'd explained. "He even has a Web site." As if that gave him credibility.

"What the hell?" he said, handing them over. "It'll make a good story." He ducked into the rental car and returned a moment later with a piece of embossed hotel stationery. "What's his name?"

"Gerry."

He scribbled:

Gerry—
Enjoy the socks.
John Landis.

I wanted to hop on the subway and head straight for Gerry's, but I was afraid he'd want Monica's ring back, and as far as I could determine, it hadn't yet completed its journey through Tallulah's lower intestines. Better to wait until I had the ring safely in hand. Besides, I wasn't sure the A train was the best place for Tallulah.

As I walked home from Starbucks, Tallulah clinging to my back, I ruminated about the strange set of circumstances that had twice led me to thrust myself into strangers' lives. By nature quiet and reserved—except when I'm onstage, when an altogether different side of my persona emerges—I usually remain on the fringe of activity until I get dragged along by the current created by other people's dramas. For as long as I could remember, I'd just been trying to stay afloat, treading water without making waves.

I let myself into my building and climbed the six flights to my apartment. Tallulah was gripping my hair and making excited peeping noises as we climbed. As I reached the sixth-floor landing, I saw Brian kneeling down in front of my milk delivery door. I called out to him and he looked up, startled.

"Hey, Holly." He stood up and approached with a wave. "Hi there, monkey girl," he cooed at Tallulah.

"Were you leaving me something?" I asked.

"Oh, uh, yeah. I was going to write you a note, but since you're here I can just ask you."

"Ask me what?" I unlocked the door and Brian followed me into the apartment. After shutting the door behind him, I let go of Tallulah's leash. She jumped to the floor, then hopped onto a chair at the kitchen table and sat, hands in her lap, as though patiently waiting for the maid to serve dinner.

Brian was standing near the door, bouncing on his heels. He still hadn't mentioned what he had come for, so I asked, "Are you going away? Need me to watch Kramer?"

"No, it's not that. You're good with computers, right?"

"I guess so."

"Mine crashed. I was wondering if you could take a look at it."

"I'm not much of a techie. I can give you the number of a guy who's a real computer whiz."

"Nah, I don't want to call anybody like that. I have a lot of . . . um, personal stuff on it. I don't want to bring it to a repair shop or let some stranger mess around with it. I just thought maybe you could check it out sometime."

Hmm. Must be pretty darn personal if he didn't want a repair tech peeping into his files. I doubted I could be of any help to him since my primary method of computer repair involved whacking my Mac with my fist when it misbehaved. But if working on his computer brought me one step closer to scoring another pair of socks for Gerry's collection, it was worth a shot. "I can't promise anything," I said. "But I'll try."

"Great. I'll call you later."

Dan, the delivery guy from the Hong Kong Palace, promised extra egg rolls on my next delivery if I'd let him pet Tallulah. While I've never been one to turn down free Chinese food, I didn't want to set a precedent. After being rushed by a mob of onlookers in front of Starbucks, all wanting to pet the monkey, I had decided that I would not allow any strangers—other than famous film directors, of course—to touch or hold Tallulah. After all, I was responsible for her health and well-being. And aside from letting her swallow costume jewelry, I was doing a pretty good job of safeguarding her so far.

Unfortunately, "my house, my rules" means nothing to a monkey. Even as I was turning down delivery Dan's bribe, Tallulah leapt at him, wrapping her arms and legs around his head and pushing her belly against his face. Though startled, the delivery guy seemed to enjoy the attention. Tallulah was enjoying it a bit too much, if you ask me. What at first seemed like an overenthusiastic hug soon began to resemble more of a mating ritual, as Tallulah squeezed tight and began grinding her body up and down, up and down against Dan's face. She made a throaty noise unlike the squeaks and titters that made up the bulk of her vocal repertoire. She was clearly in the throes of passion, and though Dan the deliveryman seemed a willing, if not fully aware, participant, I had to put an end to it. As I pried Tallulah off the deliveryman's face, I scolded, "That's not how we tip the delivery guy."

Dan picked downy brown hair from between his teeth and grinned widely. "The monkey likes me." A severe understatement from my perspective.

Once disengaged from the object of her affection, Tallulah hopped onto my back and buried her face in my hair, occasionally peering around my shoulder to cast loving glances at Dan, who wouldn't leave until I promised to order from Hong Kong Palace again soon and to request that he make the delivery. "I'll bring you some *platanos*," he promised Tallulah as he backed out of the door.

Tallulah and I dined informally in front of the TV, a couple of primates kickin' back and watchin' the tube. Tallulah seemed far more interested in my moo goo gai pan than in her monkey chow, but who could blame her? For a lower primate, she had decidedly human sensibilities—probably a natural outgrowth of spending her life with people. I tried to picture her in the South American rain forest—sans polka-dot dress—and had to laugh. Tallulah had never known the jungle, and would probably be appalled by its lack of modern conveniences. I could relate, after all, having turned down fieldwork in Africa because it was outside of Village Pizza's ten-block delivery radius.

After dinner, I left Tallulah tethered to the sofa while I booted up my computer. Although the Writer's note said he was in no rush for the typing, I was eager to read what he'd written, especially in light of Carter's emotional response. Carter, who'd remained dry-eyed through both *Beaches* and *Steel Magnolias,* while I'd bawled like a baby beside her. In all my years of typing medical reports for handwriting-impaired doctors, scripts for aspiring screenwriters, and résumés for unemployed actors, I'd never been moved to tears by an assignment. This could be a first, I thought, positioning a box of Kleenex near my keyboard.

I picked up the yellow pages, found the spot where I had left off, and began typing.

"That's not how Mommy does it," my daughter says, watching as I dump Shake 'N Bake mix into a plastic bag weighted down with chicken parts. She is sitting cross-legged on the counter, in what has become her usual position when she watches me make dinner. Her reference to her mother takes me aback, and I look up. Her face flushes and she instantly turns away. "I mean, how she did it," she corrects herself, and her lower lip trembles. She doesn't want to hurt me, but the truth often does.

"I can't do anything the way Mommy did it," I say, my tone matter-of-fact. "But that's O.K., right?" Then half the seasoning mix spills onto the kitchen floor and I curse.

My wife would no sooner make chicken from a box than she would serve it on paper plates in front of the TV, another habit we've fallen into lately. I push aside a pile of dirty clothes to make room for us on the couch but my daughter plops onto the floor two feet from the set. She flips purposefully through the channels until she hits on an I Love Lucy rerun she likes. I know I shouldn't let her sit so close, know it will probably cause irreparable damage to her hearing or her eyesight or both, but when a wisecrack from Lucy makes her crack a barely perceptible smile, I can't take it away from her.

On a commercial break, she looks up at me. "It's O.K.," she says, and I don't know whether she means the chicken, or Lucy, or what has become of our life. She forces a smile in my direction before turning back to the TV. "It sure is," I say, but it's a lie. None of it is O.K.

I was so absorbed in my work I didn't notice that Tallulah had stopped watching television and had begun pulling the stuffing out of my sofa cushions. I yelled, "Knock it off!" and she looked up at me sheepishly. I instantly regretted my harsh tone. Though she was the one demolishing my divan, I felt guilty. I knew I should take a break and spend some time with her, but I couldn't pull myself away—not even to save my secondhand sofa.

Now, having read most of the Writer's latest installment, I could understand why Carter had been crying—and why she'd said the Writer's destiny was intertwined with mine. I wouldn't go so far as to say that fate was involved, but I was feeling a mounting sense of déjà vu. The Writer's account of his wife's death had moved and intrigued me. Now that he was describing his daughter's struggle to deal with the loss of her mother, he was delving into painfully familiar territory. My own dad had done his best to ease my grief, but in the end, nothing he could do or say made a dent in my pain.

Another reason I was loath to take a break from typing was that should the Writer happen to call to check on my progress, I wanted to tell him I was all done and eager for him to come pick it up. Then I'd bar shut the milk cubby door, forcing him to ring my bell.

The thought of the unknown Writer ringing my bell sent a curious chill down my spine. I still had no idea what he looked like, or even a general idea of his age, occupation, or ethnicity. Yet a picture was beginning to form of a tall, broad-shouldered man with blond hair, deep-set eyes, and a haunted expression. I figured he rarely smiled, and when he did, it was restrained. Because he had lost his wife, laughter probably didn't come easily. Like his trust, it would be hard won.

The picture was fuzzy at first, but the more I typed, the more clearly I could visualize him—right down to the thin gold band he still wore on the ring finger of his left hand.

The phone rang, snapping me back into reality—a reality in which my sensitive Writer could well be a balding, sixty-something man with chronic halitosis.

"Yeah?" It was my personal line, so I didn't bother with formalities.

"Yo, Holly. It's me," my cousin's voice boomed over the phone. "Find out Monica's name yet?"

"No. I'm still working on it." Truth is, though I'd been all gung-ho about tracking down Monica Broccoli that afternoon, my enthusiasm had since waned, replaced by my obsession with the Writer of unknown identity. Discovering who wrote the words that so moved me was far more compelling than pinning a name on Gerry's pushy girlfriend—who, come to think of it, had grated on my nerves ever since my grandmother's funeral.

"Maybe it's for the best," I offered. "Maybe she's not cut out for our family."

"Watch it! You're talking about the woman I love."

Yeah, I thought, good ol' What's Her Name.

"Listen," Gerry continued. "I'm working a catering gig tonight in your neighborhood. I'll stop by on my way to pick up the ring."

I shot a quick glance at Tallulah, silently cursing her for taking her sweet time in digesting the diamonelle. I'd checked her diaper after dinner and was dismayed to find it was still clean and dry. Before today I could never have imagined a day when changing a monkey's doody-filled diaper would be something I actually looked forward to.

"Uh, not good. I have to go out."

"That's O.K. I'll use my key. Just leave it out on the table."

"Uh . . . well . . ." I stammered, trying to think my way out of this one. "Actually, I'm not going out. I'm having someone over. A date."

"Not your suicidal friend, I hope."

"Danny's not suicidal, just depressed. And no, not him. It's someone new. I planned a romantic evening and I don't want you showing up in the middle of it."

"No sweat," Gerry said. "Just leave it in the cubbyhole and I'll pick it up. I won't even knock on the door."

"I can't do that. What if it gets stolen?"

"Who's gonna steal it?" he laughed. "You got parades of people peeping in your milk box? No offense, Hol, but it's not like that business of yours is headed for the Fortune Five Hundred." This from a man who was staking his future on a couple pair of socks.

"Why are you in such a hurry to get the ring?" I shot back. "No offense, Gerr, but it's not like you have a fiancée to give it to."

He was silent for a moment, then mumbled, "Yeah, thanks for reminding me. Appreciate your support." And he hung up.

I replaced the receiver and fought the urge to call him back and apologize. If I smoothed things over with him, I'd still have to come up with a reason why he couldn't have his ring. I hated having Gerry mad at me, but at least this way he wouldn't be stopping by.

I picked up the phone and punched in Monica's number. Maybe I've been going at this the wrong way. Time for a head-on assault. After three rings, an answering machine picked up and Monica's strident tones announced, "You know what to do, and when to do it." *Beep.*

"Mon—" I started, then hesitated. Using her fake name probably wouldn't win me any points right now. "*Mon chéri,* it's Holly calling. I wanted to apologize for last night. If I'd known what Gerry was up to, I would have just let him choke." Wait, that didn't come out right. "I mean . . . I wouldn't have tried to save him. . . . You know what I mean. Anyway, the real reason I'm calling is—"

"Save your breath," Monica said, picking up the phone. "I'm not going to tell you my name just so you can get Gerry off the hook. I'm pissed at him and I have every damn right to be."

"You're right. You do. That's not why I'm calling, actually. I was just thinking, even if you and Gerry are through, you and I can still be friends, can't we? How about getting together for coffee?" If I could get her to use a charge card at Starbucks, Carter could lift her name off the receipt. It wasn't much of a plan, but it was a start.

"You and I aren't exactly friends, Holly. You've never invited me for coffee before. Why start now, just because you shot my marriage proposal to hell?"

"Yeah, well, I was just trying to save my cousin's life. Trust me, it will never happen again." I tried to remember how to do one of those deep cleansing breaths Carter demonstrated and reminded myself that Monica might be family one day. "I've been meaning to call you for some time now, but I keep getting bogged down with work. Ever since you entrusted your snake to me"—foisted it on me is more like it—"I've been wanting to get to know you better."

"Why? You and I aren't exactly cut from the same cloth. Anyone who keeps that many power tools in their broom closet is a bit freaky, if you ask me."

Last week, my possession of power tools made me a lifesaver in Monica's book; today she calls me a freak. I took another cleansing breath. "Come on, how about lunch tomorrow? My treat?"

"I don't think so."

"Okay, well, maybe you could stop by and visit with Rocky sometime." *And while you're busy stroking the snake, I'll take a quick peek in your pocketbook and check out your ID.*

"No, thanks."

"You sure? It might be your last chance to see him."

"What's *that* supposed to mean?"

I had no idea what it was supposed to mean, since I was totally improvising, but since it was the first thing I'd said that had gotten a rise out of her, I pressed on. "It means I'm not keeping your snake. You dumped my cousin, I'm dumping Rocky. Turning him over to Animal Control."

"You're bluffing. You love animals."

"I don't love *snakes*. I agreed to keep him as a favor to Gerry. But you two aren't together anymore. And like you said, you and I aren't exactly friends. I don't even know your name. . . ."

There was a prolonged pause where I thought she was going to cave. Then she said flatly, "Do what you have to do."

This was going to be tougher than I thought. I couldn't even use her beloved boa as bait. I scanned the apartment, looking for inspiration. My eyes stopped on Tallulah, who had entirely relieved one of my sofa cushions of its stuffing and was starting on another. "Just stop over tomorrow for a few minutes, O.K.?"

"Give me one reason why I should," she challenged.

"I'll let you play with my monkey."

Capuchins are arguably the most dexterous and intelligent of all monkey species. In the wild, they apply their manipulative skills to extracting embedded food resources like seeds, nuts, and insects.

But in captivity, without the need to forage for their food, they quickly grow bored. Which is why good zoos and sanctuaries provide monkeys and apes with various kinds of enrichment activities to stimulate their minds and keep their bodies active. Knowing this, I shouldn't have been surprised that Tallulah, when left to her own devices, resorted to performing a cushionectomy on my couch. Despite everything I'd learned in "monkey school," I had neglected to consider Tallulah's need for opportunities to explore and manipulate items in her environment. What kind of tax-preparing comic primatologist was I?

Once I had secured Monica's promise to stop by soon to visit Rocky and meet Tallulah, I resolved to rectify my neglect of Tallulah's psychological well-being. I went to my broom closet and hunted around for my drill, various-size drill bits, and a scrap of pine lumber. The wood was an inch thick and about one foot long, perfect for crafting a raisin board.

I decided to put Tallulah into her cage before undertaking my construction project. One near-fatal encounter with power tools was enough for one week. The monkey was reluctant to abandon her de-stuffing duties, but I lured her into the cage with a few gummy bears and the promise that I'd let her out as soon as I was finished. Before locking her in her cage, I gave Tallulah a few pieces of junk mail to play with, then removed her diaper, taking no small delight in the fact it was soiled. It was too soon after dinner to go combing through its contents for Monica's ring, so I set it aside for later examination.

I took advantage of Tallulah's confinement to let Grouch out of the bedroom. He'd been sequestered all day—with a snake, no less—and even though I'd moved his food, water, and litter box into the bedroom, I felt bad about keeping him locked up. I also checked on Felix and Rocky, both of whom showed no signs of psychological distress. Grouch, meanwhile, was more than living up to his name. He ran from the bedroom hissing at everything in sight. He circled the apartment as though reestablishing the boundaries of his territory, sniffing the ground as he went. He obviously detected a foreign scent, which he followed until he located its simian source.

Tallulah looked up from her junk mail, registering only mild interest in the lower mammalian life-form before her. I wondered if there was any etiquette for interspecies introductions. Grouch, I'd like you to meet Tallulah. Tallulah, Grouch. Miss Manners never wrote about that one.

Cat and monkey sized each other up; then Grouch raised his hackles and emitted a low growl. Tallulah banged on the side of her cage and gave Grouch an openmouthed screech that sent him scurrying back into the bedroom and under the bed, where he remained the rest of the evening. All in all, it wasn't bad for a first meeting, I thought. Tallulah had quickly and bloodlessly asserted her dominance—though I wondered how bloodless her coup would have been had she not been caged—and Grouch had been sufficiently cowed into submission.

Tallulah was unperturbed by the sound of the power drill and apparently uninterested in what I was doing with it. As I drilled several holes of varying depths and widths into the narrow board, she remained focused on her department store circulars and no-annual-fee credit card offers. Perhaps all she needed after all was reading material. She finally took notice when I fished a package of raisins out of her suitcase and began stuffing raisins into the holes.

I opened the cage just long enough to slip the raisin board inside. Tallulah grabbed it eagerly and began poking at the morsels with her fingernails. I found some toothpicks in the kitchen and gave one to Tallulah to use as a tool. She took to the task like a pro, using the toothpick to dig out a raisin, then licking it clean.

With Tallulah thus occupied, I turned my attention to her diaper. There was no putting it off any longer—it was time to hunt for buried treasure. With a pair of chopsticks as excavation tools, I combed through the contents of Tallulah's diaper. But, like the time I spent half my allowance on a bum box of Cracker Jacks, I was dismayed to find no cheap plastic ring at the bottom. I was doubly disappointed now. Not only was I still minus one faux diamonelle engagement ring, but I'd have to repeat the excavation process the next time.

The phone rang. I quickly washed my hands and picked up the receiver. Please don't be Gerry, I thought.

It wasn't.

"Hi . . ." Tom was speaking low, his voice almost a whisper. "I hope it's not too late to call. I just wanted to hear your voice."

I felt a rush of emotions, not the least of which was guilt. I'd spent half the evening daydreaming about someone else—a man I'd never met, no less. Mixed in with the guilt was a flurry of more positive feelings, including a tangible sense of relief. Despite the fact that I'd managed to include both a famous director and a monkey in our first date, Tom was calling me. Just to hear my voice.

"Really?"

"Yes. Is that O.K.?"

"Absolutely."

"Good. So what are you doing?"

"Um, I was just . . ." I stumbled, wondering whether I should lie or evade the question. I felt curiously comfortable with Tom and my instinct was to tell him everything, but in this instance, evasion seemed the most advisable course. "I was . . . looking for something. What are you up to?"

"I just put my daughter to bed. Oops, spoke too soon. Hold on, please."

He set down the receiver, and in the background I heard Nicole entreat, "Daddy, can I have a cookie?" I listened as Tom fulfilled her request and led her back to bed. Something about the exchange left a lump in my throat. Tom was kind and patient with his daughter; they had the kind of relationship I hoped to have one day with my own children.

When he came back on the line, he said, "Sorry for the interruption. You said you were looking for something?"

"Uh, yeah. Not anymore."

"You found it?"

"No. I gave up. What about you—" I began, trying to change the subject.

"Is it something you lost?" he pursued.

"Well, not exactly. I know where it went. I'm just not sure I can get it back."

"You're not going to tell me, are you?"

"Well . . . no."

"O.K., then, twenty questions. Is it bigger than a bread box?"

I sighed. He wasn't going to give up. "No."

"Animal, vegetable, or mineral?"

"Mineral, I guess."

"Does this have anything to do with the monkey swallowing your cousin's engagement ring?"

"How do you know about that?"

"You told me. This afternoon, when you were explaining why you wanted that director's socks."

"Oh. I forgot." I must have let my guard down. Very odd first-date behavior for me, but then again, I'd been distracted. Oh, what the hell. "Yes. I was looking for the ring . . . in the monkey's diaper."

Tom laughed, a deep, rolling laugh that seemed to have no end. Part of me thought I should be annoyed or embarrassed, but Tom's laughter had no malice or judgment. He was simply tickled. I couldn't help but chuckle, too, and soon my laughter was blending with his.

It felt good.

We talked for two hours, and I found myself openly sharing stories about myself and my family—warts and all. Things I usually tried to hide from would-be boyfriends, I threw out on the table. After all, if he was going to run screaming for the hills, I'd rather he did it now, before my heart became inextricably linked with his.

There was decidedly less dysfunction in his family, but he made up for it by sharing details of his increasingly contentious divorce from Nicole's mom, Bianca. It turned out they'd already been separated for three years, but it had taken that long for the lawyers to hammer out a custody arrangement that both sides found tolerable—if not ideal.

After describing a long-running feud they'd had over Nicole's Gymboree schedule, Tom said, "I hope I'm not scaring you off. But if you and I get serious, you should be prepared—Bianca may try to cause problems."

"Does she own any weapons of mass destruction?" I asked.

"No."

"Had commando training?"

"Negative."

"O.K., then. I'll take my chances."

"Good."

"To be fair," I said, "I should warn *you* that if you have dinner with my relatives, my aunt may bite you."

"Does she have rabies?" he asked.

"No."

"Other life-threatening communicable diseases?"

"Is psoriasis life-threatening?"

"I don't think so."

"Then no."

"O.K., then. I'll take my chances."

"Good."

*   *   *

It was after midnight when we hung up. Tallulah was sleeping peacefully in her cage, curled up in a ball and clutching her tattered blanket. I was grateful she'd allowed me to talk on the phone without expressing her displeasure at being ignored. Obviously the raisin board had done a good job of focusing her attention. Its holes were now empty and the surface had been licked clean.

I made a mental note to dig up my old notes from my primatology courses, to look for more ideas on how to keep Tallulah occupied and amused. Since my apartment had precious little storage space—and what it did have was crammed with beauty supplies and power tools—I had stored all my school papers in Kuki's attic, along with my old Barbie collection, ballet slippers, and other assorted remnants of my childhood. Unfortunately, I couldn't show my face in Brooklyn until Tallulah liberated Monica's ring.

With Tallulah more or less tucked in for the night, I could return to my typing. But as I looked over at the lined yellow pages stacked next to my computer, I realized that the urgency to finish the job had passed. That's what it was after all—a job. Not my destiny. It could wait until morning.

What couldn't wait, however, was the restoration of my sofa to some semblance of its former self. Chunks of stuffing were scattered everywhere. It looked like Snuffleupagus had exploded in my living room. I cursed myself for letting it get so out of hand. The fact that I had been so immersed in my typing that I allowed a mischievous monkey to mangle my sofa was further proof of my irrational obsession with the Writer.

I gathered up as much of the material as I could and stuffed it back into the gaping opening in the mutilated cushion. Then I stitched the hole closed and beat the pillow into something faintly resembling its intended shape. The second cushion still had most of its innards, so I could get away with just stitching over the hole

Tallulah had made. As I stuck the sewing needle through the fabric, its progress was halted by something solid embedded in the pillow's stuffing. I tugged at the hole, trying to get a better look. A flash of light bounced off the surface of something shiny— something, if my eyes didn't deceive me, I'd just searched through monkey shit to find.

I yanked at the hole, enlarging it, and there it was: one genuine faux diamonelle ring. Tallulah hadn't swallowed it, after all; she'd secreted it away inside my couch cushion and would probably have returned it if offered a piece of candy. Mrs. Lipton had said it was just a game to her, after all. I wondered if she'd been trying to find it all evening, and my other cushion had just been a casualty of her search. I glanced over at her, still serenely sleeping in her cage, and decided to give her the benefit of the doubt.

Monkey in the Middle

Like most performers, I often dream of being onstage unprepared, not knowing what I'm supposed to do or say next. To top it off, in these dreams I am usually naked, or at least having a really bad hair day. The morning of the comedy showcase was no exception. Except, unlike previous assaults from my subconscious, this time it seemed my nightmare was about to come true—except for the naked part.

In the past week, I'd left dozens of messages for Danny, who had not returned a single call. I'd resorted to cornering him at Starbucks during his shift, but he'd slithered away, claiming Starbucks' policy forbade fraternization with customers—which I knew for a fact wasn't true, having practically memorized the employee manual when Carter was up for store manager and made me drill her to prepare for her interview with the big coffee kahuna from the regional office.

The showcase was ten hours away and I had no idea if Danny was intending to show up. I wasn't all that sure I would even go. We hadn't prepared any material, and there was no way I was going to wing it on my own. I'd never done a solo act and wasn't about to start now, when all I had was a handful of one-liners scribbled on napkins and envelopes.

All week I'd told myself I should work up some material, but between caring for Tallulah and keeping up with a steady stream of snip-and-style clients, it had been hard enough squeezing in time for lunch dates with Tom. Besides, I had truly believed that Danny—one of my two closest friends in the world—would not leave me in the lurch. The more I thought about it, the more it rankled me that Danny was still angry at me. After all, he was ready to forgive Carter, whose sin was far more serious. I'd kept Carter's pregnancy a secret, but she was the one who'd been secretly pregnant.

Carter, meanwhile, had resumed working at Starbucks but she and Danny were at a stalemate. She told me they'd spent a night talking and crying and in the end had decided to make things work. But the following morning, she'd sat down to chart her astrological forecast and decided that her moons and planets were not aligned properly for a reconciliation attempt. She informed Danny that not until Venus was in the seventh house would she even think of reuniting.

I usually gave Carter the benefit of the doubt when it came to her New Age beliefs, but this time was different. She had a baby on the way and a man who loved her. If her planetary poppycock prevented her from settling down with Danny, I'd give her a swift kick in her astral projections.

My hair was still looking ragged, but I'd hit upon a hairstyle that managed to hide most of the damage—as long as I didn't make any sudden movements or walk into a strong breeze. If I decided to do the showcase tonight, I'd have to use a gallon of hairspray to keep up the facade.

Tallulah banged on the side of her cage to get my attention. I looked at the clock—five minutes to nine. How that monkey knew when it was time for Regis to come on, I will never figure out, but every morning about this time, she'd begin rattling her cage and demanding to be let out. Like much of Mrs. Lipton's advice regarding Tallulah, her comment about Tallulah liking Regis Philbin turned out to be a gross understatement. Tallulah likes Regis like I like Mocha Frappuccinos. In both cases, it's infatuation, pure and simple.

Over the past week, Tallulah and I had settled into a pleasant morning routine. Pleasant, that is, once I stopped trying to get her to adjust to *my* schedule and decided to adjust to *hers*.

The monkey's arrival had rendered the Sleepblaster Plus virtually obsolete. She'd sleep soundly through the night, but once she woke in the morning she seemed duty-bound to wake everyone else in the building, too. Her chattering, clattering, and screeching would rouse me from the deepest sleep, and I'd haul myself out of bed, largely driven by fear that one of the neighbors would call Animal Control if I didn't silence the beast. That, and the very real possibility that if I ignored her for too long, she'd find a less vocal way to express her displeasure.

Once I trudged out of the bedroom, I'd pop some monkey chow into Tallulah's cage on my way to the bathroom. She'd take the food, drop it on the cage floor, and greet me with a raspy "he he he." Her disinterest in the monkey chow made it clear that it wasn't hunger that compelled her to blast me out of bed each morning. Monkeys are social creatures, and Tallulah just didn't like to be alone. Once I was up and moving around, Tallulah was content to sit and watch me feed Grouch, make coffee, and get ready for the day. Then she would settle down, nibble her food, and peacefully play with her toys.

Until nine o'clock. Whether she actually knew how to interpret the readout on my digital kitchen clock or whether some kind of internal sensor alerted her to the time, somehow she knew when *Live with Regis & Kelly* was about to begin. She'd make an ungodly racket until I came around to unlock her cage. Then she'd be uncharacteristically cooperative while I put a fresh diaper on her and clipped her leash onto her harness. Usually, putting a diaper on Tallulah was like wrestling an octopus—she'd lash at my hands with any available combination of hands, feet, and tail, repeatedly wriggling out of my grip. But there was no time for such foolishness when Regis was waiting.

Once properly attired, she'd plant herself on the sofa and randomly press buttons on the remote until she hit on ABC. Then she'd bounce impatiently during the *Live with Regis & Kelly* theme music and voice-over introduction. As soon as Regis Philbin's image filled the screen, she'd leap off the sofa and heave herself at the television set. Then she would wrap her arms and legs around the TV so that her abdomen was pressed against the screen, whereupon she'd thrash about ecstatically. The whole display resembled her overture toward the Chinese food delivery guy, only more intense—and without the benefit of free egg rolls.

After a minute or so of this greeting ritual, she'd settle back on the sofa and, aside from commercial breaks and film clips, during which she'd get visibly agitated, remain attentive until the end of the hour. All throughout, she'd bob her head and prattle at the screen as though joining in the banter between Regis and his guests.

Mrs. Lipton had said that Regis had a calming effect on Tallulah. He had an effect on her all right, but "calming" wasn't the word I'd use to describe it.

While Tallulah flirted with Regis, I took care of household and business chores like paying bills and setting appointments. This morning, my calendar was empty. I purposely hadn't scheduled any hairstyling clients, for fear I'd be in a mad dash to get ready for the showcase. So much for that. I'd resolved that if Danny didn't show up, I would go onstage just long enough to announce the cancellation of the show and, not coincidentally, the end of my comedy career. We'd mailed flyers to more than a hundred agents and casting directors, a handful of whom had called to R.S.V.P. If we failed to put on a show tonight, word would get around and we'd be through.

I supposed I could sit down and start calling the hundred or so people on the invite list and tell them the showcase was canceled. But if Danny did show up, we'd be playing to an empty house and our reputations would still be sunk.

I could already hear my aunt Kuki's I-told-you-so. "Thank God you have a trade to fall back on. First it was monkey school, then stand-up comedy. Now you can do something sensible for a change." Like go to work with her in the barbershop—a fate I'd spent my entire adult life determined to avoid. I'd sooner join forces with Gerry in his sock venture, maybe be his executive vice president in charge of sweat socks.

I shuffled to the pantry and opened my milk cubby door. It was empty. Earlier in the week, I'd finished the Writer's last batch of typing and left it in the cubby. Two days later, when I returned from running errands, the cubby was bare. I'd missed him again. I still felt a curious connection to him and wanted to know what he looked like, but my relationship with Tom was heating up and I didn't want to jeopardize it over some romanticized notion of a man I'd never met. At least not yet . . .

I cringed, remembering how I had impulsively included a flyer for the showcase in with the first typing job I did for the Writer. Now I was regretting it. If he didn't show, I'd feel silly for having extended the invitation, and if he did, it would only be to witness the death of my career.

Thankfully, I hadn't invited Tom to the showcase, so I didn't have to worry about him seeing me flounder. Our last few dates had gone so well that I had been tempted to invite him. But one thing I'd learned from other comedians over the years was never to bring a date to a gig until the relationship is stable. Stand-up is nerve-racking enough without the added pressure of trying to impress a new squeeze. And since so many comics use their relationships as fodder for their act, there's always the danger that you'll end up offending or embarrassing the ones you love. With the exception of Gerry, I never invited my relatives to my gigs, because if I cut all the jokes about my family out of my act, I'd barely have enough left to fill sixty seconds. Gerry was thick-skinned enough to take being the butt of some of my jokes; in fact, he seemed to enjoy the minor celebrity it gave him afterward to mill about the crowd and claim ownership for one of his funny faux pas.

The phone rang as Regis was coming back from a commercial break. I took the phone into the bedroom so I wouldn't upset Tallulah by talking over Reege.

"Yo, Hol, how's it goin?" Gerry asked.

"Just swell. The showcase is in ten hours and I don't have an act."

"You'll think of something. Anyway, listen, my Web site is racking up hits. Yesterday the hit counter was at thirty-seven—and I'm pretty sure most of them were from me. This morning I logged on and the counter's at 2,963!"

"Maybe it's broken," I said.

"Thanks a lot, cuz."

"I'm sorry . . . but why would three thousand people wake up this morning with a sudden desire to check out stinkysocks.com?"

"It's celebrity-socks.com. And I don't know why, but the counter doesn't lie. Look, it just got bumped up to 2,964!"

"Are you sitting there watching it?" Some people stared at the stock market tickers scrolling across the bottom of the news channels. My cousin was going to spend his day watching a tally of how many computer geeks, loners, and perverts logged on to his site.

"It's not like I'm *just* watching the counter. I was working on the site. I'm putting a new page up. Highlighting my American directors series."

O.K., so I was partly responsible for this. Without my acquisition of John Landis's socks, there would be no American directors series, just one American director's stolen Armani socks. Instead of bringing my cousin back to reality, as I'd once hoped to do, I'd added fuel to the fire by giving him Landis's socks—not to mention the autograph, which Gerry immediately had mounted, next to the socks, in a gold-plated frame. Now he was even more convinced of his entrepreneurial genius at cornering the previously untapped celebrity sock market.

The good news was that the addition to his collection had taken his mind off his broken engagement. He'd barely mentioned Monica Broccoli all week. The faux diamonelle, which I'd turned over the morning after I'd discovered it squirreled away in my sofa cushion, was probably gathering dust in the bottom of his sock drawer.

"That's great, Gerry."

"I'm gonna upload the new page soon. Check it out and tell me what you think."

"Okeydoke." With no clients scheduled and no showcase to prepare for, it's not like I had anything better to do.

"Show it to Tallulah, too. See if she likes it."

I wasn't sure I wanted Tallulah to like anything she saw on my computer screen. Humping my TV was bad enough—the little decades-old set was on its last legs anyway—but I wasn't going to stand by and let her sexually abuse my iMac.

"One more thing," Gerry said before hanging up. "I told my mom about your show tonight. She wants to go."

I peeked into the living room to check on Tallulah; then I picked up the phone to call my aunt.

"Bad news," I told Kuki. "The showcase has been canceled."

"Canceled, my foot. You just don't want me to come. Why don't you ever tell me when you're having one of your jigs? I had to find out about it from Gerry. Even Betty has seen you perform," she added in a wounded tone.

Once, early in my career, while Kuki was on vacation and she'd asked me to look out for Aunt Betty and my grandmother, I'd taken them along to an open-mike night and loaded them up with enough banana daquiris that they wouldn't be offended by the inevitable foul language and sexual innuendo of modern-day comics. Suitably soused, they loved the show, laughing so hard that Betty experienced a lapse in bladder control.

"They're called 'gigs,' not jigs. And I didn't think you'd be interested. The comedy scene can be a little raunchy. Lots of drinking and cussing."

"You think you young people cornered the market on drinking and cussing? I could teach you a thing or two." Having once overheard Kuki chewing my father out for missing my ballet recital, I had no doubt of her cursing abilities.

I sighed. Kuki's stubbornness was legendary. I wasn't going to be able to talk her out of going to the showcase.

"I swear it's canceled. Remember how Danny ran out of the house at dinner last week? He hasn't spoken to me since. He's half the act—I can't go on without him."

"Sure you can. Just do something else. What about that little skit you did in school?"

" 'I'm a Little Teapot'?"

"Well, what about your little monkey? Doesn't it do tricks?"

"She's not a circus animal." True, Tallulah did have a few tricks up her polka-dotted sleeve, but nothing the crowd at the Cracker Factory would pay a cover charge and two-drink minimum to see. "Besides," I told Kuki, "I'm supposed to be babysitting her, not exploiting her for the sake of my career." Exploiting her for the sake of my cousin's sock collection was another matter entirely.

"Well, I'm sure you can come up with something. You're a resourceful girl. Besides, you don't want to let down all those people who come to see you perform."

"Sure I can." Actually, lately I'd gotten pretty good at letting people down.

I joined Tallulah on the sofa for the last few minutes of Regis. We were debating what to watch next when the phone rang again. It was Tom. His voice was unusually animated. "I have a meeting with the dean in an hour. Actually it's a job interview for that full-time position I told you about. I'm a little nervous and I was hoping to see you. Do you think I could stop by? Maybe for a good-luck kiss?"

My cheeks flushed hot at the thought of kissing Tom, but I hesitated so I could take stock of my surroundings. While my apartment wouldn't win *Good Housekeeping*'s seal of approval, it was passably clean and absent of any embarrassing piles of laundry or dirty dishes. Tallulah was still tethered to the sofa, busily shredding my *TV Guide* while watching a Tampax commercial. There were no fires to put out, no snakes to recapture, no pools of blood to mop up or crime-scene tape to take down. Aside from a mounting sense of dread about the showcase, all was in order in the house of Holly.

I was about to say yes when Tom, probably thinking my hesitation was a sign of apprehension, added, "I'll pick you up a Mocha Frappuccino on the way."

Bribing me with my favorite drink certainly wasn't necessary— I'd wanted to kiss Tom for days but had been waiting for him to make the first move—but it earned him bonus points. "Mmm. Sounds good."

"The kiss or the coffee?"

"Both."

Twenty minutes later I buzzed Tom into my apartment. I'd spent most of that time tidying up my apartment and concealing my bald spot. Now I turned my attention to Tallulah, wondering if I should put her back in her cage and risk earning her displeasure, or leave her loose and risk having her manhandle Tom the way she did the Chinese deliveryman. I opted to leave her out, giving her a pile of toys and a bowl of trail mix to keep her busy in case she got bored with morning television.

Tom's face was glistening with perspiration when I opened the door to greet him. He handed me my Frappuccino and took a long sip from his own. He exhaled loudly. "My heart's racing."

"I know. It's six flights." I nodded sympathetically. "In the summer I can barely make it all the way without passing out. But it keeps my aunts from visiting too often."

He made his way into the living room and sank onto the sofa next to Tallulah. She cocked her head to one side and regarded him intently. He certainly didn't inspire the same instantaneous affection that Dan the deliveryman had. That much was a relief.

I stood near the sofa trying to decide whether to pull up a chair or take the bold move of sitting beside Tom. He made the decision for me, reaching out and taking my hand and guiding me to sit next to him. When our eyes were level, he said, "It's not the climb that's making my heart race."

Now my own heart felt like it was going into overdrive. I took a deep breath and tried to steady my nerves. "The job interview, then. You said you're nervous."

He gave my hand a gentle squeeze and I felt my fingers tingle. "It's not the job interview either."

I spotted the Frappuccino cups sitting on the coffee table. His was half empty, while I'd barely touched mine. "Caffeine has that effect on some people," I offered weakly. "You know, heart palpitations."

He looked over at the cups; then he turned back to me and shook his head. "Nope, not the coffee."

He leaned forward and our knees touched. Now my legs were tingly, too. I couldn't imagine what would happen when our lips finally made contact. But I was ready to find out. "What is it, then?"

"The kiss," he said, leaning forward.

I leaned into him and our lips met. The tingly sensation shot through my entire body. I abandoned myself to the feeling, losing myself in his kiss. He was still holding my hand in his. He wrapped his free arm around me and pulled me closer. I felt his hand caress my cheek. Then another hand stroked my hair, gently at first and then forcefully. No, wait. It wasn't stroking—it was pulling. Hard.

"Ow, you're hurting me."

"What?" Tom sputtered. "You're the one pulling my—"

Then thin, bony fingers clamped onto my upper lip and yanked. I jumped backward, startled. It took me a moment to realize that the hairy thing attached to my face wasn't Tom—it was Tallulah. She had positioned herself between us on the sofa back and was trying to pry us apart—tugging at our hair, lips, and nostrils, until finally she just stuck her tiny fingers into our mouths and pulled in the opposite direction. Now she was swatting at Tom's face with both hands, while her tail wrapped itself around his head.

Tom looked dazed and confused. He jerked backward, toppling over the coffee table, and landed flat on his back on the floor. Tallulah jumped back onto the sofa and resumed watching television as though nothing had happened.

Tom clutched the back of his head in pain. His face was covered with thin red scratch marks and his hair was completely disheveled.

I crouched by his side. "Are you O.K.?"

"I think so." He was gazing at me as though trying to make up his mind about something. Then he reached out and pulled me down to the floor. He wrapped me in his arms, rolled me a few feet away from the sofa—out of Tallulah's reach—and kissed me again. This time the kiss was slower, deeper, and gloriously free of third-party intervention.

I heard Tallulah strain against her leash and grunt in frustration at her inability to reach us. A small object hit the back of my head, then another. I was pretty certain she was throwing trail mix at us. But I didn't care.

The tingling sensation I'd felt earlier had been replaced by an overall feeling of warmth and well-being. I felt all gooey inside, like my blood had been replaced by melted butter.

Tom broke from the kiss and flashed me a lopsided grin. I looked into his gold-brown eyes and knew that this relationship would be different from any other I'd ever had. He took everything in stride; nothing about my crazy life seemed to faze him. Even being mauled by a monkey during our first kiss didn't dampen his enthusiasm for dating me.

"I think the monkey's jealous," I said, my tone apologetic.

"What monkey?" He pulled me closer and pressed his lips against mine.

Tallulah went wild.

Head over Heels

After Tom had cleaned himself up and dashed off to his appointment, Tallulah and I lunched on leftover moo goo gai pan. I tried out a few jokes for the showcase on her but she just stared at me blankly. When we were done eating, I put her back in her cage with a few toys, righted my overturned coffee table, and began picking trail mix out of my carpet.

With Tallulah locked away, Grouch felt safe enough to venture into the kitchen. Over the past few days, he and Tallulah had reached a tenuous peace accord based on his acknowledgment of her supremacy. I no longer felt it necessary to sequester him in the bedroom—he stayed out of her way on his own.

The key to living with a monkey, I had discovered, is understanding your place in the pecking order. Like dogs, primates are very hierarchical. In the wild, dominant monkeys get more food and more access to mates, and they pretty much get to boss everyone else around.

Hand-reared, solitary primates like Tallulah, lacking a social network of monkeys, instead rank the people around them. I assumed that her owner, David, was Tallulah's "alpha," the highest-ranking person in her circle. From what I gathered of Mrs. Lipton's feelings toward her brother's cherished companion, she ranked considerably lower on the totem pole. In my position as temporary surrogate to David, Tallulah regarded me with a mixture of respect and indifference. She didn't treat me as subservient—like Grouch clearly was—but she also didn't feel obligated to kowtow to my desires. Hence the frequent games of diaper derby, when my attempts to wrangle her into her Pampers often resulted in the loss of both the diaper and my dignity.

Come to think of it, my place in Tallulah's hierarchy bore a strange parallel to my relationship with Kuki. I loved and respected her, but I didn't have the same eager-to-please attitude toward her that had characterized my relationship with my mother. With Kuki, I felt the need to please, not to make waves, to express my gratitude for her taking me in. But whenever we had a clash of wills, which was increasingly frequent as I reached adulthood, I became less compliant and more willing to assert my own dominance.

Still, though, I was always careful not to take it too far. Heaven forbid I be accused of biting the hand that fed me—just as Tallulah had so far refrained from inflicting bodily damage on me, despite her ability to do so.

The more I got to know her, the more I realized that Tallulah was not the alien creature I thought when she first arrived. In fact, aside from her fondness for fecal art, I was beginning to think the little monkey and I had a lot in common.

My buzzer rang. I wasn't expecting anyone and half feared it was Dan the deliveryman, back to score a second date with Tallulah. Or maybe it was Tom, back to score a second kiss with me.

I pressed the intercom button and Monica Broccoli's voice boomed through the speaker. "So I'm here."

I hadn't heard from Monica in days, so I'd figured she wasn't going to take me up on my invitation to visit Rocky and meet Tallulah. I guess she had a change of heart.

"Ya gonna let me up or what?"

I pressed the buzzer and waited while Monica clomped up the six flights. She took almost as long as she had when her leg was weighted down with a plaster cast. I wondered if she was having difficulty climbing the stairs because her leg hadn't properly healed. I leaned over the railing and saw her one flight down, gripping the railing for support as she scaled the stairs on what looked like six-inch stiletto heels—hardly appropriate footwear for someone still recovering from a fractured fibula.

The twinge of guilt I felt over removing Monica's cast before it was medically advised disappeared the moment she reached my landing and barked, "If this is some scheme to get me and your numb-nuts cousin back together, forget about it. We're kaput."

I'm the first to admit that Mensa wasn't beating a path to Gerry's door, but what he lacks in IQ points, he makes up for in other ways. He's what my Brooklyn-Italian relatives would call a "stand-up guy." No way I was going to let some bra-modeling floozy call him numb-nuts.

"No scheme. Gerry doesn't want you back. At least he hasn't mentioned it to me." Not in the last few days, anyway.

"Fine. Where's the monkey?"

She brushed me aside and pushed her way into my apartment. I followed her in and closed the door behind us, trying to remember why I'd invited her in the first place. Oh yeah, I wanted to find out her name so my numb-nuts cousin could win her back. Huh.

Tallulah was in her cage, tearing up some junk mail I had given her. She looked up when Monica approached the cage.

"Whaddya know? You do have a monkey. I thought you were just yankin' my chain." She leaned over and peered intently at Tallulah, who retreated deeper into her cage—a natural reaction to having your personal space invaded by Monica Broccoli. "Can I hold her?"

"Maybe in a little while. Let her warm up to you first. Wait till she gets used to the sound of your voice." That could take a while. I'd known Monica for nearly two years and I still wasn't accustomed to it.

I put some coffee on to warm and offered Monica a snack of trail mix, courtesy of Tallulah. What can I say? The little monkey's suitcases were stocked better than my kitchen cupboards would ever be.

Monica sat at the kitchen table and grabbed a handful of trail mix. It was a hot day and her hair was pulled up and fastened atop her head with a big pink plastic clip. I cringed, thinking of the hours I'd spent rolling her long locks into curlers, only to have her waste a perfectly good 'do by shoving it into a ninety-nine-cent hair clip.

She gestured to a flyer for the showcase that was sitting on the tabletop. "Your thing's tonight, isn't it?"

"The showcase? Yeah."

"Break a leg."

You, too, I thought to myself. But I said, "Thanks. It's probably not going to go off."

She shrugged disinterestedly. "Whatever."

We were silent for a few beats. Truth is, with the topic of Gerry off-limits, I didn't have much to say to Monica. "Any news about the audition?" I finally asked.

"What audition?"

"The one you were so desperate to get your hair done for." She was staring at me blankly. "Remember? You, me, beauty supplies, a power saw . . . ?"

She nodded. "That's right. And your pregnant friend bouncing all over the place getting in the way."

Yeah. *Carter* was the one in the way.

"So? Did you get the part?"

"Nope." She shrugged. "No biggie. It was small-scale anyway. I really wasn't that interested, but my agent insisted I read for it."

I could understand Monica wanting to save a little face, but didn't she recall that she'd turned my entire evening upside down for the sake of her "small-scale" audition?

"Your agent, huh? What agency are you with, by the way?" O.K., so part of me still wanted to crack the case of Monica's true identity.

She started to speak but then bit back her words. "Why?" She narrowed her eyes at me.

"Danny and I are splitting up the act. I'm gonna go solo, and I need an agent. I thought maybe you could refer me to yours."

"Good try, Nancy Drew." She gestured in the direction of my chop job. "Or should I say Kojak?"

She stood, brushed trail mix crumbs off her lap, and looked around my apartment. "Where's Rocky? You didn't starve him to death, did you?"

"He's in the bedroom."

"Can I see him?"

"Knock yourself out."

The phone rang just as Monica disappeared into the bedroom. It was Tom. The sound of his voice immediately brought back the memory of our kiss and sent shivers up my spine.

"How'd the interview go?" I asked.

"Great. Until the dean asked how I got the scratches on my face."

"Oh, no!" I cast an accusing glare in Tallulah's direction. "What did you say?"

"I told him my girlfriend has a jealous monkey."

Girlfriend? While I let that one sink in, I asked, "How did he respond?"

"He said his wife has a possessive poodle. Then he showed me the scars around his ankles."

He laughed and I breathed an audible sigh of relief.

"Do you have plans tonight?" he asked.

I gritted my teeth. I hated lying, and I especially didn't want to lie to Tom. But which would be worse: a little white lie or a big fat disaster like having Tom show up for the most mortifying evening of my life? "Yeah. I kind of have plans . . . to see my aunt." There, that was O.K. Not exactly the truth, but not a lie either.

"Too bad. I was hoping you'd want to have dinner."

"Sorry. How 'bout tomorrow night?"

"Can't. I have Nicole tomorrow."

"Oh." I paused, wondering if I should invite the two of them over for dinner. I knew that as a freshly divorced dad, Tom had to be careful involving his daughter in his personal relationships. If she got to know his girlfriends and things didn't work out, she could get her heart broken as much as he did. One divorced friend of mine wouldn't let her boyfriend meet her kids until she'd been dating him for a year. I rolled my eyes. A year? With my track record, I'd be lucky if Tom and I weathered the three-month mark.

"Speaking of Nicole," he said, "I'm actually dreading picking her up tomorrow."

"Why?"

"She has—or had—a goldfish she keeps here. Sammy. He was floating at the top of his fishbowl this morning."

"Oh, no. How do you think she'll take it?" When I was growing up, there were always some kids in the neighborhood who'd go all out for a dead pet—a shoebox coffin, burial in the backyard, a cross made out Popsicle sticks marking the grave site. Other kids would callously flush the deceased or toss it in the trash with last night's dinner. I always took pet deaths hard. Still do.

"Not well. She was planning to bring him to school next week for show-and-tell. She's been talking about it for days, planning what she was going to say."

"Poor Nicole!" Not only did her fish die, but now she's got to get up in front of her class with nothing to show or tell. It was a predicament I could relate to. I knew all about having to face an audience empty-handed. "Hey, maybe I could help. I have plenty of pets. She could borrow one for show-and-tell."

"That's O.K. I'll take her to the pet store tomorrow and let her pick out another goldfish."

"All right, but let me know if you change your mind." I eyed the closed bedroom door. Probably I should check on Monica and Rocky. Problem is, I wasn't too keen on seeing another of their snake-stroking sessions. I spotted Monica's purse on the kitchen table and decided that I could make better use of my time rifling through it looking for her identification. "I have to go," I said into the receiver.

"O.K. Call you later."

I dropped the phone and was reaching for Monica's purse when the door to the bedroom opened wide.

I suppose I should have warned Monica to stay in the bedroom with Rocky, but I never suspected she'd bring him out into the kitchen. After all, she knew full well I was terrified to be anywhere near him when he was uncaged. The only reason I'd been able to sleep since I'd moved him into my bedroom was that I'd added yet another locking mechanism to his already supersecure aquarium. But there she was, walking toward me with the boa constrictor draped over her arms. She was making kissy faces and cooing noises.

Tallulah and I started simultaneously freaking out.

"Get him out of here!" I screamed at Monica. "The monkey's afraid of snakes!"

Tallulah was baring her teeth and emitting an ear-piercing screech. The hair all over her body was standing on end, making her look nearly double her normal size.

Instead of beating a hasty retreat, Monica stood her ground. "Maybe she just hasn't had the chance to warm up to him yet, since you've had him hidden away in the bedroom." She took a few steps closer to Tallulah's cage, holding the snake out in front of her. "He won't bite. Will you, baby?"

Tallulah screeched again, then looked at me, her face twisted up in anguish. I knew how she felt. My skin crawled every time I encountered a snake that wasn't on the other side of an impenetrable barrier. I wished I could crawl inside Tallulah's cage with her. But as scared as I was, I knew I had to put an end to Tallulah's distress. She was in my care, and it was my job to protect her from the big bad snake and the bigger badder Broccoli.

I stepped between Monica and the cage and thrust both arms out to my sides in an attempt to shield Tallulah. "Back away, Broccoli," I said, as I walked slowly forward, forcing Monica to back up into the bedroom. I kept up a brave front, but I almost lost it when Rocky's head angled toward me, his beady black eyes appraising me hungrily—probably thinking I'd make a good change from those puny frozen rats.

I took a deep breath. "I should have warned you, but snakes and monkeys are natural enemies. That's why Rocky is hidden in here."

"Doesn't he get bored in here all day, all by himself?"

"I haven't asked him."

"Do you at least take him out once in a while? Hold him?"

I looked at her incredulously. "Have we met? I'm the one who didn't want your freaking snake in the first place because I'm terrified of him."

She snorted. "I thought maybe when you got that hole in your head it knocked some sense into you." Before I had a chance to react, she was coming toward me, backing me into a corner of the bedroom. "He's harmless," she said, pushing the snake onto me. His long, muscular body glided across my shoulders and twisted around my arm. My stomach quivered and I became light-headed. I reminded myself to breathe. The only thing keeping me conscious was the fear that if I fainted, I'd wake up in the emergency room with another gaping head wound. I was a decent hairstylist, but no way could I camouflage two bald spots.

I took a few deep, cleansing breaths and looked down at the reptile in my arms. I was shocked to realize that his skin was smooth as leather, not slimy or scaly or slippery. And while he wrapped himself around my arm, he was putting no more pressure than a blood-pressure cuff—certainly not enough to amputate the limb.

"See, it's not so bad." Monica gripped the snake and lifted him off me. Then she thrust his face toward mine and said, "Give Holly a kiss."

"Yikes!" I jumped back, grabbing blindly for the bedroom door so I could make a quick escape. I admit I may have given the snake a bum rap, but kissing it was definitely out of the question.

I fled to the kitchen, where Tallulah was still looking a bit agitated. I talked to her in my most soothing voice and stroked her hair through the cage bars. I tossed a small handful of trail mix into the cage and she began snacking.

After a few moments, Monica came out of the bedroom and shut the door behind her. Upon seeing her, Tallulah began rattling her cage door and uttering a stream of what were probably the monkey equivalent of obscenities.

"Did you lock the aquarium? *All* of the locks?"

"Yeah." She walked to within a few feet of Tallulah's cage and stood facing me, hands on hips. "Rocky is a people snake, Holly. He's used to being handled, so he's good around people. But if you never take him out and hold him, he'll turn mean. He'll start trying to bite people. Even feeding him could be dangerous."

"You're right," I said. "This is no home for Rocky. I took him in as a favor to you and Gerry, but since you two are kaput, you won't mind taking him back." I stood and headed for the freezer. "It'll just take me a minute to pack his things."

"But—"

I turned and narrowed my eyes at her. I wasn't going to let her slither out of this one. I was putting my foot down: Monica Broccoli was taking her snake and stomping out of my life . . . today. "No buts. You said the only reason you couldn't keep Rocky was Gerry didn't like seeing you two slobbering all over each other. Now that the numb-nuts is out of the picture—"

"He's not a numb-nuts." She bit her lip and looked down. When she spoke, her voice was unsteady. If I wasn't dead certain that Monica Broccoli's heart was as hard as her steel-toed Gucci boots, I'd have sworn she was about to cry. "I . . . love your cousin, Holly. I want to marry him. I just want him to be really sorry first."

Ah, cripes. Now full-blown tears were falling down her cheeks. My plan to get rid of Rocky and Broccoli in one fell swoop was doomed. I sighed. "He *is* sorry. He feels terrible."

"Really?" She wiped tears from her eyes.

Tallulah emitted a throaty cackle that seemed to suggest she wasn't buying into Monica's emotional display.

I sighed. "He's been miserable. He's been racking his brain trying to remember your name. He says you're his little . . . 'Brockly-wockly' "—I fought the urge to roll my eyes as I repeated it—"and he can't think of you any other way."

Monica looked up at me. An expression of relief washed over her face, which was quickly replaced by wide-eyed shock—the look of someone who just realized she'd left her baby on the bus.

"What is it?" I asked, but before she could reply, the answer came whizzing past my head in the form of a brown blob that hit Monica's forehead with a squishy splat. I heard a breathy "he he he" behind me and turned to see Tallulah slapping her sticky brown fingers against her cage, looking inordinately pleased with herself.

Monica shot bolt upright and stumbled into the kitchen. She grabbed a dish towel off the counter and wiped her face. Then she ran the faucet and stuck her head under the sink. She was simultaneously sputtering, spitting, and swearing. When she finally stood, her face was red, her mascara was smudged, and she looked ready to kill.

She pointed stiff-fingered at me. "You have problems with my *snake,* but you don't mind taking care of this *ball of shit*?"

I should allow Monica some latitude, I told myself. After all, she's just been pelted with monkey feces. But still, I thought "ball of shit" was a bit extreme.

"I'm sorry. She was just . . . expressing her displeasure at seeing the snake."

Monica pushed past me, heading straight for the front door. She opened the door, looked over her shoulder, and shot back, "Save your breath. Tell your numb-nuts cousin to forget it. I don't want to marry into this crazy family."

I watched her slam the door, then noticed that she had forgotten her purse. I grabbed it off the kitchen table and raced to the top of the stairs. "You forgot—"

I stopped myself before I finished the sentence, suddenly realizing I had the key to Monica's identity—and Gerry's potential happiness, God help him—in my hands. I unzipped the handbag and stuck my hand in, fishing for a wallet. I felt a hairbrush, lipstick, keys, pens, but so far, no wallet.

Monica had heard me and was headed back up the stairs toward me. "Hey!" she yelled. "Get your hands outta my purse!"

I jumped back, trying to buy myself time. My fingers closed

around something that felt like a checkbook and I was about to pull it out of the bag when Monica reached the top of the stairs and snatched at her purse. "Let go!"

Suddenly realizing how foolish—not to mention criminal—I looked, I let go of the bag and lifted my hands in a gesture of sur-render.

Apparently Monica hadn't counted on my giving up so easily. Just as I was about to release her bag, she yanked harder. With nothing to counter the force of her tug, she was thrown off balance. For a split second, she teetered at the top of the stairs, struggling to regain her balance. If I wasn't frozen dumb with shock, I may have been able to reach out and pull her onto the landing—but more likely she would have taken me down with her. Monica was model thin, but she was also model *tall*. She had a good ten inches on me, not counting her stiletto heels, and outweighed me by at least fif-teen pounds. At the moment, she also had the benefit of gravity, which was using its full force to suck Monica downward.

She made a desperate attempt to grab on to the railing for sup-port, but just as her fingers brushed the banister, she toppled down the stairs, a crashing jumble of arms, legs, and stiletto heels.

12

A Merry Chase

Lately I seem to keep letting other people drag me into their problems, somehow making them my own. Carter and Danny's breakup had somehow made them angrier at me than at each other. And Gerry had me feeling so guilty over ruining his proposal to Monica that I'd run myself ragged investigating Monica's identity and searching for her stinking ring. All in all, I'd spent more time trying to reunite Carter and Danny and Gerry and Monica than I'd invested in my own budding relationship with Tom.

This time, though, I had to accept liability for my own actions. I was responsible on so many levels for what happened to Monica. She lost her balance because I was going through her purse without permission. Her vision was blurred because *my* monkey charge had thrown feces in her face. And her leg was weak to begin with because *I* had hacked her cast to pieces with my power saw.

O.K., so *she* had been the one who insisted I remove her cast. And *she* had provoked the monkey by brandishing her snake in its face. And *her* stubbornness over her name was the only thing keeping her and Gerry apart. Yet I had to accept my share of the blame.

I thought of all this as I walked the twelve blocks from my apartment to St. Vincent's Hospital. The paramedics had told me I could ride in the back of the ambulance, but Monica had loudly vetoed that idea. After watching the ambulance drive off, I dashed back up to my apartment to check that all animals were accounted for and all cages secure; then I locked the door and headed off to the hospital to check on Monica.

According to one of the paramedics, Monica's leg was probably broken, but it didn't appear she'd sustained any other injuries, with the possible exception of a concussion. He said she was slightly disoriented and her pupils were dilated. I refrained from mentioning that there were other possible explanations for both symptoms, having already provided way too much incriminating information to the 9-1-1 operator, who was probably dispatching men in white jackets to my apartment at this moment.

At St. Vincent's, I entered through the emergency room entrance and stood in line at the information desk. If the crowded waiting room was any indication, the ER was having a very busy day. The desk clerk looked like he'd already been working a twelve-hour shift and was ready to go postal. Veins in his fat neck were bulging as he spoke to the old woman in front of me. When it was finally my turn, I told the clerk I was there to see a friend who'd been brought in by ambulance.

"Name?" he asked.

"Huh?"

"Your friend's name?" His fingers hovered impatiently over a computer keyboard.

Shit. "I don't know."

"You don't know your friend's name?" His neck veins throbbed visibly.

I sighed. "She answers to Monica Broccoli."

His fingers pecked at the keys. "Broccoli like the vegetable?"

"Yes, but it's just a nickname."

He shook his head. "There's no patient named Broccoli in my system."

"I know, I know. She was just brought in here. I was going to ride in the ambulance but I walked instead. I have to see her. Can you just look up which patients came in within the last ten minutes? She has a broken leg. Maybe two."

He crossed his massive arms over his chest. "I can't do that."

"O.K., then just let me back there"—I gestured to the large metal door separating the waiting room from the rest of the emergency unit—"and I'll find her."

"No one goes back without a pass. And I can't give you a pass unless you're visiting a patient whose name is in my system."

I craned my neck so I could see his computer screen. "Let me just see a list of patients currently being treated. Maybe I can pick her out."

"No!" He turned his monitor away from me. "Are you crazy? That's against security regulations. I'm going to have to ask you to leave." He gestured at me to step aside so the next person could come forward.

I slunk over to the waiting area, where the *Jerry Springer Show* was blaring from a TV in the corner. I wondered if I'd left the TV on at home. Jerry's topic, My Grandma's a Ho, featured elderly, mostly obese, women crammed into sequin-studded outfits made for people half their size. It was hardly the type of programming I thought Tallulah should be exposed to. I hoped I'd remembered to turn the set off.

I went to a bank of pay phones, fished loose change out of my purse, and called Gerry. I figured he'd still be home watching his hit counter, but after three rings, his machine picked up. Of all the times to get a life.

I left a message telling Gerry that Monica was at St. Vincent's, most likely having a cast put on her rebroken leg. I doubted he would have better luck charming his way into the ER, but he'd at least want to give it a try.

I hung up and dialed Kuki's house. No answer there, either. I left a vague message stating that I needed to speak to Gerry right away. No need to let everyone know I had maimed Monica Broccoli just yet.

I blew out a sigh. I considered camping out in the ER waiting room, hoping to catch sight of Monica when she was released, but I couldn't be certain that there wasn't another exit she might leave through. Or, worse, they could decide to keep her overnight, and I'd have wasted my day watching trash TV. If I was going to spend my day watching trash TV, I might as well do it at home, where I could pretend to be working on my business concerns.

Once outside the emergency room, I realized that there was someone else at St. Vincent's I could pay a visit to. I swung a corner, went in through the main entrance, and marched up to the information desk.

After showing my ID, I was issued a visitor's badge and directed to room 328 on the third floor. I stopped off at the gift shop and bought a small potted plant. That way, if my unannounced visit turned out to be totally awkward, I could say I was just coming to drop off the plant and leave.

David Marquette was in his late thirties with short-cropped brown hair and wire-rimmed glasses. His hospital bed was raised to a sitting position, but he was lying back with his eyes closed. All sorts of wires connected him to monitors at the far side of his bed. The television was tuned to the *Jerry Springer Show* and the granny hos were still strutting their scantily clad selves across the sound-stage. I guess I needn't have worried about Tallulah seeing Jerry at my house; her owner was apparently a fan.

I tiptoed to a table, hoping to deposit the plant and slip away without disturbing him.

"Hello?" His voice startled me and I spun around.

"Hi," I said. "I didn't mean to wake you."

"You didn't. I've just been waiting for them to come change the channel. I can't watch this crap."

I smiled, oddly relieved that David wasn't watching Jerry and the slutty seniors. It hadn't even occurred to me that he was unable to change the channel on his own. I'd never met a quadriplegic and hadn't thought about what it would be like to lose the use of all four limbs. David was a prisoner in his own body, dependent on other people for his every need.

"Let me." I reached for the remote control on the table.

"Just turn it off," he said.

I nodded and clicked the POWER button.

"Do I know you?" he asked.

I shook my head. "We have a friend in common."

He looked at me expectantly.

"Tallulah."

His face broke into a huge grin. "You must be Holly!"

I nodded, unable to speak because of the lump in my throat. I'd been so afraid of disturbing him that I hadn't expected he might actually be glad to see me.

"Holly, sit down. How is my Tally?"

I pulled a chair up to the side of the bed. "She's doing great. We had a little scare when I thought she swallowed my cousin's engagement ring, but it was a false alarm."

He chuckled. "I bet she hid it somewhere."

"Yep."

"She can be so naughty!" he said, smiling.

I nodded my head in agreement.

"I miss her terribly," he said. "It's so hard to be away from her.

It's like I have no one to talk to." He looked down, then back at me. "I mean, the nurses here are supersweet and everything, and my sister comes by every day, but it's not the same. Tally's my constant companion. You don't think I'm weird for talking to a monkey, do you?"

"Of course not. I've been talking to her lots. She's a good listener."

"She is! Oh, Holly, I'm so glad you came. You're good for Tally, I can tell. My sister said you were nice, but I was so worried about Tally being in good hands. Now I can relax."

"Well, don't get too used to it here. Tallulah misses you. She and I are getting along fine, but I can tell she's just putting up with me. She'd rather be home with you."

His head dropped and he started sobbing. I looked away, uncomfortably, not knowing what to say. I'd hoped to reassure him, not make him cry. There was a box of tissues on the bedside table and I started to reach for one, but stopped short. Would he want me to wipe his eyes for him, or would he resent it?

Finally he looked up. "Can I tell you something, Holly? What Tallulah does for me?" He broke down again.

"I know all about the program," I said. "The monkeys are trained to use the remote control, open containers, retrieve objects, turn off lights, and stuff like that."

"Tallulah is my best friend," he said, his voice shaky. "That may sound strange for a grown man."

"No—"

"She can do all those things for me. So can my nurse. And my sister lives in my building and she's there anytime I need something. But Tallulah opened up the whole world for me. When you're in a wheelchair, people feel awkward around you. They don't know what to say, or they're so afraid of staring at you that they won't even look you in the eyes."

I frowned, knowing it was true. I was guilty of those things myself.

"When I go out with Tallulah, people come right up to us. They're curious about her. They ask me questions and pretty soon they forget I'm in a wheelchair. We always draw a crowd. Tallulah loves it just as much as I do."

"She's a crowd pleaser, all right."

"I have friends all over this city that would've been afraid to even approach me if it hadn't been for Tallulah. And another thing, she gives me independence. Most of the day, my nurse takes care of me. But with Tallulah, I can have some time alone, just me and her. If I need little things, she can help me. And if there's an emergency, she knows how to dial 9-1-1."

Good to know. Living with me, that particular skill could come in handy.

He continued. "You don't know what a relief it is sometimes just to be alone, and not have to feel like a burden to my family and friends."

Tears welled in my eyes and I wiped them away with the back of my hand. I may not comprehend what it's like to be paralyzed, but I did know what it was like to be a burden to your family, having felt that way since my mother's death and father's abandonment.

"I didn't mean to make you cry, Holly."

"It's O.K." I stood and stretched my legs. "I didn't realize how much she does for you. I knew about all the 'tasks' she could do, but I have to admit—"

"What?"

"I don't mean to sound disrespectful, but it always seemed a little—"

"Silly?"

I shook my head. "Unfair. To Tallulah. I'm a primatologist, or at least that's what my degree says. I've always been opposed to people having monkeys as pets, and I know this is different, but I had to wonder about a few things."

"Like?"

"Like how they're trained, what they get out of it, and if all those people who come up to you in the streets decide they want to have a pet monkey, too. People think having a monkey would be fun but then they can't deal with the reality of it and those monkeys suffer a terrible fate. Do you realize—" I stopped myself, fearing I'd gone too far already. David was recovering from surgery and the last thing he needed was a tirade from his monkey sitter. "I'm sorry," I said.

"Don't apologize, Holly. I had those questions, too. My sister and I visited Tallulah at the place where she was trained and watched the training sessions. It's all done with positive reinforcement. They're not forced to do anything they don't want. Monkeys won't do anything they don't want to! They won't work when they're bored or tired. Doing little things for me is like a game to Tally. And I always tell people that monkeys don't make good pets. If they don't believe me, I just tell them how Tallulah—" He paused as though searching for the right words.

"Expresses her displeasure?" I offered.

He smiled. "Exactly. That turns them off every time!"

David and I talked for another twenty minutes; then a nurse came to do tests and I said good-bye. As I exited the hospital, I ducked my head into the ER entrance, hoping that the clerks had changed shifts.

Drat. The same big-necked guy was manning the information desk. There may have been a chance I could pry information out of a different clerk, but this guy already had my number.

Since I couldn't do anything more about Monica Broccoli, I headed out of the ER in the direction of home. I checked my watch. Four hours till the showcase. If I was smart, I'd march home and work up some material for a solo act. Instead of wallowing in self-pity over being abandoned by my partner, I could seize the opportunity to advance my career. Instead of playing second banana to Danny, I could grab the spotlight for myself. There would be agents and casting directors in the audience and, who knows, maybe one of them could propel me to stardom, taking me away from the daily drudgery of being a hairstyling, tax-preparing pet sitter.

Or better yet, Tallulah and I could finish off the last of the Rocky Road while watching *Dr. Phil.*

As I neared my building, I saw a sheriff's patrol car outside and had a stab a fear that the cops had come for me, that Monica Broccoli had filed criminal charges against me from her hospital bed. Then I reminded myself that this was New York City. There are seven million inhabitants in the naked city, at least half a million of them more guilty than me.

I let myself in and climbed the six flights. As I approached my landing, I saw a uniformed officer turn away from my door. I tried not to panic. He could have the wrong apartment, I told myself.

"Are you Holly Heckerling?" he asked.

Ohmigod. He was going to arrest me.

I nodded. "It was an accident," I said. "She slipped."

"I'm Deputy Sheriff Beckman." He opened a thin metal case and extracted a sheaf of papers. He made some scribbles on the top page, tore it off, and handed it to me with a wide smile. "You've been served. Have a good day."

He floated down the stairs while I stood, mouth agape, staring at the piece of paper in my hands. My heart was pounding in my ears and I couldn't make sense of anything. If I was being accused of maiming Monica, why didn't he take me in for questioning? When my eyes focused and my heartbeat slowed to a million beats per minute, I finally realize that I was holding a subpoena with my name on it. I scanned the page, thinking that at least this nightmare would have a bright spot: Monica couldn't file legal documents under an alias. If she sued me, she'd have to use her real name. It was little consolation, but at this point, I'd settle for anything.

But the name at the top of the page wasn't Monica's. It was Tom's. I was being subpoenaed to testify in the case of Hansen v. Hansen.

I let myself in to my apartment. Tallulah's chirps of greeting elevated my mood only slightly. I reflexively checked the milk cubby, but it was empty. There were no messages on my business line, and one on my personal line. I prayed for it to be Danny, but instead I was greeted by Gerry's ebullient voice. "Hey, Hol. You won't believe this, but my Web site is up to 4400 hits! It's incredible. And I owe it all to you. No time to talk. I gotta book. Look in yesterday's *Post*."

He made no mention of Monica or whether he'd gotten my messages about her fall. Maybe he truly was over her. Or maybe he was just too wrapped up in his sock-induced fantasy to notice what was going on around him. I doubted there was anything in the *Post* of immediate relevance to my life, so I put it out of my mind. I wasn't going to bust my butt rushing to the corner newsstand for a copy.

After being confined all morning, Tallulah was happy to be let out of her cage. She slipped free of my grasp before I had a chance to tether her to the sofa, and I spent a good ten minutes chasing her around the apartment while she cackled gleefully. Exhausted and emotionally spent, I gave up and collapsed on my sofa with a grunt. "You win!"

Once she lost her pursuer, the game ceased to be of interest to Tallulah, and she leapt onto the sofa next to me. She cocked her head to one side and stuck her tongue out at me. My day had been so disastrous that one more insult would have been enough to put me over the edge. But I'd just learned from David that the outthrust tongue was something Tallulah reserved for people she truly liked.

I cocked my head to one side, mirroring the monkey. I smiled, then stuck my tongue out at her. "Thank you," I said.

I grabbed the phone and dialed Carter's number. I needed to call Tom, to find out what this subpoena business was all about, but I wanted to wait until my nerves had settled.

Carter wasn't home, so I tried Starbucks. Barista Bob put me on hold when I asked for Carter. She came on the line a few minutes later.

"When do you get off?" I asked.

"Not until six. Just enough time to change clothes before the showcase. You want me to meet you there?"

"I was hoping you could come over before then. I've had a killer day. First Monica broke her leg falling down my stairs. Then the sheriff came and gave me a subpoena to testify at Tom's custody trial."

"Holy hakama," Carter said. "I wish I could, but I'm short-staffed and we're in the middle of a rush. Come down here and I'll see if I can take a break."

"Maybe. I need to get my thoughts together first."

I heard paper rustling and looked over to see Tallulah chomping on a corner of the subpoena, which I'd left on the coffee table. I whipped my hand out and snatched it from her before she could destroy it. But once I had it safely tucked under a sofa cushion, I entertained second thoughts. Maybe I should let her gnaw it to pieces. Maybe "my monkey ate my subpoena" was sufficient grounds to be excused from legal proceedings.

Then again, maybe not.

Carter was saying, "If I don't see you, I'll be front row at the showcase."

"Showcase?" I snorted. "Have you talked to Danny? Do you know if he's intending to show up?"

"No. Why? Haven't you two rehearsed?"

"He still hates me! He hasn't returned my calls."

"I knew he was still holding a grudge, but I didn't think he'd sacrifice the show for his pigheadedness." So sayeth the woman who would sacrifice her future happiness for her pigheaded belief in astrology.

"Danny's not working today?" I asked.

"No. He took himself off the schedule this week, except for my days off."

"Hmm."

"So you'll just do the show alone," she said, as if this was no big deal.

I balked. "I've never done stand-up alone. I need a partner to bounce off."

"You'll just bounce off the audience."

"What if they don't like me?"

"Of course, they'll like you. You're the poster child for likability. That's why people trust you with their animals, their kids, their apartments, and their hair. Everybody likes you."

"Monica Broccoli doesn't."

Carter made a disgusted sound. "Forget her. I knew she was a nut job ever since she made a stink at your grandma's funeral."

I groaned, remembering how Monica Broccoli—hardly the epitome of propriety even under the best of circumstances—had disrupted Gerry's eulogy of our grandmother to object loudly to his characterization of her as a virgin. Gerry, in his own embarrassing way, was trying to compliment Monica by telling the crowd how pleased my grandmother would have been that he'd found himself a "nice" girl. Instead of sitting politely through the curious stares and then beating the crap out of Gerry in private—as I would have done had the virgin shoe been on *my* foot—Monica stood and began shouting expletives at him that caused representatives of the younger generation to blush and the older ones to fumble for their nitroglycerin tablets.

Despite desperate attempts to erase it, the image of Monica at my grandmother's funeral was seared into my memory forever. *So why didn't I think of it sooner?*

"Oh, my God, Carter, you're a genius!"

"You're gonna do the show?"

"Maybe. But first I have to go to Kuki's."

I dialed Gerry's number and left a message asking him to meet me at his mother's house. Then I dialed Kuki's. There was no answer, which was just as well. This way I could let myself in and get what I wanted without having to face a barrage of questions.

I shoved some makeup and a change of clothes into my knapsack in case I ended up going straight to the club from Kuki's. Then I went to make sure Tallulah was locked in her cage before leaving the apartment. But the cage was empty. Of course, I reminded myself, I'd let her out as soon as I returned from the hospital. After our merry chase, I hadn't secured her leash to the sofa leg as was my custom. While I was talking to Carter on the phone, she was sitting on the sofa, cheerfully chomping on Sheriff Beckman's bombshell.

I looked over at the sofa. No monkey. The table, chairs, and bookshelves were also monkeyless. There was no monkey doing the bump-and-grind with my TV set. Panic set in.

I raced from one end of my apartment to the other, trying not to hyperventilate as I opened every door, drawer, and cupboard looking for Tallulah. I called her name sweetly, then sternly, then pleadingly, but there was no response. I opened the bedroom door and peeked inside. From Grouch's relaxed legs-in-the-air, belly-exposed-to-the-world pose, it was a safe bet that Tallulah hadn't passed his way.

I made another circle through the apartment, ending in the pantry. My heart skipped several beats when I saw that the inner door to the milk cubby, which I usually kept locked, was wide-open. I'd opened it to check for deliveries when I got home, but must've neglected to lock it again. I walked a few steps closer, clutching my chest so my heart wouldn't leap out of it. The outer door, which I always left unlocked so my clients could drop things off day or night, was also ajar. The space was easily big enough for a full-grown capuchin monkey to slip through.

I stared through the open milk cubby for a full beat as the enormity of the situation sank in. Tallulah had escaped.

I flung open my front door and started running up the stairs like a madwoman. I knew the bigger danger was in Tallulah reaching street level, but I figured I'd try going up first, if for no better reason than to enlist Brian's help in the search. When I reached the seventh-floor landing, I pounded on his door and called his name. Then I turned and started running back down.

When I heard Brian's door open, I yelled up, "Tallulah's on the loose! Help me look for her."

"Which way should I go?" he shouted back.

"Up! Go up!"

The noise attracted the attention of Mrs. Mete, the building's resident busybody. She stuck her head over the railing and called down, "What's going on?"

"Did a monkey run past your door?" I shouted up at her.

"A monkey? Heavens, no. How on earth would a monkey get into the building?"

This from the woman who'd let Quasimodo himself in if he rang her buzzer at midnight.

I kept running, calling Tallulah's name, and shouting, "Monkey on the loose," for the benefit of my other neighbors, who were probably wondering what all the ruckus was about. A door opened and an older man peered out suspiciously. "Have you seen a monkey?" I asked.

He shook his head and quickly shut the door.

As I bounded down the next two flights, I tried to mentally calculate how long Tallulah had been gone before I realized she was missing. It was possible she'd had at least a five-minute head start. Combined with her natural speed and agility, a five-minute lead meant Tallulah could have made it to midtown Manhattan by now.

I hit the second-floor landing with a thud and paused only an instant to take a big gulp of air. "You find her?" Brian called down.

"No!" I yelled back. "Keep looking!"

I turned the corner and began sprinting down the last set of stairs. In my blind rush to reach the front door, I almost didn't see the man who was standing in the front entryway, looking as though he hadn't made up his mind whether he was coming or going. Through my sweat- and tearstained eyes I could have sworn the man was holding a monkey.

"That's . . . my . . . monkey," I panted, pointing at Tallulah, who tipped her head and stuck her tongue out in greeting.

Tallulah's new friend was a familiar-looking man who looked to be in his midfifties—hair graying at the temples, slightly balding, a bit of a paunch. Probably one of the many neighbors I'd passed on the stairs dozens of times but had never stopped to learn his name.

"This little guy was just about to leave the building when I came in," he said, cracking a slight smile. "Had a feeling he might be on the lam."

I nodded forcefully. "Her name's Tallulah. She got out. . . . I didn't realize. . . ." I bent over, struggling to catch my breath.

He handed over Tallulah's leash, then turned and reached for the front door.

"Wait," I said. "I didn't thank you."

He turned back to me and nodded. "Wasn't nothing."

"Yes, it was." I looked at Tallulah and my eyes filled with tears, the reality of how close I'd come to losing her hitting me with full force. "She belongs to a man who's a quadriplegic. She's his best—" I paused, choking back tears.

He smiled and wrinkles creased the corners of his eyes. "Don't cry, sunshine. It'll be O.K."

His gentle reassurance only made me bawl more. "I've been screwing up a lot lately, but if I'd have lost her . . . it would have been unforgivable." I wiped my tears on my sleeve.

Brian, dressed only in silk boxer shorts, came flying down the stairs and ground to a halt at the foot of the stairs. "You found her!" he said, looking almost as relieved as I was. He must have really been smitten with Tallulah to have dashed out of his apartment in his skivvies. He gave Tallulah a playful pat on the head. "You gave us quite a scare, monkey girl."

Tallulah bobbed her head and made chattering noises, as though telling him all about her daring escape.

Meanwhile, the man who had effected Tallulah's capture looked like he was trying to make a getaway of his own. He'd inched closer to the door and was gripping the knob, an awkward smile fixed on his face. He was probably shy, I figured. Either that or he didn't feel comfortable standing around with a half-naked man, a hysterical woman, and a monkey. Though I felt I should do something for the man to show my gratitude—invite him up for coffee perhaps—he obviously wanted to leave as desperately as I wanted to see Tallulah back inside her cage, safe and secure.

"Thanks again," I said.

He nodded, gave a slight smile, and disappeared out the front door.

Ha Ha, Holly

Cold sweat. Fear-induced nausea. Disoriented and dizzy. That's how I felt just before taking the stage at the Cracker Factory. It had taken fifteen minutes for me to get up the courage to go inside the club, and another ten for Carter to coax me onstage. It wasn't so much that she convinced me; it was more like she refused to yield to my incessant begging and pleading that she go on and announce the show's last-minute cancellation.

I'd taken a last glance around the club. It was more than half full, with a few stragglers still making their way to their seats. A respectable showing for no-name talent, which, let's face it, is what Danny and I were. We had a small, local fan base, but hadn't yet landed so much as a national TV spot.

"You think Mr. Sensitive is out there?" Carter whispered to me.

I'd been scanning the crowd since I arrived, half hoping I'd see the Writer, whom I figured I'd recognize by instinct alone, but I hadn't seen anyone who looked the type. The other half of me was praying that the Writer—along with everyone else I'd ever known or cared about—wouldn't show up. I was relieved to see no sign of

Aunt Kuki, but worried that Gerry's absence meant there was more trouble in Broccoli Land.

One of the late arrivals was making his way to an empty seat near the stage. As he moved closer, I was startled to realize it was Tom.

I gripped Carter's sleeve. "What's *he* doing here?" Not only hadn't I invited Tom, but I wasn't ready to face him. I was still reeling from being subpoenaed in his custody case.

She turned and looked, then shrugged. "Aren't you dating him?"

"Yeah, but I didn't invite him. I didn't even tell him about it. I was afraid it would be embarrassing."

"He probably saw the flyers around your apartment, duh."

"I don't think so. He was never at my place until this morning. And I didn't have any flyers out."

"Maybe he just—" She stopped midsentence, her forehead scrunched as though in deep contemplation. "You don't think he's—"

I waited for her to complete her thought. I don't think he's what? *A spy? A comedy stalker? A mind reader?*

She nodded her head as though it all made perfect sense. To her anyway. I was still left hanging. "He's what?"

"The Writer."

It wasn't possible. Or was it? I needed time to think it all through. Problem was, the lights had dimmed and Roger, the club owner, was approaching the stage.

Could Tom be the Writer? I had met him the same morning the Writer had picked up his first typing job. And only a block away. It was quite possible that he'd decided to stop in Starbucks after leaving my building. Also like the Writer, Tom had a daughter.

"But the Writer's wife is *dead*," I reminded Carter. "Tom's is very much alive."

She arched one eyebrow. "Maybe he'd rather think of her as being dead. Maybe all that writing is his way of working through the divorce. It could be cathartic. I did that when Joey Jarzen dumped me. I wrote this whole poem about his untimely death. Made me feel much better to imagine him rotting in his grave." She smiled serenely. "Of course, I've moved past that kind of thing. I inhabit a higher plane of consciousness now."

"Of course."

Roger was winding up his big intro. "Usually she performs with her partner Danny Crane, but tonight Holly Heckerling is going solo, so maybe she'll have a chance to get a word in edgewise. Let's give a big hand for Holly!"

I grabbed Carter's sleeve. "I can't. I'm going to be sick. If I hurl onstage, it will *really* be the end of my career."

"If you don't go on, that'll be the end. Now quit whining."

"Meeee? Whi-i-ine?" Okay, so whining was one of my best things. "I can't do it alone. I need Danny."

"Screw Danny. He left you stranded. Now go up there and be funny."

Be funny. Easier said than done. As I walked onstage and took the microphone, Monica Broccoli's words echoed through my head: *Gerry's always saying how funny you are, but I just don't see it.* At the time I just took it as evidence of Monica's ill-mannered ignorance, but now I feared it was true. Danny's the funny one. I always play the straight guy; I just bounce off of him. Who do I bounce off now?

Lacking any prepared material, I started off by casually talking about recent events in my life. "I have to admit I haven't had much time to prepare for tonight," I admitted ruefully. "But I've had a houseguest staying with me. You know what it's like to have someone come, stay in your house, eat all your food, watch your TV, and not clean up after themselves?" A few audience members nodded and groaned in commiseration. I singled one out in the front row, a sweatshirt-clad man in his early thirties. "You've had a similar experience?"

He nodded and shouted out, "Mother-in-law!"

One of his buddies gave him a sympathetic slap on the back.

"Mother-in-law, that's a tough one," I said, nodding. "But I bet my houseguest was worse. Did your mother-in-law wake you up every morning demanding to be fed?"

"Oh yeah."

"Did she chitter chatter all the time, until you couldn't think straight?"

He nodded. "Yak, yak, yak. All day long."

I put hands on hips, goading him on. "Did she hog the television set, insisting on watching Regis every day, regardless of what you wanted to watch?"

He shook his head and blurted, "Oprah!"

The crowd chortled, clearly enjoying the challenge.

"Okay. While watching *Oprah,* did your houseguest ever try to hump your TV set?"

Huge laughter from the crowd. The guy in the sweatshirt waved his hands in a gesture of surrender.

"No? Well, mine did," I said. "And if that wasn't bad enough, my houseguest—her name is Tallulah—has an unusual way of expressing herself when she's angry. You've heard the expression 'throwing a shit fit'? Well, Tallulah threw a lot of them. All over my walls."

At this point I confirmed what most of the crowd already suspected—that Tallulah was no ordinary houseguest. On a roll, I shared of few of the more colorful things I'd learned in my week of cohabitating with a monkey, ending with her swallowing my cousin's engagement ring. So what if she was innocent of that particular crime? It's called comedic license.

"To be honest, I was more worried about the monkey than the engagement ring. My cousin's no big spender. We're talking about the kind of ring that turns fingers green. I could just imagine what it would do to a little monkey's innards. She'd probably get intestinal gangrene.

"But still, I knew my cousin would be upset if he found out. Even though he only paid about twenty bucks for the ring, he acts like it's the Hope Diamond." I adopted an overblown Brooklynese. "Uh, Hol, dis here's da real thing. One hunnerd percent gen-u-ine foe diamond."

I paused for a beat, then nodded. "Yeah. One hundred percent genuine faux diamond. That's like saying something is authentically simulated . . . or an original replica." I approached an older woman in the front row. "You an art lover? How'd you like to buy a gen-uine first-edition reprint of a mock masterpiece?"

I returned to the stool and sat for a beat, thinking I'd exhausted this topic, but not knowing where to go next. Then I remembered something Betty had told me. "Speaking of diamonds," I said into the mike, "I just heard of this new thing where when a loved one dies, instead of burying or cremating them, you can have their corpse turned into a diamond."

Laughter was mixed with groans of disbelief. "No, no, it's true. The human body contains carbon, which is what diamonds are made of. So they extract the carbon from the body—I don't want to think about how exactly they do this—and compress it under thousand-ton weights, and voilà—your uncle Charlie is now a lovely fourteen-karat diamond tie clip."

There was a woman in a bright red dress seated near the stage. She looked to be in her midfifties. Seated next to her was a woman who looked closer to eighty. "Is this your mother?" I asked the lady in red.

"Aunt" came the reply.

"What's your name, hon?" I asked the elderly woman.

"Edna."

I turned back to the red-dress lady. "Can you imagine turning your beloved family member into a diamond ring?" I mimed putting a ring on an imaginary finger. "With Aunt Edna, I thee wed."

I had to wait until the howls of laughter died down before continuing. "Now this is not for everyone: I understand it's a very expensive process. And I would think, if you had decided to do this—say, when your husband dies, you want to have him made into a diamond so you can wear him around your neck—you want to get your money's worth. You don't want to spend ten grand and end up with a puny little diamond. So you start trying to fatten him up, like a turkey in October. 'Here, honey, eat another T-bone, drink your milk, have some chocolate cake. Mama wants a big fat brooch.'"

The crowd roared and I took a deep breath, my mind racing to come up with something to play off the diamonds of death, when I saw Roger motioning me from the side of the stage. I scrunched my forehead to show my confusion—I didn't think it was possible I'd gone over my time limit. Then Roger mouthed something, and pointed to his left. I followed his gaze and saw Danny.

I was flooded with a mixture of relief and anger. I felt like I'd been walking a tightrope and barely hanging on. It would be so easy to go back to being Danny's second banana. But then again, he had a lot of nerve showing up here and expecting to go on like nothing had happened.

Roger had one arm outstretched; it looked like he was holding Danny back until he got the go-ahead from me. I appreciated his sensitivity. Roger had done years of stand-up himself and knew what it was like to be thrown for a loop when you're in the middle of a set.

The crowd had quieted to low-level squeals and titters. I'd let them wait too long. I had to come back with something. Problem is, seeing Danny had knocked me off-balance and my mind was blank. I nodded to Roger, who allowed Danny to climb the steps to the stage.

"Ladies and gentlemen," I said, "you came here tonight to see two comedians, and I'd hate for you to feel shortchanged. It seems my partner, Danny, was able to make it after all, so please give him a warm welcome."

Danny hopped onstage, tipped his head to the audience, and launched into a bit I usually found trite but which now felt refreshingly familiar—a riff on my name. He looked over the audience and said, "Looks like a tough crowd. Have they been giving you a hard time?"

I shook my head no. "You sure?" He approached a front row table. "This one looks feisty," he said, pointing to Aunt Edna. Everyone laughed, but no one harder than Aunt Edna, who was obviously enjoying the attention.

"I have to look out for Holly, you know," he told the crowd. "Sometimes people in the audience give her a hard time. It's not her fault," he said over the shouted objections from a table in back. "It's her name. Holly Heckerling."

He pretended to field a question from the crowd. "Of course, it's her real name. Why would someone make that up? But my question is, being burdened with that name, why would anyone go into comedy? Holly Heckerling. Sounds like Holly Heckle-Me. So who can blame the poor schlep who comes in here happy to oblige?"

He turned to me but still addressed the crowd. "She's cute as a button, isn't she? With that name, and that face, she could be a little furry doll. Heckle-Me Holly, from the makers of Tickle-Me Elmo?" In a dead-on impersonation of the *Sesame Street* character, Danny said into the mike, "Elmo likes Holly." Then he tickled my belly.

The crowd was howling now. I sat back and relaxed into my role as second fiddle while Danny trotted out a few more of our over-played routines. I didn't feel the same adrenaline-pumping excitement I'd had when I was trying to carry to show on my own, but that was O.K.

It wasn't long, though, before Danny steered the act into some new—and very uncomfortable—territory. Namely, my life. He'd paraded my dirty laundry out onstage before, of course, but I always knew what was coming and had given my permission, albeit reluctantly at times. I had strict ground rules for the inclusion of my foibles in our follies. First, current inhabitants of my love life were off-limits. Second, while I didn't mind coming off as klutzy or kooky, I objected to being made to look downright dumb.

Tonight, however, Danny tossed the rules aside and launched into a manic monologue about my dating debacles, right up to my "infatuation" with a mysterious writer of unknown identity. "She doesn't know who he is or what he looks like. He comes in the dark of night and leaves his tattered manuscripts for her to read."

My temperature shot up at least ten degrees at the mention of the Writer. I hadn't even told Danny about him! Apparently, Carter had filled him in during their brief reconciliation. I scanned the crowd. For all I knew, the Writer was out there somewhere. My eyes landed on Tom. Was he the Writer? Either way, my relationship with him was doomed now. If he was the Writer, he'd been keeping secrets from me and I couldn't trust him. If he wasn't the Writer, he'd just been alerted to the fact that I was "infatuated" with some-one else.

I prayed Danny would drop the subject, but he continued. "How does he send you his writing?" he asked.

I rolled my eyes. I didn't want to follow his lead, but couldn't think of a way to derail Danny. "He leaves it in a cupboard in my pantry."

He turned back to the audience. "I know it's a little sad, our Holly falling for some guy she's never met, but you have to cut her a break. She's a single woman living in New York City whose relationships have the shelf life of a Bartlett pear. Who wouldn't be aroused if someone started showing up mysteriously and leaving things in her panties?"

"Pantry!" I corrected him, shouting, but my objection was drowned out by the peals of laughter emanating from the audience.

It took a while but I finally managed to steer Danny away from my love life by setting him up for one of his favorite topics: my family. He tossed off a few quick jokes at Aunt Kuki's expense before turning his sarcastic wit loose on Gerry's recent fixation on famous footwear. I was glad my cousin wasn't in the crowd to hear Danny mocking him. "Martin Scorsese's socks! Martin Scorsese's socks!" he said, waving the imaginary relics over his head. I know I hadn't been completely supportive of Gerry's endeavor, but this was going too far.

Thankfully, Danny soon turned his focus back to the target du jour—me.

"When Holly was living with her aunt and uncle," he said, his voice edgy, "they came home one day and found her bra in the cookie jar."

My temperature spiked even higher as I flashed back to the night I brought Danny to dinner at Kuki's. He'd heard enough of Uncle Bernie's stories to inflict permanent, irreversible, career-disabling humiliation upon me. This felt even worse than my nightmares of being onstage naked. *Thank you, Uncle Bernie.*

I shot a pleading look at Danny, but he plowed ahead. "Turns out our Holly had read in *Cosmo* that if you want to attract a man's attention, you should put a dab of his cologne in your brassiere. He'll be attracted to the familiar scent and be drawn to you without knowing why."

He paused in his story to approach Aunt Edna. He pointed a scolding finger in her direction. "Now, now, I saw you taking notes over there. You *are* a feisty one, aren't you?"

After grabbing a sip of water, he resumed. "Trouble is, Holly was only twelve at the time, and none of the boys in her class wore cologne. The boy she really liked . . ." He looked at me to supply the name, which I did, despite my better judgment.

"Robby Francomano," I muttered.

"So this boy, Robby Frankly Homo, didn't wear cologne. But he had a real jones for chocolate chip cookies. So Holly figured if she stuck her training bra in her grandma's cookie jar for an hour or two, her bosoms would be infused with enough savory chocolate aroma to make Robby follow her around like a lovesick puppy dog."

A woman sitting near the front bent forward in paroxysms of laughter, grasping her stomach and gasping for air. The rest of the crowd was equally exuberant. If I wasn't in the midst of a flashback, vividly reliving my prepubescent mortification at being called Tollhouse Tits by my entire sixth grade class, I would have taken a moment to appreciate the fact that the act was a hit.

The rest of the act was a blur, but judging by the reaction of the crowd, it was an unparalleled success for the comedy duo of Crane and Heckerling. Afterward, as people pushed their way toward the stage to offer their congratulations, I was separated from Danny.

One of my hairstyling clients approached me and gave me a quick hug. "Great show, Holly."

"Thanks, Danielle. I'm glad you could make it."

She stepped aside and I was surprised to see Marcus, with a pretty brunette on his arm. He gave me a quick hug and congratulated me on the show.

"I didn't expect to see you here," I said truthfully.

"After stuffing all those flyers in all those envelopes, I figured I should at least see what I was advertising."

I smiled, half wishing I'd felt something more for Marcus. He was a decent, kind man who would probably make any sane woman wildly happy. But I'd never been able to connect with him romantically. The fact that he'd brought a date to the show so soon after our breakup didn't even spark any jealousy on my part.

Marcus said he enjoyed the show and was glad to see that his saliva had been expended for a good cause. Then he left with his date.

My neighbor Brian was next. "Hey, Holly. Where's your simian sidekick?"

"At home. She's not into the club scene."

"At least you got a good showing from the building."

"Really? Who else?"

"I saw Pete the super. And that guy, the one who found Tallulah."

"Where is he? I should say hi."

"He was standing in the back. Probably left when the show ended."

I turned and looked around the club. The tables were clearing. Several people were hanging out by the bar, but none looked like the man who rescued Tallulah from the mean streets of Manhattan. My heart jumped when I spotted my aunts sitting at a table near the door. They'd obviously been late arrivals. With any luck, they'd been very late.

Tom was still sitting at his table, sipping his drink. I had so many questions for him, but at that moment I wasn't sure I wanted to hear the answers.

As I debated who to face first—my aunts or Tom—a more attractive third option presented itself: ducking out the emergency exit and running all the way home. Just as I was about to step in that direction, I felt a tap on my shoulder. I turned around and saw Danny, grinning widely, his eyes big and wide.

"What a show, huh?" He gripped me in an awkward hug, made all the more awkward by the fact that I was not hugging back. "We killed 'em!"

"*You* killed them," I said. And *me,* I might have added.

"A guy from NBC just gave me his card. This could be our big break."

"I don't know about that."

"What's with you?"

"You threw me for a total loop, Danny. I didn't think you were coming. Then you barge in just when I'm on a roll—"

"Sorry about that. I couldn't decide whether to come. I had a last-minute epiphany. I've been taking my anger and frustration out on you, when it wasn't your fault. I was hurt that you lied to me, but I should have known you'd keep Carter's secret. She's your best friend. It's just, you're *my* best friend—"

"I am?"

He hit my arm. "You know you are. Since the Bistro days."

"I wanted to tell you about the baby, but Carter—"

"I know. She wouldn't let you. I realize that, and I'm sorry for freezing you out the past few weeks. My whole world felt upside down. But up there"—he gestured to the stage—"we were sizzlin'!"

"Still," I protested, "you were pretty mean-spirited up there."

"Oh, come on, it was all in good fun. Whatever gets a laugh is fair game."

At that moment, Carter came up and put an arm around each of us. "The great comedy duo is back together again! Let's go celebrate. Molly Malone's?"

"Sounds great," Danny said, "but what about the baby?" He put one hand on Carter's not-yet-bulging belly.

"Hey, I can still have a good time even if my body is a booze-free zone."

"You two go," I said. "I'm sure you have a lot to talk about. Besides, my aunts are here and I don't see my cousin, so I may have to see them home to Brooklyn."

"I saw Gerry," Carter said. "He was talking to a guy from the Leno show about booking him and his socks."

I rolled my eyes. "Why can't I have a normal family?"

Danny slapped my back. " 'Cause then we'd have no act!"

He took Carter by the arm. "Hey, Holly, say good night to your aunts for me. I'd go over there, but I haven't gotten my rabies vaccination yet and Aunt Betty looks hungry." He laughed at his joke and bounced toward the door, stopping every few moments to accept a congratulatory slap on the back or high five.

Tom hadn't left his table to join the well-wishers at the stage, so I made my way through the crowd to his table. "I didn't expect to see you here," I said.

"Why didn't you tell me about it? I didn't even know you did stand-up."

"I didn't want you to be here, in case it was awful. As you can see, it can be pretty embarrassing."

He shook his head. "You shouldn't be embarrassed. You were funny. Especially in the beginning, before your partner showed up."

"Really?" I felt myself brighten at the compliment. Then I remembered I was still upset about the subpoena and the fact that he might be the mysterious Writer. "How did you find out about it?"

"There was a flyer on the bulletin board at Starbucks."

Oh yeah. I had plastered my neighborhood with flyers advertising the showcase. I just hadn't counted on Tom seeing one. Maybe he wasn't the Writer after all. "So when you asked me out to dinner tonight, it was a test, to see if I'd tell you about the show."

He shrugged. "I was curious why you would keep it a secret." He took a slow sip of his drink, then said, "It doesn't have anything to do with that other guy, does it? The Writer?"

I blew out air, unsure how to respond.

Betty was waving her scarf in the air and calling, "Yoo-hoo, Holly, over here!" I waved at her and gestured that I'd be over in one minute.

"I have to go say hi to my aunts," I told Tom, "but first I want to tell you that I'm really upset about the subpoena."

"The what?"

"A sheriff came to my apartment today to subpoena me for your custody trial."

"What?" Tom looked genuinely shocked.

"You didn't know?"

"Of course not! My ex-wife must have done it. But I don't know how she could even have found out about you."

"Maybe she's having you followed."

"It doesn't make sense. So we've been on a few dates. What is she trying to prove?"

I shrugged. It didn't add up for me, either. It's not like we were having a torrid affair. Maybe Nicole spilled the beans about her impromptu haircut and her mother was going to use it to paint Tom as an incompetent father. And now, testifying on behalf of the petitioner, Holly Heckerling, otherwise known as the scissor-wielding stranger from Starbucks. "I thought your divorce was settled. Why is she issuing subpoenas?"

He sighed. "She won't sign the final papers. She's not contesting the divorce itself. She's fighting over the custody arrangement. I thought we'd reached an agreement, but now her lawyer is demanding a hearing." He reached over and put his hand over mine. "This doesn't concern you, though. I'll take care of it."

I got to my feet. "This is too complicated. I thought you were divorced, free and clear. But obviously there are still issues to be ironed out, and I don't think I can be in the middle of it."

He brought his fingers to his temples and rubbed as if fighting off a migraine. Almost under his breath, he said, "Don't let her ruin this, too." Then he looked up at me. "I like you, Holly. A lot. I want to give this a chance."

I felt a lump in my throat. I hadn't started this conversation with Tom intending to put an end to our relationship, but right now it seemed like the right thing to do. "I like you, too. But my life is complicated enough without getting in the middle of your divorce. I just can't do it."

I walked away in the direction of my aunts' table, afraid to turn back and look Tom in the face. I leaned down and kissed Kuki on the cheek. She stiffened against my embrace.

Then I stepped over to Betty, whose arms were outstretched in my direction. I leaned down expecting a hug, but instead she reached up, gripped my cheeks, and gave them a painful tweak.

Betty was even bubblier than usual. I assumed her good spirits had more to do with the assemblage of empty glasses in front of her than the evening's entertainment. "I haven't been in a nightclub in ages." She gripped my arm as if to steady herself. "This was a real hoot, Holly."

"I didn't see you guys when the show started," I said. "When did you arrive?"

"Not too late," Betty said.

"Not late enough," Kuki added, between tight lips. Clearly she disapproved of what she'd seen. I dealt with her signs of obvious disapproval in my usual manner, by not asking her outright what she thought. I wasn't going to give her an easy opening. If she wanted to rain on my parade, such as it was, she'd have to be direct.

"Is Gerry here?" I asked.

Betty turned and pointed. "I saw him talking to a gentleman over there. I'm surprised you didn't notice him during the show. He was laughing so hard I thought he'd bust a gasket."

Kuki's lips curled down even farther at the edges. Not only was her niece an embarrassment onstage, but her own son found it amusing.

"I'm glad he enjoyed himself," I said.

"We all did, sweetie! That was something else, seeing you up on stage, with all those people watching, applauding. I'm real proud of you, honey." Betty hiccupped. "I laughed so hard I almost wet myself!"

Kuki rolled her eyes. I congratulated Betty on maintaining bladder control.

Just then Gerry came up behind me and slapped me on the back. "Hey, Hol, that was terrific. I laughed my ass off."

"You didn't mind the jokes about the socks?"

"Hey, there's no such thing as bad publicity. People are talking about the collection! Did you see the *Post*?"

Between the showcase and Monica's injury, I'd forgotten Gerry's urging to pick up a copy of the paper. "Sorry, I've been busy."

He reached into his back pocket and pulled out a laminated square the size of an index card. It was a clipping from the *Post*. I read it aloud:

Director John Landis, in town to receive an award from the Veritas Foundation, arrived fashionably late for his acceptance speech but delighted the crowd at the Waldorf with a tale that anyone living outside Manhattan—where the bizarre is de rigueur—would be hard-pressed to believe. On his way to the luncheon, Landis dropped his car keys down a subway grate and would have been stranded had it not been for the timely arrival of a monkey, who obligingly reached down where human hands wouldn't fit and retrieved the keys. Landis could have rewarded the helpful ape with a kingdom's worth of bananas, but the creature's owner had something else in mind—the director's socks! Landis good-naturedly obliged, taking his socks off in front of the startled crowd, without questioning the young lady's assertion that the socks would be part of an Internet site devoted to the footwear of the rich and famous. Only in New York, kids!

Gerry was beaming as he took the card back and returned it to his pocket. "My Web site is up to nine thousand hits as of a few hours ago. People are talking, and I owe it all to you, Holly."

I gulped, taking it all in. "Tallulah's a monkey, not an ape," I said. "People always get them mixed up."

Gerry shook his head. "It's the *Post,* not the *Encyclopaedia Britannica.* Don't take it so seriously."

He'd laminated the clipping and I was the one taking it too seriously.

I still couldn't figure out how Gerry was going to make any money off his collection, but he'd obviously succeeded in piquing people's curiosity. He was so thoroughly enjoying his fifteen minutes of fame that I hated to bring up the subject of Monica Broccoli, but the guilt over possibly maiming her had been eating at me all day. "That's great, but . . . how's Monica? Did you get in to see her at the hospital?"

Both my aunts spoke at once. "The hospital?" Betty gasped. "Good Lord, what did you do now?" Kuki asked.

"We were having a disagreement and she fell down the stairs."

"Oh, heavens!" Kuki said. "She's so tall and lanky, she probably came down pretty hard."

"Like a tossed broccoli salad," Betty added.

Kuki wagged a finger in my direction. "You better get your affairs in order in case she sues you. Do you have money for an attorney? If you still lived at home, this kind of thing wouldn't happen."

Betty nodded in agreement. "Yeah, on account of there's no staircase, just the front stoop."

Gerry waved his hand dismissively. "She won't sue, Ma. If I know Monica, she's fine. She's tough. She takes a lickin' and keeps on tickin'."

"So you haven't seen her?" I asked.

He shook his head. "I couldn't get any information from the hospital, and I've been calling her apartment all day. She's not answering."

That's probably because she's in traction, I thought.

The club lights dimmed. I glanced over at Tom's table, but it was empty. A waitress was wiping it down. Most of the other tables had also been cleared. "We'd better go," I said.

Roger, the club owner, was making his way toward us, carrying a large cardboard box and a spiral-bound book—items I'd asked him to hold backstage for me before I went on. He congratulated me on the good turnout and receptive crowd.

"Thanks. I'm sorry if we're keeping you from closing."

"Take your time," he said. "I just didn't want you to forget your stuff."

After striking out at the hospital, I'd taken the subway to Brooklyn and gone to Kuki's house, letting myself in when no one answered the door. It took me an hour of sifting through dusty boxes in the attic before I found what I was looking for: the guest book from my grandmother's funeral. Carter's reminder that I had first met Monica Broccoli at the funeral prompted my realization that it was likely she had signed her name—her *real* name—in the guest book. With barely enough time to make it back to the Village to change before the showcase, I'd grabbed the book without looking through it. As I was about to close the door behind me, I'd spotted the familiar box containing my father's belongings and decided I'd never have a better opportunity to find out what was inside, since

Kuki was usually hovering over me whenever I went into her attic. So I tucked it under my arm along with the guest book and made my escape.

Now, standing in front of my aunts with the evidence of my attic raid, I feared reprisal from Kuki. Surely she recognized the box she'd striven to keep from me for so many years. But if so, she said nothing.

I clutched the box and guest book protectively. "The club is closing and I need to talk to Gerry for a few minutes," I told them. "Why don't we all go out for some coffee?"

Kuki stood and grabbed her handbag. "Coffee at this hour? Nonsense. Just help us into a cab and we'll be fine."

As Gerry helped Kuki and a still-tipsy Betty into a Brooklyn-bound taxi, I stood on the sidewalk waving good-bye. If I kept my distance, Kuki wouldn't feel compelled to offer her true opinion of my performance and I wouldn't feel compelled to choke the living daylights out of her. Not that I'd be spared her analysis in the end. I knew that, after a few days, Kuki would find a way to work into a conversation her opinion that I was wasting my life in comedy and I'd be well advised to keep my cosmetology license up-to-date. But by then I hoped I'd have mentally sorted out all the angst of the past few weeks and I'd be better able to deal with Kuki's criticism.

Before he slammed the cab door shut, however, Gerry did what Gerry does best in such circumstances. He stuck his foot in it.

"So, Ma," he said with a grin, "what did ya think of Holly's show? She rocked, didn't she?"

Over the noise of the passing traffic, I was able to hear each crisp syllable of her reply. "I just thank God her mother wasn't here to see it."

14

I'm No Superhero

For the first time since the introduction of the Writer into my life, I didn't check the milk cubby first thing when I got home. I'd taken the bold move of inviting him to the showcase in hopes that I'd finally learn his identity. But either he didn't show up, which meant he didn't have the least bit of interest in meeting me, or he was there and had his own reasons for not introducing himself. Like maybe the fact that he already knew me. I thought again of Carter's suggestion that Tom and the Writer were one and the same. Certain elements fit—like the fact that when the Writer was on vacation, I didn't hear from Tom that week either. But other things didn't make sense. Like why would he keep his identity a secret?

I didn't have time to puzzle it all out now. I had to solve the Monica Broccoli mystery once and for all. I'd been harboring such guilt over her fall—not to mention her breakup with Gerry—that I had to set it straight, if only so I could get back to obsessing over my own life and forget about hers.

Gerry was poking his fingers into Tallulah's cage. She had her belly pressed up against the side, allowing him to stroke her. I popped a few raisins into her cage and promised to give her a surprise later if only she'd behave while Gerry and I got to work.

I opened the spiral-bound guest book and set it on the kitchen table. My grandmother was beloved in the community and her funeral had been very well attended. This was going to take a while. I grabbed a couple of sodas from the fridge and snagged a bag of gummy bears from Tallulah's suitcase.

"O.K., I'm going to read off names of people I don't know," I told Gerry. "You tell me if any of them sound familiar." I scrolled down the first several entries—mostly relatives and neighbors—until I reached an unfamiliar woman's name. "Pamela Loveday?"

Gerry's forehead scrunched in thought. Then he said, "I think she's one of the bingo ladies from church."

"You sure?"

He shrugged. "No, but I know that's not Monica's name."

"How can you tell?"

"Loveday? I wouldn't have forgotten that. I'd have had a field day with that name."

"O.K., O.K. How 'bout Tricia Kokoszka?"

"How do you spell it?"

"Does it matter?"

He looked over my shoulder at the page. "Looks like old lady handwriting. Why don't you skip the ones where the handwriting looks like they were having a stroke when they signed the book."

I skipped past a few names I recognized as former customers at the barbershop and stopped at the last entry on the page. "The handwriting looks young, but that's an old lady name if I ever heard one. Esther Collins." I shook my head and began to turn the page.

"That's it!" Gerry yelled, grabbing the book from my hands.

"What?"

"I remember now! That's her. Esther Collins."

He kissed my cheek, grabbed a handful of Tallulah's gummy bears, and dashed out the door.

For the first time, I noticed that the message light on my answering machine was blinking, but I uncharacteristically chose to ignore it. I was worn-out, physically and emotionally, and there was only one thing I wanted to do before falling into bed.

I pulled a chair up to Tallulah's cage and unfastened the lock. She hopped onto my lap and let me clip on her leash. Then she began combing her fingers through my hair. She'd begun this grooming ritual a few days ago; every time I returned to the apartment, she'd spend a few minutes carefully picking through my hair as though removing insects or debris. I felt honored by her attention. Since grooming is a major form of social bonding for nonhuman primates, and monkeys prefer to groom higher-ranking individuals, I thought it might be an indication that she held me in good esteem. Then she reached the back of my head, where I'd vainly attempted to hide the ragged patch of shorn hair, and I could swear she uttered a disapproving "Tsk, tsk."

As she plucked at the patch with vigor, I reached for the phone book and flipped through the pages until I found the number for St. Vincent's. "Hello," I said to the tired-sounding operator who answered, "do you have a patient there named Esther Collins?"

"Hold please."

A few moments later, the operator returned. "Treated and released."

I breathed a sigh of relief. That Monica had been released already was definitely a good sign.

"Can you tell me if her leg was broken?"

"I cannot release patient information over the phone."

"O.K., O.K. Could you put me through to room 328?"

"One moment, please."

The phone rang once; then a woman's voice answered. I recognized it at once. "Mrs. Lipton? Hi, it's Holly Heckerling. Tallulah's . . . uh . . . babysitter."

"Hello, Holly. David told me you came to visit him today."

"Yes. How's he doing?"

"Oh, fine. The doctor might release him tomorrow."

"That's great! Can I talk to him?"

"Sorry, he just fell asleep. I was just about to go home when the phone rang. I only answered so the ringing wouldn't wake him."

"I hate to disturb him. It's just . . . I thought he might want to say good night to Tallulah. I'm sure she'd like to hear his voice."

There was a pause, as though Mrs. Lipton was considering. Then she cleared her throat and said, "Oh, I'll wake him up for that."

A few moments later, David was on the line, sounding groggy but curious. I said a quick hello and turned the phone over to Tallulah. She licked the receiver, then threw it on the floor. O.K., so maybe I was giving the monkey too much credit, thinking she would know what to do with a telephone. I retrieved the receiver and held it up to her ear. I could hear David's voice coming through the other end, talking to Tallulah in a singsongy voice. Tallulah became still. She regarded the phone intently, then began noisily chattering and bouncing up and down. She grabbed the receiver from my hands and began rubbing it vigorously all over her body.

I suppressed a laugh. Tallulah was clearly overjoyed to hear her master's voice, even if her method of expressing it was a bit unusual. I tried to take the phone from her, but she would have none of it. I watched a while longer, as she squealed, bounced, and finally, settled down on the floor, cradling the phone in her arms.

I kneeled down next to Tallulah and put my ear to the phone. David was singing what sounded like a lullaby. Suddenly feeling like a third wheel, I crept away silently.

* * *

After getting ready for bed, I returned to find Tallulah fast asleep on the floor, the phone receiver dismantled beside her. I wondered whether she'd merely grown bored or if she'd taken the receiver apart trying to find the source of David's voice. In either case, I didn't mind this latest act of destruction. In fact, I thought it was kind of sweet.

At some point during the past week, the tide had turned in my relationship with Tallulah. I no longer thought of her as a meddlesome monkey who was always in the middle of things. I was beginning to think of her as a friend. I remembered Mrs. Lipton's announcement that David might be released from the hospital tomorrow. While this was undoubtedly good news, I had to admit feeling a little sad. Tallulah's departure would leave a monkey-sized hole in my life.

As I lifted Tallulah back into her cage, I noticed something shiny buried in some shredded newspaper near the back of her cage. What has she stolen from me now? I wondered, digging through the paper until I came upon the object in question. It was a small silver medallion. A woman, probably a saint, was pictured on one side. I drew a blank on the saint's name. A wave of Catholic guilt passed over me as I remembered my mother struggling to teach me about the lives of the saints at a time when I was more interested in the adventures of the Teenage Mutant Ninja Turtles.

I'd never seen the medallion before and couldn't imagine who had been the victim of Tallulah's latest act of thievery. I stuck it in a kitchen drawer, out of her usual roaming range.

As I headed toward the bedroom, I spied the box of my father's stuff sitting on the kitchen table. Though I'd lugged it all the way from Brooklyn, my curiosity over its contents wasn't strong enough to overcome my extreme exhaustion. I carried the box to the hall closet and put it in on a shelf. It had been collecting dust for over fifteen years; it could wait one more day.

*   *   *

Finally, I went into the pantry and checked the milk cubby. I felt a rush of emotion when I saw the now familiar handwriting on the manila envelope. Another installment from the Writer. I carefully opened the envelope and withdrew its contents. There was no note accompanying the half dozen lined yellow pages. Nothing to give a clue as to the Writer's identity or whether or not he'd taken the bait and attended my showcase. Nothing to indicate when he'd be back to pick up the finished job.

At first, I'd blamed my own carelessness for the fact that I didn't know who my mysterious client was. But now that I was on my third job for him I was certain that he was purposely keeping his identity secret. He never knocked on my door when he was picking up or dropping off work and never enclosed any identifying information with his manuscripts.

I quickly skimmed the lined, dog-eared pages. In this installment, the Writer described his difficulty handling the day-to-day domestic duties of caring for his young daughter in the weeks after his wife died. *She needs me to be strong,* he wrote midway down the second page, *to shoulder the burden of our grief so that she can go on being a child, carefree and protected. But I cannot absorb her pain. I cannot lessen her sorrow. I cannot diminish for one moment her suffering because my own is too much to bear.*

Preoccupied as I was by my own suffering, I was in no mood to read the Writer's innermost thoughts. I put the pages back in the manila envelope and left it on my desk. Then I crawled into bed, pulled the covers up to my chin, and started to cry. I wasn't sure what was making me so miserable. By all accounts, the showcase had been a success. Danny and Carter had left the club together— a hopeful sign that they would work things out. And now that Gerry knew Monica's name, they'd probably get back together, too. Even his harebrained sock scheme seemed to be picking up steam. Everyone was happy. Except me.

Kuki's parting remark had stung, but I was used to her barbs and rarely let them get to me. Tallulah's impending departure may have had something to do with my funk, but although I would miss her, I knew she belonged with David. And, while I understood her importance to him, I still thought that the only monkeys that truly belonged in Manhattan were the plastic animatronic types that decorated theme restaurants and toy stores.

Lacking other obvious causes, I deduced that my malaise must have owed its origin to my once-again dead-as-a-doornail love life. A week ago, I'd been torn between Tom and the Writer, and though the latter relationship existed solely in my own fantasies, it still hurt to see the daydream end. Come to think of it, my relationship with Tom had also been the stuff of fantasy. From the moment I first spotted him in Starbucks, I'd created an idealized image of him based on his interactions with his daughter. I could see myself fitting neatly into the hole left by Nicole's mother. I'd be the superhero who saved their world from cocoa stains and split ends. But in reality, bad hair and spilled cocoa were the least of Tom's problems. He was embroiled in a seemingly bitter custody battle with a seemingly bitter ex-wife, whose departure had surely left more than a neat little hole. I had done the right thing, putting an end to our relationship before it got too serious.

Then why did I feel so bad?

Bunking with Betty

The following week, my already crowded apartment gained three new residents. My aunt Betty had had a fight with Uncle Bernie and announced that she was moving in with me. As much as I loved Betty, I couldn't imagine sharing my cramped apartment with her, even temporarily. But before I had a chance to talk her out of it, she was on my front stoop, unloading several suitcases from a taxicab. The number and dimensions of the suitcases made me severely doubt the veracity of her statement that she planned to stay "just a few days."

During their thirty-five-year marriage, Betty had left my uncle on more than a few occasions. Their spats usually lasted no more than a few days—which is about how long it took Uncle Bernie to work his way through the prepared casseroles Betty left in the fridge. This time, however, he was insisting he'd had enough. What had pushed him over the edge, he said, was Betty's blathering on about what kind of jewelry she would have his body turned into after he died. She was torn between a diamond pendant and a pair of teardrop earrings. Neither idea sat well with Bernie, who preferred that his remains be quietly interred at Green-Wood Cemetery after his demise.

"He never buys me anything now that he's alive," Betty told me as I hauled her luggage up the six flights to my apartment. "The least he could do is let me have something pretty after he goes."

Normally, in these situations, Betty would stay with Aunt Kuki, but this time Kuki refused to take her in. "On account of she doesn't like me to walk around the house naked in front of Leo," Betty explained to me. Betty was suffering from a severe case of psoriasis, a condition that caused her skin to itch uncontrollably.

"Clothing irritates my skin," she said, tugging at her blouse as though she was going to rip it off right there in the stairwell. "I can't stand to wear anything for more than an hour or two."

I had tried to tell her over the phone that I, too, refused to ac-commodate her desire for round-the-clock nudity, especially since I regularly had clients who came to my apartment. A few of my more skittish hairstyling customers had been put off by Tallulah's pres-ence in my dining room—a naked, scaly-skinned old lady would definitely be bad for business. But Betty didn't register my protests. She thanked me and hung up the phone, scurrying off to pack her bags while I sat wondering how, once again, I had somehow "agreed" to something without actually saying yes.

The morning before Betty arrived, Virginia at PAPS had called to tell me that Armand, a man in my neighborhood whose pets I watched whenever he was hospitalized, had died of acute kidney failure. Armand's brother, Jean-Claude, took in his dog, Fritz, and Virginia wanted to know if I'd adopt his bunny, Jack, and a gold-fish, a new and apparently unnamed acquisition. I accepted without hesitation, my heart saddened at Armand's sudden passing. Be-cause I knew how he loved his animals, it was the least I could do to provide them a good home. And since Tallulah had left, they could be assured a relatively sane and stable environment.

Tallulah's departure had been strangely anticlimactic. Mrs. Lipton and Virginia had come to pick her up the morning after the showcase, packing up her cage and suitcases with a brisk efficiency that belied the emotional impact of the event. Saying good-bye, I fought back tears, but Tallulah seemed unfazed. She cocked her head, stuck her tongue out in my direction, and was gone.

Tallulah's absence meant that Grouch was once again king of the manor. His dignity reclaimed, he no longer spent his days hiding under my bed. Now he strutted around the apartment hissing at nothing in particular, as though reasserting his dominance to whatever unseen beings might want to rise up and issue a challenge. Fortunately, Jack the bunny and the goldfish I'd named Whoopi would pose no threat to his supremacy. I wasn't so sure about Aunt Betty.

As I dragged her suitcases into my apartment, I tried to fight off a growing sense of dread about Betty's visit. My most recent roommate had been a monkey, after all. Surely my dealings with Tallulah had prepared me to handle anything Betty could throw my way.

For someone who was presently averse to wearing clothes, Betty sure brought a lot of them. In anticipation of her arrival, I had emptied two drawers in my bureau, but it wasn't nearly enough. I had to empty two additional drawers and a third of my closet to accommodate her belongings.

Once she was unpacked, she began taking stock of her surroundings. "Is this where I'll sleep?" she asked, pointing to my sofa.

"No, you'll take my bed. I'll sleep out here."

"Nonsense! I can't kick you out of your bed. This is your home."

Ordinarily I might have given in, but I'd already contemplated the possibility of stumbling through the living room during the night on my way to the bathroom and tripping over Betty, spread out au naturel on my sofa bed. Much better to let her take the bedroom, where she could display her wares behind closed doors.

As Betty was unpacking her things, the phone rang. I hoped it was Uncle Bernie, calling to beg her to come back. No such luck. It was Monica Broccoli, now known to the world by her given name, Esther Collins. My stomach churned at the sound of her voice. I hadn't seen her since the paramedics whisked her away after her tumble down my staircase. Though Gerry insisted she wasn't planning on pressing charges, I still feared some kind of reprisal would be forthcoming.

"What do you want?" I asked.

"I need a favor."

A foreboding sense of déjà vu drifted over me. "I'm booked up today. No time for a perm or a haircut. And I am definitely not removing your cast again."

"It's not that."

"And no more snakes. The zoo is full."

"It's nothing like that, Holly. It's for your cousin."

While the thought of doing a favor for Monica Broccoli filled me with fear and dread, helping my cousin was another matter entirely. I let out a sigh. "What is it?"

"It's his sock thing. I know it's crazy, but he believes in it, so I have to support him."

"Of course. Marry the man, marry the sock empire."

"All he talks about is how you got John Landis's socks for him. You're like his hero because of that. He even made it in the Post."

Actually it was Tallulah who'd been immortalized on the paper's gossip page, but why quibble. "So . . . ?"

"So I want to do something like that for him, to help him with his business and show that I'm behind him a hundred percent."

"Okay. But what does that have to do with me?"

"That superstud in your building. You could get me his socks, for starters."

"Not that again. I've told you both I'm not stealing my neighbor's socks. Besides, you said *you* wanted to do something for his business. How would me getting Brian's socks show Gerry how much you're devoted to him?"

" 'Cause I'll be the one who gives them to him. It'll be an engagement present. You know Kuki's throwing us an engagement party Friday night. I'll give them to him there."

"Why don't you go hang out at Sardi's? I'm sure you could charm the socks off of any celebrity that comes in."

"I would do that if I could, but I'm stuck in this cast, thanks to you."

Oh, good grief. Monica was playing the guilt card, but it wasn't going to work this time. I groaned.

"Is that a no?"

Ding, ding, ding, give the lady a prize.

She breathed a heavy sigh. "I was going to wait to ask you this Friday. At the engagement party. But I might as well do it now." She paused dramatically, then continued. "Will you be my maid of honor?"

I smelled a rat, and it wasn't Felix. Monica and I had never been close; surely she had at least a dozen dancer friends she'd rather have stand beside her on her wedding day in a hideous hot pink dress.

"Gee, Monica—I mean, Esther—I'm honored. But it doesn't change the fact that I'm not giving you Brian's socks."

"That's not why I'm asking," she pouted. "You're going to be like my cousin-in-law or something. We're family."

And there's no escaping family, I thought, casting a glance at Betty, who was buck naked except for a pair of hot pink granny panties.

"I'll see what I can do," I said, knowing I'd live to regret it. "Good-bye, Monica."

"My name's—" I hung up before she could finish her sentence.

* * *

As soon as she was settled, I left Betty alone so I could run some errands. Business had been busy in the days since the showcase. I'd had a record-breaking week for haircuts and typed several patient files for my psychiatrist client, Dr. Handelman. I'd even sold some of my handcrafted jewelry to one of my wash-and-set clients and picked up some extra money running errands for Mrs. Mete, whose rheumatism was acting up, making it impossible for her to hike the seven floors to her apartment. This morning I had to pick up her medication and a few personal items from the pharmacy.

From there, I stopped in at Starbucks to get my daily caffeine fix and catch up with Carter. As expected, she and Danny had reconciled after the showcase, and they'd been so busy making plans for their future together that neither had had much time for me. Not that I was complaining. I was so relieved to be on speaking terms again with both my best friends that I'd take what little face time with them I could get.

By the time I reached the front of the line, Carter had my Frappuccino prepared and waiting on the counter. "Saw you coming," she said, taking my five and handing me back five singles. She looked ragged and tired.

"You O.K.? Is it morning sickness?"

She shook her head. "I'm sooo tired all the time, and it's killing me to be around coffee all day and not drink any. Sometimes I just sniff the coffee grounds, hoping to get a buzz." That would explain the little brown flecks stuck to her upper lip.

"Take a break?" I asked.

She gestured toward the line forming behind me. "Can't. But I'm off in two hours. I'll come up."

"O.K., but be forewarned: There may be a naked old lady in my living room." I took a sip of my drink and looked around the store. "Danny in?"

"He's on a delivery. But I'll bring him with me. We both want to talk to you." She bit her lip and I sensed she was holding something back.

"What is it?" I asked. "You guys getting married?"

She shook her head, then leaned over and addressed the next customer in line. "Can I get something started for you?" As she scribbled the order on a paper coffee cup, she glanced up at me. "Can't talk now. Later."

"O.K.," I said, stepping aside to make room for the guy behind me. Carter set his drink on the counter, but didn't let go. She stared, trancelike, as she white-knuckled the cup, and for a moment I feared she was going to arm wrestle the guy for his triple-shot espresso.

I climbed the seven flights to Mrs. Mete's apartment, grateful that my yoga-induced groin injury had healed. The hike took enough out of me as it is—I was amazed that Mrs. Mete had been able to manage it all these years.

By the time I hit the fifth-floor landing, she was already looking down over her banister, watching my progress. "The young couple in 4A got some new furniture. Looks classy. He musta got a raise or something."

I looked up and nodded, unwilling to contribute to her latest gossip report, and unable to speak anyway, due to my exertion.

"And you know the guy in 6C? His wife's a ballet dancer? She's away on tour and wouldn't you know he had a young lady over last night?" She paused as though allowing ample time for this latest tidbit to float down and reach me on the floor below.

"It's not right, I tell you," she continued.

I took a deep breath and rasped, "Maybe it was his sister."

"Hmph! Word in the building is he's taking an acting class and she's his scene partner."

I shrugged. "I'll buy that."

"You're so naive, Holly. But I've lived a lot longer than you. I know what really goes on. I can take one look at a person and have him pegged."

I nodded in agreement, not wanting to bring up the fact that Mrs. Mete once had *me* pegged as a drug dealer, after observing several of my clients picking up and dropping off packages in my milk cubby, sometimes late at night. She spread word of my illicit activities to everyone in the building, earning me strange looks and disbelieving stares from several of my neighbors. I finally learned what was going on after a young college student approached me in the laundry room and asked if I'd sell him a dime bag of powder. Thinking he was trying to bum some laundry detergent, I offered him a cup of Tide, but insisted he keep his money.

Eventually, Mrs. Mete conceded that neither my clients nor I looked like drug fiends, and she came to believe that I was carrying on a legitimate business. Ironically, delivering Mrs. Mete's assorted prescription drugs brought me closer to being a "dealer" than any of my prior activities.

I reached her door, breathless, and handed over a bulging package of pills and ointments.

She reached into her purse and pulled out a twenty. "Care to come in for some coffee?"

"No, thanks. I just came from Starbucks."

"Eesh." She grimaced. "Four bucks for a cuppa coffee. Well, I guess it's your money. You can do what you want with it."

From downstairs, we heard the asthmatic buzz of the front door and someone pushing it open. Mrs. Mete pushed past me, gripped the banister with both hands, and leaned over, her upper body dangling dangerously far over the railing. I reached out and grabbed her by the arms to prevent her from taking a nosedive.

"Careful, Mrs. Mete!"

She hushed me, then scrunched her face up in a look of deep concentration. I heard lumbering footsteps climbing the first flight, then a jangling of keys. A few moments later, a door opened and closed. Mrs. Mete leaned back and released her grip on the railing.

She talked in a whisper. "That was the big fellow in 2D." She glanced at her watch. "Home in the middle of the day. Musta been fired from his job at the dry cleaners. I wouldn't be surprised. Twice this week he was late for work. Heard him running out the door at five minutes after nine, cursing himself."

I shrugged my shoulders disinterestedly. Mrs. Mete was always passing along this kind of minutiae about my neighbors, despite my protests that I really didn't want to know anything about them. Aside from Brian, I'd never made friends with anyone in my building, and he was more of a client than a friend. Manhattan was filled with strange people; I always thought it was best to keep a polite but safe distance. I hoped that when I reached Mrs. Mete's age I would have enough other interests that I didn't become engrossed in the lives of my neighbors—tracking their comings and goings, hirings and firings, breakups, late-night rendezvous, and presumed drug deliveries. What possible relevance or value could there be in having that kind of information, anyway?

As I considered this, a dangerous thought lurked in the back of my head. I tried to dismiss it, but, seized by a sudden impulse, I abandoned my vow to never fuel Mrs. Mete's gossipmongering fire.

"Do you watch everyone who comes in and out of the building?" I asked her.

"Certainly not!" She looked offended. "Just when there's nothing good on TV, or when people make too much noise, or if I *happen* to be at my door. And if someone buzzes me to let them in to the building, I have a right to know who I'm letting in, so I take a quick peek."

In other words, she probably witnessed eighty to ninety percent of the traffic in and out of the building.

"There's a guy who's been coming by the last few weeks. Dropping off work for me in my milk cubby. I've never seen him and I was wondering—"

"Big manila envelopes?" she interjected.

I nodded, trying to contain my excitement. "You've seen him? What does he look like?"

"Suspicious. He raised my hackles, creeping up the stairs like he didn't want to be seen."

"Really? But what does he look like?" I felt my face burning. Now was my chance to find out if the mysterious Writer and Tom were one and the same. But with the information so close at hand I suddenly wasn't sure I wanted to know.

She shrugged. "Nothing special. He's kind of medium."

"Medium build?"

She nodded. "Medium height, medium weight."

"What color hair?"

She looked thoughtful. "He was wearing a hat. And hunched over. I didn't see his face."

My heart sank. This was going nowhere. Maybe it would help if I described Tom. "If it's the same guy I think it is, he's got dark hair, brown eyes, and sometimes he has that sexy two-day stubble thing going on. He's about five nine, five ten, in his late thirties."

"That's not him. I'd put this guy in his fifties, easy. Something about the way he walks."

I sighed, defeated. I wasn't sure how much faith I could put in Mrs. Mete's statement, but it seemed to imply that Tom was not the Writer. I trudged down the stairs toward my apartment, no closer to finding out who the Writer was.

On the way down, I passed Brian, who was dressed in sweats and carrying a gym bag. "Good workout?" I asked.

He nodded. "How's Miss Tallulah?"

The corners of my mouth turned down. "She's gone back to her owner."

He raised both eyebrows. "I didn't get a chance to say good-bye."

"It happened pretty fast."

"Well, I'll miss the old girl."

I nodded sadly. "So will I."

I started down the stairs again but stopped when Brian called to me, "Hey, do you have a few minutes to take a look at my computer? It's freezing up on me again and I don't want to bring it to a repair shop."

I'd forgotten about my promise to play computer tech to spare Brian from allowing a real technician to peek into his probably pornographic files. "Right now?"

He flashed me the same picture-perfect smile that had once graced the cover of *Soap Opera Digest.* "If you're not too busy. Last night I was working on something for my creative writing class and the damn thing died on me before I had a chance to save. Probably the first decent thing I've written, too."

While computer repair was not my forte, I had two hours to kill before Carter's shift ended and I was in no hurry to renew my acquaintance with Aunt Betty's bare breasts. "Sure. I just can't promise anything. I'll give it a try."

"That's all I ask."

I followed him back up the stairs and waited while he unlocked his door. "Come on in." He dumped his gym bag on the counter and led me to a desk in the corner, where a battered IBM clone was making an odd whirring sound.

"I left it on all night," he said, "hoping it would magically unfreeze by morning. But no such luck."

"Does it always make that noise?" I asked.

He nodded. "For a while now. But it worked fine until last week."

I sighed. It was obvious that Brian's computer was on its last legs. If it had been a horse, someone would have put it out of its misery by now. "I'll see what I can do."

I rebooted the machine and took a deep breath. PC repair wasn't my area of expertise, but I used to work on a machine just like Brian's, and I knew my way around a hard drive.

As I went to work examining the system files and scanning for viruses, Brian disappeared into the bedroom. Remembering Monica's entreaty that I steal a pair of Brian's socks, I stole a long glance around the apartment. The decor was sparse but tasteful. Everything was tidy. Unlike the apartments of most single men I knew, there were no stacks of pizza boxes or newspapers by the door, no dirty laundry piled in the corner or on the sofa. No socks lying haphazardly on the floor. Most likely Brian's socks were all lined up neatly in a dresser drawer in his bedroom.

Having redeemed myself with Gerry by my acquisition of John Landis's socks, I told myself there was no need for me to try to obtain Brian's. Monica could find another engagement present. It wasn't my responsibility. Still, as I defragmented Brian's hard drive, I found myself entertaining thoughts of thievery.

Kramer nudged his head against my leg and I bent to scratch his head. "Hey, big guy," I said, as the cat flopped onto his back and began purring.

Brian emerged from his bedroom, having changed into khaki shorts and a tank top. He walked over to the window near the desk. "I'm sorry it's so hot in here," he said, drawing the curtains and opening the window wide. "It gets stuffy if I keep the windows closed." He turned on a ceiling fan and within minutes the place began to cool.

I looked out and noted that he had the same view as me, only from a slightly higher angle. We were both in the back of the building, facing the back side of another apartment building to the south. The same smell of rotten garbage wafted up from the alley below.

I returned my attention to the computer. It didn't take long to pinpoint the problem: Brian's old model lacked the storage capacity required to hold the numerous files he'd downloaded from the Internet, mostly JPEGs and GIFs from gay porn sites, which he kept in a subdirectory labeled PRIVATE. Brian sheepishly pointed out which directories contained his important documents, then gave me carte blanche to delete as many other files as necessary to get the machine running again.

"I'm gonna bop down to the market. You want me to pick you up a Coke or something?" Brian asked.

"No, thanks."

He grabbed his keys off the counter and was gone.

I sat still for a moment, considering. The market was directly across the street from our building, but since Brian lived on the seventh floor, he'd be gone for a while. Plenty of time for me to surreptitiously seize his socks.

I shot up from the desk and darted toward the bedroom. I opened the door and slipped inside the stylish boudoir, pausing only momentarily to admire his prints of vintage movie posters. A large mahogany bureau abutted the king-sized bed. A crystal frame atop the bureau held a photo of Brian and his lover, Patrick, a model I'd met once or twice. I hastily crossed to the bureau and opened the first drawer. It was filled with T-shirts, all neatly folded and arranged in symmetrical stacks. The next drawer held a similar assortment of shorts. I was just about to reach for the knob of the third drawer down when Brian's voice stopped me cold.

"What are you doing?"

Damn. I knew Brian was athletic, but I'd seriously miscalculated his agility if he'd managed to make it down seven flights and back in the same time it took me to traverse his one-bedroom apartment.

I froze, my outstretched arm betraying my criminal intentions. I turned to face Brian, who was standing in the doorway and regarding me warily. My heart pounded in my chest as I wondered what penalty petty larceny carried in the state of New York.

"Um, I, well . . ." I hedged, silently cursing myself for having acted impulsively. From now on, Gerry would have to score his own socks. I wasn't getting involved. "I . . . wanted to see Kramer. I thought I saw him come in here."

He raised one eyebrow. "Kramer's on the sofa. I'm surprised you didn't see him."

"Oh!" I feigned surprise and quickly retreated to the living room, Brian close on my heels.

I planted myself on the couch next to the cat. "Changed your mind about the market?" I asked, affecting a nonchalant tone.

"Forgot my wallet," he said, crossing to the counter and fishing it out of his gym bag. "Luckily I remembered before I got too far."

"That *is* lucky." I nodded, forcing a fake smile.

Brian pocketed his wallet but showed no signs of leaving, his trust in me having evaporated along with my moral rectitude.

After a few minutes of obligatory cat scratching, I'd managed to regain my composure, if not my dignity. I returned to the computer and finished cleaning up the hard drive. Brian slipped into his bedroom, no doubt to check his drawers for missing items. A few moments later his phone rang. I heard him answer; then his bedroom door shut.

As I dragged file after pornographic file to Brian's electronic recycle bin, I began to wish I had asked Brian to bring me a Coke. It was an unusually hot day and the apartment was stuffy despite the whirring ceiling fan and occasional waft of warm air coming through the window. I got up from the computer and went into Brian's kitchen. As I filled a glass with tap water, I spied his gym bag sitting on the counter. The bag was partially unzipped, and through the opening, I could see a pair of gray sweat socks. I stopped in my tracks, tantalized by their nearness.

Ignoring every rational impulse in my brain, I reached into the bag and snatched the socks. An illicit thrill surged through my body as I clutched them to my chest. Now I just had to hide them. I was wearing sweatpants and a formfitting T-shirt. No pockets on my person, and my purse was all the way on the other side of the apartment, by the front door. I could hear Brian's muffled voice coming through his bedroom door. I kept my eyes trained on the door as I tippy-toed toward my purse. I was halfway across the apartment when the bedroom door popped open and Brian came out, cradling the phone to his ear.

"All right, Manny. Catch you later," he said into the phone.

Panic seized me. Brian may have believed my excuse for poking through his bedroom earlier, but there was no way I could talk my way out of this one. With no time to get the socks back into the gym bag, I was stuck with a hot potato in my hands. I looked around the neat apartment. There were no piles of clutter, no potted plant or trash can within reach, no place to stash the socks without them sticking out like a sore thumb.

I spun around so that my back was toward Brian. Then I reached under my T-shirt and stuck the socks the only place I could think of: my bra.

"Holly?"

I turned back toward him, my breasts jutting out unevenly in front of me. "I'm just about done with your computer." I spoke quickly, hoping to deflect his attention from my suddenly voluptuous chest.

"I streamlined the hard drive and cleared up about two gigs of storage space. I was able to salvage most of your documents. A couple files were corrupted though. If you want to download any more photos, you should upgrade to a better machine."

He nodded sheepishly. If he noticed that I'd gone up several cup sizes since I'd arrived, he said nothing. I took comfort in the fact that Brian was probably not accustomed to checking out women's breasts.

As I was leaving, he handed me a couple of folded twenties and awkwardly intoned, "Let's keep this between us." I wasn't entirely sure if he was referring to his cache of computer porn or my being caught red-handed in his inner sanctum, but I readily agreed.

I was as eager to vacate the scene of my crime as Brian must have been to see me go, but something stopped me just short of the front door. A small bookcase stood to one side of Brian's entryway, its shelves filled with paperbacks neatly aligned by height. I'd set my purse atop the case when I arrived. As I stooped to pick it up, my eyes fell on a large manila envelope sitting on one of the shelves. I'd only managed a quick glance at it before Brian ushered me into the hall, but I was certain of what I'd seen. The front of the envelope bore a single word in all-block letters: HOLLY.

I stood in the hallway for a long moment, too shocked to move. *Brian* was the Writer? My homosexual neighbor, the soap opera star, was the author of the passages that had so captured my imagination? But why would he be writing about a dead wife and motherless daughter? I guess it was fiction, after all. It had seemed so real, so convincing. Or maybe I had just read too much into it because of the parallels to my own life. Brian had mentioned something about a creative writing class. The impassioned prose I had gotten myself so worked up about, that had kept me up nights fantasizing about the man who had written it, that had caused me to hold back in my relationship to Tom . . . was nothing more than Brian's *homework*?

But why had he kept it a secret? Why wouldn't Brian just ask me straight out to do his typing, as he'd asked me to fix his computer and babysit his cat? Why the secrecy?

I descended the staircase in a daze, my elation at having acquired Brian's socks instantly dissipated, replaced by shock and embarrassment. Brian had been present at my comedy showcase and had heard Danny tease me about my infatuation with the mystery Writer. My infatuation with *him*.

I unlocked the door to my apartment, momentarily forgetting that earlier that morning I had acquired a roommate. I remembered the moment the door swung open and I was greeted by a smell I could best describe as Bengay mixed with mothballs. Aunt Betty was standing stark naked in my kitchen, poking her head into my refrigerator. She turned when I entered, blotchy, sagging flesh hanging loosely on her small frame. I averted my eyes, uncomfortable with the unabashed nakedness of my octogenarian aunt. "Hi, Aunt Betty," I said, addressing the ceiling.

"There you are, sweetie. I was just looking for something to fix us for lunch." She had her head in the freezer now. She pulled out a pair of Ziploc Baggies and held them up. "I was going to take a few of these out to thaw, but I wasn't sure how you prepare them."

I snatched the Baggies from her and put them back in the freezer. "Those are rats! They're for the snake."

"Oh, thank goodness. I've heard stories about how you starving artists live. But then I figured, when in France . . ."

"I haven't had a chance to go shopping this week." More like this *year*. "We'll order in. But you'll have to put some clothes on." I wondered if we'd score any freebies from Dan, the deliveryman from the Hong Kong Palace, if Betty answered the door in the buff. Maybe he only went in for monkeys.

"I can't get dressed yet. I just put my ointment on. I have to air-dry."

"At least put on a bathrobe," I pleaded.

She shook her head. "Not for twenty minutes."

She closed the freezer door and turned around. I stared down at the cracks in my linoleum floor.

"Holly honey, what happened to you?"

My hand instinctively shot to the back of my head, even though the bald patch rarely merited comment anymore. "What do you mean?"

She pointed at my bulging bustline. "You didn't have those when you left this morning."

I looked down. My artificially enhanced breasts were straining against the fabric of my T-shirt. I reached into my shirt and extracted the sweat socks, tossing them onto the table. "They're my neighbor's socks. I stole them for Gerry."

"Heavens to Betsy, I never thought you would do such a thing." Betty's disapproving tone surprised me. Though the theft was already weighing heavily on my conscience, I'd expected Betty and the rest of my family to be proud.

"But at dinner last week, you said I should do it. The whole family ganged up on me!"

"I know. I just never thought you'd do it."

The buzzer rang. I pressed the intercom button and Carter's voice sounded over the speaker. "It's me!"

I pressed the button to let her in. "Please go get dressed," I urged Betty. "We have company."

Betty shrugged a bony shoulder. "It's just little Carter. She's practically family. She can handle it."

"I *am* family, and I can't handle it," I said. "Besides, Danny is probably with her. She said they would both stop by."

"Your young man?"

"He's *not* my young man, remember? And throw something on or you'll freak him out."

She rolled her eyes and disappeared into the bedroom.

* * *

Carter looked a bit wan, probably a result of morning sickness. Danny, meanwhile, looked positively radiant. Expectant fatherhood apparently agreed with him.

I gave Carter a hug. "How are you feeling?"

"Like Mercury is in retrograde," she said, as though I was supposed to know what that meant. I nodded uncertainly.

Danny put one arm around my shoulders and squeezed. "Gotta use your facilities," he said as he bounced toward the bathroom.

I pulled Carter aside. "I found out who the Writer is," I whispered. "It's Brian, my neighbor."

She gaped at me. "The homosexual hottie upstairs?"

I nodded. "Can you believe it?"

"Frankly, no. Are you sure?"

I told her about the envelope I'd seen in Brian's apartment.

"Did you ask him about it?"

"No. It happened so fast. I was on my way out the door, and I just caught a glimpse of it. It was a pretty awkward moment, anyway, on account of—"

"What was an awkward moment?" Danny interrupted, returning from the bathroom.

"Never mind. I'll fill you in later," I told Carter.

She winked conspiratorially. "What's that smell?" Danny said, crinkling up his nose at the Bengay-and-mothball scent that filled my apartment.

"Aunt Betty," I replied, just as the door to my bedroom opened and Betty sauntered out in a skimpy red nightie I immediately recognized as one of my own. Purchased back when I had better romantic prospects, it was a sexy, silky number that didn't cover much. When I'd splurged on it at Macy's, I was envisioning a night of passion with Marcus, to celebrate our three-month anniversary. I'd barely blinked at the eighty-dollar price tag after seeing how it complemented my milky-white complexion and enhanced my nothing-to-brag-about bustline. Now, loosely draping Betty's sagging breasts, the same neg-ligee brought out the color of her patchy scales and liver spots. There goes eighty bucks down the drain, I thought. Not only could I never wear the little red number again, but the image before me would neg-atively impact my entire relationship with lingerie.

Danny looked at me aghast while Carter managed a polite smile in Betty's direction. "Um, hi, um, Mrs. Brosniak," she said.

"Hello, dear," she said, squeezing Carter's cheek between her thumb and forefinger. "You know you can call me Betty."

"I thought you were putting on a bathrobe," I said.

"My robe covers too much territory. I told you, my skin needs to breathe." She waved her arms in the air and her territory flapped in the breeze. "Hope you don't mind I borrowed it."

"Keep it," I said. "It's yours."

"Gee, thanks. Wonder what Bernie will make of it."

She made her way toward Danny with outstretched arms. He flashed a deer-in-the-headlights look in my direction, but I just shrugged. Even if I could do anything to prevent him from being mauled by my scantily clad elderly aunt, I wasn't sure I wanted to.

She reached out and grabbed a fistful of Danny's hair and tugged forcefully. "And you! You were such a stick in the mud at dinner, I never thought you'd amount to much on stage." She released his hair and smacked him across one cheek. "But you were dyna-mite."

Danny rubbed his cheek. "Thanks." He turned his gaze toward me. "Actually, Holly, that's what I wanted to talk to you about."

"The showcase?" I brightened, thinking he was going to apolo-gize for publicly humiliating me. "What about it?"

"I was right—we killed that night. My phone's been ringing off the hook." He was grinning widely and bouncing on his heels, barely able to contain his excitement.

I looked over at my own phone, the red light on my answering machine unapologetically unblinking. The only calls I'd gotten on my business line all week were from people interested in my hair-cutting, typing, or pet-sitting services; not a single caller commented on my dubious comedy career. "It has?"

"Yeah. Mostly congratulations, but a coupla clubs are interested in our act. We're a hot ticket."

I smiled. This was good news indeed. The comedy duo of Heck-erling and Crane, formerly floundering in obscurity, was poised on the brink of success. No more scrimping to get by on my meager earnings from word processing, hairstyling, and tax preparing. If I'd known it would boost our popularity, I would have allowed Danny to degrade me sooner.

"That's great, honey." Betty beamed at me. As I flashed a victory smile in her direction, I was already wondering how Danny and I would work her and her psoriasis-induced nudist phase into our act. This time I wouldn't pull any punches. Any guilt I'd had over exploiting my family's foibles for fame and fortune had vanished the moment Danny said "hot ticket."

"And best of all," Danny continued, "a guy from CAA wants to represent me."

I blinked, the smile frozen on my face. Did he say represent *me*? Not *us*?

"Isn't that great?" Carter prodded, though I could tell by her plastered-on smile that she knew the news was not what I'd hoped to hear.

"Just you?" I asked Danny, hoping I didn't appear as crestfallen as I felt.

He nodded. "He thinks you're cute as a button, but he's not in-terested in the act. Comedy teams are a hard sell in today's market, he says. He called me 'edgy and sardonic.' He wants me to put to-gether a demo tape with some solo material. And he's gonna send me out for some acting gigs."

Carter patted my shoulder. "You'll find an agent, too. Danny'll help you."

I nodded, numbly. My head was spinning. It was all happening so fast. In mere seconds I'd gone from half of a hot ticket to all alone and cute as a button. I lowered myself into a chair. "But we'll still do the act, right? You said a couple of clubs are interested."

"I'd love to, but—" Danny turned toward Carter and a private moment passed between them. Then he turned to face me. "We're moving to L.A. Pilot season starts in a few weeks and Brent—he's my agent—thinks I should be there." He took one of Carter's hands in his. "If all goes well, we'll stay out there."

Carter blinked back tears. "The city is no place to raise a baby," she said, patting her stomach.

"But—" I tried to speak but I couldn't squeeze any words past the lump in my throat. I gripped the edge of the kitchen table in an attempt to quell my nausea. I remained wordless as the enormity of the situation sunk in. I was losing my comedy partner and my two best friends in one fell swoop.

Down Memory Lane

Within twenty-four hours of my cohabitation with Aunt Betty, my apartment was already transformed. Signs of her occupation were everywhere: support hose drying on the shower rod, Geritol on the bathroom counter, dentures in a glass by the bedside. It wasn't these artifacts of old age themselves that were bothering me; it was the fact that they—like their owner—showed no signs of departing. By the second day of her stay, Betty was talking about having her mail forwarded. She'd even taken to calling me "roomie."

That night, after Betty turned in, I placed a furtive phone call to my uncle Bernie. I'd already tried to talk sense into Betty, but she wasn't budging. Bernie's refusal to be turned into diamonds after his death was the final straw, she said, the last in a lifetime of disappointments. "He didn't even buy me an engagement ring," she confided to me. "We couldn't afford it then, but he promised to make it up to me one day. And he's gonna keep that promise if it's the last thing he does."

Bernie was no less obstinate. "After working hard all his life, a man deserves to have some say about his final resting place. I always pictured a nice little plot, next to Betty, with a headstone that says, 'beloved husband,' that kind of thing. Nothing fancy, but a place you and your cousins and your kids could come visit. Maybe bring flowers. If she turns me into a pair of earrings, how are people gonna pay their respects? Go into the bedroom and sit around her jewelry box?"

I was uncomfortable playing mediator in their marital woes, but someone had to do it. Kuki was busy planning the engagement party for Gerry and Monica, and Gerry was preoccupied with promoting his collection. And as long as he could mooch meals off Kuki and Uncle Leo, Bernie seemed to be in no rush to get Betty back. It looked like she was here to stay.

Betty and I quickly settled into a routine that rivaled the one I had with Tallulah for its predictability. As with the monkey, things went more smoothly once I relinquished any notion that I was in control. Betty woke at dawn and within minutes the clattering of pots and pans in the kitchen would awaken me. Then she'd sing "Oh, What a Beautiful Morning" in a key Rodgers and Hammerstein never intended. I'd roll myself off the couch and stumble into the kitchen to join her for tea. Afterward, she'd plant herself in front of the television to watch a steady stream of talk shows, soap operas, and reality programming. Like Tallulah, she was a big fan of Regis, but her displays of affection were much less exuberant. This was a good thing since she was perpetually naked.

Looking over at Betty, who was sitting on the couch in just her underwear, I thought fondly of Tallulah's little dresses and modified diapers. Earlier in the week, I'd called David to see how he and Tallulah were doing. Owner and monkey were fine, Mrs. Lipton reported, but both would be delighted if I'd stop by for tea one day soon.

Despite the many awkward moments Betty's nudity caused, I had to admit, having her around was keeping my mind off my other troubles. Like my abortive relationship with Tom.

I hadn't spoken to Tom since the showcase, though he had left a message on my answering machine the following day, saying that I could tear up the subpoena. He'd contacted his ex-wife through her attorney and they'd reached an agreement to share joint custody of Nicole. Apparently Nicole had told her mother about her father's interest in the crazy hair lady, and a few questions to the employees at Starbucks had yielded my name. She'd had her lawyer issue the subpoena not so much because she cared whom Tom was dating, but because she hoped to scare him into agreeing to her terms. He'd ended his message with a plea that I'd leave the door open to the possibility of a relationship in the future. Despite his assurances that the custody issue was settled, I still thought it best that I keep my distance for the time being.

Meanwhile, I was still reeling from the news that Carter and Danny were moving to Los Angeles, taking with them my dreams for comedy stardom, not to mention their unborn child, whom I had hoped to spoil rotten in my role as doting Aunt Holly. "What about your job?" I'd asked Carter after they'd dropped the bombshell. "You made assistant manager."

She looked at me like I was batty. "They have Starbucks in L.A., you know. I can transfer and still keep my benefits."

"But the yoga studio. You were gonna do that new prenatal class."

"They also have yoga studios there. Lots of them. I've already checked out a couple."

She had it all figured out. Of course Los Angeles offered as many if not more opportunities for Carter, and she was probably right about it being a better place to raise children. But was all that worth the price of our friendship?

I couldn't blame Danny for jumping at the chance to further his career. He had, after all, aspired to stardom even before he met me. Playing the comedy clubs had been *his* dream; on my own, I probably never would have stepped up to a microphone. Danny's wit and enthusiasm were infectious; I'd gotten caught up in his energy and wanted to be part of it. He was rocketing toward stardom and I was caught up in his tailwinds. Now our partnership had run its course and it was time for him to move on. No, I couldn't blame him one bit.

But Carter's desertion was another matter entirely. She'd seen me through my mother's death, my father's abandonment, and the angst of my teen years. Not to mention half a dozen failed relationships. Now she was leaving, too.

"What about me?" I asked sharply, looking from one to the other. "You're my best friends. I've always been there for both of you. And now you're abandoning me?" My biting tone belied the depth of my emotions. I was fighting to maintain a semblance of control while everything was falling apart around me.

Carter blinked back tears. She looked genuinely stricken. I realized I was being selfish. "You're my best friend, too," she said, her lower lip quivering.

"And mine," Danny added, squeezing my hand. "But that's the problem. Carter and I turn to you for everything. Every mess we've gotten into in our relationship would have been solved a lot sooner if we just talked to each other instead of coming to you. We need to be each other's best friend now."

His words had the ring of truth, but they stung. I was always in the middle of their problems precisely because I was the closest friend either of them had. It had been a lot easier before they became a couple. When they first began dating, I'd been thrilled; I naively thought my friends' blending would mean I'd see more of each one. Ultimately, it meant I'd lose them both.

Throughout our exchange, Betty had been tugging at the red nightie and intermittently scratching the scales on her arms and legs. "Is anyone else hot in here?" she said, clearly ready to rip the silky material from her body. Finally, her scratching became vigorous. She looked at the clock. "My ointment's worn off. Time for a new application." With this, she lifted the nightie over her head.

Once Betty bared all, Carter and Danny left abruptly, citing a string of errands they had to run in preparation for their big move. In the two days that elapsed after their visit, I didn't speak to either one.

Monica, meanwhile, called daily, renewing her plea for me to snag Brian's socks. I'd neglected to tell her that I'd already done just that. I was having second thoughts about turning the socks over to Monica. Brian was no stranger to cyberspace, after all. What if he stumbled upon Gerry's site and saw it touting the acquisition of *his* footwear?

Since stealing the socks, I'd been suffering serious pangs of guilt. I'd not only committed a theft, I'd also violated the sanctity of the pet sitter–client relationship. I could never be trusted again.

Betty understood my moral quandary but suggested I consider the greater good of maintaining family harmony. "It's not like it's a mortal sin, anyway. You won't go to hell over a pair of socks."

On Thursday morning, Monica called again. Her voice had a desperate quality. "The engagement party's tomorrow night," she reminded me. "I need to get something today."

"I can't help you," I told her.

"I'll go talk to him myself. I know where he lives. I was in his apartment, remember? I can be real persuasive."

No one was more convinced of Monica's persuasive abilities than me. Just ask Rocky, my reptilian roommate. Yet there was no telling what sort of mayhem would ensue if I allowed Monica to darken Brian's doorstep. "No, you can't—"

"Sorry to interrupt." Betty's voice crackled over the bedroom extension. "I thought it might be Bernie."

"Hi, Aunt Betty," Monica said. "Holly and I were just talking about her neighbor's socks."

"So she told you she stole them?" Betty said brightly.

"She did what?" Monica asked.

"It was a mistake," I insisted. "I'm going to return them."

"Don't you dare! I'll be right over to pick them up!"

"No, don't—" I cried, but she had already hung up.

I probably could have stopped Monica from coming over, but I still felt partly responsible for her fall. If giving Monica Brian's socks would put me back in her good graces, I supposed it was a small price to pay. Whatever her name was, she was soon going to be a member of the family, after all.

"Looks like we're going to have company," I told Betty when I hung up the phone. "Monica's coming."

"You mean Esther," she corrected me.

"Oh yeah, Esther," I repeated, wrinkling my forehead. I didn't think I'd ever get used to Monica's new moniker. It might be easier if her nickname bore any similarity to her real name, but Monica Broccoli was about as far from Esther Collins as you could get, except in Gerry's lopsided logic.

"The first few times I met her, I kept forgetting her name," Gerry had explained to me the morning after he reconciled with the fiancée formerly known as Monica. "I really liked her and didn't want to blow it, so I made up things to help me remember. Esther sounds like Easter, and Collins sounds like cauliflower. So I told myself to think of people eating cauliflower at Easter. The next time I saw her, I remembered that her name sounds like a holiday and a vegetable. But I thought it was—"

"Hannukah and broccoli," I'd said, as the pieces of the puzzle finally fit together.

It took a little prodding, but I managed to convince Betty to put on a bathrobe by the time the buzzer signaled Monica's arrival. I unlocked the front door and went around tidying up my apartment. I had plenty of time, since Monica was once again weighed down by a cast. Just as I was tossing a week's worth of ice cream containers into the trash, the phone rang.

"When did they start putting the grapes in fruit cocktail again?" my uncle Bernie asked.

"Huh?" I put my hand over the receiver and called to Betty. "It's for you. Uncle Bernie."

"I don't want to speak to that grave robber," Bernie said. "I'm just asking a simple question about fruit cocktail. You eat fruit cocktail, don't you?"

"Once in a while."

Betty was slowly making her way to the phone, her speed hindered by the metal hinges in her hips. I shrugged my shoulders and whispered, "He has a question about fruit cocktail."

Bernie wheezed in my ear, "Forty years ago, they stopped putting grapes in it. Now they're back. Why did they put them back?"

I was no fruit cocktail connoisseur, but I was pretty sure the basic recipe had never changed. "There's always been grapes in it," I said. "And peaches and cherries and little pieces of pineapple—"

Betty grabbed the phone from my hand. She shouted, "Moron," into the receiver and hung up. Then she turned to me. "When I was dating your uncle, we went to a picnic. They had fruit cocktail. I fixed him a plate. Instead of thanking me, he complains." She mimicked his voice. " 'I hate fruit cocktail. I don't like grapes.' " She shook her head. "For forty years I've been picking the grapes out of his fruit cocktail and he doesn't even know it. He thinks they stopped putting them in at the factory."

I wondered how many other little things my aunt did for my uncle that went unnoticed by him. I didn't have to wonder long, for she poured forth a litany that continued until Monica stuck her plaster-casted foot in my door.

"And he thinks his underpants are magically transported into the hamper when he leaves them on the bathroom floor," Betty concluded as she turned to greet Monica. "Don't ever pick the grapes out of fruit cocktail for your husband," she said. "You pick one grape, you'll be pickin' grapes for forty years. And he'll never appreciate it."

"Gerry loves grapes," Monica said with a shrug, missing Betty's larger meaning. She stood in my doorway and peered in, hesitantly. "Gerry said you got rid of that monkey?"

I nodded. "Tallulah went back to her owner." I wished I could say the same for Rocky, who'd become a permanent fixture in my life.

"Good," she said, limping into my apartment and dumping her purse on my table. "If you ask me, that stinkball overstayed her welcome."

"I didn't."

"You know, Holly, I don't know how you get yourself into these things," she said without the slightest hint of irony. She gave Betty a quick hug and emitted a yelp when Betty responded with a finger flick to the forehead.

"How are the wedding plans going?" I asked.

"Your idiot cousin wants to put 'Monica Broccoli' on the wedding invitations. He says if we put my real name, no one in your family will know who he's marrying."

"He has a point."

"What about my family? They're not going to trek up from Florida to go to the wedding if my name isn't even on the invitation."

"What about putting Esther Collins and then Monica Broccoli in parentheses?" I could envision fine parchment embossed with gold-leaf lettering: *You are cordially invited to witness the nuptials of Esther Collins aka Monica Broccoli and Gerald Corelli aka Numb-nuts.*

"What about minding your own business?"

The phone rang and I grabbed the receiver. "Hello?"

It was Danny. "Hey, partner," he said, despite the fact that he had peremptorily dissolved our partnership. "I'm packing up my place and I've been searching everywhere for my running shoes. Then I remembered that night at your aunt's house. I left without them."

"I have them. They're in my closet."

"Great! I'll swing by and pick 'em up on my way to work. Be there in a few."

He hung up. The ten-second exchange had to be the shortest phone conversation in the history of my friendship with Danny. There'd been no pleasantries or idle chitchat, no snide remarks about my family or wicked gossip about his coworkers, and most pointedly, no inquiries as to my health or mental state. After dumping me, both personally and professionally, the least he could do was ask how I was doing. I guess he didn't care.

Apartments in Manhattan are notoriously small, and closet space, if it exists at all, is even smaller. The little broom closet in my hallway was absurdly overcrowded. Squeezed in among scads of jackets, boots, and scarves were the accessories of my many trades, including my old barber chair and a battery of power tools. It was no small task to find what I wanted.

I had tossed Danny's sneakers into the closet a few weeks back, when Gerry brought them from his mother's. It was the morning of Tallulah's arrival. What with minding the monkey and orchestrating the demise of my comedy career, I'd forgotten all about them. Now I was on my hands and knees, picking through a jumble of umbrellas, shoes, and cleaning supplies. I finally found them toward the back of the closet, squashed under a cardboard box I immediately recognized as the one containing my father's belongings.

I hadn't forgotten about my dad's box; I was just waiting for the right time to open it. Now I realized there would never be a *right* time. In the eighteen years that had elapsed since I'd last seen my father, my interest in the box had ranged from indifference to idle curiosity. I had a million questions about the man who had sired me, but I wasn't naive enough to think I'd find any answers in a cardboard box.

I lifted the box and carried it out of the closet. On one side in faded magic marker, RICHARD'S THINGS was written in Kuki's handwriting. The masking tape that had sealed the box had turned brittle; pieces of it fell away as I set the box on the kitchen table.

"It's now or never," I said under my breath as I gingerly lifted one of the flaps.

Betty titled her head inquisitively. "Isn't that the box Kuki was keeping for you?"

"Keeping *from* me," I corrected her.

"When did she give it to you?"

"She didn't. I took it."

Betty emitted a disappointed sigh. "Oh, honey. First the socks, now this." She shook her head, no doubt envisioning the life of crime that lay ahead of me now that I was on a roll.

"Yeah, I'm on a crime spree. You'd better watch out or I'll take you down with me."

I opened the box. Its contents smelled vaguely like cedar chips, the same aroma that permeated Kuki's attic. The box was loosely packed, mostly with papers. I picked up a heart-shaped piece of pink construction paper.

"Looks like a valentine," Betty said.

"It's an invitation to my Valentine's Day dance recital." I opened it and read. " 'Wednesday, October 16, 1986. Miss Lanette's School of Dance in Brooklyn.' "

"I remember those recitals of yours." Betty smiled. "Kuki would spend weeks sewing those costumes, then complain that they had you all the way in back so you couldn't see the detail work."

I hadn't been the most graceful of ballerinas, but I loved performing. I'd continued taking classes after most of the other dancers my age outgrew their prepubescent ballerina fantasies and moved on. I fingered the crinkly pink paper, remembering the recital. It was the last one I took part in. Miss Lanette had finally assigned me a leading role, moved more likely by pity than my imperfect pirouettes. I'd been staying at my grandmother's house while my father "sorted things out" at home. He'd sold the house I was born in and was moving us into a small apartment in Queens. The night of the recital, he was to pick me up and take me back with him. It would be my first night in my new bedroom, a fresh start for us both.

My family filled a whole row at the recital—Kuki and Leo, Betty and Bernie, Gerry and Ronnie, and Grandma. At the end of the row was an empty seat they'd reserved for my father. Though Miss Lanette had instructed us not to pay attention to the audience during the show, I couldn't help but notice that the seat on the end remained empty the whole time. My father never showed. I never saw my new bedroom, never saw my father again, never heard his voice, aside from a brief message on the answering machine the next day: "I'm sorry, sunshine. Daddy has to go away for a while. Be a good girl and don't make waves."

My mind was racing, careening down memory lane. Though it was more than half my lifetime ago, the memory of that evening was still fresh. Yet the distance of intervening years allowed me to view it with detachment. I'd grown a hard shell over the years since my father's abandonment. I would examine these relics with the dispassion of a scientist.

I set aside the heart-shaped cutout and sifted through several layers of documents pertaining to the state of my father's finances circa 1986—bank statements, credit card bills, receipts. The bank

balances were low while the bills were high. As I recalled, my
mother's funeral expenses had taken a hefty bite out of their sav-
ings; after several months of struggling to make it on one salary,
he'd been forced to sell the house.

Monica had limped over to the table and was standing over me.
"What's the big deal about a bunch of old bills?"

"Beats me," I said, setting the bills aside and fingering a faded
family photograph that lay underneath. I felt a shock of recognition
when I saw the man standing beside my mother, his long brown
hair tucked behind his ears, his full beard unkempt. His "hippie
look," my mother had called it. Though pictures of my mother were
abundant in Kuki's house, there wasn't a single photo of my father
anywhere on display. It had been years since I'd seen his picture; I'd
almost forgotten what he looked like.

As I was scrutinizing the photo, Monica reached into the box and
grasped a leather-bound book with *1986* embossed on its cover. "This
could be interesting," she said. "Looks like an appointment book."

"Don't touch it." I grabbed it from her, feeling oddly propri-
etary of these items I'd let wither away in an attic for eighteen years.
I felt a cold shot of adrenaline rushing through my veins as I flipped
through the pages of the tattered book. My limbs went limp and I
lowered myself into a chair.

"What is it, honey?" Betty asked. "You look pale."

"Uh—" I began, but I couldn't speak. My throat constricted, ar-
resting my words.

"What's it say?" Monica craned her neck to look over my shoulder at the book. But it wasn't what was written there that had un-
nerved me, rather it was how it was written. On page after page, my
father's notations were lettered in crisp, precise handwriting.

The same handwriting I'd come to know as belonging to the
Writer.

17

Fools Rush In

I shot up from the table and pushed past Betty and Monica, heading for the door.

"Where are you going?" Betty called after me, but I hadn't yet regained the power of speech.

I dashed up the stairs and rapped on Brian's door. I hadn't planned out what I would say when he answered, but I knew I had to confront him about the envelope I'd seen in his apartment. If the Writer was my father, as the handwriting in the date book clearly indicated, then what was Brian doing with one of his envelopes? Brian was at least two decades younger than my dad, and I doubted they traveled in the same circles. Then again, I had no way of knowing what circles my father traveled in these days.

I knocked again and waited, but there was no response. I was about to turn away when the door to the next apartment opened and Mrs. Mete popped her head out.

"You're looking for Brian?" she asked. "He left early this morning. Softball in Central Park. It's some kind of benefit. His show against the cast of *All My Children*. Susan Lucci's gonna be shortstop."

"He told you that?" Knowing how Brian tried to maintain his privacy, I was surprised that he'd shared this much with Mrs. Mete.

She cocked her head to one side. "The wall between our apartments is thin."

I turned to start down the stairs. "You want me to give him a message?" she asked.

"No. I'll come back later."

"He won't be home tonight. He was carrying an overnight bag and I heard him on the phone making plans with his boyfriend."

"O.K."

I took a few more steps and she called after me, "I saw that big-mouthed girl go into your apartment. You're not going to take her cast off again, are you?"

"Nope," I said, shaking my head. "I learned my lesson."

"Good. You shouldn't let people take advantage of you, Holly. By the way, I called the pharmacy. My prescription will be ready by three. Don't keep me waiting."

When I returned to my apartment, Danny was standing at the table with Betty and Monica. He was wearing jeans and a dress-shirt, his green Starbucks apron slung over one shoulder. The three of them were leafing through the contents of the box.

"Whoa, look at that hair! Get your head caught in a weed whacker?" Danny asked, pointing at a picture of me at age eleven. My choppy 'do was the result of my father's first and only attempt at giving me a haircut. I remembered Kuki's protests—"I own a barbershop, for Christ's sake!"—and my father's insistence that he could take care of it himself. Money was tight and he didn't want to bring me to a salon. So he performed a crude rendition of the bowl cut, positioning a plastic cereal bowl atop my head and tracing around it with a pair of dull scissors. The results were so disastrous that he didn't let his stubborn pride stand in the way the next time Kuki wanted to cut my hair.

I snatched the photo out of Danny's hand and put it back in the box. Snapping the lid closed, I said, "Show-and-tell's over."

Danny's face was apologetic. "This is all you have from your dad?"

I nodded. "It's just some random stuff that he happened to leave in the guest room at my grandmother's house. Kuki tossed it in a box for him but he never picked it up. There's even loose change in the bottom and some twenty-two-cent stamps."

"He must have had a good reason for not coming back," Danny said.

"A good reason?" I turned on him. "You're about to be a father," I shouted. "You tell me: What would be a *good* reason for walking out on your kid and never looking back?"

That's when it struck me. My father *had* looked back. He obviously knew where I lived and what I did for a living. He'd hired me to do his typing not because he actually wanted anything typed. He just wanted me to read it. I recalled those lined yellow pages in which he chronicled his pain over my mother's death and his subsequent attempts to raise me on his own. I'd been so moved by them, not only because of the poignancy of the writing, but because of the painful familiarity of the situations. I'd never stopped to wonder *why* they were so familiar, never considered the possibility that they were not recent events but decades-old chapters out of my own life story.

In his own way, my father was trying to reach out to me through those lined yellow pages, trying to make me understand what he'd gone through and why he had left.

Now I knew why the Writer had wanted anonymity, why he never knocked on my door when making his pickups and deliveries, why he paid in cash. I struggled to recall the first phone call, when he'd inquired about my services. If I was talking to my father, why hadn't I recognized his voice? It was a brief phone call, and I'd been in a hurry to get out the door. And now that I thought about it, there was something odd in the way he spoke, in a hushed monotone, like he'd been deliberately trying to disguise his voice. Most of all, eighteen years had passed since I last saw my father. I could barely remember what he *looked* like, let alone the sound of his voice.

"I'm sorry," Danny was saying, but I waved him aside as I made my way over to my desk in the living room. Propped up by the computer was the last typing job the Writer—my father—had left in my milk box. Since his no-show at my showcase, finishing the Writer's typing had lost its sense of urgency. I'd only made it through the first two pages. I skipped ahead to the last page and read:

My wife liked to garden. She lavished such care, attention—and money—on her plants that I used to joke we should list them as dependents on our tax returns. When our daughter was born, she compared her to a flower bud—tiny and full of potential. Under my wife's loving care, our little bud blossomed and flourished, growing strong and confident and brightening the landscape around her with every sweet smile and goofy giggle.

Without proper tending, the garden withers. I am an ineffectual gardener. Under my stewardship, the beautiful flower that was my daughter is slowly turning to a weed, devoid of vitality, drained of spirit. Her listless walk and low-slung head, her unkempt hair and clothes, her cries in the night for which my shoulder provides no comfort—all give witness to my inability to give her the nurturing she requires. I know now that if I want this tiny flower—my beautiful, budding Holly—to thrive, I must leave her in the hands of a better gardener.

My eyes stung. I tried to choke back the tears, but this time I could not. They rolled down my cheeks and fell onto my shirt.

"What is it?" Betty asked.

I brought the yellow pages back to the table. "This is from my client, the 'mysterious' Writer." I opened the cardboard box and withdrew my father's date book, letting it fall open to a page in the middle. I set it down next to the yellow pages. The writing was identical.

Danny did a double take. "The Writer is your *dad*? That's who you got all hot and bothered about? Kinky!"

I walked over to where Danny's tennis shoes were sitting on the floor outside my closet. I grabbed them and returned to the table.

"Here are your sneakers," I said, thrusting them into Danny's chest. "And there is the door!"

"Hey, I'm sorry." He let the sneakers fall to the floor. "But I don't get it. Carter said that the Writer was your gay neighbor."

"That's what I thought. He has one of his envelopes upstairs in his apartment. I saw it the other day. That's why I went up there just now, to ask him about it, but he's not there."

"Too bad you don't still have his key," Monica said, stating the obvious. "Then you could just go check it out for yourself."

Monica's statement spurred an idea that I knew at once to be reckless and foolhardy. Yet knowing this didn't prevent me from giving it serious consideration. What I wanted more than anything right now—even more than a Mocha Frappuccino and an apartment free of family and friends—was to get inside Brian's apartment and see what was in that envelope. I glanced over at the open window in my living room. Since Betty had moved in, the window was constantly open, "on account of my skin needs fresh air," she'd said. Brian had said he kept his windows open in hot weather, and it had been unseasonably warm the last few days. I charged toward my window and climbed out onto the fire escape. I sat there for a moment, looking up. Brian occupied the apartment directly above mine. From where I was perched, it looked as though his window was open at least half a foot. I started to climb.

Betty, Monica, and Danny crowded around my window, peering out at me.

"You're not gonna jump, are ya?" Monica asked, her tone more curious than concerned.

I reached Brian's window and peered inside. The apartment was empty. A portable screen was propped in the window. It didn't have a lock and was obviously meant to keep Kramer in rather than burglars out. I pushed it aside and swung my legs in. I hesitated. If I crawled through the window, I'd be breaking and entering. Or at least entering. Either way, it was definitely criminal activity. Snatching socks from a gym bag may not have been my best move, but it wouldn't have gotten me arrested.

I took a deep breath and hopped off the windowsill, and I was in Brian's living room. I tiptoed toward the entryway bookshelf. I was halfway across the room when I heard someone calling my name.

I spun around and saw Aunt Betty sticking her head through Brian's window.

"Aunt Betty! What are you doing?"

"I came to ask you the same thing. You're not really on a crime spree, are you?" She lowered herself in through the window. She was dressed in only her underwear.

"What happened to your robe?"

"It's too bulky. Not good for climbing." She shuffled over to me. "Are we just here for the envelope? Or are we stealing more socks, too?"

"Just the envelope. And it's not stealing if it's addressed to me."

"Yeah. The cops'll buy that."

I reached the bookcase and my heart sank. The other day, the envelope had been sitting on the top shelf, but the shelf was now bare. "It's not here!"

"Well, let's find it then," Betty said, crouching to look under the couch. "Maybe it fell on the floor."

I crossed to the desk and looked through some papers stacked there. I struck out there, and was headed for the kitchen when there was a knock on the door.

I froze. Betty was on all fours on Brian's lime green throw rug, her pink panties pointing skyward. She looked at me, her mouth agape.

"Holly, you in there?" Monica whispered through the door. I rushed to the door, threw open the lock, and pulled her inside.

"What are you doing here?" I shut and locked the door behind her. "Did anybody see you?"

"Your aunt scaled the fire escape in hot pink undies and you're asking if anyone saw *me*?"

I knew having Monica and Betty in Brian's apartment portended disaster, but both refused to leave without me and I wasn't about to go until I found the envelope. So we split up, Monica taking the bedroom, Betty the living room, and me the rest of the apartment. "Don't touch anything," I warned. "Just call me if you see the envelope."

"Since we're here," Monica said coyly, "we might as well take—"

"No!" I interrupted her. "You so much as touch one argyle and I'll throw you down another flight of stairs."

We'd been at it a few minutes without success when I heard heavy footsteps on the stairs. They stopped just outside Brian's apartment. I held my breath as someone pounded on the door.

Betty stared at me, openmouthed. Monica stuck her head out of Brian's bedroom. I put a finger to my lips and we all played at being statues.

The pounding resumed and a man shouted, "Open up! I

know someone's in there." The voice was much deeper and more authoritative than Brian's. It could have been Pete, the building's superintendent.

"You sure you heard a break-in?" the man said.

A woman responded, "I heard voices and people moving around inside." It was Mrs. Mete, who must have alerted the super the minute she heard us. "And I heard the fire escape rattling. I looked out my window and saw someone climbing in."

"What'd they look like?"

"I couldn't see a face, just legs. It happened pretty fast, but I don't think the burglar's wearing pants."

Pete pounded one more time and shouted, "The police are on their way."

All color drained from Monica's face. "I can't go to jail," she whispered. "Tomorrow night's my engagement party!"

There was a jangling of keys. The super was going to let himself in using his pass key. We were toast.

I grabbed Betty and Monica by the elbows and pulled them over to the open window. "Go out the window. Quick!"

Betty hoisted herself onto the window ledge, but Monica was balking. She pointed to her cast. "I can't climb down the fire escape!"

"It's the only way," I said, shoving her headfirst out the window. "I'll try and stall them." I wasn't trying to be heroic, sacrificing myself so that Monica and Betty could get away. I was just being practical. If all three of us went down the fire escape, Pete would easily find us before we reached the floor below, especially with Monica's cast causing a logjam. I had to stay behind to keep him from looking out the window.

The sound of sirens in the distance spurred Monica into motion. She pulled herself through the window, her cast clanging against the rusted metal of the fire escape. I winced. This was going to be one of the worst getaways in the history of petty crime.

I yanked down the shade to shield Monica's retreat just as the front door burst open and Pete the super stomped in, gripping a pipe wrench in his outstretched hand. Mrs. Mete peered out from behind him.

"Hello," I said, waving my arms above my head in surrender. "It's just me. Holly Heckerling. Apartment 6B?"

He nodded. "My wife and I caught your showcase last week. It was pretty good."

"Thanks." I pointed at the wrench and laughed uneasily. "Is that thing loaded?"

"Holly?" Mrs. Mete stepped out from behind Pete's protective shadow. "For heaven's sake, what are you doing here?"

Pete relaxed his grip on the pipe wrench but still looked ready to rumble. "You break in here?"

"No," I insisted. "I . . . uh . . . watch Brian's cat when he goes away."

Mrs. Mete frowned. "But when I saw you this morning, you didn't know he was gone."

I heard the scraping of metal against the side of the building and coughed, hoping to cover the sound.

"You have a key?" Pete asked suspiciously.

"Yes." I nodded. "Well, not right now." I'd seen the I♥NY key chain hanging on a peg in the kitchen when I was searching for the envelope and wished I'd pocketed it. "See, here's what happened. . . ." I drew a deep breath, not sure where I was going. Then Kramer rubbed up against my leg. I bent and scooped him up in my arms. "Brian must have left his window open 'cause of the heat. Kramer got out and climbed down the fire escape to my apartment. I recognized him, you know, 'cause I pet sit for him all the time. I knew Brian wasn't home, so I carried Kramer back up here on the fire escape. I was just going to leave when you came pounding on the door."

Pete leveled an appraising stare at me. "Why didn't you open the door?"

I shrugged. "I got scared when you mentioned the police."

Pete walked over to the window and stuck his head out. He looked up, then down. I silently prayed that Monica had made it in through my window. Pete pulled his head back inside and lowered the window. "He should keep his window closed if he's gonna leave his cat alone."

"You're right." I nodded. "Do you mind if I go now?"

"The cops are gonna want a statement." He looked around the apartment once again and seemed satisfied that nothing was out of the ordinary. "I guess I can take care of it."

I breathed a massive sigh of relief. Conning Pete and Mrs. Mete was one thing; I wasn't so sure I'd stand up under the scrutiny of New York's finest. Besides, the cops give me the heebie-jeebies and my nerves were rattled enough as it was due to my whole world being turned upside down.

Pete opened Brian's front door, and I followed him and Mrs. Mete out into the hall.

"There's just one thing I don't understand," Mrs. Mete said after Pete had disappeared down the stairs. "When I saw you climbing in the window, I could have sworn you had no pants on."

When I returned to my apartment, Monica was standing over my kitchen sink, splashing water on her face. She was flushed and her hair was wild. The fire escape apparently hadn't agreed with her.

"Nice trip?" I asked.

"I nearly broke my other leg," she hissed. "Hanging out with you is hazardous to my health. I'm gonna think twice the next time you invite me over."

I wrinkled my forehead, trying to remember if there had been a *first* time I invited her over. Monica's visits tended to be unwelcome and unexpected. "You got what you came for," I said.

"And then some," Betty chirped.

Monica glared at Betty and I felt suddenly sick.

"Tell me you didn't take anything from his apartment," I said to Monica.

She shook her head. "Nah. You saw me leave empty-handed. What could I have taken?"

It was true Monica hadn't been holding anything when she climbed out of Brian's window. Nor was she carrying a purse. I looked her over. She was wearing baby blue elastic-banded cotton shorts and a matching short-sleeved T-shirt. It wasn't Monica's most stylish ensemble, but then again, it was probably hard to find outfits that fit on over a leg cast. There were no pockets and nowhere she could have hidden surplus socks. Unless . . .

I cast an appraising stare at Monica's T-shirt. Was it just my imagination, or did it fit a little more snugly than before? She'd always been buxom, but today she looked like she was ready to burst.

I turned to Betty. "Did she steal anything?"

Betty looked from me to Monica, then down at the floor. "You girls are just going to have to work this out for yourselves."

"What's in there?" I asked Monica, pointing at her chest.

Monica gaped at me. "You're not suggesting I smuggled socks out of Brian's apartment in my bra, are you? That's the stupidest thing I've ever heard."

"It's not so stupid," I said defensively. "Hand 'em over."

She put her hands on her hips and faced me. "Make me."

I lunged toward her, my hands poised to grab the stuffing out of her overstuffed boobs. As I made contact, she jerked away. We both went down to the floor, Monica hitting me with both hands and kicking me with her good leg.

My arms flailed wildly as I tried to make a grab for her breasts while deflecting her blows. Within seconds Monica had me pinned. If Carter's yoga class had raised questions as to my physical fitness, being tackled by the partially disabled Monica Broccoli removed all doubt. I was pathetic.

18

Show-and-Tell

The next morning I rose and dressed quickly before Betty awoke. I'd learned that if I wanted access to my bathroom before she began her lengthy morning ritual, I had to get up pretty darn early. Thus the Sleepblaster Plus had come out of retirement.

As I brushed my teeth and slapped on some makeup, I marveled at the agglomeration of transgenerational toiletries arrayed on the shelves and countertop. My products were quickly losing ground to Betty's; her Depends had already displaced my Tampax in the cupboard underneath the sink while her wrinkle creams were crowding out my acne remedies. After accidentally brushing my teeth with Polygrip, I resolved to do something about our living situation.

But first, I had bigger fish to fry. I was determined to get some answers from Brian regarding the envelope I'd seen in his apartment. I slipped out the front door and charged up the stairs to his apartment. I knocked on his door. Still no answer.

I returned to my apartment and checked my milk cubby for the tenth time since discovering the Writer's identity. The night before, after Monica left, clutching her boobs and rescinding her offer to make me her maid of honor, I'd taken the Writer's—my *father's*—last batch of writing and put it back into its manila envelope. I scrawled *I know who you are!* on a piece of paper, slipped it inside the envelope, and left it in my milk cubby to await pickup. I'd been on edge ever since, alert to the slightest sound coming from the direction of my pantry. Every creak on the stairs sent me rushing to the front door, ready to pounce on my father before he could sneak away.

The manila envelope was still in the cubby, untouched. And though I instinctively knew that my father wouldn't be returning, I also knew I would keep checking the milk cubby as I had checked Kuki's mailbox every day for months after my father's no-show at my ballet recital, looking for some kind of message from him, some reason why he'd been delayed.

I clicked the milk door shut and reached for a can of cat food. I was just emptying it into Grouch's bowl when the phone rang. I grabbed the receiver. "Yeah?" It was my personal line, so no need to adopt a professional tone.

There was a brief pause and then a familiar voice said, "Hi." I hadn't heard from Tom since the night of the showcase. His voice sounded apologetic. "I probably shouldn't be calling you . . . ."

I had to admit it was good to hear his voice, even though I hadn't changed my mind about dating him. "It's O.K. How are you?"

"I'm fine," he said. Then he laughed. "Actually, I'm a wreck. I don't know what to do and you're the only person I could think of to call."

"What is it?" I heard crying in the background. "Is that Nicole?"

"Yes. Today is show-and-tell and she still doesn't have anything to show."

"I thought you were going to buy her a goldfish."

"Her mother bought her one, but she doesn't like it. I offered to buy her a different one, but she refused. She spent all last night going through her toys looking for something to bring, but she couldn't make up her mind. Now she wants—"

Nicole's cries elevated in pitch, drowning out Tom's voice. My heart went out to Tom. He'd told me once that he was afraid to discipline Nicole lately: The divorce and the adjustment to living in two homes had been hard enough on her; he didn't want to be the bad guy who always said no. So until things settled down, he would bend over backward to please her. Tom's devotion to his daughter was one of the things I admired most about him. He wouldn't be like my dad, who had bailed after only a few months of trying to care for me on his own.

"I can't hear you!" I screamed. "What does she want now?"

"An animal," he shouted back. "But not a fish. Could you . . . I mean, would it be too much to ask . . . ?"

I hesitated for a moment, considering. If I helped Tom out, would it be opening up a door that I wasn't ready to open?

Nicole's screams had died down. I heard her say between sniffles, "Pleeease, Daddy!"

Tom gave an exasperated sigh. "Just a minute, honey. Daddy's working on it."

I knew I should probably tell Tom that I couldn't help him. After all, it wouldn't be the end of the world for Nicole to show up at school with nothing for show-and-tell. There were far worse things that could happen to a kid these days. But, as on the morning I met them at Starbucks, something compelled me to get involved, to be the superhero who saved Tom and Nicole from cocoa stains, split ends, and show-and-tell.

"How about a bunny rabbit?" I said into the phone.

I hung up the phone and began straightening up my apartment. I hadn't expected visitors so early in the day. Nicole had to be at school by eight thirty, so at least their stay would be brief. Betty was in the bathroom, gargling Listerine to the tune of "Oh, What a Beautiful Morning." I knocked on the door and warned her not to come out unless she was fully dressed; otherwise she'd be giving Nicole the shock of her five-year-old life.

The buzzer rang. I pressed the intercom button and spoke into the little box. "Come on up." Then I unlocked the front door and looked around my apartment. It wasn't first-date clean, but then, I reminded myself, this wasn't a date. I heard two sets of footsteps climbing the stairs; then a small voice said, "Hurry, Daddy!"

My phone rang as I was readying Jack the Bunny for his first day at school. Probably Mrs. Mete, I thought, calling to give me instructions for my daily pharmacy run.

"So you're alive," my aunt Kuki said. I'd been avoiding Kuki since the night of the showcase, when she'd thanked heaven my mother hadn't been alive to witness my performance. "I need to talk to you about the party tonight."

"I promise to stay away from the marinated meatballs," I said.

"It's not that." She took a deep breath and continued. "I know it's short notice, but I was hoping you and your friend could do something from your jig."

I couldn't believe my ears. "We do 'gigs' not 'jigs.' And we don't do gigs anymore. Danny broke up the act. He and Carter are moving to L.A."

"Carter's moving away? Oh, honey, I'm so sorry. I know how much you'll miss her."

She didn't know the half of it. Then again, maybe she did. Kuki had not only been a second mother to me; she'd also helped to raise Carter, who spent more time at our house growing up than at her own. I'd once overheard Kuki telling my uncle Leo that she felt sorry for "that little waif Carter," whose parents were divorcing around the time of my mother's death.

"I'm dealing with it," I told Kuki. "Why would you want Danny and me to perform anyway? I got the distinct impression you didn't care for our act."

"That's not exactly true," she said. "Besides, this is Gerry's big night, and he loves your comedy. Especially the stuff about him. He'd get a big kick out of you performing a little show for his friends."

"You want me to perform my act, even though you hated it?"

"I didn't hate it! Why would you say such a thing?"

"I heard what you said to Gerry in the taxi: 'Thank God her mother wasn't here to see it.'"

There was a long silence. When Kuki spoke, her words were measured. "You misunderstood."

"I didn't misunderstand. You've always looked down on my choices. 'Monkey school,' stand-up comedy—nothing I've done was ever good enough for you. But you're wrong about my mother. She would have been proud to see me up onstage."

"Of course, she would," Kuki said. "And so was I."

"You have a funny way of showing it."

"It's just that I think you could do better. You were funnier when you were on your own. You sparkled. Then your friend showed up. He got laughs at your expense while you shrank into the background."

Tom and Nicole appeared at my door. Tom was breathing hard, his face flushed from the climb, while Nicole was bouncing energetically and tugging on his arm. "Come on, Daddy!"

I gestured for them to come in and covered the phone with my hand. "I'll be with you in a second. Jack is on the shelf." I pointed to a corner of the living room that was beginning to resemble a roadside zoo. Tom dropped his briefcase and Nicole's book bag, and they walked over to the shelf. Nicole squealed with delight when she saw the bunny.

"I have to go," I said into the phone. "I have company."

"Your mother raised you to be strong and independent, Holly," Kuki said. "I don't think she'd like to see you playing somebody's patsy. That's all I meant."

"I'm not Danny's patsy," I insisted before hanging up.

At least not anymore.

I joined Tom and Nicole in the living room. Nicole was like a kid in a candy store, looking from Jack's cage to Felix's to Rocky's aquarium.

"Where's the monkey?" she asked. "Daddy said you have a monkey."

"The monkey doesn't live here anymore."

"Oh." She scratched her head. "Does your kitty still live here?"

I nodded. "His name is Grouch. Do you want to pet him?"

"Uh-huh."

I reached for a container of cat treats and shook it—the universal call for hungry cats. Predictably, Grouch came running. I popped a few Pounce on the floor, and while he snatched them up, Nicole bent down beside him and began stroking him.

Betty emerged from the bathroom, fully dressed in a beige pantsuit and matching shoes. Relieved, I introduced her to Tom and Nicole. Nicole extended her hand for a shake and then withdrew it with a yelp. "Daddy, she bit me!"

"Ah, this must be the famous Aunt Betty," Tom said. "Holly's told me a lot about you." He examined Nicole's hand and bent to kiss it. "Okay, honey, we have to be going. Do you want to take the rabbit?"

She tilted her head. "Can I take all of 'em?"

"All of them?" Tom and I said simultaneously.

I gawked at her. "You can take the bunny. Or the goldfish. But you certainly wouldn't want to bring a snake to school, would you? Or a rat!" I made faces to illustrate how distasteful I found either idea.

"Yes!"

Tom tried to reason with her, explaining how kids in her class might be afraid of a snake or a rat, but they'd love to see a bunny rabbit or even a goldfish. His voice firm and parental, he told her she had one minute to decide between the fish and the rabbit or else they were going to leave empty-handed.

She looked up at me, the corners of her mouth downturned and her eyes brimming with tears. When she spoke, her voice was shaky. "I . . . could take . . . good care . . . of them."

Looking at Nicole, I suddenly saw a two-decades-younger version of myself. Like me, she was a wounded bird. Her world was shifting, changing, in ways bigger than she could possibly comprehend. But when you're five, you don't worry about the big picture. It's the little things that matter. Like show-and-tell. And ballet recitals.

I made a decision there and then to not be one more grown-up who disappointed her. As irrational as it might seem, I would help her get through her parents' divorce by helping her get through just one day at school. A day that she would probably forget all about in a year or two if it was a success, but which she would remember forever if it was a failure.

I put my hands on my hips. "O.K., then. We don't have much time if we're going to do this. I'm going to need everybody's help."

Having been rendered speechless by my announcement that we would all go to Nicole's classroom, with all of my pets in tow, Tom helped to load their cages onto a luggage cart I hauled out of the closet. Felix's and Jack's cages were small enough to transport easily, while a small plastic cage that housed a long-ago hamster would serve as temporary lodgings for Rocky. Transferring him was no great joy, but it beat carrying his ten-gallon aquarium through the streets of Manhattan.

"You want to bring Whoopi, too?" I asked Nicole.

"Yes!"

I secured the cages to the luggage rack with bungee cords and filled my carryall bag with assorted pet food so that Nicole's classmates could have a chance to feed the critters. "O.K., then, I think we're all set."

We made our way to the front door, Tom eyeing me with the same baffled yet amazed look he'd given me that morning at Starbucks. I was about to turn my key in the lock when Nicole shouted, "Wait!"

"What is it?" Tom asked her.

"You forgot the kitty," she said matter-of-factly.

Twenty minutes later, we pulled up in a taxi in front of Nicole's school. I had borrowed Tom's cell phone to make a few calls on the way. While I was solving Tom and Nicole's problems, I decided to take care of a few of my own.

First up was Gerry. "I need you to do me a favor," I told him. "Take Uncle Bernie to your jeweler and have him buy the biggest diamonelle he can afford on his pension check. Today."

Then I phoned Bernie. His voice brightened when I told him my plan to bring Betty back home. Apparently, late-in-life bachelorhood didn't agree with Bernie, who asked if I was aware that one wasn't supposed to put metal in a microwave. "Yeah," I said. "And while we're on the subject, I'll let you in on a little secret about fruit cocktail."

My last call was to David. His nurse told me he was doing much better since the surgery; then she put him on. "Hi, Holly, how are you?"

"Great," I said. "I thought I'd take you up on that offer for tea."

*   *   *

Nicole's teacher was flummoxed by the flurry of furry creatures taking over her classroom. After chastising Tom for not giving her advance warning, and making him sign a release protecting her and the school in the event of an animal-related emergency, she corralled the children into a large circle on the floor to listen to Nicole's presentation.

Red-faced with embarrassment, Nicole stood at the front of the room. In a timid voice, she said, "These are some pets I brought for you to see. 'Cause I like them very much. Thank you." She turned and pointed to the cages, which we had aligned on the teacher's desk. Tom and I stepped back, finding a place to stand near the door so we wouldn't be hovering over Nicole.

The teacher, Mrs. McGrail, said, "Why don't you tell us their names and what kind of pets they are?"

"Um, that's a rabbit and that's a fish and that's . . . um . . . a big mouse, and that's a snake."

At the word "snake," several of the girls gave high-pitched squeals, while a few boys shouted, "Cool" and "Awesome."

"And that's a cat in there," she said, pointing to Grouch's carrying case. "But he's not happy 'cause he thinks he's going to the vet." Grouch, more than living up to his name, had hissed and wailed through the entire cab ride, and I warned Nicole that he was probably not going to be happy to be accosted by a bunch of first graders. "So don't stick your fingers in there, 'cause he might bite them," she said authoritatively.

Nicole fell silent, so Mrs. McGrail asked the class if they had any questions. A brown-haired girl raised her hand. "What do you feed them?"

Nicole shrugged. "I don't know. Different foods, I guess."

Another hand shot up and a blond boy asked, "What kind of snake is it?"

"I don't know," Nicole said, turning to me with a pleading look in her eyes. I wanted to step in and answer the kids' questions, but this was Nicole's show, her assignment. Her turn to stand in the spotlight.

"Well, what *do* you know?" a boy's voice rang out from the back.

Mrs. McGrail put a hand on Nicole's shoulder protectively. "You must really like animals, to have so many pets at home."

"They're not mine," Nicole said. "They're hers." She pointed at me. "Her name's Holly, and she cuts hairs at Starbucks."

I waved hello to the class but stayed at my post by the door.

"What kind of snake is it?" the blond boy repeated.

"Can I touch it?" another boy yelled.

"Me, too!" several voices shouted in unison.

"I want to pet the kitty," a girl cried out.

Nicole looked dazed. She twisted her hair in her fingers, clearly at a loss as to how to handle her classmates' demands.

Tom leaned toward me and whispered in my ear, "Why don't you take over?"

I hesitated for a moment. As much as I wanted to see Nicole spared further embarrassment, I wasn't all that eager to face a roomful of first graders. They were even more intimidating than the crowds at the comedy clubs. At least the club patrons usually had consumed a few drinks by the time I took the stage, the liquor serving to lighten their moods and lower their standards.

I took a deep breath and walked over to Nicole. "Why don't we introduce them to Jack first?" I said, reaching for his plastic cage.

"O.K."

I held the cage up to the class. "This is Jack Bunny. I named him after the comedian Jack Benny." The blank stares shouldn't have surprised me; most people my own age didn't even know who Benny was. What did I expect from a bunch of first graders? "Sometimes I feed him carrots, but mostly he eats rabbit pellets."

Some students nodded, others wriggled and squirmed in their seats. I was losing their interest already. "Let me show you how I feed him."

I set the cage down and reached into my bag to find the rabbit food. I'd done a couple of hairstyling housecalls the day before, and my bag was bursting with various hair accessories, not to mention the odds and ends I usually carried. I fished through hair clips and styling gel, MetroCards and business cards, but came up empty. I dumped the bag on the teacher's desk and stuff began tumbling out, eliciting laughter from the kids. Finally I found the rabbit pellets and popped a few into Jack's cage.

As I began scooping up the contents of my bag, I spotted a black macramé scarf I'd been carrying since the weather was cooler. Inspiration struck and I ran with it, figuring I'd either win these kids over or completely humiliate myself and, by association, Nicole. Either way, I was going for broke.

I draped the black scarf loosely around my head, letting the ends hang down at either side so that they resembled dreadlocks. Then I picked up the goldfish bowl and held it up to the class. "This here is Whoopi Goldfish," I said, my voice doing as close an imitation of Whoopi Goldberg as I could manage—which I thought was pretty good for an uptight white chick.

I shook my head, tossing the scarf's loosely knotted tendrils from side to side for effect. The kids laughed.

"Whassup, dudes?" I said. "Whatch'you laughing at? Ain't you never seen a black goldfish before? Well get used to it, baby, 'cause we're here to stay. We're takin' over the fishpond."

I pointed to a girl in braids. "Come up here, baby. Let me show you how to feed Whoopi."

The girl trotted up and held out her hand. I dropped a few fish flakes onto her open palm; then she turned and dumped them into the fishbowl. "Glug, glug, glug," I intoned, Whoopi-like, trying to mimic a fish eating. "Hey, man, what's with the flakes? That stuff's nasty! How'd you like it if instead of your cheeseburgers or pizza I gave you some nasty little pieces of sawdust that taste like ground-up worms?"

I winked at Nicole, who beamed proudly. The students were laughing and talking to one another. The laughter stopped and several kids pointed toward the doorway. I looked up as David rolled through the door in his wheelchair, Tallulah perched on his shoulder.

Mrs. Lipton entered behind David and closed the door. She unclipped Tallulah's leash and the monkey hopped off David's shoulder and bounded over toward me. I held out my arms and she leapt into them, noisily chattering away.

"And this is my friend Tallulah," I said to the class. Tallulah turned toward the students, tipped her head to one side, and stuck out her tongue. "Tallulah Bunkbed."

"Could we take a break here?" Tom asked, panting. After stopping for tea, we had dropped David, Tallulah, and Mrs. Lipton off in front of their building before continuing on to my place. Though I'd wanted to part company at the curb, he insisted on helping me lug all the animals and accessories back up the six flights to my apartment.

Grouch hissed and growled during the entire cab ride home. I should have known better than to bring Grouch—who wasn't very social in the best of circumstances—into a classroom filled with screaming kids, not to mention his nemesis, Tallulah. My other critters came through the experience none the worse for wear. In fact, Rocky and I had reached a whole new level in our friendship. I thought nothing could top Tallulah—who stole the show by pulling her yellow sunflower dress over her head to reveal her Pampers to the class—but the boys in the class wouldn't be satisfied until they'd gotten to touch the snake. Throwing caution to the wind, and momentarily forgetting that I was deathly afraid of Rocky, I agreed to take him out of his aquarium.

Mrs. McGrail had eyed me nervously, but, remembering what I had learned in my Internet search, I told her that the kids would be perfectly safe as long as they approached one at a time, quietly, and did as they were told. Unless provoked, Rocky wouldn't bite; now that he was on a regular feeding schedule, receiving one ratsicle every three to four days, he wasn't hungry enough to try to take a bite out of anyone. I'd carefully lifted Rocky out of his aquarium and slung him around my shoulders like a stole. Then, keeping a watchful eye over his head, I let one child approach at a time and touch his midsection. Only three or four boys and one girl were brave enough to touch Rocky. The other students barraged them with questions: "Is it slimy?" "Were you scared?" "Did it feel like seaweed?"

Keeping in the spirit of the rest of the presentation, I also incorporated some shtick, doing Sly Stallone with a serpentine twist. "All I wanna do is go the disssstance," I hissed, throwing my voice to the snake and bellowing, "Adrian! Adrian!" The movie dialogue was more for the benefit of Tom and Mrs. McGrail, but the kids liked it, too, even if they weren't old enough to get the references.

"Nicole seemed happy," I said to Tom, as we rested on the third-floor landing.

"She was thrilled. I haven't seen her smile like that in a long time." He reached over and put one hand on mine. "Thank you for that. For putting a smile on my little girl's face."

I withdrew my hand and shrugged. "It was nothing."

I knocked on my apartment door to give Betty a warning. The last thing I wanted was for Tom to walk in on Betty in the buff. I unlocked the door and stuck my head in. "We have company. Are you decent in here?"

"We're both fully clothed," my uncle Bernie's voice boomed back. "For now."

I pushed the door open and saw Betty and Bernie sitting on my love seat, holding hands. She was wearing a very becoming peach-colored dress and a matching shade on her cheeks. She'd either put on some makeup or she was blushing.

"Uncle Bernie!" I pushed my way through the door and wrapped my arms around him. "This is my friend Tom."

Tom shook hands with Bernie and Betty. Then he dragged the critter caravan inside and we began putting everything back in its proper place.

As I was repositioning Rocky's aquarium on the shelf, Betty tapped me on the shoulder. I turned and she waved her arm in front of my face. Dangling from her wrist was a silver bracelet dripping with what I assumed were 100 percent genuine faux diamonelles.

"Check it out," she said. "Isn't it dazzling?"

"It's gorgeous," I agreed. "Does this mean you two have patched things up?"

She nodded. "Bernie just showed up out of the blue a little while ago. He dropped down on his knees—"

"I passed out!" Bernie interrupted. "That's quite a climb you got there. Six flights!"

Betty waved her hand dismissively. "He said he didn't want to wait till he was dead to shower me with diamonds. And he gave me this." She held her wrist up and the light from the overhead lamp danced off the fake gems.

She gestured toward her suitcases, which were lined up outside the bedroom door. "He's taking me home."

"First we're going to stop at Green-Wood," Bernie said. "To pick out adjoining plots. Not that we're in any rush to use them, mind you. But a man likes to know where he's gonna end up, you know?"

He picked up two of Betty's suitcases and started for the door.

Betty gathered up her handbag and overcoat and reached for another small suitcase. "Oh, I almost forgot," she said, setting down her handbag and heading toward the kitchen. "I was looking through your drawers to make sure I didn't forget anything when I was packing, and I found this." She lifted a small, oval-shaped object off the counter. "Your mother's Saint Catherine medal. I don't think you mean to keep it in your junk drawer with your takeout menus and ballpoint pens and mustard packets."

I shook my head. "It's not my mother's. It's just something I found in the monkey's cage."

She pressed the silver medallion into my hand. "What would a monkey be doing with Saint Catherine?" She held it up to the light. "It's your mother's, I'm telling you. Or one just like it. Catherine of Siena was her patron saint. Put it away in a safe place, O.K.?"

I nodded and slipped the medal into my pocket. I kissed her on both cheeks, then winced as she delivered a surprisingly strong punch to my left biceps.

Tom was checking his watch and shifting his weight from one foot to the other. "I have a class in half an hour," he said, his tone apologetic.

I felt a lump in my throat and realized that despite resolving that dating Tom was a bad idea, I didn't want him to see him go.

"Thanks for lugging all that stuff upstairs," I said.

He nodded. "No problem."

He turned to open the door, paused in the doorway, then turned back to face me. For a split second, I was expecting one of those movie moments where the hero admits there are insurmountable obstacles in the way, but what the hell, let's give love a chance! Our eyes locked. My lips trembled. Then Tom looked over at Bernie. "I'll help you carry these bags downstairs."

"That's a good fellow," Bernie said, stepping aside to let Tom pick up two of the suitcases.

I closed the door behind them. Over the sound of footsteps re-treating down the stairs, I heard Bernie shout, "Hey, Tom, let me tell you about the time Holly hid her bra in the cookie jar."

Though I'd been eager to rid myself of my rheumatic roomie, my apartment felt strangely empty once Betty had gone. I stood slumped in the doorway, watching them leave, absentmindedly fin-gering the medal in my pocket. I pulled it out and examined it again. I vaguely recalled my mother wearing a medallion but didn't know which saint it pictured. Even if it was Saint Catherine, there's no way the medal could have made it into my apartment for Tallu-lah to find it, since it wasn't among my mother's keepsakes I had kept. The medal had to have come with Tallulah, I thought, even though I knew that was impossible. I'd cleaned her cage daily and would have noticed a shiny medal object among the shredded newspaper or tucked away in her tattered blanket.

Maybe she'd picked it up off a stranger that day I brought her to Starbucks. That was the only time I'd taken her outside. Then I re-membered there had been one other time she was out of my apart-ment: when she escaped through the milk door. She'd almost made it to the street when she was stopped by that kind man. I pictured his face, the shy and almost apologetic smile as he handed me Tallu-lah's leash. *"This little guy was just about to leave . . . had a feeling he might be on the lam."*

I sank to the floor as a wave of nausea washed over me. The man had looked vaguely familiar, like someone I should have known but couldn't quite place. It was like seeing the counter guy from the corner deli working out at the gym or in line at the post office. I know you, but I'm not sure why. Overwhelmed by nearly losing Tal-lulah, I hadn't pursued the puzzle that day. I'd just figured the man who'd saved her was one of my nameless neighbors, people I passed without bothering to get to know.

I smacked myself in the forehead with my palm. It was so obvious now. My father had aged quite a bit in the nearly twenty years since I'd last seen him—his hair had thinned and gone gray—and I don't think I'd ever seen him clean-shaven before, but I should have recognized his broad brow and deep-set eyes, his strong jaw and sad smile. I crawled to the hall closet, pulled out the box labeled RICHARD'S THINGS, and found the faded family photograph. Behind the full beard, underneath the long hair, there he was: the man in the stairwell.

"Don't cry, sunshine," he'd said when I cried over Tallulah's near escape. *"It'll be O.K."* But I was remembering those same words spoken to me on another occasion. My mother's funeral. I closed my eyes, remembering the days after my mother's death. My father and my aunts packing up my mother's things, sorting stacks of clothing and other items into separate piles for storage, the Salvation Army, and the church. There were some arguments between Kuki and my dad over whom my mother would want to have certain things. He'd finally thrown his hands up and told Kuki to take everything. But he must have kept at least one item: the medal that Tallulah somehow stole from him.

I heard footsteps on the staircase and opened the door, my hands trembling. If I caught my father returning for his envelope, what would I say?

But it was Brian bounding up the stairs, a large duffel bag slung over one shoulder. He smiled as he reached my landing. "Howdy, neighbor. Pete just told me how you saved Kramer. He must have pushed the screen out of the window. I can't thank you enough!"

I stared at him blankly, wondering if I should confess my crime or let him go on believing the cat-rescue story. "No problem." He had his secrets—why shouldn't I have mine?

He resumed his climb. When he was halfway up the stairs, I called out to him, "Wait. I saw an envelope in your apartment the other day. It had my name on it."

"Thanks for reminding me." He skipped back down to my landing. He unzipped his duffel bag and reached inside. He pulled out the envelope, which was now bulging. "This is for you. For your cousin, actually."

I took the envelope and opened the clasp. It was filled with socks, at least five pair.

"Ever since I saw your act, I've been meaning to give you some socks. For your cousin. I figured that's what he was after that day in your apartment, when he was trying to get me to take off my shoes. Anyway, I kept forgetting. And you've done so much for me lately, watching Kramer and fixing my computer, that I had an idea. Yesterday I did a softball benefit with all kinds of soap stars and I got a bunch of them to donate their socks, too. I told them it was for charity."

I opened the envelope and gaped at its contents. It had never held my dad's writing after all. I looked at the front of the envelope, where my name was written in block letters. Now I could see what I hadn't noticed on first glance in Brian's apartment: the handwriting was different. My father's strokes were precise and upright, while Brian's were bold and slanted, the "y" in my name ending with a little curlicue.

I peered into the envelope again. Brian had been at the showcase, so he'd heard about Gerry's sock obsession. All the subterfuge had been unnecessary.

Then I remembered something else about that night. "You said the guy who found Tallulah was also in the audience. Are you sure?"

He nodded. "Standing in the back. I said hello but he just nodded and backed away. Kind of shy, like."

My father had come to see me perform. He'd been invited, after all, though I had no idea whom I was inviting when I slipped the flyer into the envelope with the Writer's first job. He'd stood in the background so as not to be spotted by me—or more to the point,

Betty or Kuki, who were more likely to recognize their former brother-in-law.

Though I wasn't ready to forgive my dad, knowing he'd come to my show made me feel somehow lighter, as though a long dormant cloud had lifted.

"Thanks for the socks," I told Brian. "Gerry's gonna flip."

He nodded proudly, tugging at a pair of panty hose tucked in among assorted sport socks. "Susan Lucci even donated a pair of nylons."

19

Turning the Tables

Gerry dangled Susan Lucci's stockings in front of everyone who came to the engagement party that evening, boasting of his fiancée's unprecedented procurement. I'd allowed Monica to take full credit for the acquisition on two conditions: that she let me keep calling her Monica and that she *not* make me a member of her wedding party. Time spent with Monica Broccoli usually led to physical violence, and I could only imagine the mayhem that would ensue if I had to endure gown fittings, bridesmaids' teas, and other wedding preparations with her.

I dropped the soap star sock collection off at Monica's apartment on my way to Carter's place, where Danny and I were meeting for a last-minute rehearsal. Though I was a little leery of reteaming with Danny after our showcase, I agreed with Kuki that the farewell performance of Heckerling and Crane was a fitting engagement gift for Gerry, especially if the jokes were centered on him. It was easy enough to come up with ten minutes' worth of material about Gerry, the inauguration of his sock museum, and his engagement to a woman whose name he didn't know. Gerry relished the attention, laughing louder than anyone present with the possible exception of

Monica. My future cousin-in-law conceded that she enjoyed the act, telling me, "Gerry's always saying how funny you are, but I didn't see it . . . until now."

Kuki even gave the act her kudos, taking me aside to let me know that my mother—"God rest her soul"—would be proud of me and that I should continue to pursue a career in comedy.

"Thanks for saying that, but tonight was the last time I'm doing stand-up. The gig—I mean, the 'jig'—is up."

Carter came up behind me and put one arm around my shoulder. "No, it's not. Danny and I have been talking and we want you to come with us to California. We'll rent a house together. You and Danny can keep doing the act while you both go on auditions and stuff. And you'll be around to watch the baby grow up."

"Whaddya say, Holly?" Danny embraced me from the other side. "Let's take the show on the road!"

Kuki looked aghast at the notion that I would consider leaving New York. After all, she'd put up a bitter struggle when I left Brooklyn for my apartment in the city. "You can't—" she began, then bit her lip.

I gritted my teeth. "Can't what?" I challenged, fire in my eyes.

We locked gazes and I thought Kuki would unleash a torrent of reasons why I couldn't leave New York, abandon my family, and traipse across the country to follow a foolish dream. Then her eyes flickered and she smiled. "You can't make such a big decision on an empty stomach." She led me by the arm to the serving dishes she'd arranged on the sideboard. "Have a marinated meatball."

Kuki's meatballs had never tasted better. I ate four while pondering what to tell Danny and Carter. The adventurous part of me was ready to drop everything and move to L.A. with them, to start anew in the company of my two best friends. The cautious part warned that I'd be no more likely to make it big on the comedy cir-

cuit in L.A., and I wouldn't have Holly's Hobbies to support me—
at least not until I developed a West Coast clientele.

Bernie and Betty held hands and gazed lovingly at each other
throughout the evening. Now that Betty had her long-awaited diamonds and Bernie's mind was at ease as to his final resting place,
they were like newlyweds. They looked so happy together that I decided to ignore the gnawing guilt I felt over suggesting my uncle ap-
pease her with fake jewels.

Leo uncorked a bottle of champagne and Kuki toasted Gerry
and Monica. After several more toasts, Ronnie shouted, "Have you
guys set a date?"

"I always wanted a June wedding," Monica said. "But the doctor isn't going to remove my cast until July. So I guess I have to wait.
Unless Holly is willing to—"

"Not on your life!" I shouted to a chorus of laughter.

I noticed that Monica's bigger-than-life engagement ring was
gone, replaced by a smaller version, of which she seemed equally
proud. Gerry explained to me that while shopping for Betty's
bracelet, he'd picked out a more delicate, more expensive ring for
his bride-to-be. "Uncle Bernie told me that 'faux' means fake."

I arched one eyebrow. "Really?"

"Yeah. And if he could buy all those diamonds for Aunt Betty,
I could at least shell out enough for a genuine diamond engagement ring."

"Betty's bracelet is *real*?" I asked. "It must be worth a fortune!"

Gerry nodded. "That's love for ya."

I was looking at Bernie with renewed admiration when Carter
and Danny appeared at my elbow. "Say you'll come with us, Holly,"
Carter said. "We'll be the three musketeers."

"Three-and-a-half," I said, patting her belly.

"Is that a yes?" Danny asked.

There was a pronounced hush and I realized that Kuki, Betty,

Gerry, and Monica had gathered closer to hear my answer. Gradually all conversation ceased and everyone turned to face me. Carter and Danny were staring at me expectantly. My two best friends, I thought, looking at them. Then I remembered Danny's admonition that he and Carter needed to be their own best friends. More than that, I realized they needed their own space to grow as a couple and as parents. And there was still much I needed to do in Manhattan. My family drove me crazy, but they loved me. My business wasn't making me rich, but it paid the bills and kept life interesting. Living in the city, I'd never have a shortage of clientele. There would always be hair to cut, taxes to prepare, and monkeys to mind.

And somewhere out there was my father, who, in his own way, had been laying the groundwork for a reunion. The night before, I'd removed the untouched manila envelope from the milk cubby. I tore up the paper on which I'd scribbled accusingly, *I know who you are!* and replaced it with another sheet on which I wrote carefully,

I know who you are. I don't know if I'll ever forgive you for
leaving . . . but I am glad you're back.

I slipped my mother's Saint Catherine's medal inside the envelope, sealed it, and replaced it in the cubby. I crossed out my name on the outside of the envelope and wrote above it in block letters that mirrored my father's handwriting, *DAD*.

Around six a.m., over the sounds of Grouch trying to claw his way into the cabinet that held his food, I heard a faint click coming from the pantry. Jolted from sleep, I quickly slid from beneath the covers and tiptoed across the floor. I stood in the pantry, listening to footsteps retreating down the staircase. Then I went to my window and looked out, as I had that first day, trying to pick the mystery Writer out from the anonymous crowd passing below. This time, I knew exactly who I was looking for, and I spotted him as soon as he emerged from my building, the manila envelope tucked under one arm. Though his graying hair was hidden beneath a weathered fisherman's cap and an oversized navy Windbreaker obscured his frame, I recognized the man whose bedtime stories and nightly tickle fights eased the pain of my mother's death. If only he'd known how much.

"So?" Danny nudged me back to the present. "Is Holly Heckerling ready for Hollywood?"

All eyes were on me. I shook my head. "Maybe. But I don't think Hollywood is ready for Holly Heckerling. I'm staying in New York."

The relief on Aunt Kuki's face was palpable. "Are you still quitting comedy?" she asked.

"Come work with me," Gerry offered. "I'm tellin' ya, my collection is gonna be big."

I nodded in acknowledgment. Celebrity-socks.com had topped thirty thousand hits and people were paying Gerry to place banner ads on the site. That morning, he'd been interviewed on a local radio station, daring the deejay to doff his socks on the spot. A few weeks ago, when he'd shoved Martin Scorsese's Armanis in my face, I'd never have imagined Gerry's foot folly would take him this far. Now I knew anything was possible. I wouldn't be surprised if Gerry's collection got him onto all the talk shows and entertainment newsmagazines. And I couldn't be happier for him.

"Thanks anyway, but I have another idea."

I heard voices coming from the parlor and then Tom appeared in the entryway. Bernie leaned forward. "I hope it's O.K. I invited him. He's a good fellow."

Under normal circumstances I'd be mortified. I generally tried to keep my love life completely separate from my family, for obvious reasons. But like the evening Tom and I talked on the phone for hours, sharing the no-holds-barred stories of our lives, I felt I didn't have to hide anything from him. "That's O.K., Uncle Bernie."

I also had to admit that there was more to my feelings for Tom than my desire to help his daughter get through her parents' divorce. He stirred something in me that I hadn't felt with Marcus or my previous paramours.

Recent events had brought home the fact that since I'd lost my parents, I'd been bumbling along through life, making the best of what other people threw at me, but rarely a propelling force in my own right. To quote my father's parting words to me, I tried to be a good girl and not make waves. Like tumbleweed tossed about in a windstorm or debris caught up in tailwinds, I bounced along, driven by the needs of those around me—Monica Broccoli, Gerry, Carter, Danny, Kuki, Betty, even Tallulah. I was always getting swept up in other people's dramas, with the end result being, more often than not, chaos.

Things had been different with Tom. That first day at Starbucks, in the wake of my disastrous evening with Monica's cast and Carter's pregnancy test, I'd plunged headfirst into his problems, but instead of a belly flop, I'd pulled off a perfectly executed swan dive. My creative, if unconventional, approach to his dilemmas left me feeling almost heroic.

Maybe I was just having a good day. Or perhaps Tom had inspired the confidence I felt that morning, a confidence that was also present the day I rescued John Landis's keys from the sewer and again when I played Dr. Doolittle to the denizens of P.S. 132. I supposed my life would always have a frenetic quality, as I bounced from one thing to the next like an unruly monkey, but I was beginning to feel like I could be in control.

So far in my dating history I'd alternated between two types of men, which Carter and I had labeled "the studs" and "the duds." In the first category were self-obsessed actors and other neurotic types for whom I'd fall into a mad, frenzied kind of passion at the slightest indication of interest from them—and who'd drop me cold the moment someone taller, blonder, or bustier turned up. These brief but dazzling interludes always left me feeling emotionally spent, struggling to repair my bruised and battered ego.

In the second category were men like Marcus, good, decent guys who'd follow me like puppy dogs to the ends of the Earth if I asked them to, but for whom—not for lack of trying—I just didn't feel any passion. With both types of men I was always trying to be someone I'm not.

Tom gave me the best of both worlds. Being with him gave me that fluttery feeling in the pit of my stomach like I was on a roller coaster—but it wasn't the nausea-inducing fear of losing him three months down the road that had me breaking out into a cold sweat. He'd already seen the best—and worst—of me and he wasn't running. In fact, *I* was the one who'd tried to run at the first hint of trouble.

Tom edged forward. "Am I interrupting something?"

"I was just telling everyone about my new business venture. I'm quitting the comedy circuit."

He furrowed his brow. "That's too bad. You were a real hit with Nicole's class. Her teacher called me this afternoon. She told some of the other teachers about your animals, and they want to know if you'll give the same presentation to their classes."

I laughed. "Great! They can be my first clients. What I was just going to say is, I decided to do an act for kids. I'll go from school to school teaching kids about animals and conservation, using my pets as props. It'll be educational and humorous."

"Finally you can use all that stuff you learned in monkey school," Kuki said approvingly.

"Maybe I should stick around," Danny said. "And partner up with you."

"I already have a partner. I spoke to my friend David and he loved the idea. He'll bring Tallulah and educate the kids about disabilities and working animals."

Monica put her hands on her hips. "Not that monkey again! Tallulah Stankhead? I hope you know what you're doing, Holly."

I nodded. "I do. For the first time in many years." I looked around the room, at my family and friends, at the perfectly polished knickknacks and delicate lace doilies, at the framed family photographs lining the walls, at the decades-old floral-print upholstered furniture that still looked brand-new because it was perpetually shrouded in plastic, except for special occasions. I'd spent the latter half of my childhood in this house but I never felt at home until this moment. I was always trying to do what was expected of me, trying to help out, trying not to make waves. I hadn't paid much attention to what made *me* happy.

Obviously I was drawn to animals. I never would have coaxed Kuki into helping put me through "monkey school" if I hadn't felt a particular passion for primates. My aunts' admonitions had proved prophetic. "Whaddya gonna do with a degree in monkeys?" they'd asked, and the truth was I still didn't know even after I had my diploma in hand. There aren't a lot of monkeys in Manhattan, and not a lot of career opportunities for urban primatologists.

As for my other career, I'd stumbled into comedy through my friendship with Danny, and while I never truly expected to make a lasting career out of it, there were moments when I felt I was in my element. Though I'd been utterly unprepared and horrendously nervous, the first half of our showcase—when I was flying solo—was probably the most exhilarating experience I'd ever had onstage. I had drawn a blank, so I just started talking about Tallulah, the little monkey who turned my life upside down—and somehow in the process made everything all right.

Carter wrapped her arms around me. "I have to admit, it's perfect for you. Combining comedy and your critters."

"That's what you can call it," Danny said. "Holly's Critter Comedy."

"Working with you prepared me for it," I said to Danny.

After a few more congratulatory hugs, my friends and family went back to toasting Gerry and Monica and pressing them for wedding details. Tom and I worked our way through the buffet line and found a quiet corner at the far side of the parlor.

"I know you wanted to hold off seeing me until things settled down," he said, spearing a meatball with a toothpick. "And they're beginning to. The custody papers are all signed. Starting next month, Nicole will be with me three days a week and every other holiday."

"That's great."

"There's more. I got the job at NYU. It's a full-time, tenure-track professorship. My life is finally falling into place." He set his plate on a side table and took my hands in his. "I'd like you to be part of it."

I felt a warm rush surge through my body. "How will Nicole feel about that?"

"She adores you. But be forewarned: I'm sure Bianca will cause problems from time to time."

"She still doesn't own any weapons of mass destruction?"

"No."

"Mafia connections?"

"Negative."

"O.K., then. I'll take my chances."

"Good." He smiled, the same slightly crooked smile that had disarmed me that first day in the coffee shop.

"But are you sure you can handle *my* life?" I asked. "My unpredictable work schedule? My friends, family, and animals?"

"Do any of them bite?" he asked.

"Just Aunt Betty."

"I'll take my chances."

Photo by Norman Abbey

ABOUT THE AUTHOR

Brenda Scott Royce is the author of five nonfiction books, including *Hogan's Heroes: Behind the Scenes at Stalag 13* and *Party of Five: The Unofficial Companion*. A former book editor, she is Director of Publications for the Greater Los Angeles Zoo Association and editor of the Zoo's award-winning quarterly magazine, *Zoo View*. It's the ideal job for this animal lover, who once worked as a chimpanzee caregiver at a wildlife sanctuary.

Brenda earned a bachelor's degree in anthropology, specializing in primatology, from Cal State Fullerton, where she was awarded a Think Different Technology Scholarship and a Humanities and Social Sciences Life Achievement Award. She's also the recipient of a California Predoctoral Scholarship and numerous writing honors.

Her writing credits include magazine articles, encyclopedia essays, film reviews, short stories, DVD and video liner notes, and more than one hundred audiobook adaptations.

Like Holly, Brenda has a debilitating Starbucks addiction, a mortal fear of snakes, and a working knowledge of power tools. She lives with her family outside Los Angeles. You can visit her Web site at www.brendascottroyce.com.